Sleeping Cutie

Sara Caspian

CORONET BOOKS
Hodder & Stoughton

First published in Great Britain in 2002
by Hodder and Stoughton
A division of Hodder Headline

A Coronet paperback

1 3 5 7 9 10 8 6 4 2

A CIP catalogue record for this title
is available from the British Library.

ISBN 0 340 76957 2

Printed and bound in Great Britain by
Mackays of Chatham plc, Chatham, Kent

Hodder and Stoughton
A division of Hodder Headline
338 Euston Road
London NW1 3BH

THANKS TO

FROM FIRST word to final draft, I have once again enjoyed the support and enthusiasm of my superb agent, Simon Trewin. A huge vote of thanks for your ongoing kindness and encouragement – they make a real difference. Thank you also for at times being there above and beyond the call of duty. Finally, cheers for always managing to make me laugh, even on those days when my sense of humour threatened to go AWOL!

Heartfelt appreciation to my wonderful friend Phil Saunders for all his patience, advice, and for being so staunch throughout everything – please be advised that if you try to return to Sydney I shall staple your feet to the floor!

To the one and only Tamara Kley-Leslie, my partner in both crime and bad hair days – you make the good times more fun, and the bad times better. A massive thank you for always being there for me, for never failing to see the hilarious side of life, and, not least, for continuing to make me literally cry with laughter on a regular basis.

For their invaluable support and friendship, thank you also to the fabulous Annie Fine and the lovely Lorraine Kaye; also to Hagit and Alastair Taylor, Phil Stein, Adam Lamb, and Steve

Mathieson, for the journalistic advice. Finally, a special thank you to Deborah Costello, for all our shared memories and history together.

For medical expertise, I was fortunate to have the help of Dr Paul Bentley, whose patience in answering all my questions was greatly valued.

And thank you so much to the very helpful and extremely knowledgeable Peter Saunders, of the Narcolepsy Association, who was kind enough to spend part of his Saturday afternoon answering my queries.

My thanks to Sarah Ballard at PFD for being ever-helpful and super-efficient – also for being a voice of sanity when deadlines were looming!

And a big thank you to everyone at Hodder who has put time and energy into my second novel!

To my family, thank you doesn't seem to cover it. Over the past two years my brother John has shown more confidence in me than I will ever have in myself. Your unwavering optimism has meant a lot to me, and your pep talks are the best! And I will never forget how you drove me round every garage in North London at one a.m. to find a copy of the first review of *The Next Big Thing* – glad we were together for that.

Love and thanks to my father for being the quirkiest dad a girl could ever have, and for your belief in me. Love to Nana and Betty for being there for me, for all their generosity and understanding, and also for all the chocolate – keep it coming!

Finally, I reserve a special mention for my mother. Those who know you will understand why there are no words to adequately convey your courage, your unfailing sense of hu-

mour, and your unrivalled kindness and gentleness of spirit –
for which I'm sure a certain family of squirrels is eternally
grateful . . . ! ! ! Thank you so very much for all your love and
understanding. You are, quite simply, the best.

SLEEPING CUTIE

Part One

Part One

1

It's My Party and
I'll Cry if I Want to

'Is this a private dream, or can anyone join in . . .?'

Isobel opened her eyes and looked up to see her ex wearing a suggestive smile. The party was packed and since she'd spent most of it curled up on a sofa, fantasising about being somewhere else, she hadn't realised Jon was here. Now she blinked back tears. This was more than just the office Christmas bash, and everyone else was enjoying it. Why couldn't she?

'I wasn't asleep, I was just . . . you know . . .' Isobel blushed.

Jon nodded gravely, all too aware of her tendency to wander off into an imaginary world when the real one let her down. He accepted two glasses of champagne from one of the waiters hovering nearby and handed one to Isobel. 'But this party is to celebrate the launch of *Primadonna*, and the magazine's your baby – why aren't you joining in?'

'I am!' Jumping up she gave him a blinding smile. 'I'm fine. And the party's great.' Gesturing merrily at the people milling around the room, she waved her hand a tad too energetically and succeeded in throwing her drink over the person standing behind her. Jon fixed her with a sceptical blue stare. 'Come on. Tell me what's going on.'

'JON, BABE!' A sudden shriek from across the room made them both jump. 'YOU MADE IT!' Lexie, the features editor, came sashaying over to stand between them. Turning her back on Isobel, she fluttered her lashes at Jon so fast it created a cross-breeze. Dressed as one of Santa's elves, she wore a tiny green tunic that barely covered her butt, and sheer tights revealing tanned, toned legs.

Isobel sighed. She'd been so tempted to confide in Jon, especially as she knew it might be her last chance to do so for a while. His photographic assignments took him all over the world, and later that night he was heading out to Brazil, after which he'd probably return to the States where, according to American *Vogue*, he was fast becoming the next Steven Meisel. Now Isobel watched as Lexie leaned towards Jon, flaunting her cleavage. She had been vocal about how much she adored her new breasts. None of that 'old saline crap' for her, she'd announced proudly. No, *her* implants were top-notch Swiss silicone. Now, as Lexie continued to thrust her chest forward, Isobel blinked. The girl's bras could have doubled as parachutes.

Brandishing a mistletoe sprig the size of a small Christmas tree, Lexie flashed Jon a predatory smile. 'Give me a kiss and maybe *I'll* come down your chimney this year . . .'

Jon grinned, then turned quickly back to Isobel, only to find that his ex-girlfriend had vanished.

*

Seeking refuge in the deserted lobby, Isobel pressed her face against a window that had been left ajar. Although it was only five o'clock, it was dark, and a thin dusting of snow covered the ground like icing sugar. Gazing at her reflection, she wondered if Dominic, her boyfriend, would like her new haircut. She hadn't planned on a change of image but that morning, when she'd turned up for her two-monthly trim, the stylist had declared that Isobel's hair looked 'So *yesterday*, sweetie.'

Isobel had rather liked her hair; she'd been growing it for ages, and now it was finally past her shoulders. But she was at the trendiest hair salon in London, so who was she to argue? Instead she'd just nodded meekly, then agonised while her scalp was smothered in various lotions, potions, colours and creams. And she definitely hadn't liked the way the stylist's eyes had gleamed as she'd brandished the scissors.

When eventually the stylist had stood back with a proud smile, Isobel was so disappointed her spirits could have dived for Britain. Her lovely, luxurious mane of chestnut curls had gone. Instead she sported a short, spiky bob, jagged bits of hair falling into her eyes and round her jaw, obscuring her tiny face. It was the wrong style for her. She looked dreadful.

'It's perfect,' Isobel had lied, smiling. As usual she was too nervous of confrontation to be candid. At least the colour was pretty, slices of copper and gold now warming her rosy complexion. But Dominic loved long hair. Dominic had intense likes and dislikes. Dominic was going to hate this.

Now, imagining his reaction, Isobel gazed at her reflection in the glass and berated herself for not being more assertive.

'You hiding again?' Jon sauntered into the lobby. He observed her glum face and raised an eyebrow. 'Come on, out with it. What's wrong?'

'Everything!' Isobel sighed, slumping back against the glass and almost falling out of the window. Jon grabbed her just in time. She perched on the reception desk.

'We both know I have ways of making you talk . . .' teased Jon. 'Come on, what's the story?'

'How long have you got? For a start, work's a nightmare!'

Jon glanced round as a group of girls stumbled out of the party, their laughter raucous as, arms linked, they lurched away in the direction of the cloakrooms. He caught the wistful gaze Isobel gave them. 'Friends of yours?' he probed.

She shook her head dolefully.

'Why are you out here, instead of celebrating with the others?'

'I get the feeling they don't see me as part of the team.' Isobel attempted a blasé shrug but couldn't quite pull it off. 'Maybe I'm not cut out to be a journalist.'

'Don't say that, it's all you've ever wanted to do.'

'Maybe wanting isn't enough. I don't fit in here.' Her voice caught. 'Or anywhere. It's been the same with every job I've ever had.'

When Isobel had set her heart on journalism, she had resolved to find out how far she could get on her own merits. But her father had, as usual, taken control. Although Isobel had begged him not to, he'd started frantically pulling strings with contacts in the media and his connections opened doors like a charm. Besides which, many of the women's glossies had loved the idea of having Isobel de RoseMont, Deb of the Decade and darling of *Hello!*, as one of their contributors. Also, since both her parents were known to be supremely confident and have shrewd business minds, everyone expected her to display the same qualities. But Isobel was nothing like either her high-profile father or her glamorous mother. She lacked confidence, and was the least worldly of all her friends. The fiery, feisty women she met on the glossy magazines scared the hell out of her. Truth be told, she envied them.

And, as Isobel herself was painfully aware, she wasn't the most *practical* of people. 'Ditzy' was a word often used to describe her. And having all her employers constantly comparing her with her parents turned her into a bundle of nerves, making her even more scatty than usual. Eventually, inevitably, she always got the sack. Each time she lost a job, the media gleefully reported on how she'd 'failed'. It was excruciating, having to read about her own shortcomings in the national press.

Then, on her twenty-eighth birthday, her favourite godmother had generously given her a large cash gift. An extremely large cash gift. And Isobel knew exactly what she wanted to do with it.

A few months earlier, she'd read an article on Byron Harrington, former deputy editor of *Totty*, the women's weekly tabloid magazine. Seething after losing out on promotion to editor, Byron had launched his own, rival publication, *Primadonna*, for girls who loved to be spoilt! It was an irreverent, tongue-in-cheek read, with features, gossip, beauty and health. But although he'd secured a hefty bank loan, Byron was in financial trouble: one of his investors had unexpectedly pulled out and as a last resort he was considering remortgaging his house. Through a mutual friend, Isobel managed to meet him, for she had the perfect solution. She'd provide the money – if he gave her a job and agreed to take her under his wing so she could learn the skills of the trade from him.

Their initial meeting had been a nightmare. Stony-faced, Byron had spent the first fifteen minutes cross-examining her, barking questions, interrupting and generally making Isobel so edgy she was stuttering and stammering all over the place. But eventually, he agreed to her proposition – as long as Isobel accepted that he would retain complete editorial control. Yet even once *Primadonna* was in the shops, Isobel knew that most of her family and friends expected her to fail in her quest to make it as a 'real' journalist. And it was starting to look as if they were right.

Now she made a face. 'Honestly, I dread coming into work each day. No one takes me seriously – they treat me like a Girl Friday. I hate it.'

'Come on, chin up.' Jon gave her a quick, fierce hug, then found it hard to let go. 'They just need time to get to know you.'

'I'm misunderstood!' lamented Isobel, throwing up her hands in despair. Jon lunged forward and just managed to catch the vase of flowers she'd knocked over without noticing. 'It's true! Everyone believes what they read about me in the papers.' Most people thought that Isobel was a superficial society gadabout. Her cause hadn't been helped when, depressed after being sacked, she'd started dating a famous soap star. When she broke things off he'd gone to the press for revenge, portraying her as a vapid It Girl whose main aim in life was to create a totally colour-co-ordinated wardrobe. 'She spends so much money, even her Gold Card has metal fatigue!' the newspaper had announced. It was a pack of lies, as her friends knew. But Isobel's reputation was sealed.

'Hang on – think that's my phone.' Jon pulled out his mobile and Isobel watched him walk back across the dimly lit lobby, speaking softly, one hand straying to his mop of sun-streaked brown hair. His inability to focus on one thing for more than five minutes was legendary. Jon got bored faster than anyone she knew. Not for the first time she reflected that being a freelance photographer suited him perfectly.

She compared him with Dominic, who was always immaculate, effortlessly smart – unlike Jon, who looked as if he'd grabbed the first clothes to fall out of his wardrobe. Today he wore a pair of faded denim jeans, a blue T-shirt, which admittedly enhanced his sky-blue eyes but also boasted a tiny hole in one shoulder, and a pair of old trainers that looked as if they were about to fall apart. His tawny hair curled over his collar and was crying out for a brush. He'd also allowed stubble to obscure his chiselled jawline.

Isobel knew how attractive Jon actually was, but it was as though he played it down, for if there was one thing that made him see red it was people who judged others by their looks. One of his pet hates was women who risked their health through dieting. He'd once made headlines for cancelling a cover shoot after discovering that the model hadn't eaten for two days.

Now, when she heard him snap his phone shut, Isobel wondered how long it would be before she saw him again.

'That your latest girlfriend?' she blurted out, before she could stop herself.

'Yep. Maxine.'

Isobel wrinkled her nose.

Jon gave her a sideways glance, and sat down close beside her on the desk. 'Yeah, Maxine's great. She's a student in the photography class I teach. Bright girl. Superb technique.' His smile widened. 'Always manages to get the perfect amount of exposure . . .'

'I'm sure.' Isobel began playing idly with the stapler. Fascinated, Jon watched as she somehow managed to staple her dress to the desk, then tried to tug it free without his noticing.

He continued chattily. 'Only problem with Maxi is she's insatiable. I'm permanently shagged. As it were.' Gently, he began to massage Isobel's neck and shoulders, and she let herself enjoy it, relaxing into his touch for a minute, then pulling away.

'Somebody's tense. Let me guess. Dominic is shit in the sack, right?' Jon nodded gravely. 'Figures. He's such a terrible dancer. No rhythm. Isobel, poor baby. No wonder you're tetchy.'

'I really don't think my sex life is any of your business,' replied Isobel demurely.

'But we're old friends, there's nothing we can't talk about. No need to be shy, not with me. Never with me.'

For a moment Isobel looked confused. 'Guess not.' Again, she tried surreptitiously to free her dress, then caught her ex's amused smile. 'So, what does Marvellous Maxine do, when she's not busy fiddling with your tripod?'

'She's an aerobics instructor. But her real passion is languages. She's fluent in five.'

'Well, she'll need them if she's going to traipse round the world after you. She must be looking forward to Brazil.' Isobel began gently kicking the desk, imagining it was Maxine's head, then feeling guilty for doing so.

Jon got up and slipped the mobile back into his pocket. 'I haven't asked her to come with me.'

'Oh, but, well, you'll miss her. Won't you?'

He looked at Isobel still wriggling around, her dress stapled to the desk. 'Terribly,' he said softly.

Suddenly self-conscious, Isobel kicked the desk a tad harder than she had intended. Her shoe flew off and went sailing through the air to land in the giant yucca plant on the other side of the lobby. She jumped up to get it but her dress held fast, yanking her back against the desk.

Isobel's bemused expression was almost more than Jon could bear. Trying desperately not to laugh, he freed her dress, retrieved the shoe, then gently took her foot and slid it back on, joking, 'Always thought you'd make a gorgeous Cinderella.'

She looked at him. 'Are you Prince Charming?'

'Wasn't he in Sleeping Beauty too? Or, in your case,' he looked at her fondly, recalling his old nickname for Isobel when they were together, 'Sleeping Cutie'.

For a long moment they stared at one another and Jon knew he was *this* close to doing something he shouldn't.

Like kissing her.

Isobel broke the eye-contact.

'So, how *is* Dominic?' asked Jon briskly.

Isobel flashed him a mega-watt beam. 'Wonderful.' She spent the next five minutes cataloguing the numerous gifts her boyfriend had bought her recently, most of which were adorning her neck, wrists and fingers.

'So, we're both happy,' Jon stated flatly, pulling on a battered brown leather jacket.

'Totally. I love Dominic, and you've got Magnificent Maxine with her multi-talented tongue. Things couldn't have worked out better.'

'Agreed. Anyway, I'd better make a move. You know, Isobel, you're looking pale. You spend way too much time inside. Why not take a break, come with me on this assignment? Do you the world of good.'

His tone was challenging, his smile a taunt. Isobel's hands clenched over the edge of the desk. He was testing her. And, for a weird, wonderful moment, she was sorely tempted to take him up on the offer.

But it was too late. There were some things you only got one shot at, and where Jon was concerned she'd had hers.

'Thanks. I'll take a raincheck. When will you be back?'

'Six months, longer if it goes well.'

Isobel's hand brushed Jon's, her touch tentative. 'You'll get some stunning pictures, I know you will.'

'Brazil is certainly beautiful.' His eyes were distant, and Isobel smiled in resignation. This was what he loved, this was what he lived for: roaming the world with his camera, taking the breathtaking photographs that only he could. When it came down to it, Jon travelled light, and any woman was just so much excess baggage. He'd never needed her, and he never would.

'Here, a goodbye gift.' From the vase, Jon took a pretty, long-stemmed white flower and offered it to her. Isobel raised it and pressed it softly against her full lips, her dreamy green eyes gazing into his.

Jon stared. Did Isobel have any idea how utterly cute she looked at that moment? Suddenly he grabbed a camera from his bag and snapped her picture.

'What are you doing?' Embarrassed, she laughed, and covered her face with one hand.

He scribbled something on the back of the Polaroid and handed it to her. 'Look, if you need anything, get in touch, okay? These are my numbers.'

Isobel gestured at the palatial offices. 'I've got a great job, and a fabulous man. What could I possibly need?' Her voice darkened. 'You forget. I'm the girl who's got it all.'

'Are you?' murmured Jon. 'Look, just don't be a stranger, that's all. I'm only ever a phone call away.'

As he continued watching her, curled up on the desk, Jon felt uneasy, as though someone was walking over his grave. Stamping on it, more like. Isobel looked . . . *fragile*. He didn't believe in intuition or premonition but, right then, it was all he could do to leave.

Choosing the stairs over the lift, he scolded himself. Isobel was fine. And even if she wasn't, she had Dominic to look after her now. Not that Jon would stop worrying about her. It was three years since their break-up, yet he still loved Isobel as much as he ever had. More, if anything. But it was too late. He'd had his chance, and he'd ruined it. Now he battled the urge to turn and look at her one last time, hurrying down the stairs before he weakened.

*

Watching Jon walk away, Isobel smiled wryly. He hated lifts, loathed any enclosed space. She'd known him walk down fourteen flights of stairs rather than get into an elevator. As he vanished from view, without even giving her one last glance, she experienced a sense of loss so acute her throat ached.

For the first time in ages, Isobel allowed herself to remember how she'd felt after they'd broken up. Broken up? She corrected

13

herself. They hadn't broken up, that implied a mutual decision. In fact, Jon had left her. Usually she tried not to dwell on this. It had hurt so badly, and she'd been so unhappy, that sometimes she'd doubted she'd ever get through it.

Before Jon, all the men she'd dated had been cast from the same mould as her father. Witty, wealthy and sophisticated, they'd all had a certain surface charm that concealed a streak of coldness. For them, Isobel was the perfect trophy girlfriend. With her malleable nature, ditzy ways and sweet smile, she was the most popular girl on the society circuit. Jon alone had seen through the 'perfect' life that the media and public assumed Isobel enjoyed. He'd been furious over the way her father icily dismissed her opinions, and saddened when her mother never had time for her. Jon had shown Isobel that things could be different. He'd encouraged her to speak up for herself, to try new things, to dream of having a career. He had shown Isobel that *she* could be different.

And he'd shown her how dysfunctional her family truly was. Isobel had seen her parents through his eyes, and it wasn't a palatable sight. He'd also shown her how superficial many of her friends were. Isobel was sure she was a better person for knowing Jon. But she was also more lonely because, compared with him, everyone else seemed lacking.

During their relationship, Isobel was surprised she didn't have permanent neck ache, from constantly gazing up at the pedestal on which she'd placed him. She knew she was doing it, yet was powerless to stop. But the intensity of her feelings for Jon scared her. She was convinced that he'd never, ever love her as much as she loved him.

And eventually, he proved her right.

Now she winced, recalling the night he'd turned up at her flat and announced he couldn't stay long since he was *en route* to the airport. She'd assumed it was some kind of joke, albeit a cruel one. But Jon was serious. He'd been offered a big assignment in Morocco; it was a last-minute offer, and he was needed immediately to replace a more experienced photographer who had pulled out. He had to leave within a matter of hours.

Isobel had realised that it wasn't a case of his having to choose between his career and their relationship. The choice was clear-cut: he wasn't prepared to kiss goodbye a chance this good, so he'd kissed her goodbye instead. He'd assumed she'd understand, that she would wait. But that night, Isobel had known it was over between them. She also knew that Jon would probably never understand why. But it was really very simple. Isobel didn't want to be left, and Jon was always going to be leaving.

*

His train was late. Not caring, Jon sat huddled on a shiny yellow seat, staring down at the platform with unseeing eyes. Like Isobel, he too was lost in the past. Going to Morocco had been a mistake. He knew that now. There would always have been other career opportunities, but there would never be another relationship like he'd had with Isobel.

Now, for the umpteenth time, he cursed himself: in his own, selfish excitement, he'd underestimated the impact his actions would have upon her. And, of course, being Isobel, she'd never expressed her anger and hurt. Maybe if she had, they would have found a way through.

Instead he'd returned ten long months later to find that Isobel had changed. She was still as sweet and genuine as ever, yet she seemed distant. He couldn't reach her. Gradually and with intense effort on his part, she'd allowed him into her life again, as a friend. But each time he tried to move things beyond friendship, she had reacted with such distress he'd quickly backed off.

So he'd stopped trying. If pretending they were purely platonic was the only way to keep her in his life, so be it. He'd always assumed that one day the perfect moment would arrive when they would finally resolve things and get back together. But he'd been wrong. Instead, Isobel had met Dominic.

*

Isobel knew it was time to stop thinking about her ex, and rejoin the party. She walked across the lobby and down the plushly carpeted hall, pausing to give herself a pep-talk. She was part of the team, whether the others liked it or not, and she was going to walk into that room as if she owned the place.

Which she did, having bought the entire building.

She pasted a wide if wobbly grin across her face, counted to five, then to ten, just for good measure, and threw open the door, entering the crowded room just in time to collide with a waitress and send a tray of canapés hurtling through the air.

2
Two's
Company

'Oh, God, I'm so sorry!' Isobel tried to help the waitress clean up, but the girl tutted irritably, and she realised she'd just trodden more canapés into the carpet. Then she became aware of the silence that had descended, and looked up to find everyone watching her. At this point, Isobel knew that if she blushed much more her head would explode. This would, she mused, be a *terrible* waste of her new albeit awful haircut.

That thought, combined with her embarrassment, made her giggle, and her colleagues stared at her in surprise. She knew she absolutely *must* stop laughing and stuffed her fist into her mouth, but to no avail. Tears of mirth streamed down her cheeks, and soon she was doubled over, the room silent but for her howls of hysteria. The stares of surprise became stares of alarm.

Finally, Isobel headed for the makeshift bar and, with her back to everyone, shoulders still shaking with laughter, she knocked back a stiff drink.

Gradually, conversation resumed and, when she deemed it safe, Isobel turned round. A burst of coquettish giggling caught her attention. There, in the far corner of the room, was a group of women, and at their centre, as usual, was the magazine's editor, Byron, otherwise known as Lord B, owing to his penchant for reciting poetry, his mane of sandy hair and haughty good looks. There was something leonine about him, Isobel thought. Maybe it was that lazy smile, or the deep rumble of his laughter.

'Isobel!' A hand exerted a vice-like grip on her arm. 'Just the person.'

She turned to find Lexie smiling sweetly at her. Beside her were two of the other feature writers, Jess and Pandora. 'We thought you might like to do a piece for the next issue,' offered Lexie.

'I'd love to!' Isobel beamed. 'Would you like me to jot down some ideas? I could get them to you by tom—'

'No need,' interrupted Lexie smoothly. 'We've got just the thing. We want to take one reader from an inner-city council estate and swap her with you. It'll be a colour piece. So, reckon you're up to it?'

Oblivious to the conspiratorial looks being exchanged by the other women, Isobel nodded. 'Definitely!'

Pandora put down her drink. 'Let's say three thousand words. Now, Isobel, you *do* realise these estates have no electricity?'

'No! How *appalling*!' Isobel was horrified, unaware that behind her back Jess was smirking.

'And you're okay with the curfew?' Lexie tapped her watch. 'Because you'll have to be tucked up in bed by nine every night.'

Still not twigging that they were winding her up, Isobel listened wide-eyed. This was going to be a serious article. At last, a chance to prove herself.

'We'll have to load her up with some gear,' Jess reminded the other two, who instantly adopted solemn expressions.

'Gear?' Isobel echoed weakly.

'Oh, you know,' Pandora waved a hand dismissively, 'drugs. The local currency.'

Isobel gulped.

'Probably be crack,' continued Lexie cheerfully. 'I mean, we could hardly send you in there without any, could we? 'Cause you know what they'd do to you . . .' Suddenly she leaned forward, and made a slicing motion across Isobel's throat. Isobel squealed with fright.

'Sexy Lexie, you up to mischief again?' Byron stepped forward from where he'd been listening quietly, and gave Lexie a brisk smack on the bottom. 'I'll deal with *you* later.'

'Promises, promises . . .' Lexie linked arms with the other women, and disappeared into the crowd.

'They were teasing you, Isobel,' Byron pointed out drily.

'But I am still doing an article?' Her voice quivered. 'Aren't I?'

Instantly Isobel saw a familiar expression cross Byron's face. Where she was involved, he always seemed caught between exasperation and amusement. She'd seen that look the first time they'd met, in fact. When Isobel had initially broached the idea of funding the magazine, Byron had made it clear that to him she was just another society babe with more cash than common sense. He'd obviously assumed that Isobel wanted to play at being a journalist until she reeled in a husband, and his blatant cynicism had caused her to be painfully shy. She'd guessed, correctly, that Byron was used to more spiky women who oozed ambition and who could hold their own on any topic he cared to raise.

Byron, meanwhile, was also recalling their first encounter. He hadn't known whether to hug or to shake Isobel, with her dreamy green eyes and fidgety manner. He wasn't surprised when, ten minutes into the meeting, the reams of paper that she'd been clutching on her lap began sliding towards the floor. To his surprise, Isobel had suddenly dived under the table to retrieve them, leaving him talking to an empty chair as she'd abruptly vanished. By this time Byron had been on the verge of leaving. He'd waited impatiently while Isobel had collected her papers; she'd then sat up, bumped her head on the table, yelped with pain, and finally reappeared looking highly vexed and, Byron had to admit, downright cute.

Finally, and to his relief, she'd collected her wits enough to talk business. He'd realised that she was genuinely enthusiastic about *Primadonna* and he couldn't deny that he needed financial help. So he'd agreed to make Isobel associate editor, figuring it would be an empty title but would keep her happy. And for a split second, he had found himself strangely touched by the look of sheer delight on Isobel's face.

Now, though, while the party got even louder around them, he regarded her with unconcealed exasperation.

'So, do I still get to do the article? I do, don't I?' Agitated, she tugged on his sleeve, then realised what she was doing and snatched her hand back, blushing. 'Sorry.'

'Forget the article. It's not going to happen. But you and I have something important to discuss, don't we?'

'Er, do we?'

'I gather you're not happy with my plans for the next issue.' His lips twitched with mirth at her surprise. Isobel had never voiced her disapproval but he'd caught the reproachful little looks she'd angled his way during staff meetings. Now that he'd put her on the spot, Isobel felt cornered. *Coward*, she accused herself.

'My office, five o'clock tomorrow,' Byron stated.

'I can't, I'm really sorry.' She smiled placatingly. 'Could we please make it earlier?'

'Why can't you do five?' he demanded, intrigued by what Isobel did outside work.

'Because Dominic's new gym opens tomorrow,' she explained. 'I promised I'd be there.' At thirty-one, Dominic was a real success story, having created the most trendy chain of gyms in the country, a franchise called Fit-U-Up. The business was worth a small fortune, and he was undoubtedly London's most eligible bachelor.

Byron shrugged. 'You'll just have to see him later.'

'Couldn't you and I just meet earlier?'

'No. Five.'

'I *can't*.' Isobel felt panicky. Dominic would be furious if she let him down.

Byron glared. He had no patience with people who liked the idea of being a journalist but wouldn't make the necessary sacrifices. All the other women on the magazine worked fourteen-hour days, accepting that they had to put their social lives on hold if a deadline loomed or decisions had to be made. Isobel tended to flit in and out of the office when it suited her.

'It's a question of priorities,' he said brusquely. 'You have to decide which is more important: meeting me or Dominic. You might want to bear in mind that if we don't talk tomorrow, we don't talk at all. There's a deadline to meet. Your call.' With that he wandered off to join Lexie, who had observed the entire exchange through narrowed eyes.

Isobel bolted for her office and flopped on to her little red swivel chair. She located the previous issue. She and Byron had disagreed over that one too.

She'd already given way over the cover, which featured a picture of the hottest actress around, Kitty Kay, a nineteen-year-old so feline she positively purred. Daughter of one of Britain's wealthiest property tycoons, Kitty had run away from her exclusive boarding-school, aged fifteen, following flings with two teachers. The story had hit the papers, and a star was born. Right now, Kitty was taking a break from the soap in which she played a leading role to appear in the pantomime *Dick Whittington* as the cat.

Isobel gazed miserably at the cover: it showed Kitty wearing a pair of fur-trimmed wellingtons, a matching fur-trimmed bra, with a tiny black kitten draped coyly across her lap where her knickers should have been. The caption, dreamed up by Byron, read: '**Puss in Boots**'. Isobel had longed to veto the picture but, as usual, had lost her nerve, turning into a stuttering wreck when she'd tried to broach the subject with Byron.

Now she flicked through the glossy pages, scanning the rest of the magazine thoughtfully. *Primadonna* was unique. Its ethos was that women should be spoilt rotten by men. The *Primadonna* girl wanted – indeed demanded – equality, but she didn't open doors, hail taxis, or light her own cigarettes. Chivalry needed to be resuscitated, and *Primadonna* was there to make sure it happened. So while other women's magazines insisted that women should be able to cope with everything, *Primadonna* suggested that men take care of anything stressful, leaving women free to behave like the princesses they truly were. Isobel glanced at the title of one of the articles: and smiled. 'Is Your Man Being a Royal Pain? How to Make Him Worship the Ground You Walk On!'

From the feedback so far, it seemed their readers liked the magazine's message, although inevitably a number of the more outspoken feminist writers were talking of boycotting it. But that was cool. Controversy meant publicity, and publicity meant sales.

She was so deep in thought that it took Isobel a good few minutes to register that the phone was ringing. 'Isobel de RoseMont speaking.'

'It's me,' croaked a voice, and coughed violently.

'Gems?' Isobel frowned. 'Oh, God, you're not smoking again? Thought you'd quit.'

'I did. Then I began chewing my nicotine patches and started getting hooked on those instead.'

Isobel's smile was anxious. She worried about her friend, and with good reason. Gemma was far too dependent on drink, drugs, and men. Isobel had watched her stumbling from one destructive love affair to the next, propping herself up with one chemical fix after another, and falling apart a bit more at the seams with each passing year.

But, given her circumstances, maybe it wasn't surprising. Gemma's childhood had been marred by not one but two tragedies. The first was bizarre, and Isobel knew it still haunted her friend. For when Gemma was nine, her mother had gone away to visit friends for a weekend, and vanished. No one ever heard from her again and no clues ever surfaced as to her whereabouts. A few years later, Gemma's father, not the most

23

stable man at the best of times, had taken his own life. Gemma had been raised by an aunt, who though well-intentioned, had adopted her niece through a sense of obligation, rather than genuine affection.

Because Gemma's father had been a successful businessman, and her mother a former model, the media had never forgotten the story. Gemma was a beautiful blonde society girl, and the paparazzi were enchanted by her. Even now, years later, increasingly exotic theories were proposed as to her mother's disappearance.

Isobel, also in the media spotlight, could relate to Gemma's unhappiness over the intrusions into her private life. And although, unlike Gemma's father, Isobel's was there physically, he'd always been emotionally absent. The girls spent a lot of time talking about their family backgrounds.

As they'd become friends in their twenties, Isobel had not known Gemma through the unhappy, formative years of her life. But Isobel's boyfriend, Dominic, had. In fact, he and Isobel had met through Gemma.

Now Isobel reminded her friend: 'You're still coming out with me and Dominic for dinner tonight, right?'

'You bet I am!' Instantly Gemma's voice brightened. 'The bastard hasn't called me all week!'

Isobel laughed. Dominic's parents had been friends of Gemma's aunt, and as children the two had been inseparable. They learned to swim together, ran away from their respective homes together, even took their driving tests on the same day. At seventeen, after being dumped in a rather spiteful manner by her first serious boyfriend, Gemma had ended up in hospital with alcohol poisoning; Dominic was the first person by her bedside, and the one who took care of her when she was discharged. He'd also given Gemma's ex a black eye for treating her so badly.

By the time Isobel met Gemma, Dominic was living and working in the States. Isobel gathered he had been a friend, brother and mentor, all rolled into one sublime package. Certainly, his letters and phone calls always seemed to be the high point of Gemma's week, and she positively counted the days between her regular visits to him. To Isobel, Gemma and Dominic were the definitive proof that men and women could enjoy purely platonic friendships. It was clear that Gemma idolised him. And Isobel couldn't help wondering: what was so special about this man that his approval was so precious, so vital, to Gemma?

She'd finally found out when, three years ago, Dominic had returned to London. Ecstatic, Gemma had organised a special dinner party for her closest group of friends. She spent days agonising over the menu and seating arrangements, worrying over every detail.

Isobel had been going through a difficult time, having had a miserable, lonely year after Jon had left for Morocco. Well-meaning friends urged her to get out there and play the field. She refused, too scared of being hurt again. And the one man she did date briefly, the actor, had betrayed her by going to the media. So Isobel stayed single. Besides, Jon was an impossible act to follow.

Until she met Dominic. The attraction was instant, intense, and mutual. But then, Isobel had mused, what woman wouldn't have noticed Dominic? With a mixed, part-French ancestry, he had striking, swarthy looks, with a smooth olive complexion, and raven hair cropped short.

But it had been Dominic's eyes that had really intrigued her. She could hold most people's gazes and find a hint of what they were truly thinking, hoping, fearing. Not with Dominic. Those black-as-midnight eyes were so guarded, sometimes Isobel knew she could stare into them for a lifetime and still never know what was going on behind them.

Gemma had, naturally, seated herself beside Dominic, while Isobel was at the other end of the table. Nevertheless, within an hour of meeting him, and though they'd not yet had a proper conversation, Isobel recognised that Dominic was her total opposite. Where she was shy, he exuded confidence like some kind of force-field. Where Isobel doubted her own intuition, Dominic had unshakeable self-belief.

And all through that dinner party, Isobel had experienced a delicious, shivery excitement, because each time she dared glance his way, it was to find Dominic's dark, inscrutable eyes studying her.

He'd asked her out within the week. Isobel had insisted on checking with Gemma first, sensitive to her friend's feelings. After an initial, surprised look, Gemma had encouraged her to go for it. Still, the three of them had gone through a slightly tense phase when Isobel and Dominic had started getting serious, and Gemma had retreated from her friendships with them both for a brief time. But she soon appeared to adjust, and Isobel took care to make her feel included in any plans the couple made. She also knew that Dominic would always look out for Gemma, whom he seemed to adore like a younger sister.

And Isobel was happy with Dominic. While Jon had challenged her, Dominic accepted her timidity and sought to protect her. He liked her fragility. By the time they'd been together for three months, Isobel couldn't imagine how she'd ever managed without him.

Now Gemma's voice dragged her back to the present. 'Where are we going tonight, by the way? Oh, God, not Kabaret again! B-O-R-I-N-G!'

'Actually we thought we'd try Pumpkin, that new restaurant? Anyway, I need to go home and change first. Want me to pick you up? Say about eight thirty?'

'What about Dom?'

'He's having drinks there first with some mates from work. They've got all this stuff to talk about, what with his new gym opening tomorrow.'

'Let's see . . . I'll probably meet you there, I think,' Gemma decided. 'I'm coming straight from a friend's, and it's nearby.'

'Oh. Well, if you're sure.' Isobel shrugged. 'See you later, then.'

'Bye.'

Isobel hung up and stared into space for a moment. Gemma sounded a bit deflated. Recently, her reliance on drink had become evident again. Every time the two girls went out, Gemma disappeared with a different man; on one occasion, she reappeared two days later looking pale and shaken, refusing to reveal where she'd been. Isobel was becoming uneasy. Gemma had a restless, reckless streak, and it was deepening.

*

Jon tilted his seat back as far as he could without maiming the person behind him. He hated flying: it always brought on a touch of claustrophobia and today he felt particularly edgy. Bored, he began to study one of the in-flight magazines, and found a feature on Brazil. But he couldn't focus on it. He gazed out of the window at the sheet of dull grey Tarmac beneath the plane, and chuckled as he recalled how cute Isobel had looked stapled to the desk. He closed his eyes, fatigue overtaking him. He could run to Brazil, from one beautiful location to another . . . but what difference? Isobel wouldn't be there.

He opened his eyes and watched a voluptuous brunette wearing a bright red dress walking confidently down the aisle, her hips swaying as she moved from row to row, scanning the numbers. Finally she stopped beside him, and glanced at the magazines which were taking up the vacant seat.

'Mine, I believe?' She rolled her eyes in mock irritation. 'You blokes – so untidy!' Jon caught a glint of fun in her eyes, and cleared the seat swiftly. As she sat down, she smiled in a way that confirmed what her walk had suggested. 'Hi, I'm Marie.' Her smile widened. 'So, are you a frequent flyer . . . ?'

Suddenly he was feeling a whole lot better.

*

Isobel was staring at the flurry of inserts that had slipped out of the magazine. Then she peered closely at one in particular: a crumpled piece of paper covered in Byron's untidy scrawl.

She shoved aside her scruples, smoothed it out and read it quickly. It contained Byron's notes on future issues of *Primadonna*. One regular feature was the celebrity interview, for which Isobel had put forward a superb candidate. It was easily the best idea she'd come up with so far. But, according to this bit of paper, Byron was assigning the interview to another journalist without even telling her. And not just any other journalist. Lexie.

Isobel got up and walked over to the glass wall. She gazed out at the party, then began to gnaw a fingernail. She deserved to do this interview, no two ways about it, but it wasn't going to happen, was it? Because she couldn't confront Byron. Because she was a *wimp*.

*

Byron saw that Isobel was peering out of her office and looking fretful. He saw the magazine in her hand and frowned. Groaning inwardly, he remembered all the mad ideas Isobel had entertained over recent months. Like those voice-activated computers she'd ordered. Byron had walked into the office one morning and stopped dead in his tracks. He had let out a low whistle at the sight of the gleaming new hardware. It had cost a small fortune, and it was, he had insisted, a waste of precious funds. But Isobel had simply looked at him in surprise.

'You can't expect us just to sit and type all day!' she'd protested. 'It'd wreak havoc on our nails!'

Convinced she was joking, Byron had waited for her to crack a smile, but when Isobel had just gazed back at him earnestly, he'd blinked in sheer disbelief.

Worse was to come. Isobel's next brainwave was to have a car park built alongside their office block. Byron had put his foot down.

'What? You want me to commute twice a day? In the *rush* hour?' Horrified, she'd stared at him. 'It would positively *kill* me.' Once again Byron had shaken his head in total disbelief but Isobel had looked so perplexed that he'd again found himself hovering somewhere between anger and amusement. Anyway, when push came to shove, it was she who signed the cheques. And, if truth be told, all Byron cared about was having editorial control. So if she wanted to waste her money, he wasn't going to waste time arguing with her.

Until Isobel ordered corporate credit cards, providing one for each member of the sales team and also the writers, so they could take clients and freelancers out for lunch. 'How can I put this tactfully?' mused Byron, then fixed her with an icy glare. 'Oh, that's right – I can't! Isobel, you're a fool. This lot will go mad with them – our expenses are going to be horrendous.'

'Oh, but they're such *dinky* little things.' Isobel had run her fingers over the shiny new cards. 'And all the girls love them!'

'No kidding.' He gave her a shrewd look. 'I know you want them to like you, but we're running a magazine, not a popularity contest. You can't buy their friendship.'

Seeing her eyes darken with hurt, he'd shrugged. 'Well, it's your money. Just don't come crying to me when it's all gone and the magazine folds.'

Now, oblivious to the party raging on around him, Byron watched Isobel chewing her fingernail and gazing out at her colleagues. Nice, the way that dress just skimmed her shapely thighs. Eye-candy, that was Isobel. Sweet, fluffy, ditzy beyond belief. Not his type at all.

Just then Isobel's eyes locked with his, and Byron smiled lazily, enjoying the way she blushed, before he turned back to Lexie, who had been watching him watching Isobel, and who was now looking at him uneasily.

*

As Byron had met her eyes, Isobel had smiled automatically. Because Isobel always smiled, no matter how she was feeling inside. Once he'd turned away, she looked again at his scribbled notes on the celebrity interview. Time to return to the party, right this minute, and confront him. Isobel nodded grimly. She must get tough!

She gripped the door handle and willed herself to turn it. But it was no good. She couldn't. For Isobel had lost her temper – *literally*! Mislaid it somewhere between ballet classes and boarding-school. Expressing anger was physically impossible for her.

And it was no wonder. In the de RoseMont family anger – even legitimate anger – was a gatecrasher, banished the moment it appeared. Isobel had never been encouraged to develop even the most basic assertiveness skills. Instead she'd watched as, over the years, her father had manipulated people into doing whatever he wanted. Her entire life, Isobel had kept her true emotions bottled up: hurt, disappointment, sadness, and especially anger. She simply never voiced them.

Oh, but she could feel them, all those repressed emotions, scuttling around her psyche, frantically searching for a way out.

And one day, Isobel suspected she was just going to SNAP!

Quietly.

3

Ménage
à Trois

If there was one thing Isobel dreaded, it was having to walk
alone into a crowded room. When she arrived at Pumpkin,
she scanned the dimly lit bar for Dominic. The place was
crammed with immaculate-looking couples, many draped over
low sofas. It occurred to her that all the women worked in PR
for leading fashion-houses, or wrote columns for glossy magazines. Plenty didn't work, but just drifted through a cocaine-
clouded round of socialising.

The huge dining room, in muted shades of yellow and
orange, was almost full. As Isobel entered several people looked
up and she averted her eyes, staring at the floor as she tried to
squeeze between the tables without attracting any more attention while searching for her boyfriend.

She couldn't see him anywhere, and glanced around with
rising panic. The *maître d'* was in conversation, and Isobel
didn't dare interrupt him. None of the staff looked very
approachable either, as they rushed around the busy restaurant.

Isobel froze. She felt an overwhelming urge to turn and
leave, to get away from all those appraising stares – no doubt

all the women were smirking at her horrible new hairstyle. Just then, the strap of her bag caught on the back of someone's chair. Desperately, she tried to tug it free but failed. Her face burned as everyone at the table watched her in amusement. Eventually one of the men reached over and, with a smirk, released the strap in seconds. Two of the women tittered. Mortified, Isobel scuttled off, heading blindly for the back of the room where she'd glimpsed an exit.

'Isobel! Darling, over here!'

She'd never been so happy to hear Dominic's voice. He and Gemma were sitting close together at a tiny table at the far end of the restaurant.

Dominic was by far the most attractive man in the room. He worked out regularly and was also a martial arts fanatic who taught women's self-defence classes, so he was extremely fit. As Isobel approached, she could see that Gemma was, as usual, hanging on his every word, her face resting on one hand, her long fair hair falling forward. Isobel remembered how, when she and Jon were a couple, he'd laughed at her reluctance to enter places alone, and pushed her to get over it, purposely arranging to meet her in busy pubs, clubs and restaurants. He'd always forced her to confront situations she found hard.

Dominic never did that. And from the fond look he now gave her, Isobel knew that he found her shyness endearing. As she reached the table, he got up and pulled her into a hug. Then he pushed her back slightly, dark eyes appraising her. 'Your hair's different.'

Isobel gave her new hairstyle a self-conscious pat. 'Had it done this morning.' She grimaced. 'What do you think?'

'You always look beautiful to me.' Dominic kissed her again, and Isobel clung to his hand as they headed for the table. He didn't like her hair, she knew, but, as always, was being diplomatic.

'I have good news.' Dominic pulled out a chair for her and beamed. 'I managed to get the *Lady Luck*!'

Isobel clapped her hands in delight and sent a bottle of Dom Perignon toppling over. Quickly she began to mop up the tide of champagne but Dominic summoned a waiter with a flick of his hand, then hugged Isobel who by now was feeling like a total klutz.

Again she found herself comparing Dominic with Jon. Her ex wasn't the type to hang on a woman's every word, or to be consistently attentive. Isobel remembered one particular occasion, when they'd been having dinner, and Jon had struck up a conversation with the elderly Italian matriarch who owned the restaurant. At first Isobel had sat quietly, listening to their conversation, smiling politely. After ten minutes, her smile had become strained; Jon was fascinated by the woman's stories, and wanted to come back and take her photograph. While Isobel admired his ability to connect with strangers, she wasn't sure where she fitted in at times like this. They were supposed to be having a romantic dinner, yet Jon seemed to have forgotten that she was there. Eventually, she got up and headed for the ladies'. When she returned ten minutes later Jon was still deep in conversation. He hadn't even noticed she'd gone. Not wanting to sound like a possessive girlfriend, Isobel had seethed silently until, finally, Jon focused on her again. She couldn't imagine Dominic behaving like that, but she had to admit that she and Jon had gone on to enjoy many evenings at the cosy little Italian restaurant where, from that night on, they were treated like family.

Right now, Dominic was certainly concentrating on her, beaming as he continued with his news. They'd been planning a holiday for months, just waiting until Dominic could arrange the use of his father's luxurious yacht. 'It's all arranged – two months in the Caribbean! I've already told Lucy and Charles, and Natalie and Rob are definitely on board. Nigel's said yes, and Richard's not sure but I'm working on him. And, of course, Gemma can't wait. We'll leave at the beginning of December and come back at the end of January.' Dominic hugged her again.

'But, Dominic, you know I can't go away for that long! What about my job?'

He looked at her wryly. 'Right. Of course, the magazine will grind to a halt because you're not there, but still . . .'

Isobel knew his sarcasm wasn't intended to hurt but this remark stung. Truth was, no one at *Primadonna* would care if she disappeared for good.

'Now, you realise I won't let you say no. I'm quite sure Byron can look after things while you're away.'

Isobel took a deep breath and tried to reason with him. 'I have to be at work. Can't we just change the holiday dates?' Desperate for some support, she turned to Gemma. But her friend's eyes were on Dominic.

Now he covered Isobel's hand firmly with his, trapping it against the table. 'Are you saying you'd rather be stuck at work than on holiday with me?' Dominic always spoke quietly, so it was hard for Isobel to ascertain how he was really feeling.

When she failed to answer, he let go of her hand. 'Do you have any idea how excited I was at getting the *Lady Luck*? I couldn't wait to tell you.' He shrugged. 'But I guess your job's more important.'

As always, Isobel felt her resolve weakening. 'It's not that . . .' She glanced around the room at all the other women chattering happily, looking confident and in control. How would they handle this? More skilfully than her, for sure. She felt as if she was being torn in two. Of course she'd love to go on the cruise, but she was scared that such a long holiday would simply convince her colleagues that she didn't take her work seriously.

'Well,' Dominic sounded amused, 'talk of the devil and he instantly appears.'

Following his stare Isobel watched Byron Harrington arrive, a slender brunette dangling from each arm. He was striking in a charcoal suit, his rugged face partly obscured by the long sandy hair that fell to his shoulders. *David Ginola eat your heart out*, thought Isobel.

Entering the room just behind Byron was a photographer she recognised from *OK!*, obviously here to report on the celebrity clientele of the new restaurant.

Byron saw them immediately, pushed his brunette companions towards the bar, and sauntered over. 'Isobel, Dominic, what a lovely surprise.' He turned to Gemma. 'Now, I *know* I haven't met *you* before . . .'

Dominic poured him a glass of champagne. 'Join us?'

'Sure.' Byron slid into a chair. 'Can't leave you alone with the two most beautiful women here, must take one off your hands. The question is: which?' His eyes lingered on Isobel. ' "*But to see her was to love her, love but her, and love for ever . . .*" ' He smiled, 'Burns.'

Then suddenly his smile became a glare. 'Isobel, I'm furious with you!'

She tensed. 'What have I done?'

'Only hidden such a gorgeous friend! You could have introduced us ages ago.'

Gemma blushed while Dominic gestured at the two brunettes, still hovering by the bar and looking bored. 'Haven't you forgotten something?'

Glancing over, Byron sent a careless smile their way. 'It was just a casual drink.' He looked straight at Gemma. 'Nothing special.' His tone suggested she could be, and Isobel watched her friend melt. If Gemma got any more slushy she'd dissolve! Byron was the last man she needed: another bastard who would take what he wanted then disappear into the sunset without so much as a backward glance.

The brunette babes had grown bored at the bar and now came swaying over. Close up, it was clear they were twins, their identical curves encased in identical little black dresses, a tiny tattoo of a scarlet rose on each right shoulder.

'Byron, you swine.' One of the girls pouted. 'We're feeling terribly neglected.'

'Are you? Shame. Everyone, these are two old friends of mine, Peach and Cherry.' He grinned lazily at them and slipped an arm round Gemma. 'I've run into my favourite cousin and we haven't seen each other for ages. Not seen each other *properly*, that is.' He undressed her with his eyes. 'Not yet.'

Gemma giggled.

'Anyway, loads to catch up on, family gossip and all.' Byron tucked a lock of shiny hair behind Gemma's ear and the brunettes, thoroughly bemused, drifted off wearing identical inane smiles.

Having now finished interrogating the waiter over the menu, Dominic turned to Byron.

'Perhaps you can settle a dispute.' He outlined the cruise dilemma. Isobel watched them unhappily. Byron would love nothing more than to get her out of the way; she was always getting under his feet with her constant questions about journalism. Between them, the two men were going to make sure she had no input into *Primadonna* at all.

'Dominic, I see your problem,' Byron spread his hands in a gesture of helplessness, 'but I'm afraid that, as associate editor, Isobel cannot desert us for two whole months.' He gazed solemnly at them. 'We'd never cope without her.'

Dominic raised an eyebrow. Gemma looked amused. Isobel and Byron stared at each other, both knowing he was lying through his teeth.

Dominic smiled at Isobel. 'I'm sure we'll sort something out. Isobel knows how much this holiday means to me.'

She nodded meekly.

The food arrived and the atmosphere improved as the two men discovered they had mutual friends. Isobel relaxed; she'd work something out about the cruise. Right now she was just glad they were all getting on. Seeing the longing looks Isobel was directing at his cigarette, Byron pushed the packet towards her. 'Go on,' he whispered across the tiny table, hazel eyes glinting. '*Indulge.*'

Proud of her will-power, Isobel pushed it back to him. 'Thanks, but I don't.'

'Never?' Byron smiled slightly. 'Pity.' He pursed his lips and blew a series of perfect smoke rings towards her, then sent Isobel a knowing smile.

But Dominic, who abhorred smoking, obviously approved of her will-power. Isobel felt his hand slide up her leg under her skirt. She gazed down into her drink and tried not to wriggle around on the chair as he stroked her inner thigh, gently at first, then more insistently, sending waves of pleasure rushing through her body. His hand brushed lightly against the lacy white knickers she wore, his favourites.

Isobel glanced up to catch his eye but Dominic wasn't looking at her; he was busy chatting with the others. Then Byron sent her a conspiratorial grin . . . and the hand's pressure increased. As Byron's grin deepened and the fingers began tracing lazy circles along her thigh, Isobel paled. He wouldn't. He couldn't. *He was!*

She was so shocked that, for a moment, she just sat there. Then she twisted round sharply in her chair and scraped it back. The hand stole back down her thigh, Byron grinning all the while.

Trembling, Isobel jumped up, grabbed her bag, and looked pointedly at Gemma. 'Gems, I need to brush my hair. Come and help me find the ladies'. Gemma?'

Gemma glanced at Byron, who patted her hand. 'Don't worry. I'm not going anywhere.'

*

In the cloakroom, Isobel and Gemma stood before the mirror, both busy applying make-up. Then Gemma stopped what she was doing. 'Isobel, I need to ask you something, and I want an honest answer, okay?'

'Sure.'

'And you swear you'll be totally truthful?' Gemma demanded.

'Promise.'

'Right, then, here it is. Which suits me best, flicked ends or straight?'

'Sorry?'

'My hair, the ends. Which looks better – like it is now, dead straight, or the way I normally wear it, you know, flicked up at the ends? I really need to know, I've got that charity ball at the weekend.' Gemma turned back to the mirror, twiddling a lock of hair, a look of intense concentration on her face.

It occurred to Isobel that one of them had gone mad, but who? Was this what life, *her* life, was about? Suddenly, vividly, she pictured Jon in Brazil, charging through the rainforest, camera to the fore, doing what he loved, achieving something. She wanted that too.

She tucked these thoughts away, and looked at Gemma. 'You're not really going to see Byron again?'

'Why? Do you want him for yourself?' teased Gemma.

'Hardly!' Isobel explained what Byron had done. 'He practically assaulted me under the table!'

'How do you know it wasn't Dom?' asked Gemma sceptically.

'Gems, come on . . .'

'I'm sure Byron was only winding you up.' Gemma giggled. 'It is rather funny.'

Isobel tried another tack, telling her friend how unreasonable Byron had been over their meeting the next day, and the dilemma with which this had presented her.

'So you won't be able to meet Dominic at the gym opening?' Gemma made a face. 'He'll be really disappointed.'

'I know, I'm putting off telling him,' agonised Isobel. 'But what can I do?'

'Well, look, I don't mind going along to the gym, if that helps,' Gemma suggested. 'I'm not doing anything else.'

'Really?' Isobel beamed. 'That would be great!'

'No worries.' Lipstick half-way to her mouth, Gemma paused. 'Isobel, is Dominic The One?'

'I love him,' Isobel said softly, recalling what an emotional wreck she'd been after Jon left. Dominic had restored her faith in relationships.

'Yes, but are you *in* love with him?' Gemma persisted. 'Only sometimes I wonder if you still have feelings for Jon.'

Isobel looked her straight in the eye. 'I can tell you honestly that my feelings for Jon are nothing like my feelings for Dominic. There is no comparison.' And she wasn't lying. No one would ever get to her in quite the way Jon had. But that didn't mean for a minute that Dominic was second best. Their relationship wasn't less, or worse, just different.

Gemma nodded, and Isobel decided to change the subject. 'What happened with that merchant banker you were seeing? What was his name? Piers?'

'Oh, I dumped him. The guy named his dick after a super-hero.'

'Which one?'

'Hercules.' Gemma shot her a droll look. 'Wish he'd had half his stamina!'

They both collapsed in giggles, returning to the table with their arms linked.

*

42

Byron pulled Gemma to her feet. 'I feel like going somewhere quieter.'

Gemma kissed Dominic and Isobel goodbye, then she and Byron were gone.

'God, I hope Gems isn't going to get hurt again.' Dominic sighed. 'Byron'll walk all over her.'

Isobel leaned over and kissed his cheek.

He smiled. 'What was that for?'

'For caring. It's sweet that you're worried about Gemma. You're a true friend to her.' A thought occurred to Isobel. 'If we ever . . . you know . . . broke up, would we still be friends?'

'No,' Dominic said vehemently. 'I could never be friends with you because I'm in love with you. Anything less would hurt. I couldn't handle it, I know I couldn't.'

Isobel beamed with relief. He really did love her. And, despite what she'd thought at the time, Jon had obviously never been in love with her since he was perfectly happy to be friends. It didn't hurt *him*, did it?

'But it's all academic,' Dominic hugged her fiercely, 'because we're not going to break up. Ever. I would never let you go. Nothing and no one could ever make me.'

Isobel's face glowed as he continued to hold her close and kiss her, not caring who was watching them. She smiled. 'Shall we go home?'

They headed for Isobel's car, since Dominic's friends had given him a lift to Pumpkin. Automatically, Isobel handed him her keys. Dominic always drove. She couldn't remember a single occasion when he'd ever agreed to be the passenger.

Just as he was about to pull away from the kerb, Dominic paused, eyes fixed on the dashboard. 'What's that?'

'What?' Isobel followed his gaze. He was staring at the picture of her that Jon had taken earlier that day.

He picked it up and flicked it over. His face darkened as he noted Jon's signature. 'I thought Jon was abroad. When did you see him?'

'Today,' said Isobel casually. 'He popped in to the office party.'

'I see. The office party to which I wasn't invited.'

'You were busy setting things up for the gym's opening,' Isobel reminded him, reaching for his hand.

Dominic shrugged her off. 'So, while I've been working round the clock you've been off having fun with Jon? When were you going to tell me you'd seen him?'

'I only saw him for five minutes! Hardly worth mentioning.' Isobel's chest felt tight and it was hard to breathe. 'Dominic, honestly, we had a quick chat and then he rushed off to catch a flight.'

'Really?' Dominic looked at her searchingly.

Again she reached for his hand; again he pulled away. 'But he still found time to take pictures of you.' He hit the accelerator and they were speeding away down the street. Isobel rested her forehead against the window, closed her eyes, and wished this day was over.

*

Twenty minutes later they were walking in silence from the car to Dominic's Belgravia house. Isobel had never liked it much: it was all stainless-steel surfaces and bare white walls. Dominic sat down on the sofa and buried his head in the *Financial*

Times, while she perched on the coffee table in front of him, willing him to put the paper down. 'Dominic . . . come on . . . don't be like this.'

'Like what?' The paper didn't budge.

'So angry.' She hugged herself.

'I'm just disappointed about the holiday, and upset that you can't even tell me when you've seen your ex-boyfriend. And, frankly, I don't think I'm being unreasonable.'

For a few minutes she was silent. Then she tapped the paper. 'Did you see those girls with Byron? Their tattoos were really pretty.'

Instantly he lowered the paper. 'I *loathe* tattoos on women.'

'What about a temporary one?' Isobel placed her hand lightly on his thigh. 'I could have a little butterfly or . . .' her face lit up, green eyes shining '. . . a seahorse – I *adore* them! Just think how nice it would look on my—'

'Isobel, really, how *tacky*!' Dominic tossed aside the paper.

Isobel inched forward so that she was sitting right in front of him. 'But Dominic, it might look cute. Wouldn't you like to see me with a pretty little picture just . . .' She slipped down her skirt to reveal the creamy curve of her hip '. . . there?'

Dominic's eyes warmed slightly and she smiled with relief. Isobel couldn't bear him to be angry with her, and would do anything to make things better. She began slowly unbuttoning her blouse, looking at Dominic as it fell away to reveal her breasts in a white lacy bra, the type Dominic preferred. He leaned over, grabbed her skirt and pulled it down roughly, then covered her face with kisses as they tumbled to the floor together laughing, his fingers sliding her knickers down. 'Turn over . . .' he whispered.

She complied and heard him unzip his trousers. He entered her quickly, and started to thrust hard, one hand tight around her stomach, holding her firmly against him. Isobel's face was pressed against the cool, smooth parquet floor. She closed her eyes as Dominic began moving inside her . . . thrusting faster . . . his fingers pressing into her skin as he thrust deeper and deeper . . . She gasped with pleasure. They might have their problems, but this had never been one of them.

*

Jon was enjoying Rio, enjoying the ribbon of caramel-coloured sand, the lush palm trees. He even liked the rain, which had been falling all evening, hot and fast. But most of all, he was enjoying Marie, the girl he'd met on the plane.

Outside, along the beachfront, the market was open, and chattering voices floated towards them. He could hear music spilling from a car radio, some sultry Latin-American ballad. He ran a hand lightly along Marie's thigh. She was gorgeous. But now as she reached for him, pulled his head down and kissed him, it wasn't her face he saw, but Isobel's. Jon let his own eyes close and returned the kiss, his fingers gently stroking her face.

Marie didn't know it, but that night they were a threesome.

*

Gemma leaned back against the smooth wall of the jacuzzi, feeling the tiny bubbles burst against her skin. Something was going on here that she didn't understand: although they were naked and Byron was having a hard time taking his eyes off her, he hadn't touched her. By all accounts he was a normal, red-blooded bloke, but he hadn't made a move. She felt a flutter of sheer panic. She needed *something* tonight, and it might as well be Byron. 'So, you must be one of the youngest

editors around but then you're certainly endowed with a huge
. . .' she let her eyes flit over him '. . . *talent.*'

He chuckled, but still made no move to touch her. 'Hopefully the magazine will do okay. I'm not sure Isobel's liking
work much at the moment, though.'

Work. Gemma stifled a yawn. 'Yeah, well, she takes it pretty
seriously.'

'I'd noticed. Is she that intense over everything? Dominic,
for example?'

'Guess so.' Gemma trailed her hands through the bubbles
glistening over her milky skin.

'Although for some reason,' Byron continued casually, 'I just
don't see them as a couple. Not permanently, that is.'

'Why?' Without realising it, she leaned forward.

'Just a hunch. They're not right for each other.'

'How can you tell? You hardly know them.'

'I know what I saw tonight.'

'Which was?'

'Oh, come on, Gemma. You know.'

'No, I don't. What are you talking about?'

'Want to play Little Miss Innocent? Fine by me.' Byron
seemed amused. 'But you do know. You know that Dominic
talked to you more than he did to Isobel.'

Gemma averted her eyes, and gazed into the water. She
didn't want Byron to guess that her feelings for Dominic were
light years away from platonic. It had taken a long time for
Gemma to admit this to herself. Since the age of ten, Dom had
been her confidant, the person she ran to when life let her
down, when people hurt her.

And he had been staunch through every crisis. At twenty,

when she'd fallen pregnant, Dominic had listened endlessly while Gemma agonised over her options. And, after her abortion, he'd taken care of her, sitting up with Gemma night after night while she was wracked with guilt. Without him, Gemma doubted she would have got through the ordeal. Dominic knew her inside out and back to front. Knew all her secrets. Except how she really felt about him.

She should have realised sooner that she was in love with him. Gemma recalled how, even at the tender age of ten, she'd been breathless with excitement the first time she'd seen this handsome boy with the sooty black hair and even darker eyes walking up the driveway of her aunt's house. From then on, she would sit in school each day, watching the clock, desperate for the bell to signal the end of classes so she could go home and run over to Dominic's. Could she have been in love even back then?

It was only when Dominic announced he was moving to the States that Gemma had finally analysed her feelings for him. His decision to leave devastated her. She started crying herself to sleep each night. That was when she realised that Dominic meant the world to her. Because now that he was going, it felt like her world was surely ending.

She never told him how she felt, terrified of losing him. Also, she remembered how he'd reacted the one and only time their friendship had intensified into something more. It was the summer Gemma had turned fifteen. Dominic was a year older. They were playing happily by the pool, Dominic threatening to throw her into the deep end, Gemma's arms around his neck as she screamed and squealed with mock fear. Suddenly Dominic had stopped laughing. Gemma stopped shouting. Then they were kissing. It lasted ten seconds, but to this day Gemma could recapture the touch of his lips on hers. Dominic had been the one to pull away, murmuring something before setting her down abruptly on the grass and stalking away into his house, Gemma watching him in confusion. He'd reappeared a bit later and they'd never mentioned the incident again. And there had never been a repetition.

So even when Gemma had acknowledged her real feelings for Dominic, she'd never told him. Instead, she'd resolved that when he returned to London, things would be different. *She* would be different. Somehow, she would make him see her through new eyes.

Except that, of course, it hadn't quite worked out that way. Dominic had met Isobel, and after that, Gemma knew she didn't stand a chance. It was hard, watching him with her best friend. But she told herself that being in love with Dominic was a bit like living with a medical condition: it was something she had to accept, something that would always be with her, something that was painful at times, something she had no choice over. The important thing was that neither Isobel nor Dominic suspected. They both meant everything to Gemma. Losing either one of them would have killed her.

Now she flicked some water playfully at Byron and giggled. The coke she'd taken a few minutes ago was starting to work its magic. Gemma could feel her thoughts breaking up, her throat aching. Her heart seemed to be spinning in her chest, round and round and round, just like the room. Round and round, just like her thoughts. She was laughing and she was crying and then she was in Byron's arms, or were they Dominic's?

She tried to focus on his face, but he just smiled at her and kissed her eyes closed, and she couldn't open them again, because they were so heavy. Then he was inside her, moving slowly. Gemma could hear someone talking, but couldn't make out the words. Was it her speaking or was someone else in the room with them? Why hadn't she seen them? Oh, of course, they must be playing Hide and Seek. Soon it would be her turn to hide.

Now he was pushing her back against the side of the jacuzzi, still moving inside her, still moving slowly, too slowly. Impatiently Gemma raked his back with her fingernails, wanting him to keep up with the pounding of her heart. Then he was, and she didn't care if it was Byron or Dominic inside her any more.

Gemma didn't care who the hell it was, just as long as it was someone.

4

Obsession

Hurrying home the next morning to change for work, Isobel shook her head in despair. Last night had turned into a disaster, although initially sex had certainly improved Dominic's mood. He'd even persuaded her to wear the French maid's outfit he especially liked, complete with fluffy pink duster and frilly white apron.

But things had gone downhill rapidly after she'd told him that, owing to her meeting with Byron, she couldn't make it to the opening of the gym. Dominic had simply looked at her, then turned over and closed his eyes. Isobel wasn't sure if he was really asleep or not. She herself had lain awake for hours, feeling guilty because she'd let him down.

Then Isobel had felt a fluttery sensation in her stomach, which was the closest she ever came to anger. Why couldn't Dominic be a *tad* more understanding about her work? Instantly, though, she'd chided herself. He was a wonderful boyfriend. She was the one at fault here.

Back at her flat, Isobel had the quickest shower in recorded history, leaped into the first clothes and shoes she saw, then half fell out of the front door again. She tripped over twice on her way to the car, laddering her tights and grazing her hands. Arriving at work forty minutes late, she found the office in a state of organised chaos. A radio was playing loudly, so that everyone was shouting in order to be heard. A flurry of short-skirted girls dashed around, yelling into phones, brandishing proofs, panicking over deadlines and headlines.

Three subs surrounded one computer, gesticulating frantic-ally, embroiled in a heated row over the spelling of someone's name. Byron was in his office, typing away at his computer.

Isobel made a face. Everyone had some urgent task to per-form, except her. She was the associate editor of *Primadonna*, and she had nothing to do. Something was seriously wrong with this picture.

At eleven Julia, the health and beauty editor, appeared puffing happily on a herbal cigarette. 'Lord B says since you're not busy could you rustle up some hot drinks? We've got some potential advertisers coming in any minute now.'

Isobel smiled weakly. Wouldn't an associate editor normally be far too busy to fetch hot drinks for colleagues? But her title was an empty one and everyone here knew it. And, besides, it wasn't as though she had any real work to do, was it? She didn't know how to sub an article, and her feature ideas had all been rejected. Isobel knew that everyone would probably be relieved if she'd just go home, sign the cheques when needed, and stay away. She scuttled into the kitchen. Now she felt almost efficient, organising three scalding hot teas, even re-membering to refill the sugar bowl from the large white shaker. She congratulated herself on this newly found practical streak, and added some chocolate biscuits. Then, balancing the tray carefully, she walked slowly into Byron's office.

He gaped, then smiled with relief when Isobel left the room without mishap. Back in her own office, she watched absently as Byron, Julia and the two clients helped themselves to the drinks. Suddenly she saw four faces contorting, four people gasping and gagging, their hands flying to their mouths. Next thing she knew Byron was storming into her office, face scarlet, his large frame filling the doorway. 'Isobel! Can't you get *anything* right?'

'What's wrong?'

'"What's wrong?"' echoed Byron incredulously. 'You're asking me "what's wrong?"'

'What did I do?'

'You filled the sugar bowl with *salt*.' He rubbed his eyes. 'I swear I don't know what to do with you any more! You're *hopeless*!'

Isobel looked at him reproachfully. 'That's a slight exagg—'

'*Is* it? Let me refresh your memory.' Byron's tone was scathing. 'Yesterday I got you sorting out the filing system. Now everything after the letter E has vanished never to be seen again! Last week, I asked you to run a simple errand and buy me some painkillers and you managed, *somehow*, to get *lost* – in BOOTS!'

'It *was* one of the larger ones, you know, with *three* exits,' Isobel explained, voice trailing off as Byron's face filled with despair.

'And today you've proved you can't make a cup of tea without practically poisoning four people!' Covering his face with his hands, he let out a muffled scream of sheer frustration.

Alarmed, Isobel jumped up. Suddenly her left foot turned over sharply and, with a surprised yelp, she lurched forward and all but fell into his arms. He steadied her, then spoke more calmly: 'Isobel, I know I'll probably regret asking this, but do you feel a bit, well, *off balance* today?' He sighed. 'More than usual, that is.'

'I do, actually.' Isobel frowned. 'Can't think why, though.' She looked at him earnestly. 'Strange, isn't it, Byron? How some days you just feel more *together* than others?'

Byron was staring pointedly at her feet.

'What are you looking at?' queried a puzzled Isobel.

'Your shoes.'

'D'you like them?' She beamed. 'I got them last time I was in Paris. Divine, aren't they?'

'I'm sure they would be heavenly,' Byron smiled smoothly, 'if they matched.'

'What?' Isobel glanced at her feet, then groaned. She'd been walking around in odd shoes. Both were black, but one had a slight heel while the other was flat. No wonder she kept falling over.

To Isobel's surprise, Byron burst out laughing, and a moment later they were both wiping tears of mirth from their eyes.

Finally Byron composed himself. 'Isobel, do me a favour and cover Reception for ten minutes? Alison's gone home with a migraine and that lousy temping agency have let us down. You're the only one not writing to a deadline right now.'

Isobel knew an associate editor would normally never be asked to do this. But she flashed him a reassuring grin. 'Don't worry, I can handle it.'

'Cheers. Look, I've got to get back to this meeting, but at some point another rep from the cosmetics company should turn up. Now, Isobel, this is important. You're to show him straight in, do you understand? He's the marketing director, and we need him on side. Apart from that, I do *not* want to be disturbed, get it?'

'Relax.' Isobel patted his arm. 'I'm on the case.'

Byron shuddered.

*

'Jesus, my *head* . . .' Gemma sat up slowly, so groggy it was a good few minutes before she realised where she was. In Byron's bed, in Byron's bedroom, in Byron's flat. *Sans* Byron. She screwed up her face in concentration, and retrieved a memory of him jumping out of bed at some ungodly hour then planting a quick kiss on her forehead before leaving for work.

Now it was gone twelve. Gemma didn't usually sleep that late but then, she smiled, it had been an energetic night.

She found her bag under the bed, and tipped it upside down, desperate for a cigarette. She lit one, flopped back against the large blue pillows, and tried to piece things together. She couldn't recall much, not even how they'd made it from the jacuzzi to the bedroom. Struggling to clear her mind, she glanced round the room.

'I've heard of blokes taking their work home with them, but this is something else . . .' She hopped out of bed, her eyes on the pale beige walls. Every inch of space was filled with magazine covers, all encased in glass and surrounded by shiny black frames.

One entire wall was devoted to *Totty*, the magazine Byron had wanted to edit, and *Primadonna*'s main rival. Gemma padded over and looked at this collection more closely, checking the dates, which went back three years. Two other walls contained covers from every publication Byron had ever worked on, including several trade magazines. The far wall was home to the first three covers of *Primadonna*, enlarged to poster-size. In total there had to be around a hundred covers. One hundred glamorous women gazed down at her, eyes ringed with dark liner, lips dripping with gloss, smiles shy and secretive, seductive, inviting and challenging. Gemma felt uneasy; this place was like a shrine. But to what exactly?

Out of curiosity she tried opening a few drawers but they were all locked. She lost interest and headed for the bathroom where, beside the sunken jacuzzi, she found her clothes. Time to leave.

*

Isobel headed out into the lobby and perched on one of the chairs behind the high chrome reception desk. She took in the switchboard, and realised she had no idea how to use it.

After playing around with it for a good fifteen minutes – and accidentally calling Byron's direct line twice which further infuriated him – she gave up. Instead she amused herself by seeing how fast she could spin round on the little swivel chair before getting dizzy.

'Er, excuse me?' A smartly dressed man in his late thirties approached warily. 'I'm here to see Byron Harrington.'

The tiny chair was now spinning wildly. Arms flailing, Isobel clutched frantically at the desk, gasping, 'Name, *pleeeeeeeease*?' before she went whizzing round again.

'Michael Brooks.' Giving her a dubious look, he began edging away.

Isobel lunged for the desk lamp and clung on for dear life. The chair stopped. 'I'll just let him know you're here. Have a seat.' She gestured towards the sofa, turned back to the switchboard and began hitting buttons at random.

Around the building telephone extensions started to ring, and people cursed as their conversations were mysteriously cut off. Oblivious to the chaos she was creating, Isobel continued frantically punching buttons, wondering why nothing was happening and Byron wasn't picking up.

Five minutes later she realised it would be quicker to go and tell him personally that someone was asking for him. But just then the external line began ringing and glowing red. She grabbed it. '*Primadonna*, good morning!'

'Isobel?' It was Jon. 'I tried your office but the line's engaged. What are you doing on Reception?'

'Destroying it, probably.' She groaned but felt better for hearing his voice.

*

In Rio, Jon glanced at Marie, still sleeping, her hair streaming over the pillow. Pulling the phone over to the window he gazed out at the beach, littered with streamers and other assorted debris from last night's street party. It was nine in the morning, and already the air was so hot it stung.

'So, how goes it?' Isobel put her feet up on the desk. The mismatched shoes were making them ache so she slipped them off, throwing them carelessly on to the floor beside her chair, then made herself comfortable.

'Couldn't be better. Brazil's stunning.'

'Jon?'

'Yes, Isobel?'

'Why are you whispering?'

'Because I have company, and she's still asleep.'

'Oh.' Isobel frowned. 'Jon?'

'Yes, Isobel?'

'Why am *I* whispering?'

He chuckled. 'Because you're cute.'

'So who is she, then? Your guest, I mean.'

'Name's Marie. We met on the plane. She confided that her ambition was to join the Mile High Club, so what's a bloke to do? Except oblige, of course.'

'Didn't take you long to get over Marvellous Maxine.'

'Yeah, well, you know what they say – a change is as good as a rest.' Jon decided it was time to switch subjects. 'Seriously, though, you'd love it here. Tomorrow I'm flying south to Iguaco Falls. I hear they're amazing.' The slightest of pauses. 'Come and join me. You could hop on a plane and be here by tonight.'

'Not worried I'd cramp your style?'

'You?' His voice softened. 'Never.'

'Might take you up on the offer soon. I could do with a break.'

'What's the problem?'

Isobel explained the dilemma involving the cruise, heaping blame upon herself for not being a better girlfriend, berating herself for letting Dominic down all the time.

Drumming his fingers on the window-sill, Jon bit back a sharp retort. God, how he longed to tell Isobel what he really thought of Dominic; the bastard should be showing support, not guilt-tripping her. And Isobel was so naïve, so idealistic about her boyfriend that she couldn't even see what he was doing. Or, Jon frowned, maybe she could see it but couldn't face admitting to herself that she'd made a mistake, that she'd invested two years of her life with the wrong man.

Again.

Now Jon was in a quandary. Isobel was confiding in him as a

friend, because she trusted him. He mustn't stir up trouble between her and Dominic, tempting though it was. But how he longed to set her straight.

'So?' Isobel concluded. 'What do you reckon?'

'You must do what you think best.'

'But what would you advise me to do?'

'Only you know which means more. Your man or your mag.'

'Yes, but, Jon, what do *you* think I should do?'

'Only you can decide.'

'Gosh, Jon, those splinters in your bum must be *so* painful!'

'Splinters?'

'*From sitting on the fence!*' said Isobel lightly. 'Won't you at least give me an honest opinion?'

Jon flopped down on the bed, now so agitated he was practically tearing his hair out.

'That's the best advice I can offer. And, anyway, shouldn't you be talking to Dominic about it? Don't suppose he'd like you running to me.' Jon was disgusted with himself for not being more blunt with Isobel, and it made his tone terse.

'I thought you cared,' said Isobel softly. 'Sorry, my mistake.'

'I do care, I—'

But it was too late. She'd gone. Not that she'd slammed the phone down, for Isobel would never dream of doing that, instead had simply replaced it quietly.

Jon swore. Maybe he'd handled it wrongly. Maybe he shouldn't pretend to be neutral. After all, what did he have to lose? He'd already lost the most important thing: Isobel. Swiftly he hit the redial button, pacing up and down until she answered again.

Jon didn't give her a chance to speak. 'Okay, you want to

know what I think? I think Dominic is a selfish, superficial git who doesn't deserve you and never did. I think you started going out with him on the rebound from me, but you don't love him – it's just habit, or security or *something*! And he sure as hell doesn't love you. And, yes, I think your career is a thousand times more important than some stupid cruise. There! That's what I really, truly *think*!'

Isobel was gripping the phone so hard her fingers hurt. She couldn't bear being shouted at like this, especially by Jon, the one person she'd always assumed would be totally, unconditionally on her side, 'I love Dominic,' she insisted, determined to be loyal to her boyfriend. 'The idea that he's just a rebound from you is laughable.'

'Really?' Jon's voice was rough with rage. 'That's strange, because you don't sound amused. Anyway, you wanted my honest opinion – *now you've got it!*' Slamming the phone down violently, he cursed again. He was in a beautiful country, in a fabulous hotel, with a gorgeous girl in his bed, yet he'd trade it all for ten minutes alone with Isobel – just long enough to talk her into seeing sense.

'Morning, handsome.' Opening her eyes, Marie yawned, the rumpled bedsheets sliding down over her naked body. For a moment Jon simply stared blankly at her, then he leaned over and kissed her too hard.

*

Isobel slumped in her chair.

'Excuse me?' A slim, fair-haired man was hovering in front of her. 'I'm here to see Mr Harrington?'

Swinging her feet down off the desk, Isobel attempted a businesslike smile. 'And your name is?'

'Same as when you asked me fifteen minutes ago!' he snapped. 'Michael Brooks!'

'Oh, God, I'm *so* sorry!' Flustered, Isobel jumped up too quickly, and promptly tripped over the shoes lying by her chair. She squealed as she landed firmly on her behind.

When she looked up, Byron and Michael were peering over the desk at her.

'Isobel, there really are no words.' Byron wore a pained expression. 'Michael, I do apologise for having kept you waiting. Please come with me.'

Just as they were heading off, two men in dark green overalls emerged from the lift. Byron stared at them. 'Can I help you?'

'Hope so, mate,' the older one said. 'We're from the Tranquil Tank Company.'

'And?'

Timidly Isobel tapped Byron's shoulder. 'Er, I booked them.'

He turned to face her. 'What *for*?'

She attempted a soothing smile. 'They're going to install a flotation tank. You know, for when we all get stressed. It's supposed to be wonderfully relaxing.'

Byron's smile was sanguine. 'What a *wonderful* idea!' He turned to the workmen. 'And the cost to us is?'

'Six thousand pounds, mate,' the first workman answered cheerfully.

Byron nodded. 'And it will take exactly how long to install?'

''Bout four days,' the second workman replied cautiously, ''cause, of course, we'll 'ave to knock that there wall through to make room for the tank, like.'

'I see.' Byron's eyes glinted. 'And how deep is the water going to be? Would it be sufficient –' he scowled at Isobel '– *to drown someone in*?'

*

Gemma's sleek red car screeched into the multi-storey car park outside the new Fit-U-Up and into a parking space. She turned off the engine, then stared into the rear-view mirror. She was dressed casually, in a cropped white T-shirt and low-slung navy leggings that revealed her ironing-board stomach.

She walked quickly through the dimly lit car park, and paused outside the sports complex. Like all the branches of Fit-U-Up, this one was constructed mainly of glass and since it was slap-bang in the middle of greenbelt land, those exercising inside could gaze out over lush emerald fields and tiny clusters of willow trees. Through its transparent walls Gemma could see spacious dance studios, rows of people working out, their faces flushed, their smiles virtuous.

Though it was only five thirty, the sky was heavy with night, streaks of turquoise fading slowly, the glass windows gleaming against the darkness. Gemma smiled. The complex resembled some magical city, shimmering in the dark, miles away from everything and everyone.

Then the entrance doors were sliding open and she was entering the plush lobby, which was swarming with perfect-looking people. Behind the reception desk stood four men in bright yellow shorts and tops, all with bulging biceps and blinding smiles. For a fleeting moment she wondered if they were bionic.

'Welcome!' The nearest man beckoned her over. 'Are you a new member?'

'Er, actually I'm a friend of Dominic's.'

'Oh, terrific!' The man's smile widened as he checked Gemma's name against a list which Dominic must have provided. 'He's around here somewhere, probably working out in one of the gyms. I can page him for you?'

'No! Thanks anyway.' Gemma decided to surprise Dominic.

* * *

Isobel had spent all day psyching herself up for the meeting with Byron. She was determined to confront him over the celebrity interview, over the way he'd given her idea to Lexie. And this time she wasn't going to back down. She was going to be *assertive*.

But when it came to it, she stuttered and stammered, unable to put together a coherent sentence.

'Isobel, I fully accept that you lack my verbal ingenuity, but could you at least make an effort?' Byron gave her a pitying smile. 'Come on, let's try it in words of three syllables or less, shall we, poppet?'

Isobel felt herself wilting under his cool scrutiny. Who was she kidding? She couldn't confront Byron. She couldn't confront anyone. Be assertive? Yeah, *right*.

'Good Lord, woman, what are you waiting for – the Messiah?' Byron directed a droll look heavenwards.

Isobel cleared her throat a few times, then mumbled almost inaudibly, 'It's about the celebrity interview.'

'Yes?'

'Er, well, it's just that, this, er, this interviewee was, er, well, she was my idea,' stuttered Isobel, hands twisting in her lap.

'Lexie's a journalist and you're not. Plus the celebrity column is hers, always has been.'

'I know.' Isobel shrugged. 'Guess I was just being silly, thinking I could handle doing an article.'

Byron's eyes softened. He had been expecting Isobel to throw in the towel long ago, but she had continued to show up at work every day, despite Lexie and her cronies making it clear they'd rather she didn't.

And suddenly, Byron felt intensely protective towards Isobel. She deserved a chance to prove herself. 'Okay, we need the inside track on this celeb. Reckon you can get it?' He was touched by the expression on her face which was half hopeful, half wary.

She nodded eagerly. 'Just give me a chance.'

'You sure?' Byron was also smiling now.

'Try me!'

'Love to,' he drawled, 'but, Isobel, seriously, I hope you can handle this woman. I mean, we're talking about *Tempest St John*.'

Isobel had been intrigued by this woman for months. Tempest, aka the Gorgeous Guru, was fast becoming the most influential New Age figure-cum-psychotherapist around. Her client list included a growing number of celebs. She was also popular with wealthy young women trying to kick various habits. Clients thought nothing, apparently, of her exorbitant fees.

Born in Australia, Tempest had come to Britain six years previously. Within months, the media had dubbed her the Sexy Shaman. She was most famous for the Karmic Cleansing sessions she ran at a country retreat, from which clients returned even more enamoured of her than before. Tempest was wary about granting interviews; she'd finally agreed, after being pursued by Isobel, to speak to *Primadonna*.

Now Isobel turned an imploring green gaze on Byron.

'Please, give me this one chance. I won't let you down. Promise.'

He frowned. 'Well, I suppose, unlike Lexie, you'd have plenty of time to work on the article. Let's face it, you don't exactly *do* much round here, do you?'

Isobel was swivelling nervously on the chair, one leg tucked beneath her, her tiny checked skirt riding up slightly without her even realising. Byron tried not to stare. 'If I'm so useless,' she said, 'why did you insist to Dominic that you needed me here over Christmas?'

'Oh, I like having you around.' He paused, then went on, 'So, you and Dominic . . . Interesting, seeing you two together last night.'

'Can't think why.'

'Watching couples is always entertaining. How long have you been going out? Two years?'

Isobel didn't respond.

'And no wedding plans.' Byron looked at her quizzically. 'Why's that, then?'

'Dominic is . . . traditional. He wants to make sure he's financially secure before he asks me.'

'Bullshit. He's got more money than he knows what to do with. The bloke's a fool. If I were Dominic . . .' he was walking slowly around the office now, circling her, getting closer and closer '. . . I wouldn't be wasting time. And I certainly wouldn't risk you being swept off your feet by someone else.'

'Dominic trusts me.' Isobel jumped up and gathered her papers together with unsteady hands.

'Takes you for granted, more like.' Byron stopped pacing and stood close to her. 'If I were Dominic—'

'But you're not.' She took a step backwards.

'And don't you know it.' Byron gave her a look. 'Last night, at the restaurant, you guessed, didn't you? Guessed it wasn't him touching you. Come on, Isobel, it's just the two of us. And I won't tell if you don't . . .'

'You flatter yourself.' Isobel cursed the way her voice caught, snagged on the semi-lie. 'I'd never let you touch me.'

Before she could stop him, Byron was placing a finger gently over her lips. 'Ssh – *never* say never. It's the most dangerous word in the world. The things you think can't happen are often the things that do. *And you've just tempted fate.*'

As their eyes met, Byron increased the pressure of his finger against her mouth a fraction. His touch made Isobel shiver. She pushed his hand away. 'Didn't think you were the type to believe in fate.'

'Oh, but I do. Some things are inevitable. It's just a question of when.'

Her chin tilted in a moment of rare defiance. 'Like my interview with Tempest St John?'

'Very good.' Byron nodded approvingly. 'I like it.' He smiled. 'You want it so very, very badly, don't you, Isobel?'

Isobel wasn't sure if they were still talking about the interview, and wanted to look away, but couldn't. She nodded.

'Then it's yours. On one condition. Tomorrow I'm taking two old contacts to dinner. It's going to be bloody boring but it's got to be done. You're coming.'

'I'm busy—'

'Cancel.'

'Take Lexie inst—'

'I want you.'

'I can't, I rea—'

'You'll come, if you want that interview.'

'This is blackmail!'

'Indeed. And it's *so* underrated as a management tool,' mused Byron. 'Anyway, I'm glad we've sorted that out. Tomorrow afternoon you'll do your interview with Tempest, and tomorrow evening I'll have the pleasure of your company.' He laughed. 'It's only one night. What's wrong? Scared you might enjoy it?'

Isobel did not dignify this with a reply. She scooped up her papers and left the office without another glance at him but forgot that the glass door was shut and walked straight into it. 'Fine,' she gasped. 'I'm fine. Really.' Clutching her throbbing face, she scuttled off to her own office where she collapsed at her desk. Spend an entire evening with Byron?

Isobel shivered again, and wondered suddenly whom she didn't trust: herself or Byron.

*

Gemma had finally found Dominic on the fifth floor. Alone. He was in a massive gym, with a polished wooden floor and bright red crash mats. Leading off it were several store cupboards, with exercise bikes and other pieces of equipment spilling out of them. Outside, the sky had deepened to a beautiful midnight blue, with tiny stars like glitter against the darkness, the gym's glass walls seeming to glow under the soft silver light. At the far end of the room, in black shorts and a black vest cut low at the front, was Dominic, his skin glistening with sweat, as he circled a punchbag, laying into it with his fists, muscles rippling across his back and shoulders. Energy seemed to pour out of him as he curled round the bag, looking as if he could kill with his bare hands.

Gemma sighed at the grace and control of his movements. Gone was the rather reserved man people usually saw: this was a lean, mean fighting machine. Not that she was surprised. Gemma had always known there was a darker, more intense side to Dominic, a side revealed between the sheets.

For a few minutes she watched him move around the bag, making it swing violently with every new assault. Then she glanced down the corridor. In the studio next door, some sort of dance class was going on, music blaring, the teacher counting and shouting words of encouragement.

All the other rooms around were empty; the day classes were winding down and the evening classes weren't yet under way. Gemma slipped through the heavy gym doors and padded slowly, soundlessly to the far end. Dominic was still intent on his workout, his back to her. She waited patiently until he circled the bag again and spotted her.

His eyes widened in surprise then flitted over her appraisingly, lingering briefly on her breasts, which were just visible through her T-shirt. 'Gems! What a lovely surprise! Didn't think you'd make it here today.' He threw one final punch, then held the bag still.

'Yeah, well, Isobel was really upset she couldn't be here. I said I'd just pop in. This place is fabulous, Dom.'

'Glad you like it. Must say, I'm pleased. We've had a great turnout today.'

She gestured to the bag, which was still swinging slightly. 'God, I wish I could pack a punch like you.'

'It's not hard to learn.' Dominic frowned. 'Every woman

should know how to defend herself. You know how I feel about this issue.'

'Hey, no argument here!' Gemma fell silent, recalling a date that had gone badly wrong a few months ago. She could have used a good right hook.

Dominic wiped his forehead with a navy blue towel. 'You all right?'

'Yeah.' But her expression was sheepish.

'Gems, has something happened to you?' Now Dominic walked over to her and placed his hands on her shoulders. When she still didn't look at him, he gently tilted her chin up. 'Tell me – I'll kill the bastard! Who was it?'

'It was nothing. Sure could have done with a few pointers from you, that's all.'

'Better late than never.' Dominic clapped his hands briskly. 'We'll start now.'

'What?' She felt uncomfortable. 'Look, that's really sweet of you but it's not nec—'

'Stop arguing. This is important. Come on.' He took her firmly by the hand, led her back to the punchbag, and showed her how to stand correctly, then how to form a proper fist.

'Now, Gems, the secret is to swivel your hips when you strike. That's what puts the power into the punch. You need to throw your whole bodyweight into it. Give it a go.'

Gemma obliged, then looked crestfallen when she got it wrong. 'I'm crap.'

'No, you're a beginner. You forgot to pivot your hips when you threw the punch. Here, I'll help you.'

Standing close behind her, Dominic placed his hands lightly on either side of her waist and turned her as she punched. 'See?

Swivel those hips and . . . good girl! Much better. Now do it again. It's all right, I'm helping you. Go on.'

'But, Dominic, what if . . .' Embarrassed at what she was about to ask, she broke off and turned to face him. For a moment they stood still, Dominic's hands resting on her hips. Then something flickered in his eyes and he let go of her abruptly. 'You were saying?'

'It's just that, what do you do if an attacker has you pinned to the ground, for instance?' Gemma asked anxiously. 'I mean, there's no way to get out of that, right?'

'Wrong.' He patted her shoulder. 'I teach women's self-defence classes on just that situation. Come on,' he pointed at the crash mats, 'I'll show you.'

Gemma followed him to the other side of the gym, where Dominic outlined the technique, lying down on the mat and demonstrating it as best he could without a partner. 'See?'

Gemma remained dubious. 'You make it look so easy, but there's no way I'd be able to do that, not if someone actually had me on the floor. I know I wouldn't!' Fear stained her voice.

Dominic smiled. 'You are so wrong, and I'm going to prove it. I'll play the bad guy. Now, what you need to do is this . . .' Once more he explained the technique and Gemma listened carefully.

'Okay. Lie down.' Carefully, rather self-consciously, Dominic lowered himself over her until his body partially covered Gemma's, then put his hands round her throat, tightly enough for it to feel like a realistic threat. 'Now do what I told you. You'll see how effective it is.'

Obediently Gemma drew up her right knee, and tried to flip

her hip then roll on to her left side to overturn him. 'I can't – it doesn't work!' Again she tried the move. Again she failed.

Hands still taut around her neck, Dominic gazed down at the pale, vulnerable curve of her throat, just as Gemma whimpered softly, turning her head slightly to one side, her long fair hair streaming round her face, her chest rising and falling too quickly, her pink lips parted as she lay there helpless beneath him. Once again, she saw something flicker in the depths of those dark eyes. Dominic's body was crushing hers. Gemma's pulse leaped. She couldn't control her responses: suddenly her arms had slipped around his neck and she was kissing him. Dominic tensed for a moment. Then he was kissing her back.

Gemma felt thought dissolving. The kiss deepened and something seemed to catch inside her, and it was as though she'd never truly wanted anything or anyone until now.

'*No!*' Dominic was unclasping her hands from around his neck. 'We *can't.*'

But Gemma could hardly think straight. She pressed herself against him, her pupils dilated.

'You *know* we can't,' Dominic insisted.

'**Must**,' she murmured, pressing her body against his more insistently.

Dominic's will-power fled. Part of him simply could not believe this was happening. Part of him had been waiting for it all these years.

And in his mind's eye was an image that refused to fade: Isobel and Jon, Jon taking Isobel's picture, Isobel gazing dream-ily at her ex.

'Gems, *no* . . .' He tried again to pull away, but it was a token gesture. She kissed him again, and her hands slipped inside his shorts. She pulled them down impatiently, her soft sweet fingers teasing him until Dominic thought he'd go insane.

In the next-door studio, the dance class was winding down, and people were starting to leave. As the door opened music filtered out. Gemma and Dominic could both hear people walking to the lifts, laughing and chattering. Anyone could see them, just by glancing through the gym doors.

But neither cared. Dominic was pulling down Gemma's trousers, then her knickers, stroking between her legs until she was writhing in his arms.

Finally, when she was delirious with need, he entered her and Gemma gasped. He felt unbelievably hard and hot and thick as he moved inside her with fast, rhythmic strokes.

Dominic flicked his hips a little, enjoying the way Gemma cried out, her back arching. His fingers played lightly over her body, moving along the hollow of her back then caressing her buttocks. Gemma quivered uncontrollably at his touch.

Even while it was happening, Dominic couldn't believe it. Gemma adored Isobel, yet here she was, her skin hot and slick under his hands, her entire body sensitised to him. He also adored Isobel, but right now, his ego was as swollen as his dick. But, then, his friendship with Gemma had always been unusually intense. And over the years, he'd often looked at her and wondered what she'd be like. They were so close, so affectionate with each other, sometimes it had been hard not to respond to Gemma's vulnerability. But he cared about her too much to risk their friendship. She needed him. And though Gemma would never know, she was one of the reasons Dominic had moved to America. He'd known she was becoming too dependent on him and had recognised the need to put some distance between them.

Angry with himself, he thrust harder. Gemma's fingernails clawed his shoulders and soon he was slamming himself into her, hearing her sob with pleasure. And Dominic knew he was in trouble, knew that this was getting to him, big-time.

Because this was something else. Isobel was great in bed, always wanted sex as much as he did, but Gemma seemed to crave his touch. He knew that on some level her guilt, like his, must already be mounting, but right now, he didn't care. Right now, guilt couldn't get a look-in. Because he was fucking the brains out of his girlfriend's best mate, and she was mad for it, her sweet, supple hips snaking under his and driving him wild, her eyes closed, her lips swollen and parted, her head thrown back in ecstasy, exposing that slender white throat.

And with a sudden tantalising, terrifying certainty, Dominic knew he could have Gemma anywhere, any time, in any and every way he wanted. For if she would betray her best friend for him, what wouldn't she do?

He started thrusting even harder, feeling her hot and so incredibly tight around him. Then she was crying out his name, shuddering as a violent climax tore through her. A moment later Dominic erupted inside her.

Swiftly, he rolled off her, pulling on his shorts and getting up, hating himself. Gemma sat up slowly, watching him with a tentative smile.

'This shouldn't have happened,' said Dominic brusquely, 'and we're going to act like it didn't.'

When she said nothing, he sighed. 'Do you hear what I'm

saying? We're going to act like everything's normal. Like nothing's changed.'

'And if I can't?' Eyes filling with tears, Gemma brushed them away impatiently. 'Because I'm telling you now – *I can't!*'

Dominic felt close to tears himself. 'Gemma, *please*, I love Is—'

'Then why were you just with me?' sobbed Gemma. 'What – you're standing there and telling me you feel nothing?'

'We're friends,' Dominic protested weakly. 'Like we've always been.'

He went to put a hand on her shoulder, but she shook him off, glaring. 'Sorry, Dominic, but you can't just pretend nothing's changed! I won't *let* you!'

'Let me?' he mocked furiously. 'You don't have a choice!' He grabbed Gemma's wrists and they glared at each other, suspended somewhere between lust and loathing. For a few moments they stood there, both trembling. Then Dominic tightened his grip on her wrist, saw her lips part, her eyes darken.

It scared him, knowing what he could make her do.

It excited him, knowing what he was going to make her do.

Still they stared at each other, each knowing how wrong this was, each equally helpless to stop. Then, with an anguished cry, Gemma was stumbling towards him or maybe he was pulling her forward, or maybe it was a bit of both, because now she was on her knees, fumbling blindly with his shorts. And in that moment, Dominic didn't know whom he despised more, Gemma or himself.

He looked at her, kneeling before him, her face flaming with guilt, embarrassment, and longing. Dominic knew she wanted him so badly it made her weak. She couldn't help herself. He closed his eyes. He couldn't help her either.

Now those pretty-pouty lips of hers were closing around his dick. Dominic grasped her head with both hands, pushing it down, thrusting himself into her mouth, then deeper, Gemma taking it all, right to the back of her throat.

Dominic felt the universe shrink until all that existed was her lips around his dick. He came in her mouth and Gemma swallowed greedily, eyes still closed, long hair tumbling around her face in damp strands.

Furious with himself, Dominic pulled up his shorts as Gemma got to her feet.

A small, scared smile trembled on her swollen lips. 'Still insisting nothing's changed?'

'No. One thing has. I know now what you're really like. Call yourself Isobel's friend and then you come here and you do *this*?' He knew he was blaming Gemma unfairly yet he couldn't stop himself. 'Okay, I'll admit it. I may want you, but I'm in love with Isobel, and that's what counts.'

'Until the next time!'

'Next time?' Dominic gave her a withering look. 'You don't understand. There can't be a *next* time – there wasn't a first time! *Because this never happened!*' He grabbed a towel and stormed out of the gym.

As the doors swung shut behind him, Gemma's legs buckled and she sank weakly on to the crash mats. She was shaking. Dominic despised her. He was the most important thing in the whole world to her, and she'd just wrecked their friendship.

Then Gemma's eyes narrowed. Oh, but he'd enjoyed it, hadn't he? So all these years, she'd been wrong about his feelings towards her. He *had* found her attractive. He *did* want her.

She thought of Isobel, and cringed. Isobel would never understand what had just happened. Only someone who had been in Gemma's position could possibly know how this felt. She'd never consciously chosen to go after her best friend's man. She'd wanted him so badly that once they were lying on that mat together, she'd *had* no choice.

She dressed swiftly, left the gym and headed back down the corridor. While she was waiting for the lift, she glanced through the door at the end of the hallway; a group of girls were lounging on large, pastel-coloured cushions, listening intently to a woman striding up and down before them. Gemma wondered what she was saying that could be so riveting. Then, to her embarrassment, the speaker glanced up and caught her watching. Quickly, Gemma stepped away from the door, and headed for the lifts.

'Did you want something?' Gemma turned. The woman was approaching her. 'I saw you watching. Join us.'

'What are you all doing?' She couldn't help staring at the woman, who had a striking, hour-glass figure; her nipped-in waist and curvy hips were enhanced by a lime-green trouser-suit. Flame-red ringlets bounced round a dimpled, cherubic face, but it was the woman's eyes that mesmerised her: they were wide-set and violet, sparkling like two amethysts against perfect porcelain skin. Gemma judged her to be in her late thirties, the only clue being the deep laughter lines around those astonishing eyes.

'Oh, we're just doing some relaxation exercises. Nothing too taxing. Tell the truth, I've had a seriously shit day. Looks like you have too, actually.' She gave Gemma a shrewd glance. 'Bloke trouble, hmmm?'

Sensing the pressure of tears behind her eyes, Gemma nodded. She felt displaced, didn't know what to do or where to turn for help. She needed Isobel, but that wasn't an option.

The woman gestured at the studio. 'I'd better get back. Sure I can't tempt you?'

'Thanks.' Gemma hesitated. 'Maybe another time.'

'Sure. Feel free.' With another warm smile, the redhead strolled back down the hallway.

The panic threatened to close around Gemma again, and this time it was far more acute. She couldn't be alone right now. She hurried after the woman. 'Sorry, I've changed my mind, if that's okay?'

'That's fine. Thought you might.' She took Gemma's hand, led her towards the studio, then stopped and chuckled. 'Sorry, I forgot to introduce myself. I'm Tempest.' Her vivid violet eyes sparkled. 'Tempest St John.'

5

Love on
the Rocks

Isobel thought about Byron all the way home. She was so busy reliving the touch of his finger on her lips that she almost missed Dominic's car, even though it was parked right outside her flat. She hurried over to it and peered through the window, surprised to see her boyfriend slumped over the steering-wheel as though he was asleep.

She tapped softly on the window but got no response, so she walked round to the front, leaned over the bonnet and rapped sharply on the windscreen. Dominic sat up, his face blank. Then he wrenched open the door, jumped out and wrapped his arms around her, burying his face in her hair.

'Hey, I've missed you too!' Isobel eased herself out of his bone-crushing grasp, and smiled at his spontaneous display of affection. 'Don't keep me in suspense – how did the first day at the new gym go? I *so* wanted to be there.'

Seeing the genuine regret in those beautiful green eyes, Dominic felt sick with guilt.

'I wish you had been, too, but it went well. And don't worry, I know your meeting with Byron was important.' He brushed the back of his hand down the soft slant of her cheek, then his arm fell limply to his side.

'What's wrong?'

'Nothing!' He hugged her fiercely again, then steered her towards the flat. 'So, how *did* the meeting with Byron go?'

'Fine.' Isobel hoped she wasn't blushing as, arms entwined, they headed inside. 'Hey, are you sure you're all right?'

'I'm fine, really. But we do need to talk about the cruise.' They went into the flat, and sat down on the sofa, his arm round her. 'I know I gave you a hard time about it at dinner last night, and I'm sorry. I just don't think you realise how much I want you there.'

And he wasn't lying. He would miss her terribly. Suddenly Dominic was bombarded by images of what the holiday would be like without Isobel. Of what it would be like having Gemma within reach.

The sleek boat sliding slowly through the night . . . the star-crammed sky . . . the silver sheen of the waters . . . Gemma's naked body bathed in moonlight . . .

'Isobel, you know how long I've been trying to organise this cruise – it won't be the same without you.'

'And you know I want to be there,' Isobel fretted, 'but the others don't think I'm serious about work as it is. If I go swanning off on a two-month cruise I'll prove their point. Just as I'm starting to get somewhere.' Swiftly she told him about Byron finally allowing her to do the celebrity interview.

Dominic professed to be pleased, but Isobel could tell he didn't understand how much this chance meant to her.

'So in other words,' he went on slowly, 'you'll never be able to take a holiday?'

'I'm not saying that at all! Just that I'd rather not go away right now. And maybe not for as long as two months.'

'Sure.' He flashed Isobel a rueful smile. 'Guess I just got too excited, thought this cruise would be something really special.' He laughed. 'Trust you to be different! Most women would jump at the chance.' He was suddenly lost in thought. Then he shook himself and kissed her. 'But you *are* different, and that's why I love you. Anyway, it's just a holiday. There'll be other chances.' Somehow, though, his tone suggested there might not be.

Anguished, Isobel began to chew a fingernail, searching his face for signs that he was secretly angry. After all, he was right. Most women would kill for a two-month luxury cruise with a gorgeous guy like Dominic. And he was obviously hurt by her insistence on working instead. She must seem ungrateful. Really, it was a wonder he put up with her at all.

Now Isobel noticed that Dominic looked tired, which was hardly surprising when he worked so hard. A violent wave of guilt at her own selfishness made her wince. 'Look, *you* should still go,' she insisted, trying not to think of how bereft she'd be without him for eight weeks. 'I don't want you missing the cruise because of me. God knows, you need a break after the hours you've been putting in lately. And at least all the others are going. You'll have a brilliant time.'

'I'll probably be too busy missing you.' Dominic squeezed her hand.

*

The waves of smooth, silken sand . . . a candy pink sun setting slowly . . . Gemma in a skimpy red bikini sauntering along the water's edge, looking over her shoulder at him with that seductive little smile of hers . . .

Dominic tried to dispel the images of himself with Gemma that seemed to be seared on his brain. He couldn't do it, though – couldn't get over how badly she'd wanted him.

'Isobel, please, hear what I'm saying . . .' Dominic knew he had to make her understand, though he could never tell her one of the real reasons why he wanted her so desperately on that cruise.

Gemma in his bed . . . Gemma his, all night long . . . Gemma's hips snaking sweetly under his . . . Gemma half out of her mind with wanting . . .

'Isobel, we've hardly seen each other over the past month or so. I mean, I've been so preoccupied with getting the new gym ready, and you've been working hard at the magazine.' His eyes never left her face. 'We're drifting. We need this time together.' He played his trump card. 'Are you saying that your magazine is more important than *us*?'

Gemma kneeling before him, doing what Gemma did best.

'Please, Isobel,' Dominic gazed earnestly into her eyes, 'you have to be there with me.'

*

A throbbing pain at the base of Isobel's skull intensified. She rubbed her eyes and hoped she wasn't about to develop one of the blinding migraines she'd been suffering from recently. She couldn't hold out much longer against this emotional co-ercion. There was a blatant subtext to what Dominic was saying. He wasn't happy. He felt neglected. He wasn't sure they'd make it, not without more effort on her part.

'Leave it with me.' She smiled weakly. 'I *do* want to be with you.'

He held her face between his hands, then kissed her gently on the forehead and stood up.

'You're not staying?' Disappointed, Isobel followed him to the front door, dread unfolding within her. So he *was* angry with her. But Isobel touched Dominic's arm lightly; she knew how to make it up to him. 'Stay.'

His hand already on the door, Dominic looked at her. Isobel's coppery-brown hair was soft and shiny, her fringe falling into her wide, green eyes, making them seem lighter by comparison. She looked more beautiful than ever.

But be with her and Gemma in one day? He despised himself enough as it was. Giving her a regretful look, he opened the door. 'I'm shattered, and I have to be up at the crack of dawn.' He kissed her quickly on the cheek, then headed down the path. He glanced back, and Isobel blew him a kiss. 'Love you!'

'Love you more.' Dominic smiled sadly.

Isobel stood there, shivering in the chilly night air, watching as he drove away, then closed the door, leaning against it and wondering why lately it felt like everything was caving in around her.

Then she talked sternly to herself. Everything was fine. Nothing had changed. She and Dominic would sort things out. They wouldn't let some silly holiday come between them. Deep down, she suspected he was just resentful that she'd missed the gym's opening, and she didn't blame him: she hadn't been around for him much recently. But that was going to change. Isobel gulped. Even if it did mean going away for a whole two months and missing the most important issue of *Primadonna* yet.

For now, though, she must focus on tomorrow and her interview with Tempest St John.

In her bedroom she pulled out all her notes on the celebrity guru. At the back of her mind Isobel knew she'd be spending the following evening with Byron. She ordered herself to relax. It was just one evening. How hard could it be?

*

The offices were deserted and dark. Not even the gentle humming of the photocopier cut into the silence and Byron was glad; he liked having the place to himself. On his desk were copies of all of *Primadonna*'s rivals. It was vital to keep tabs on the competition, note the good writers, check which topics they were covering and from which angle. The market was so overcrowded that to survive you had to be several steps ahead. He sighed happily, enjoying the feel of the glossy pages against his fingertips.

Glancing at *Totty*, his smile faded. Editor Roberta Davies had recruited several new columnists and they were all excellent. The magazine was the wittiest read around. It left the others standing. The features were original, the news stories tight, the design and layout striking. Even the regular diet and beauty pieces were streets ahead. There was no doubt that *Totty* had achieved the perfect combination of serious and sexy.

God, he'd wanted to edit that magazine so badly. He had hardly been able to believe it when they'd appointed Roberta over him. Five years of loyalty and hard work on his part and they'd given the position to an outsider. Not, he admitted grudgingly, that she wasn't doing a superb job.

There were many nights like this, when Byron sat in the darkened offices, wondering if he'd done the right thing in leaving to start *Primadonna*. It had been the biggest gamble of his career. The problem was that now he'd been an editor, he'd never be able to work under someone else. He had to make this magazine a success, and that was all there was to it. The thought of failing made him shudder.

Looking up, he saw Lexie alone out in the main office, working quietly at her desk, her skin pale against the sickly green glow of the computer screen. She didn't seem aware that he was watching her but, Byron smiled, she knew all right. He could read her in a second. Lexie held no surprises for him.

Unlike Isobel.

Byron thought back to when he'd met Lexie. He was already deputy editor at *Totty* when she'd come on board as a lowly staffer. God, the way she had gone after the job of senior features writer. She'd bent over backwards – literally, when he'd demanded it – to impress him and get that promotion . . . running around in those flirty little skirts, perching on his desk and crossing those long, lithe legs. Lexie had been impossible to ignore.

It had amused Byron no end because she'd probably have got the promotion anyway but, hey, if she wanted to make doubly sure by sleeping her way into the position, that was fine. He'd enjoyed it. But being with Lexie had been less than satisfying: she had no depth, was all good looks and raw ambition. End of story.

Unlike Isobel.

Lexie had caught him staring. She hesitated, then got up, sauntered into his office and perched on his desk. 'So, how's it going, babe? Isobel still sulking over the celebrity interview?'

Shit. He'd forgotten to tell her. 'Look, there's been a change of plan. I'm letting her do it. It *was* her idea.'

'And never mind that it's *my* regular slot? Never mind that

I'm in the running for an award – which I won't get if Isobel steals my column.'

'It's just one piece.'

'For now!' she snapped. 'Assuming Isobel doesn't screw it up! What if she wants to do another? And another?'

'Lexie, chill.' Byron understood where she was coming from but it was only fair to give Isobel a chance. It was time to see what she was made of. And he realised it had been hard for her even to raise the subject with him.

'Are you going to let her carry on doing these interviews?' Lexie scowled. 'Either it's my column or it isn't. *Well?*'

'If she keeps suggesting good ideas, then yes, I will let her. There's room for both of you. Don't turn this into a contest.'

She looked away, her face sullen. Lexie had seen the way Byron had been watching Isobel lately. Well, she'd just have to work a bit harder to protect her patch, wouldn't she?

She smiled sweetly, leaning back on the desk so that her breasts were thrust forward. 'It's late, let's go for a drink.'

Byron tapped the pile of magazines on his desk. 'I've got loads to get through.'

'It's never stopped you before. Come on, babe . . .' Lexie stroked his leg with her foot and looked coyly at him through long lashes.

Byron stood up, took her by the arm and bundled her out of the room. 'I'm tired and you're tiring. Night, Lex.' He slammed the door on her and was soon engrossed in reading articles again.

*

Lexie stood there, speechless. The *bastard*. He'd fallen for Isobel. She'd have to be stupid not to see the signs. She snatched up her coat and bag, then walked slowly to the lifts, deep in thought. No way was she about to be pushed on to the sidelines by that rich bitch. She'd have to plan her next step carefully. Lexie sighed. Shame she'd burnt her bridges with *Totty* when she'd followed Byron here. But maybe there was a way to salvage something, if she could bring herself to do it. She wasn't sure she could. No. Better to find a way of rekindling Byron's interest and forget getting even. For now.

*

'Look, I'm sorry but I really can't make it tonight.' Gemma tried to sound apologetic.

'But, Gems, we booked these tickets ages ago! Come on, it's supposed to be a wonderful play, and the whole crowd'll be there,' Rachel moaned.

'I know, but . . .' Gemma searched for the right words. She had no excuse for cancelling, she just didn't feel like going out. Didn't feel like company. Or smiling. Or talking. She just wanted to be alone. It was most unlike her. 'Look, I'm really sorry. I'm just not feeling too good. An early night's in order. But I promise we'll put a date in the diary soon, okay?'

Once she'd placated her friend, Gemma turned off all the lights in the flat and lay down on her bed. Suddenly she began crying. The tears took her by surprise, for there was no apparent reason for them.

If she could just speak to Dominic . . . Gemma groaned, clenching her fists until her fingernails left tiny red weals on her palms. She craved him more than any drug she'd ever taken. Was she ever going to get over him?

6

Ghost in
the Machine

Tempest was having multiple orgasms. At least, that's what it sounded like. Isobel was sitting in the guru's Harley Street offices, wondering what on earth was going on. The door to Tempest's consulting room was shut but cries of ecstasy were clearly audible. Isobel caught the receptionist's eye and enquired, 'Some new type of therapy?'

'Yeah – retail! She's talking to her PS.' Seeing that Isobel looked blank, the girl explained, 'Her Personal Shopper.'

'Oh, right, of course.' Isobel knew many of her friends availed themselves of this service, but she'd always avoided it.

She opened her bag, and double-checked that she had the tiny, state-of-the-art cassette recorder she'd borrowed from Byron. Isobel had been too embarrassed to admit to him that she invariably ended up destroying gadgets of any kind. This particular one was super-sophisticated, with umpteen tiny buttons and numerous functions. Isobel looked at it dubiously.

Suddenly the door burst open and Tempest appeared. She wore clingy black culottes and a low-necked white T-shirt that showed off her generous curves, while her unruly Titian curls were piled up on her head. She was talking rapidly into a mobile and clutching a pair of shoes. 'Oh, *yes!* I *love* them! Oh, you *darling* man . . . Yes, be sure to send me another three pairs, one in the pink . . . *mmmmm*, the green pair were *delicious* – those too . . . Yes, I'll be seeing you *very* soon.' She clicked the phone shut, beamed at Isobel and held out the shoes. 'Jimmy Choos! Don't you just *adore* them?' She smiled fondly at her bare feet. 'You *lucky* little tootsies!' After wriggling into the shoes, she proceeded to caress them for a few seconds, her expression one of sheer unadulterated bliss.

Isobel concluded that either Tempest had a foot fetish or this was some bizarre psychometric test meant to measure her own responses. She stood up and cleared her throat nervously. 'I'm Isobel de RoseMont? Here for the interview?'

The guru's dazzling violet eyes seemed to sharpen. 'Of course.' She extended a hand. Her grip was surprisingly firm. 'It's good to meet the woman behind *Primadonna*.'

Isobel noted that Tempest's smile didn't reach her eyes. She returned the handshake warmly, then followed Tempest into her office.

'Oh, how silly of me, I forgot to organise drinks. Back in a tick!' The guru excused herself and Isobel was alone.

She looked around with interest. It was like stepping into a Persil ad, for the room was a blinding white, the only touch of colour from two large lilac sofas. Between them stood a long, glass-topped table on which lay Tempest's two best-selling books. Glancing at the jackets, Isobel grimaced. The first, *The Storm Within*, showed a raging sea under a grey, angry sky; suspended between the two, and apparently walking on the water, was Tempest, clad in a diaphanous white gown, a beatific smile on her face, one hand extended. 'A foot fetish *and* a Messiah complex,' Isobel muttered. The second book was just as bad. *Hurricanes That Heal* showed Tempest in the centre of a spinning black tornado, with her eyes closed and her arms folded across her chest, her face irritatingly serene.

Isobel sat down and set the tape recorder on the table. To be on the safe side, she'd put new batteries in it this morning. She switched it on now, rather than waiting, scared she'd get so caught up in the interview she'd forget. Just then the overhead lights began to flicker, and a moment later the room was plunged into darkness. Glancing up, Isobel saw Tempest at the door, watching her, a few Titian tendrils snaking around her pale face. Then the lights came back on.

'Hope our little blackout didn't startle you,' said the guru. 'There's something wrong with the electrical wiring in this place.' She set down a pretty china tray and smiled warmly. 'I thought you might like some herbal tea.' She gestured to Isobel to take a seat, then handed her a cup. 'So, Isobel, tell me about *Primadonna*. It's a great magazine. You must be proud.'

'Oh, well, I can't really take credit for much.'

'But it was your business acumen that rescued it, right? It would have folded without you. And you write for it as well. Come, now, no need to be so modest.' Seeing Isobel blush, she sighed. 'Why are we women so bad at accepting praise? I've yet to meet a man with that problem! Yet we achieve such a lot. It's not easy, finding the energy to keep a career and a relationship going, and still have time left over for oneself.'

'No, it isn't,' Isobel agreed quietly, picturing Dominic's expression each time she needed to work late, or when she was worried about the magazine.

'Guess that's why the weekly meditation classes I run are so popular,' Tempest continued chattily. 'They provide a safe space for women to put themselves first.'

Once again Isobel thought of the numerous times lately when she'd compromised. Swiftly she switched her attention back to the interview. 'So, how many women turn up to these sessions?'

'Oh, it varies. Anything from ten to forty.'

'And what do you actually do?'

'Whatever we want. Sometimes it's a guided meditation. Other times we just sit around stuffing our faces with chocolate. Or maybe we have, like, a problem-sharing hour, you know, if someone's got something on their mind and they need help to sort it out.'

'Are most of your clients women, then?'

Tempest took a sip of her drink and nodded. 'Yes. I'm big on the idea of women empowering themselves. My girls have *real* confidence.'

'According to my research, most of the women who come to you tend to be fairly . . . wealthy?'

'They're like you.' The guru's violet eyes flitted over her appraisingly. 'Young women from affluent families, with fabulous jobs. They seem to have everything – good looks, the right connections, gorgeous men. Never seem to be happy, though.' Her eyes returned to Isobel's face. 'Are *you* happy?'

Isobel wriggled on her chair. 'Er . . . they say you work miracles with your clients?'

'I just help my girls work out what they really want.'

'Yes, but *how* do you do that exactly?' probed Isobel. Was she imagining it or was the woman being evasive? She glanced at the little cassette recorder. It was whirring away quite happily.

'Oh, there are so many ways. Hypnosis. Relaxation techniques. Sometimes getting in touch with past-life memories can help.'

'Isn't that a potentially unsettling technique for the client?' Isobel queried. 'Surely there are more, well, "proven" methods?'

The guru gave her a cool smile. 'I assure you that in the hands of a competent therapist it's a valuable tool. Besides, it all depends on what the client brings with them.'

'Which would include their cheque-book?' Isobel smiled apologetically. 'Sorry, it's just I've heard you're rather expensive.'

'Yes, it's true. And you know why?' Tempest leaned forward. *'Because I'm the best.* So what sort of example would I be setting my girls if I sold myself short and undercharged, hmmm? How can I encourage them to have high self-worth if they don't see that I have it?'

Isobel had to give the guru full credit for the ingenious rationale behind her exorbitant fees. It would be a great angle for her article. This piece, she promised herself, was going to be the best. She'd show Byron. And Lexie. She'd show them all.

'So what motivates you, Tempest? Is it money?'

Tempest looked amused. 'To a certain extent, of course. I'm just like any other woman. I like to have nice things. But mostly I enjoy helping people.' She leaned across the table and lightly touched Isobel's hand. 'And what about you?' Now her clear violet eyes seemed to be staring straight into Isobel's soul. 'Is Isobel de RoseMont happy, hmmm?'

Again, the question startled Isobel. It was something she'd rarely thought about. Throughout her life she'd been told that she had everything a girl could want. Why on earth *wouldn't* she be happy? 'I'm very lucky,' she answered finally. This wasn't the way the interview was supposed to be going. *She* was meant to be asking the questions.

'*Lucky* . . .' murmured Tempest thoughtfully. 'The papers say you're the girl who has everything. Are you?'

'Pretty much.' Toying with her pen, Isobel accidentally snapped the end off.

' "Pretty much"? What don't you have, then, Isobel? What's missing, hmmm?' Something in Tempest's voice suggested that she already knew the answer.

'Oh, where to begin?' Isobel grinned, then added quickly, 'I'm kidding. There's nothing wrong with my life. I'm totally happy. Really.'

'Who are you trying to convince? Me or you?' challenged the guru.

Isobel's smile faltered. Actually, she hadn't felt very happy lately. She was terrified of losing Dominic. Unhappy at work. Stressed over the cruise. Resentful at the lack of support from her family. Confused by her continuing feelings for Jon. The perfect life? Hardly.

'So, Tempest,' Isobel tried to move the interview on, 'I understand you also have a practice back in Australia. Tell me about that.'

Tempest's beautiful eyes narrowed. 'If I didn't know better, I'd say you were trying to change the subject.'

Isobel fidgeted in her seat. 'Tell me about your work back in Australia.'

'It's basically an advanced therapy programme. Some clients benefit from a more intensive, more in-depth approach.'

'For which they have to go to Australia?' Isobel was intrigued. 'Couldn't they do it here?'

'Not really.' Seeing Isobel's puzzled expression Tempest explained, 'Some colleagues of mine run a clinic in Sydney which is really cutting-edge in terms of therapy. They're much more . . .' she smiled '. . . *adventurous* than many practitioners here. I refer clients there when I know they'll benefit from such an approach.'

'Could you be more specific about the type of therapy being done there?'

'Not really, it would all get horribly technical and bore you to bits.' Tempest laughed. She stood up. 'Did you get enough for your article?'

Isobel glanced at the cassette recorder; it had already stopped. The time had gone so quickly, she hadn't realised how long they'd been talking. 'Oh, yes, thank you.' She nodded. 'If I combine it with some background information on you, it should be fine. I really appreciate your giving me this time.'

'My pleasure.' As they left the office, Tempest smiled warmly. 'And look, Isobel, if you get back to work and remember something you forgot to ask, just give me a call. It's no trouble.'

'Thank you very much.' Isobel followed the guru back into the reception area.

'Feel free to drop in on one of our weekday relaxation sessions. You'd be more than welcome, and I know you'd enjoy it. I'll send you the details.' Tempest squeezed her shoulder. 'Join us.'

Somehow, Isobel doubted she ever would, but smiled back

politely. Next thing she knew, Tempest was hugging her good-bye. Isobel was normally an affectionate person, but now she found herself tensing. She was unsure why. She hadn't taken an active dislike to the guru, yet there was *something* about the woman that made her uneasy. She just couldn't put her finger on it.

The receptionist opened the door for her, grimacing at the rain. 'You're welcome to wait a few minutes until it stops,' she offered.

'I'll be fine, but thanks.' Isobel pulled her coat on, then turned as someone called out her name. Tempest was approaching.

'You left this behind.' The guru held out the cassette recorder.

'Oh, God, thank you so much!' Isobel said gratefully. 'I'd be in serious trouble without it!'

Tempest smiled. 'I know.'

*

Back in the car, Isobel was excited about hearing the interview. She hit the rewind button, waited impatiently, then pressed play. After a minute or two, when all she could hear was a static-filled silence, she hit forward, then again tried play. Again all she could find was a dusty silence. Trying hard not to panic, she hit forward again, then stopped the tape and listened, repeating the sequence until the end of the tape.

Nothing. No voices. No questions. No answers. No interview.

She wrenched open the cassette recorder and gingerly fingered the tape, making sure it was in place. Then she rewound the tape to the beginning and tried again. Still nothing.

Perplexed, Isobel stared out of the window, watching raindrops hurtling to the ground. The cassette recorder had been working. She'd *seen* it working! And she was sure she'd been using it correctly. This didn't make sense. The wretched thing hadn't been out of her sight all morning. Isobel frowned. Except for those few minutes when she'd left it behind and Tempest had returned it. But there was no reason for anyone at the guru's office to tamper with it. It was absurd even to consider the idea.

What was she going to say to Byron? 'Oh, my God,' she whispered, staring at her ashen face in the rear-view mirror. 'He's going to murder me . . .'

If she told him.

She rummaged frantically through her bag, pulling out a pad and pen. She could probably scribble down the gist of the interview, plus enough direct quotes to get by. For a moment she considered calling Tempest, telling her what had happened, and requesting another meeting. But she'd look so *stupid.* Not to mention unprofessional. Isobel shuddered. Imagine Lexie's reaction if this ever got out. No, she wouldn't tell anyone about it.

Isobel sighed. She should probably just agree to go on the cruise with Dominic and forget about *Primadonna*. Then she rallied. This article was going to be good. Good? It was going to be great. Isobel didn't care if she had to work on it all day and all night. She had something – she had everything – to prove.

7

Crush

'Right, it's official.' Isobel threw up her hands in despair. 'This is a Clothes Crisis. I am suffering from Sartorial Stress Syndrome. And I'm talking to myself. Maybe what I really need is one of those nice little jackets that does up round the back . . .'

She was sitting cross-legged on the floor in front of her walk-in wardrobe, which was more like a small shop. It was seven fifteen, and Isobel still couldn't decide what to wear. She'd almost buried herself alive under a pile of dresses, and had narrowly avoided being knocked unconscious by an avalanche of shoes. She'd tried on every skirt, top and trouser-suit she owned, but nothing felt right, probably because she had mixed feelings about tonight.

On one hand, she resented Byron blackmailing her into going, and hated the idea of being seen as some kind of ornament. On the other hand, there was *Byron's* hand, and how it had felt tracing lazy circles against her thigh that night at the restaurant . . . the touch of his finger on her lips at the office . . .

Her skin warmed at the memory and Isobel berated her fickle, foolish body: 'You traitor!' Now her imagination rebelled by conjuring up an image of Byron's mouth on hers, his hands stroking her, and instantly Isobel felt the sweet-sharp ache of lust. It was time to face facts: she was attracted to Byron.

There, that wasn't so hard to admit, was it?

'But it's wrong,' she wailed. 'I love Dominic!' And while she was with Byron, her boyfriend would be at a friend's house-warming party. Gemma was also going.

Isobel carried on rummaging through the racks of clothing, discarding outfit after outfit. A few minutes later, the ringing of the phone was a welcome distraction.

'Isobel, Byron here. Just to let you know we're ten minutes away.'

'What? But I was supposed to meet you at the restaurant!'

'Seemed stupid taking two cars. Anyway, our reservation is for eight, so I trust you're ready?'

Isobel collapsed on to her bed. 'I haven't even worked out what to wear – I need more time.'

'What do you have on right now?' Byron asked smoothly.

Isobel's eyes went to the mirror across the room and she gazed at herself, naked but for her bra and knickers; two scraps of midnight-blue lace, each held together by a whisper and a promise.

As if he could see clean down the phone line, Byron chuckled. 'Isobel, don't tell me you're sitting there in your underwear? Let's see, I bet you're the sort of girl who wears . . . white. Something pretty but simple, in white.'

'Shows how much you know,' murmured Isobel, then clamped a hand over her mouth, shocked at what he'd stung her into revealing.

'Good. I prefer something a bit more colourful.' He lowered his voice and suggested huskily, 'Don't waste time getting dressed. Come as you are.'

'Wish I wasn't coming at all! This is so unfair.'

'But such fun!' he countered gleefully. 'Now, hurry up and get ready. Bloody women – always late for everything!'

Isobel hung up and went back to the wardrobe. She waded once more through the sea of clothing then glimpsed a black dress from Voyage that she'd never worn. It proved rather more skimpy than she'd recalled, and the swell of her breasts was visible through the sheer material. It was also rather short; sitting down could involve an act of indecent exposure.

But just as she was preparing to change, she heard an engine outside. Too late. She grabbed her coat and dashed out of the flat. There was Byron, leaning against his car, eyes flitting over her. She flew down the path, clutching the hem of her dress.

Peering into the car she saw three men in suits lounging in the back. She turned back to Byron. 'Hugo, Harvey and Harry, I assume? Looks like they're already rather inebriated.'

'Totally slaughtered,' Byron responded.

Isobel glanced back longingly at her flat. The prospect of curling up before the TV with a box of chocolates was truly tempting. 'Don't make me come tonight,' she begged. 'I really don't want to.' She edged backwards down the path waving as she went. 'I'll be terrible company. I'll ruin everything. I'll just stay here inst – *Byyron!* **Put me dowwwwwnnn** . . .' He had scooped her into his arms and was carrying her to the car, but even as she protested her body was revelling in the feel of his hands, hot through her dress, which was riding up and revealing not only her thighs but, to her horror, a glimpse of her lacy blue knickers.

'*Nice*.' Byron flashed her a devilish grin. 'Edible ones, by any chance? No? Shame. Must buy you some. I've always been partial to them.'

With a strangled yelp Isobel yanked down her dress as he deposited her unceremoniously in the front seat. He shook his head sternly. 'Wearing a dress like that! Really, Isobel, it's asking for trouble. Might just have to give you some.'

Isobel narrowed her eyes and pursed her lips in an attempt to convey the full extent of her wrath.

'My, that's one *dirty* look!' Byron said admiringly. 'Can you talk dirty, too?' He reached across and deftly clipped together her seat-belt. As he did so, his hand brushed her right breast. She blushed, and saw his mouth quirk in a satisfied smile before he turned away, closed the car door and went to get in on the driver's side. In the back, Hugo, Harvey and Harry were spreadeagled across the seat, heads lolling back, words slurred. Then Byron was squeezing his bulky frame into the driver's seat and they were racing down the road.

Isobel glanced at his large, well-shaped hands, lightly controlling the steering-wheel. She imagined how those hands would feel controlling her body, Byron's hands, playing tenderly and teasingly over her bare skin . . . She risked a sidelong glance at him, and was mortified when suddenly Byron turned and grinned at her. Instantly she looked away, crossed her arms, and stared out of the window, trying to ignore Byron's hearty laughter.

*

'Just love your new place!' Dominic patted Lance on the back. 'It's fabulous.'

After a few minutes of small-talk, he left his friend to continue greeting guests, and wandered into the dimly lit hall, now heaving with bodies. He saw Gemma the second she arrived. How could he miss her in that slinky pink dress? Her hair was pulled back in an elegant chignon, and her full lips were coated with a delicate pink gloss. Hating his heart for the way it skipped a beat, Dominic watched as Gemma sauntered around with a bright smile and a breezy kiss for people she knew, which seemed to be everyone. He couldn't take his eyes off her. And Dominic knew that, if he wanted, he could get her upstairs, into a bedroom, undressed and into any position he chose, all in a matter of minutes. If he wanted.

And he did.

He rubbed his forehead in an effort to erase the image that was lodged in his mind and driving him slowly, sweetly insane: Gemma, kneeling before him, lips wet and parted, beautiful eyes brimming with anguish and wanting.

Oblivious to the fact that people were talking to him, he turned and headed for the kitchen where he slammed down his wine-glass so hard that the contents spilled on to the pristine white tablecloth. He was learning the hard way that the old adage about forbidden fruit was true; knowing it was wrong to want Gemma just made him want her all the more.

Suddenly Dominic felt trapped by his own emotions as he realised there was no way out of his dilemma. Gemma wasn't simply a girl on the fringes of his social crowd whom he could ignore. She was his best friend. And she was Isobel's best friend too. She was always going to be there, maddeningly within reach.

But there was always Plan B. Reaching into his pocket, Dominic touched the small jewel box he'd been carrying around all day. What had he been waiting for, anyway?

*

Gemma watched Dominic turn his back on her and bolt down the hallway. Did he now resent her so much he couldn't bring himself to speak to her?

She decided she must have a fever; she was burning hot and her throat was parched, no matter how much she drank. Maybe she was coming down with something. She felt tired. More than tired, weak. She had only come to this party because Dominic would be here, and now she was starting to wish she'd stayed in.

Well, she wasn't going to let him see that he was getting to her. With a blinding smile, Gemma approached a group of friends. Dominic had now come back into the hallway, and he was watching her. Instantly a cold, hard sense of triumph surged through her. He couldn't ignore her if he tried, and they both knew it. She slipped her arm through that of the man next to her and began to flirt as though her life depended on it.

*

'I'd rather not.' Isobel shuddered as Byron leaned across the table and told her where Hugo, Harvey and Harry wanted to go next. They had decided the night wouldn't be complete without a visit to Shake Your Thang, a lap-dancing club in the heart of Soho. Isobel stared glumly at her untouched dessert. She'd hardly eaten a thing, too busy fending off Hugo's greasy advances. Now she was perched on the edge of her chair, with

Hugo practically sitting on it with her, his arm along the back, his thigh jammed up against hers. Since Isobel's chair was next to a huge, ornate white pillar, there wasn't much room to manoeuvre. Glancing from the pillar to the bulge in Hugo's trousers, Isobel groaned. 'Perfect – I'm wedged between two colossal erections!'

Meanwhile, under the table, Byron's knee was pressing against hers. Lust for Byron and loathing for Hugo made a bizarre combination, and one just seemed to heighten the other. Again Isobel's gaze came to rest on her dessert. Idly, she imagined every inch of her body coated in that sticky dark chocolate, and Byron slowly licking it off . . .

'Isobel, come on, you'll enjoy it.' Byron's knee pressed against hers a bit harder, and she looked at him in horror, convinced he'd somehow read her mind, but he was, of course, still talking about the club. 'And, besides,' he continued, 'you said you'd spend the whole evening with us. I'm going to hold you to it.'

Isobel nodded meekly. Hugo, meanwhile, had grabbed her bowl and was cheerfully gobbling up her dessert.

For what seemed the hundredth time lately, Isobel wished she was more feisty. Maybe she should go along to one of Tempest's classes. The Gorgeous Guru would know how to handle herself in this situation, for sure. More, Isobel knew that if she were truly a *Primadonna* woman, she'd have found a way to stop Hugo in his tracks but, as usual, all she could do was seethe inwardly.

God, she wished she was with Dominic and Gemma at that party. Maybe she'd pop over to Gemma's later – they'd hardly seen each other for ages, and Isobel knew they'd have a laugh over her god-awful evening. She managed a smile as she followed Byron and the others from the restaurant and out to the car. Touching base with her best friend would make her feel better. It always did.

*

Dominic's stomach was knotting with tension. Gemma was plastered, her laughter so loud it seemed to fill the room. She'd spent the party flitting madly between the various groups, draping herself over every man within reach.

After edging close enough to catch snatches of conversation, he realised she was getting reckless. Understandably, she was desperate to confide in someone about what had happened between them. She couldn't tell Isobel, and Dominic had refused to talk to her. Now it was only a matter of time before she blurted out their secret. And then there would be no going back.

He watched her clinging to a girlfriend's arm and darting a sly, drunken look at him as she slurred loudly, 'Want to hear a shecret?' Gemma paused, hiccuped, giggled.

The other woman looked at her with interest as Gemma leaned in close. 'About a man . . . shomeone you know—'

'Gems, we're going to be late! Remember, we promised to meet Isobel.' Dominic removed the glass from her hand and glanced at the clock with mock alarm. He gave the other woman his most charming smile, and was relieved when she returned it. 'So sorry to interrupt. Gems, come on, we need to pick Isobel up or she'll be stranded.'

He steered her out of the room while Gemma continued muttering and mumbling. 'Dominic, I know you want me but can't you even wait till we're alone?' she scolded merrily, suddenly turning and kissing him full on the lips. A few of their mutual friends shot curious glances their way. Dominic met the looks with a self-deprecating smile. 'She always gets like this when she's pissed – I saw her trying to jump one of the waiters earlier!' Everyone laughed and he felt light-headed with relief; he'd allayed any suspicions. For the moment.

Outside, he bundled Gemma into his car and sped off into the night, keen to reach her flat as soon as possible and to leave it even faster. At the party it had been safe; they'd been surrounded by others. Now it was different. Now they were alone. And here was Gemma, slumped in the seat beside him, her hair having escaped its neat chignon to tumble around her shoulders, the moonlight playing over her troubled face.

Dominic felt attraction mingle with anxiety: he was concerned at how much she was drinking and how unhappy she looked. This girl was unbalanced, and that should serve to keep him away. So, why was it luring him in further? Because, he admitted, it gave the attraction an edge. It meant Gemma was a wild card. And it made him feel protective towards her. Glancing at Gemma again, Dominic shook his head bitterly. He was probably what she needed protecting from most.

*

Once her eyes had adjusted to the dim lighting, Isobel surveyed the club with interest, then followed the others as they squeezed between the tiny round tables, past a slim catwalk running down the middle of the room, on which a girl wearing sparkly silver knickers was gyrating so frenetically it was a wonder she didn't grind her way clean through the ground. Isobel felt dizzy just watching her.

A crowd of people was clustered around a long bar at the

back of the room. Isobel was surprised to see that several women were watching the girl's act just as intently as their male companions. The air was thick with smoke and the décor muted. Dancers were busy before various tables, and men leered and leaned forward, tucking money into the girls' costumes, their fingers lingering on the gleaming flesh.

Finally Isobel, Byron and the other three men reached an empty table in the middle of the room. As they sat down a dancer sashayed over. Isobel gaped; the woman's chest was so vast it must have entered the room a full ten minutes before its owner, whose long blue-black hair fell to her waist, while her eyes were fringed with spiky false lashes.

'Good *evenink*.' Her accent was heavy yet elusive. She slid her hands up and down her body and her crimson lips parted in a wide smile. 'My name ees Luscious Delite.' At this point one pair of her false lashes stuck together and Luscious couldn't open her right eye. Isobel bit back laughter. 'And vot ees *your* name?' Suddenly the dancer reached over and started stroking her arm. As she wriggled away Isobel muttered a reply, while Byron looked on with barely concealed mirth.

'Ah, *Eeeesobel*!' Luscious rolled her eyes in rapture. 'Vot a beeootiful name, darlink!' Angling a final coy smile Isobel's way, she turned to the men and began swaying in time to the music.

Isobel expected Byron to be as absorbed in the act as the others, but instead he was watching her, and she knew why: he wanted to see her blush. Well, she wouldn't be giving him that satisfaction. Or any other, she reminded her wayward body.

Luscious was now discarding items of clothing at an alarming rate. Her top fell off and there was a resounding crash as several jaws collided with the ground. The gargantuan breasts were now on display – complete with plastic pink tassels attached to the nipples and glowing like Christmas-tree baubles.

Byron nudged Isobel. 'Those tits wouldn't move if you lit dynamite under them. Gotta be fake, right?'

She nodded. 'Reckon she must have qualified as a weight-lifter before getting them done.'

They looked at each other and burst out laughing.

'Personally,' Byron let his gaze linger on the soft swell of Isobel's cleavage, 'I prefer the real thing.'

She waited for him to look away but his blatant scrutiny continued. 'Er, Byron, you're, er, well . . . you're staring at my breasts.' Isobel's face flamed.

He shrugged. 'What can I say? I'm just a red-blooded bloke.'

The way he stared at her was unsettling. If she didn't know better, Isobel would think Byron was genuinely interested in her. Not that she'd ever encourage him, even if it would make her life easier at work. Unlike her female colleagues, Isobel would never flirt or use her looks in any way. Now she gave Byron a cool smile. 'Don't worry, there are plenty of girls here. I'm sure you'll be able to sweet-talk one of them into bed before the night's over.'

'Is that what you think I want?' He affected a wounded look. 'Just a quick shag?'

'Don't you?'

'Absolutely not!' Byron regarded her gravely, then grinned. 'Nothing quick about me, I take my time. I can keep going all night!'

'I'm really not impressed with your prowess between the sheets.'

'How do you know? You haven't experienced it. Yet.' Byron placed his hand on top of hers, which were clasped in her lap.

Instantly Isobel wriggled out of his grasp, scared by how much his touch affected her. She looked at him, aware that her eyes were probably giving her away. She wished she could let him do something to relieve this terrible, wonderful wanting. But even though she was intensely attracted to him, she would never give in to it.

As Byron reached for her again, Isobel stood up abruptly and headed for the bar. She found an empty table and sat down, still trembling from the effort of resisting Byron's touch. Out of the corner of her eye she watched him storm from the room, his face conveying his disappointment and frustration.

Seeing her standing alone, Luscious Delite came sidling over, planting herself in front of Isobel and grinding away. Isobel tried to stare anywhere except at the mammoth breasts, which were now level with her face.

'Eeeesobel, I vant you to come dance viz me! Come . . .' Luscious grabbed her hand and tried to pull Isobel to her feet, but she refused with a polite smile. The dancer pouted and tried again. Through their drunken haze, Hugo, Harry and Harvey had noticed what was going on and were now clapping their hands and chanting Isobel's name.

Luscious's attempts became so determined that Isobel clambered on to a chair to avoid her clutches. To her dismay, the stripper took this as a good sign, thinking Isobel wished to be centre stage. She, too, began to clap and screech encouragement. 'Come on, Eeeesobel! Dance! Dance for me, Eeeeesobel! *I know you vant to*!'

'Oh, I **so** don't,' Isobel insisted, inching back on the chair as

Luscious tried to grab her round the waist. She squealed as the chair wobbled violently. Luscious was wriggling and jiggling with a vengeance, the garish pink tassels now flashing on and off as they swung wildly from her breasts, while she began shimmying round the chair shrieking, 'Come, Eeesobel – *come shak your thang viz meee* . . .'

People at nearby tables were turning round, their eyes pinned on Isobel as she balanced precariously on the chair. Suddenly Hugo let out a yell of joy and Isobel realised that he could see up her dress. 'Don't worry,' he gave her a lascivious smile, 'I know what's wrong! You'd rather dance with a bloke!' He jumped up, clasped her round the waist and swung her down, then caught her hand and placed it firmly on his crotch. 'That's more like it, right?'

Disgusted, Isobel wrenched away her hand but Hugo was clinging to her like some giant, oversexed leech.

'Let *go* of me!' Isobel implored him, realising even as she said it how feeble she sounded, but he began to spin her round and round until finally she twisted out of his grasp and made her dash for freedom, pushing blindly past the tables, with howls of derision and wolf-whistles breaking out around her.

But getting away proved no mean feat. The men at the edges of the room were laughing, trying to catch her, pushing her from one to another, tugging at her flimsy dress. Isobel could hardly see where she was going, and lashed out blindly as they groped and pawed her. But her frenzied attempts to fend them off just seemed to excite them more, their fingers moving more feverishly over her body. Soon their gleaming eyes and rasping voices started to scare her.

Meanwhile, the lap-dancers continued to undulate to the

music, their amused gazes following Isobel as she fought to escape. Then her dress snagged on a table. She yanked it free but it ripped.

The men sitting nearby cackled, one of them reaching over and slapping Isobel's thigh so hard it hurt. Isobel was panicking now; things had turned nasty. She spotted a door by the bar, dropped to her knees and crawled between the men's legs to get away, gritting her teeth as they cheered and pinched her bottom.

Biting back tears she reached the exit, staggered to her feet and skidded out into the chilly corridor. Behind her, the room erupted into laughter.

Suddenly another pair of hands grabbed her. She screamed and tried to slap them off. But the man held her tightly, and Isobel found herself staring up into Byron's steady hazel eyes. He glanced at the torn dress. 'What the fuck's going on?'

'Byron . . . I . . . they . . .'

Byron pulled her into a hug, silencing her. She couldn't help enjoying the way he gently brushed her hair from her face with one hand, keeping the other arm round her waist. His fingers moving softly through her hair were so soothing. Isobel sighed happily, felt her eyelids growing heavy, her skin warming against his. Then something in his touch changed, and she tensed.

Byron tilted her chin, and she gazed up at him with wide, frightened eyes. 'There's nothing to be scared of. I'm not about to ravish you here in the corridor.' He smiled. 'Unless you'd like me to . . .?'

The idea of Byron fucking her right there, up against the wall, left Isobel weak with wanting.

His arms tightened around her. 'You're coming back to my place.'

'No!' Isobel started to back away. 'I really don't think—'

'So don't think.' Byron pulled her towards him again.

'But the others—'

'Won't even notice we're gone. Isobel, come on. You're driving me crazy.' Byron squeezed her hand. 'And I know you want to.'

'I don't! You're wr—'

'Running out of patience!'

Gently he began stroking her hand, his thumb tracing a careless caress over the inside of her wrist, and Isobel's pulse fluttered. Now his other arm was slipping round her waist again, pulling her towards him, and she knew she was going to let him—

'*There* you are,' slurred Hugo, sloping towards them, brandishing a bottle as behind him the door to the bar crashed open.

The spell was shattered. Isobel bolted down the corridor. Byron sighed. This wasn't going as smoothly as he'd expected. Every time he was sure he had Isobel within his grasp, she managed to slip away. And it was driving him mad, the way she gazed at him with those gorgeous green eyes, unable to look away, but too scared to go for it.

Suddenly Byron chuckled. If things didn't fall into place soon, he would simply scoop her up in his arms and carry her off to bed, even if she protested all the way. She'd soon stop, once he showed her what she was missing. Watching as, further down the corridor, Isobel thanked the doormen for calling her a cab, Byron shrugged. Something told him she'd be worth the wait.

*

Dominic hurried after Gemma into her flat, not even pausing to shut the front door. He intended to leave the moment he'd made sure she was all right. He watched her stagger into the sitting room and collapse on to the sofa. Her eye make-up had smudged, and she was pale. More, she seemed dazed. Dominic recognised the look in her eyes; he had seen it before.

Abruptly he lunged forward, grabbed her slender arm and forced the sleeve of her dress up, praying his intuition was wrong. But it wasn't, and he stared in horror at the jagged red scars that lacerated her skin, like some bizarre tattoos. She'd been cutting herself again.

'Oh, Gems, not *this* . . .' He could have cried. 'I thought things were better.' He sat down next to her. 'You poor thing, why didn't you tell me?'

'Wanted to.' Gemma's smile was pained. 'Didn't know how. I don't know what's going on with me, I just feel so down – *all the time*. It's getting worse.'

'You're going to be fine, Gems.' He raised her hand to his lips and kissed it. 'I promise. We'll find someone for you to talk to, someone who can help you.' He took her into his arms and held her close, wishing he could wave a magic wand and make all of her problems vanish. How long had this been coming on? Had sleeping with her made things worse, he wondered uneasily? Gemma had seemed so sure of what she wanted that day at the gym, but maybe she'd just needed to connect, to tell him how she was feeling, only she hadn't known how to.

'Dominic.' Agitated, Gemma clasped his hand, her mouth quivering. 'Did you mean what you said at the gym? About me meaning nothing?'

'No, oh, Gems, of *course* not!' And as she began to cry silently he couldn't help it, he kissed her softly on the cheek, tasting the salty tears and knowing he couldn't keep Gemma at a distance, couldn't reject her, not when she was feeling so low. But he couldn't give her what she wanted either. To lead her on would be cruel. Whatever he did, Dominic knew he would hurt her. So he just sat there, feeling helpless, while Gemma held her head in her hands and sobbed as if her heart was breaking.

Finally, though, he couldn't take it any longer, and he pulled her close, kissing away each tear. Then, suddenly, naturally, his lips weren't on her cheek but on her lips and they were kissing so wildly that Dominic felt light-headed. Now right and wrong seemed irrelevant, absurd even, to Dominic as he held Gemma. She was still crying, and Dominic hated himself for what he was feeling but he couldn't help it; this girl was so vulnerable and available that it was getting to him all over again. And Dominic knew that if they went to bed now, the sex would be so dark and desperate he'd never get Gemma out of his system.

He pulled away. Both then and afterwards, he wasn't sure why. He told himself it was because he was about to do the honourable thing and leave, that no way was he about to take advantage of this girl. But he was never *sure*.

Never sure if maybe he pulled back because he was about to get up, take her by the hand, take her into the bedroom, and then take her the way he wanted to. Or maybe, Dominic wondered later, maybe he'd pulled back because unconsciously he'd heard Isobel quietly entering the room.

8

Only
Human

No one spoke. Isobel blinked rapidly, trying to clear her head and make sense of what she was seeing. Gemma. Dominic. Gemma and Dominic. Her best friend and her boyfriend. *Kissing*.

Isobel opened her mouth to speak, but could manage only a pathetic croak. As her face drained of colour, she turned to Dominic, then to Gemma, seeking reassurance that, somehow, she'd got it wrong. That this wasn't how it looked.

But beneath that perfect tan, Dominic had turned a chalky white. He started to speak and Isobel could see his lips moving but his voice was muffled, eclipsed by the pounding in her head. It felt like her brain was about to burst. With a stifled sob, she turned and fled.

'Isobel, *wait*!' Dominic shoved Gemma aside and tore down the stairs after his girlfriend.

Gemma's block was in a tiny cul-de-sac and, running blindly, Isobel reached a dead end. She collapsed on to a low brick wall, which bordered a pretty townhouse, and hugged herself, trying to stop shivering.

Across the road, a door opened and a crowd of people spilled into the street, laughing and chattering, splitting into couples as they headed for their cars. A few sent Isobel anxious looks as she sat slumped on the wall. Then Dominic shouted her name; the couples exchanged knowing smiles and melted into the night.

'Isobel!' Dominic sprinted over.

Isobel's eyes brimmed with tears. She felt like screaming. Sobbing. Hitting him. *Hurting* him. Surely now she'd find her temper? But, as usual, the red-hot edge of her anger was cooling and a strange numbness was setting in, as it always did when Isobel's temper threatened to show itself.

Dominic sat down on the wall beside her. Isobel looked past him and saw Gemma at the front door of her flat, her head in her hands, her long golden-brown hair catching the light. She was the picture of despair.

'Isobel, I swear, it was just a kiss! You have to believe me.'

'Do I?' She tried to wipe away her tears with her sleeve.

'I love you! You *know* how much I love you!'

He grabbed her hand but Isobel flinched and shook him off. 'I don't understand how you and she could be . . . *why* you would suddenly be . . . How long have you and Gemma . . .' Isobel almost gagged on the words '. . . how long has this been going on?'

Again he took her hand, this time not letting her pull away. 'It hasn't. It was just a kiss. I'll explain everything – just say you know I love you!'

'All this time . . .' Isobel tried to steady her breathing but she was crying too hard '. . . All this time, you wanted Gemma?' She was close to throwing up. 'All this time, the two of you—'

'*No!*' Dominic shouted. 'It's you I want. Only you.'

'Only me?' Isobel echoed incredulously. '*You were just kissing my best friend!*'

'But you didn't see how that kiss *started*. Gemma's in a real state! I don't know what's wrong with her but something sure as hell is.' He told her about the grotesque cuts along Gemma's arms. 'I was just trying to comfort her – she misunderstood, confused affection with attraction. That's all there was to it, I promise. You saw me pushing her away, I know you did. Isobel, you're the only one I care about. I love you. I've never felt this way about anyone else, not ever! And,' Dominic swallowed nervously, 'I can prove it.' Suddenly he dropped to his knees and gazed up at her with solemn brown eyes. 'Isobel, marry me. I don't want Gemma! It was just a kiss, I *swear*! It's you I love. Say yes. Say you will. Say you'll marry me.' He pulled out a tiny box and opened it to reveal a diamond solitaire engagement ring that glinted in the darkness. Isobel steadied herself on the wall. She was starting to feel as if she'd stepped on to the set of a soap opera, only to find herself trapped there.

But she was still suspicious. 'All these years, have you wanted Gemma? The two of you are so close . . .' Oh, how badly she wanted to hear him deny it. Even more badly, she wanted to believe him. Had she been a total fool for believing Dominic's friendship with Gemma was purely platonic?

Another thought hit her like a slap around the face. She blanched. 'Has Gemma been coming on to you?'

Dominic met her stare boldly. Over the past few days, he'd managed to convince himself that, actually, Gemma *had* been pursuing him. After all, she adored him. Always had. And sure, he'd given in to it that once, at the gym – what guy wouldn't have? With a bit more impressive mental footwork, Dominic had even persuaded himself that she'd come to the gym that day with the sole purpose of seducing him. She'd set him up. He, Dominic, why, *he'd* been nothing more than an innocent victim! Caught in a seductive little honeytrap all of Gemma's making.

He shifted uncomfortably and averted his eyes. 'I think Gemma may . . . have feelings for me. But she'd never hurt you, not deliberately. Tonight was a mess. *She* was a mess. She doesn't know what she's doing right now. She's all over the place.' He paused. 'Gemma doesn't know what she wants, but I do. And it's you. What I want, all I want, is you.'

Bemused, Isobel let him slide the ring on to her finger. It was a perfect fit. She got up and walked over to the kerb, her back to Dominic, and stared at the ring.

Turning her hand this way and that, she admired it, smiling as it caught the moonlight and sparkled softly at her.

So pretty.

Still, everything in her screamed at her to believe the evidence of her own eyes, to tell Dominic where to shove his proposal. He'd been kissing her best friend. She should walk away.

But his ring was on her finger and already she couldn't bear to take it off. Already, she was getting used to it. Already, images of a stunning wedding dress, of a beautiful wedding, were dancing through her mind. And twenty-eight years of social conditioning clicked slowly, surely, smoothly into place.

He must truly love her – he'd proposed.

He must be telling the truth – he'd proposed.

He must want the best for her – he'd proposed.

For wasn't the proof here, in his ring? He wanted Isobel to

take his name, wanted to declare to the world that she was his. Dominic was claiming her.

*

Dominic held his breath as Isobel gazed into space, absently sliding the ring on and off her finger. He'd wanted her from the moment he'd met her.

As for Gemma . . . He'd been weak, sleeping with her. He'd been confused, kissing her. But it was never going to happen again. If Isobel would agree to marry him – if she'd prove once and for all that *he*, not Jon, was the love of her life – then Dominic would never look at another woman as long as he lived.

*

'I have to know one thing.' Slowly, Isobel walked back to him. 'Was this the only time you and Gemma . . . you know . . .' She scanned his face for the faintest flicker of guilt. 'Have you been seeing Gemma behind my back?'

'NO!' Dominic poured as much conviction as he could into that one word. 'And frankly, I can't believe you'd even think such a thing.'

Well, he wasn't really lying about the extent of his involvement with Gemma, was he? They'd fucked once – he wasn't *seeing* her. Dominic rationalised that most men probably enjoyed a final fling before taking the plunge into wedlock. He looked Isobel straight in the eye. 'I have *not* been having an affair with Gemma! And frankly, Isobel, I'm not sure what it says about us that you even need to ask.'

Using the oldest trick in the book, Dominic neatly turned the tables on her. It was awful having to manipulate Isobel like this, but if it was the only way to keep her he would do it. He'd do whatever it took. And then some.

'Isobel, I'm gutted.' His face was pure reproach. 'In the two years we've been together, have I ever given you cause to distrust me? Well? Have I?'

Slowly, she shook her head.

'Two years of love and loyalty on my part clearly don't count for much with you, though.' Now Dominic was really getting into his stride. 'I mean, for fuck's sake! I make one mistake, get caught in a situation I can't handle, and suddenly you don't trust me! Suddenly I'm some two-timing, lying, scheming bastard! One lousy kiss and you're ready to finish with me over it!' His eyes bored accusingly into hers. 'I couldn't have meant much to you in the first place. Where's the *commitment*? Answer me that!'

'You were kissing my best friend . . .' whispered Isobel, her mind grappling with the twisted logic he was using against her. Oh, God, she clamped a hand over her mouth, had she made some horrible mistake? Was she being disloyal even to suspect Dominic of betraying her? In the face of his fury her own intuition seemed weak and foolish. She took in his livid expression. What had she *done*?

'One mistake,' repeated Dominic, shaking his head sadly, 'one mistake – in two years! Well, lucky you, *Saint Isobel*!' He looked her up and down disdainfully. 'So perfect you never screw up like the rest of us mere mortals! Know something? *I'm only human!*' Seeing her blush suddenly, Dominic played a hunch. 'Isobel, are you telling me you've never, not even once, thought about someone else?'

She looked away.

She'd imagined being with Jon, and Byron.

She'd been unfaithful, if only in her mind. 'No, not really,' she fibbed, 'and besides, I've never done anything – unlike you!'

'But you have thought about it?' Dominic's voice rang with bitter triumph. 'So who was he? Oh, wait, stupid question. *Jon*. Perhaps I'm the one who should be having doubts.'

Isobel stared unhappily at the beautiful engagement ring. 'Hardly.'

Again Dominic grasped her hand. 'Listen to me. I love you. *Only you*. Yes, I did let things with Gemma get out of hand, but only because she was in such a state, I swear! Isobel, I'm going to ask you one last time, will you marry me?' He shrugged. 'I won't ask you again. Turn me down and we're through. I love you and I want to be with you. Permanently. Properly. It really is all up to you, now.'

Again she turned away from him and stared into the night. In the distance traffic murmured, and above the faint red lights of an aeroplane cut through the darkness. What would life be like without Dominic? She tried to picture it. She failed. It seemed so bleak and black and blank. Isobel shivered again. For two years she'd been happy with him. What was a ten-second locking of lips?

And who could guarantee she'd meet someone else? After breaking up with Jon, she'd been devastated. When Dominic had started pursuing her she had not only been flattered but relieved. If she was honest, she had been waiting for him to propose the entire time they'd been together.

If she lost Dominic, who was to say she'd get a third chance?

Isobel gazed at the ring. Then she took a long hard look inside, gave herself an emotional X-ray. She didn't like what she saw, but she knew it was the truth. She wasn't a career woman. She'd tried, but who was she trying to kid? She was never going to make it. Everyone else knew that, so why was it so hard for her to accept? This ring represented the things she truly wanted. Security. Safety. A fairytale wedding. A fairytale marriage. A fairytale life. *Happy Ever After*.

And sure, maybe that made her an underachiever. But, reasoned Isobel, she would wake up every morning beside a man she loved. Surely that counted for just as much, if not more, than any glittering career?

Once again, she looked at the ring. This was what she wanted; this was what she *needed*. The alternative was too hard; she couldn't cope with being alone. And if that made her weak? So be it. At least she knew herself.

Isobel turned to Dominic. 'Yes. I will.' Her smile was shaky. 'I will marry you.' He shrieked with delight and swung her off her feet. Now they were both crying with relief and joy.

Dominic smoothed Isobel's hair from her eyes. 'No man has *ever* wanted to marry anyone as much as I want to marry you.' He kissed her, then suddenly his face turned grave. 'Isobel, from tonight things have to be different. All along, we've let Jon and Gemma get in the way. From tonight, that has to change. I know Jon will always be your friend, and I want to be there for Gemma and get her the help she needs – but it stops there. We have to let go of them.' He stroked her face gently. 'Can you do that?'

Fresh tears filled Isobel's eyes. This was it, then. For so long she'd clung on to her relationship with Jon, and she knew it had been unfair to Dominic. Now it was time to place her ex where he belonged. In the past.

'What do we do about Gemma?' Dominic glanced over to

the doorway where Gemma still stood. She saw them look her way, turned and went inside.

'We'll talk to her tomorrow.' Isobel felt wary of her best friend. She was shocked to discover that all this time Gemma had wanted Dominic. It was disconcerting, to say the least.

In silence, hands clasped, they walked to Dominic's car, where they stood and hugged, both busy telling themselves they were blissfully happy and madly in love.

They must be.

They were getting married.

9

I Just Called to
Say I Love You

'Gems?' Clutching his mobile phone, Dominic glanced round furtively. He was outside Isobel's flat, waiting while she called her parents. He'd just told his own family about the engagement. Now, despite the pact with Isobel, Dominic knew he must tell Gemma the news. It wouldn't be right to let her hear it from anyone else.

Hearing Dominic's voice, Gemma closed her eyes with relief. It didn't last long.

'Gems, you need to know . . .' Pausing, he searched for a kind way to do this then realised there wasn't one. 'I've asked Isobel to marry me. She's said yes.'

Gemma's legs buckled. She slid to the floor and slumped against a radiator, not caring that it was burning her back.

'But what about *us*?' Even as she spoke she recognised how absurd that sounded.

'Gems? You still there?' Dominic could feel her distress as though it was flowing down the telephone line between them. 'Look, I know this is all horrible at the moment, but I meant what I said about helping you find someone to talk to. I'm really worried about you.'

'Don't be,' Gemma said faintly. 'You've got a wedding to arrange.'

Catching the despair in her voice, Dominic's voice softened. 'I do care about you, Gems. Lots.'

That made her feel worse. 'Yeah, you care. You just don't care enough.'

He sighed. 'What do you want me to say?'

'Whatever you want to say.'

'Gems, you know I love you, but I'm *in* love with Isobel—'

'Then why did you sleep with *me*? Why were you kissing *me* tonight? I suppose you think we can still jump into bed whenever you feel like it.'

'You think I'd do that now I'm engaged? Don't you see this changes everything?'

'Don't you see this changes *nothing*?' Gemma stood up and began to pace. 'Dominic, for God's sake, you'll only cheat on her again. Stop lying to yourself.'

'You're being ridiculous, and I'm not listening to any more. I'm your friend and I care about you, and that's what I phoned to say. Anything I can do to help you, I will.'

'Yeah, I bet your *fiancée* will just love *that*!'

'She'll come round. Look, I have to go. I'll call you.'

'When? We can't just leave things like this! I need to talk to Isobel!'

Dominic froze.

'Don't, Gems. Promise me!'

'Why? Worried I'll tell her about our little workout at the gym?'

'She's having enough trouble coping with what she saw tonight. What's the point in hurting her more? I mean it –

you tell Isobel that we slept together and she'll be devastated. Is that what you want?'

'No,' Gemma agreed sullenly. 'Of course not. I just can't bear lying to her like this. It's doing my head in. I mean it, Dominic, it's . . .' Gemma struggled to express how she'd been feeling recently '. . . it's . . . affecting me.'

'You're not exactly lying to her, though, you're just not telling her.' Dominic was desperate to convince her. 'If she doesn't know, it can't hurt her. This way is kinder. You know that.' He paused, fatigue overtaking him. 'I have to go. We'll speak soon.'

'Dominic?' Gemma was dreading the moment he put the phone down.

'Yes?'

'I . . .' This was the last chance she'd get to say it. 'I know you probably don't want to hear this but I love you.'

'Can't think why,' Dominic smiled bitterly, 'I don't deserve it.'

'I just wanted you to know.' She hung up before he could.

Dominic snapped his mobile phone shut and sighed. His feelings towards Gemma were so confused. On the one hand, he loved her like a sister; whenever he looked at her he experienced an incredible rush of tenderness. More, he'd always felt sorry for her, for the unhappiness she'd known. Over the years, he'd seen Gemma at her most vulnerable, and even when they were children, he'd wanted to look after her, to prove to her that not everyone was going to let her down, or leave her.

But their relationship was complicated by his attraction to her. Maybe it was inevitable that he'd want her; she had a pale, almost ethereal beauty. But, as Dominic realised, it was more than purely physical. Gemma needed him. And he was uneasily aware that she would do absolutely anything for him, both in bed and out of it. With Gemma, there were no limits, no restrictions, no end to the things he could demand of her. It was a heady feeling, having such a powerful influence over such an attractive girl. Isobel was also malleable, and he was genuinely in love with her. But his relationship with Gemma was darker. There was something addictive about it, on both sides.

Now Dominic stared into space, wondering what to do. He'd already run away from the problem once, when he'd gone to America. He couldn't run again. No, all he could do now was gradually ease himself out of Gemma's life, for her sake as much as his.

And, of course, for the sake of his fiancée. Isobel was everything to him. And he was going to be the perfect husband.

*

Gemma knew she had to keep busy or she wouldn't get through this. There was one antidote for how she felt right now, and that was to find herself a man. Tonight she was scared to be alone. Quickly she changed, slipping on a tight T-shirt and a skirt so short it never failed to draw attention. She applied her make-up with an unsteady hand, using lashings of black mascara and kohl pencil, hoping they'd mask the dead look in her eyes.

Fifteen minutes later, she was chucking her keys into a bag and heading for the front door. The phone rang. She paused, her eyes narrowed. Maybe it was Dominic? Yeah, like she really needed one of his mercy calls. He didn't love her. He just felt guilty for fucking her. She slammed the door behind her just as the answer-machine clicked on. By the time the caller started speaking, Gemma was already in the lift.

'Gemma, it's Tempest St John here. Just wanted to say how much we all enjoyed meeting you the other week at the gym. And you seemed to get a lot out of the session. I knew you would. Anyway, we're all meeting up for another meditation class later this week, at my house. Join us.'

*

'Jon?' Isobel paused. 'Sorry, I have no idea what the time difference is between London and Brazil. Did I wake you?'

Jon was in a palatial hotel in Iguaço, in the south of the country, shooting pictures of the magnificent waterfalls, and having a wonderful time. Almost. He couldn't stop thinking about Isobel, and since their row he'd wanted desperately to call her. Pride had stopped him.

Now he smiled. 'Any time you call is a good time.'

'I'm not interrupting anything, I trust?' Isobel enquired politely, and Jon recalled that the last time they'd spoken he'd been with the girl he'd met on the plane.

'No. I'm alone.'

'Me too.' In London, she was sitting cross-legged on her bed, cradling the phone against her shoulder. Dominic was outside on the mobile, telling his family the news. She felt guilty. Wasn't she breaking their pact already? But she had to tell Jon the news. She owed him that.

It felt strange. When they'd been together, Isobel was so sure he was The One. Obviously, though, Dominic must love her far more than Jon, for he was the one who had proposed. Dominic, not Jon, had said the magic words.

131

'Everything all right?' queried Jon, wondering at the long silence between them.

'Actually, things are more than all right.' Isobel laughed self-consciously. 'Dominic and I are engaged.'

Jon sat very still, an icy wave of shock breaking over his head. Suddenly a mosaic of missed chances swam before his eyes; isolated moments when, maybe, there had still been a chance for them. Like the last time he'd seen her, at the *Primadonna* party, when she'd been so upset, and he'd been so close to kissing her.

Now it was too late. And all Jon could feel was the weight of a thousand regrets.

'So, when did this happen?' were the first words he managed, aware he probably sounded like he felt.

But Isobel showed no surprise at his flat response. 'Tonight,' she said. 'To be honest, it all happened rather quickly. I'm still getting used to the idea.'

'Congratulations.' Jon tried to sound excited. 'I'm thrilled for you.'

'Really? I know what you think of Dominic.'

'If he makes you happy, that's all I care about.'

'Happy? I'm ecstatic!' Isobel's voice was overly bright. 'And there are so many things to organise, you wouldn't believe it!'

'I can imagine.' Jon couldn't help smiling fondly at a vision of Isobel flying around, making a million plans, having fittings for her wedding dress.

Isobel in her wedding dress.

The idea of Isobel, *his* Isobel, in a beautiful wedding dress, looking radiantly happy as she married someone else . . . It cut him to the quick. He'd never thought this would happen.

Because deep down, Jon had always known Isobel was The One, and assumed she'd felt the same. He'd taken her for granted, then taken his chances and sat back while she got serious with Dominic. He'd never thought it would last between them.

Well, he couldn't have been more wrong. Isobel must genuinely love Dominic. After all, she'd agreed to marry him. Jon couldn't blame her; he'd always known she wanted the whole package – engagement, marriage, total commitment. And since he had never offered these things, why shouldn't she look elsewhere?

'Any chance you'll make it to our engagement party?' asked Isobel. 'It would mean a lot to me.'

'I'll try my best. Let me know the date. It'll depend on where I am at the time.'

'Sure.' Her cheerful tone faltered for a moment. 'Anyway, I'd better go. Jon, I just want you to know that I . . . I . . .' She stopped, suddenly close to tears again.

'It's okay, Isobel.' His voice caught. 'I know.'

'But *do* you?'

'I do. And I love you too.'

Isobel smiled. As always he'd understood her.

'I guess things will be a bit . . . different, between us, now, I mean,' she said tentatively, not sure whether she was telling him, or asking him.

'A bit,' lied Jon, knowing everything would be different.

Suddenly neither knew what to say next. On some level they understood that this was the moment they'd both been waiting for all these years, when one of them had to say something to put right what had gone wrong between them so long ago.

But neither spoke. Finally, unable to bear it any longer, Isobel said quickly, 'Okay. Well, 'bye for now, then.'

'Goodbye, Isobel.'

Jon put down the phone and walked over to the window. The sky was darkening slowly, sliding from the wistful blue of twilight into an inky black. In the distance he could hear the faint thundering of the waterfalls, like a million tears dashing on to the rocks below.

Suddenly he was gripped by the urge to call Isobel straight back. This was, he realised with a frisson of fear, his last chance to salvage his relationship with her. He strode across the room, smiling grimly. He'd do whatever it took. Even if that involved proposing to her.

Hardly daring to hope, and certainly not thinking straight, he punched in Isobel's number and waited.

*

In London, Isobel was curled up on her bed, staring at the phone, wondering why she felt something had been left unsaid. If Jon hadn't left her all those years ago, would it be them getting engaged now? If only she'd been honest when he'd returned, told him how hurt she'd been, how angry . . . if she'd let him get closer . . . could it have been them getting engaged now?

Somehow, Isobel doubted it. The one thing they'd always disagreed on was marriage. She had spent her whole life longing to be acknowledged by her parents, even while accepting it would not happen. They were never going to be proud of their ditzy, failed career-girl daughter. So for her, being somebody's wife meant recognition. It was a statement that this man loved her more than anyone else. It was a message to the world that he was proud of her.

Did Jon feel that way about her?

Suddenly, Isobel had to know. She snatched up the phone, and hit the redial button.

*

'*Fuck!*' In Brazil Jon slammed down the phone. The line was, like Isobel, engaged. He stared out of the window again with unseeing eyes. It obviously wasn't meant to be. Time to leave well alone. Isobel was happy. Who was he to go unsettling her just because he was suffering from a bruised ego?

And if she had answered, would he really have proposed? The instinctive shudder of pure panic that greeted this idea suggested he still wasn't ready.

Jon knew that marriage would never be as important to him as it was to Isobel. His own parents had chosen a pagan 'handfasting' ceremony rather than a wedding and it was a family joke that they weren't legally man and wife. Jon was convinced that, after all these years, they were still happy together precisely *because* they'd never married. To his mind, marriage just lulled couples into a false sense of security. It made people complacent.

He also knew that the arguments he and Isobel always had over marriage represented greater differences. Jon yearned for excitement and change; Isobel feared these things. She craved stability and security. And although they both came from wealthy backgrounds, their families were not at all alike. Isobel's was repressed and cold. Jon's was eccentric and volatile. He and Isobel shared a few mutual friends, but he could only spend a limited amount of time in her world before it stifled him.

So now he realised it was a relief she hadn't picked up the

phone. He'd never be ready for the big white wedding that Isobel dreamed of.

She was probably better off without him.

*

Isobel put the phone back glumly. Jon's line was engaged; no doubt he was calling some girl. She almost laughed. Yeah, like she even had to wonder if he'd ever have made a real commitment. Actions spoke louder than words. And when it had counted, he'd run away. The only thing her ex was committed to was freedom.

Hugging a pillow to her chest, Isobel talked sternly to herself.

Jon was the past.

Dominic was the future.

Dominic was her Prince Charming.

And their fairytale life was about to begin.

10

Everything
But the Girl

K armic Cleansing always went down a treat. And today
would be no exception; already the workshop was
packed. From the stage at the front of the lecture theatre,
Tempest St John beamed at her audience. There must be
three hundred women in front of her. Amazing, the way
people flocked to hear her speak. It never failed to thrill her,
for Tempest genuinely believed in what she taught women.
Now, six years after she'd left Australia for the UK, she was
the most media-friendly therapist in the country, which
helped make up for how terribly she missed her home:
the glorious sunshine, the stunning views, the laid-back
humour, the superb restaurants. But each time she resolved
that it was time to go back, her associates Down Under
convinced her to stay on in the UK, insisting that her work
there was far from finished, that she was really making a
difference. So she stayed.

She checked the time and saw she still had a good ten
minutes before the workshop was due to start. She pulled
out of her bag the issue of *Primadonna* that had arrived in
today's post. This was the first chance she'd had to read Isobel's

piece on her. Now she opened the magazine and flicked impatiently to the relevant pages.

Tempest wasn't sure what to expect. So far all the pieces profiling her had praised her to the skies. She was extremely careful about which reporters she granted interviews to, and Isobel had seemed perfect. She'd been so persistent about doing the interview that Tempest figured she'd be too grateful to write anything negative. And when they'd met, Tempest had smiled to herself. The girl was a novice. She probably wouldn't ask even one probing question.

But Tempest had been wrong. Because for all her nervousness, Isobel had picked up on several things she'd hoped to avoid. And at some point in that interview, Tempest had started to feel distinctly uneasy.

Now, as she quickly scanned the piece, her eyes widened. Isobel hadn't, as she'd feared, gone away and started digging further into her background. Tempest's worries on that score were unfounded.

But that didn't mean she was happy with the article. As she continued reading, Tempest began cracking her knuckles, a childhood habit to which she only returned when extremely angry. Isobel had *ridiculed* her. She was making fun of her. Oblivious to the women seated before her, the guru cracked her knuckles more violently. If there was one thing Tempest was touchy about, it was her reputation. She'd started from nothing and succeeded through sheer hard work and talent. How *dare* Isobel mock her?

Oh, but she was going to regret it, all right.

Because Tempest was going to wipe the floor with her.

Starting with her speciality. A nice little mind game . . .

*

'It's a good piece.' Byron chuckled as he looked at Isobel's profile of Tempest in the latest *Primadonna*. 'I'm impressed.'

'Cheers.' Isobel glanced at the double-page spread. She'd succeeded in putting a humorous spin on the interview, managing to capture Tempest's incredible self-confidence. Juxtaposed with her extravagance and her love of Jimmy Choos, the image was comical. Her secondary angle was Tempest's outrageous fees, and Isobel had found the perfect picture of the guru, showing her wearing a complacent smile above the caption: 'Of course money motivates me – and I charge the earth. Know why? Because I can . . .'

'I still can't believe you got her to admit that on record.' Byron shook his head in wonder. 'Bloody brilliant!'

Isobel fidgeted uneasily. She had a nagging feeling that she may have *slightly* altered Tempest's original comment. But it was close enough. And besides, wasn't journalism all about playing with words?

Byron watched Isobel lounging on the window-seat, sliding her engagement ring up and down her finger. 'I ran into Gemma the other evening,' he said casually.

Isobel didn't respond.

'She told me you two haven't spoken properly for a month. She's very upset.'

Isobel shrugged.

He decided to change tack, and gestured at the magazine. 'You don't seem that excited about your article.'

'I'm just tired.'

He sat quietly, waiting for Isobel to break the silence, but she didn't seem to notice that he was still there. He looked at her thoughtfully. Isobel was not herself: he'd noticed a change ever since she'd got engaged. At first she'd seemed enthusiastic, a little jumpy but happy enough. Then the wedding date was announced – and the preparations had gathered momentum. The newspapers were going crazy, hailing it as the Society Marriage of the Millennium. Every detail that emerged about the Big Day was gobbled up by a media ravenous for glamour and gossip.

Every newspaper had something to say on this fairytale union, and they all profiled Isobel, the girl who had captured Dominic's heart. The *Express* ran a piece with photos of all his ex-girlfriends, chronicling how long each had held Dominic's affections for. Isobel read the article, then tore it into little bits, scattering it like confetti. The press had also discovered she was dieting so she could fit into her wedding dress, which was being specially made. Her weight became a national obsession, and Isobel became the subject of criticism when female pundits pointed out that she was not, by any standards, fat. They accused her of setting a bad example to young girls by trying to shed stones when she didn't need to.

As he watched her now, Byron was disconcerted to realise that, somewhere along the line, he'd started to care about Isobel. 'So, you must be looking forward to your engagement party tomorrow night,' he probed.

'I'm sure it'll be lovely.' She looked at her watch, and made a face. 'Sorry, I have to go. Dress fitting. Again.'

'Sure. But, hey, at some point this week, we should talk about your next article.' Byron smiled encouragingly.

'There may not be another for a while. I have to cut back the hours I work.'

'Why?'

'Dominic wants me to take things a bit easier and spend more time on the wedding arrangements. He's right, really. It's crazy, what I've been trying to fit in. No wonder I'm always tired.'

'You're tired because you're not eating,' scolded Byron. 'Look at you – if you lose any more weight you'll be classified as a missing person.'

His eyes lit up as Isobel laughed for the first time in days. 'Shows how much you know about weddings, Byron! All brides-to-be lose weight!'

'Yeah, well, I only care about *this* bride-to-be.'

'I'm fine. Never felt better.'

Byron moved into the doorway, barring her exit. He looked at her shrewdly. 'You're such a bad liar. You're *not* fine.' As weariness surfaced briefly in Isobel's face he took her hand, and pulled her over to the sofa and sat down beside her. 'Talk to me . . .'

*

Isobel bit her lip, staring at the floor. How could she tell him what was wrong when she didn't know herself? At first, things had seemed fine, and Isobel had been genuinely excited about planning the wedding. Then Dominic's family had hijacked the arrangements.

Isobel knew when she was beaten: it was hard enough to hold out against her fiancé, but impossible against his parents and two elder brothers as well as her family. They were all the same. Confident. Controlling. They just kept finding reasons for doing things their way, from the wedding dress to the choice of venue for the reception. Isobel never got what she wanted. Someone else's preference always took priority.

She simply didn't have the energy to keep arguing, especially when they were so nice to her all the time, until she ended up feeling like she was being unreasonable. Soon she accepted that all anyone wanted from her was to show up on the day and say, 'I will.' People seemed to care more about how she looked than how she felt. Where the wedding was concerned, they cared about the tiniest details imaginable. They all cared about everything – everything but the girl who was getting married.

Byron noted the dark shadows beneath Isobel's eyes. 'Are you sleeping?'

'Not that well.'

'Why?'

Embarrassed, Isobel looked away. She'd started sleepwalking, which she hadn't done since childhood. It meant something was very wrong, but she didn't want to look too closely at what it might be. Instead, she kept telling herself she was just overly excited. Dominic was being wonderful, she couldn't ask for a more caring fiancé. Now they were engaged, they spent more time together than ever, doing all the things engaged couples do. But when they slept together, Isobel felt strangely detached, as though she was merely a collection of limbs moving beneath his.

'I don't know, I'm just jittery, I guess.' For Byron's benefit, Isobel smiled, then got up quickly, not wanting him to probe further. She was about to say goodbye when he began to look her up and down. Slowly.

Isobel blushed. She was wearing a loose jade dress that brought out the green of her eyes and shimmered over her body. Since she was going straight to a fitting she hadn't bothered with a bra, and she was acutely aware of the soft material clinging to her pert breasts. The way Byron was watching her made her nipples harden against the fragile fabric and, yet again, Isobel cursed her treacherous body for giving her away.

'Isobel . . .' Byron finished his visual inspection and met her eyes again '. . . don't you ever . . . wonder?'

'About what?' she asked unsteadily.

'You know.' He smiled. 'Tell me you've been imagining what it would be like. What we would be like.'

'Why?' She looked at him unhappily, not even caring any more that he knew. 'What's the point?'

'I want to hear you say it,' he insisted, leaning back on the sofa, while Isobel stood there before him, trembling.

'Okay, yes! I have!' Face scarlet, she crossed her arms. 'Satisfied now?'

'Hardly,' said Byron wryly, 'but I haven't given up on you.'

She looked at him in exasperation. 'I'm getting *married*!'

'Like that bothers me!' He took her hand and ran a finger over the ring then slid it off. 'See? *It doesn't fit!* You silly girl – you've lost so much weight that your own engagement ring is too big.'

Isobel held out her hand. 'Give it back!'

His fist clenched around it. 'Make me.'

'Byron, come on, I'm running late, this isn't funny.' Isobel knew he was relishing her discomfort.

'Tell me about us, what we would be like. Then you can have

the ring back.' Byron watched as Isobel stood there, her face anguished.

Finally she shook her head wearily. 'Keep it, then.' She walked quickly from the office. As she passed him, Byron caught her hand and pressed the ring into her palm. His face was pensive as he watched her leave.

*

In the car park Isobel found Gemma waiting for her. They hadn't spoken much since the night Isobel and Dominic had got engaged. Gemma had phoned countless times, but Isobel had always cut short the conversations.

Now Gemma's expression was resolute. 'Look, I know you don't want to talk to me, and I don't blame you, but we can't carry on like this.'

'I'm listening.' Unable to look at her, Isobel rummaged through her bag for her car keys.

Gemma sighed. 'They'll be in your pocket.'

Ignoring her, Isobel continued to search her bag, finally tipping it upside down on the car bonnet and sighing when the keys failed to materialise. Eventually, reluctantly, she shoved a hand into her pocket and, sure enough, there were her keys.

'Isobel, please.' Gemma stepped between her and the car. 'I don't blame you for hating me but, *please*, it was just a kiss! I was upset – really, really upset! I got confused and, yes, I admit,' Gemma looked sheepish, 'I do have feelings for Dominic.' She took a deep breath. 'I'm in love with him. I know you don't want to hear that but I'm being honest. Normally I can cope with it, but that night it had just become too much for me.'

'Are you saying that all this time . . . all these years . . . ?'

Isobel shook her head in bewilderment. 'I mean, I knew you two were incredibly close, but I never realised. Why didn't you tell me?'

Gemma looked at her ruefully. 'I was embarrassed. It took a long time before I could even admit to myself that he meant more to me than just a friend. And when the two of you met, it was so obvious you liked each other. How could I say anything? You hadn't gone out with anyone for ages – you were still talking about Jon the whole time. No one could connect with you. Then you met Dom and suddenly you were smiling again! What was I supposed to do? Ruin it for you?'

Isobel's heart went out to her friend. 'All this time, it must have killed you, seeing us together,' she said quietly. 'And I never guessed how you really felt about him. Doesn't say much for my powers of perception, does it?'

'Dom didn't guess either,' Gemma pointed out. 'I put on a good act.'

Isobel nodded. She still found it disconcerting that Gemma had managed to conceal her true emotions so skilfully. 'Gems, where do we go from here? How can we carry on like everything's fine when you're in love with Dominic?'

'It's up to me to get over him, to make him a smaller part of my life. I'm getting help.'

'What do you mean?'

'I'm seeing someone.'

Isobel frowned. 'You mean a therapist?'

'Yep. And she's really good. Magic, in fact. I've only been a few times but already she's helped me. Wish I'd seen her years ago.' Gemma looked pleadingly at Isobel. 'Isn't that a start? Can't we put this behind us? If my feelings for Dominic ever get too much for me again, I'll be upfront about it and tell you. I promise.'

As usual, Isobel felt her temper scuttling away. Truth be told, she was still in shock over seeing her boyfriend and best friend kissing.

And though she accepted Gemma had good reasons for not confiding in her, still Isobel couldn't quite shake the feeling that she'd been duped. Nothing was ever going to be the same again. Where once Isobel had trusted both Gemma and Dominic implicitly, now she felt unsure, and wary.

But here was Gemma starting to cry. Isobel couldn't bear it. 'Oh, Gems, you idiot, come here!' Next minute they were hugging.

'Where are you off to now?' Gemma linked her arm through Isobel's as they walked to her car.

'To try on my wedding dress – again!'

'Listen, about your engagement party. I'll understand if you don't want me there. Really I will.'

'Don't be daft!' Isobel slid her key into the car door. 'Of course you'll be there. We're going to get through this.' But as they hugged again, Isobel sighed inwardly. As usual, she wasn't expressing her true feelings. Instead, she was putting someone else's feelings before her own. It was second nature.

*

As Isobel got into the car, waved, and drove off, Gemma said a silent apology to her friend. She, Gemma, didn't deserve such kindness. Not when she'd slept with Dominic behind Isobel's back.

She turned and walked slowly towards her own car, wondering if she'd ever be able to like herself again.

11

Black
Magic

'B-L-O-N-D-E,' said Meredith de RoseMont curtly, holding
out a strand of her hair, 'spells *blonde*. I think we can agree
that, right now, *my* hair is *not* blonde! My hair is *bland*!' She
scowled into a three-way mirror so big it filled an entire corner
of her bedroom. Behind her, André, the hair-stylist, scowled
right back.

Over by the window, Isobel smiled wanly at her mother,
then anxiously checked her watch. Her engagement party
started in two hours' time. Her mother had suggested they
spend the day together, and it had been enjoyable until at
lunchtime Meredith had let out a bloodcurdling cry and
declared that her highlights had faded. Since Chantal, her
usual hairdresser, was away, she'd had to make do with
André.

André was the most highly strung hairdresser Isobel had ever
encountered, and things were not going well. The party would
be packed with paparazzi, and Meredith was determined to
look her best. Now she looked reproachfully at the stylist.
'*Champagne* blonde – that's the shade Chantal normally uses!'

'Really?' André's voice oozed sarcasm. 'You should have said.

Oh, that's right, you did – *eleven times*!' Isobel didn't like the way he was twisting a spiky, lethal-looking hairbrush.

Meredith spoke through clenched teeth. 'I know what's happened. You've gone and used *Butterscotch*! That's why my hair's so dark!'

'I – used – *Champagne!*' André picked up a hairdryer and pulled the cable taut between his hands. A vein throbbed alarmingly in his high forehead.

'Then you didn't leave the bleach on long enough, did you?' Meredith announced, with the air of a woman who had solved one of life's enduring mysteries.

'If I'd left it on any longer your hair would be falling out!' André was flexing the cable ever closer to her neck.

Meredith's eyes widened. 'Are you *arguing* with me?'

'No.' André grinned. 'I'm correcting you.'

'Am I or am I not the client?' hissed Isobel's mother.

'Indeed you are,' agreed André, adding softly, 'unfortunately.'

Meredith threw one hand dramatically up to her eyes and turned away from the mirror with a shudder. 'I can't even bear to look. You'll have to add some more colour, then wash and blow-dry it again. And this time, give it some *body*.' She tossed her head. 'A bit of *movement*.'

'Oh, criticising my brush control now, are we? Fine! You're such an expert – do your own bleeding hair!' André threw down the hairdryer and stalked towards the door, pausing long enough to fling a pitying look at Isobel. Then he smiled maliciously at Meredith. 'Oh, by the way – *you've got split ends!*'

Spluttering with anger, Meredith turned to Isobel and ordered, 'Find my address book! We have to get another stylist!'

'Er, Mum?' Isobel edged over to her. 'We're, er, rather short on time.'

'Then what are you waiting for?'

Sighing, Isobel switched on her mobile. Instantly it started beeping frantically, alerting her to the fact that she had a text message. Isobel stared at the tiny screen and frowned as the words appeared:

> **Isobel. Tonight will be pure magic. For an extra treat, meet me at midnight. Room 100. East wing of the hotel. You'll be glad you did. Promise.**

Perplexed, Isobel searched for the number of whoever had sent the message. Somehow they'd withheld it, leaving her with no clue. It was probably just someone's idea of a joke. She racked her brains. Could it be Jon? Her pulse fluttered. Trust him to surprise her by turning up tonight with some special treat. Maybe he was going to ask her to call off the wedding? Isobel smiled wryly. As if. So maybe it was Dominic? Although this wasn't really his style. She looked at the message again. It was strange. It was intriguing. It was impossible to ignore.

*

When they finally arrived – Meredith still self-consciously fussing with her now gleaming blonde locks – Isobel discovered that her father had arranged the perfect engagement party. He'd insisted it be held at his favourite hotel, and the lavish pink and gold ballroom was full of glamorous guests and tables laden with divine-looking food. But outside the weather was in a bad mood, rain lashing the ground and thunder grumbling ominously in the distance.

Isobel's mood wasn't much better. She felt as if she were in a time loop, forced to listen to the same questions, jokes, and remarks over and over again. Everyone was waxing lyrical about Dominic, the Perfect Man. Isobel frowned. How would they react if she announced that she'd caught the Perfect Man kissing her Best Friend?

'I couldn't be happier for you, darling.' Isobel's father appeared at her side, his stony brown eyes misting with – Isobel gaped – was that *emotion*?

'Yes, really couldn't be more delighted,' murmured Harold again. 'Dominic's wonderful.' Smug smile. 'Better match for you than that idiot photographer you were so hung up on a while back. What was his name? Jim?'

'Jon,' she said quietly.

'Whatever. Never took to him.' He patted her shoulder. 'Always knew you could do better.'

'I loved Jon.' Isobel felt a sudden intense loyalty to her absent ex. God knows he'd had to put up with enough rudeness from her family while they were a couple.

'Rubbish! Infatuation, that's all it was. Not like Dominic. This is the Real Thing,' her father declared.

Isobel stared at him resentfully. He knew best. Always. About everything. No wonder she was so unsure of herself; her opinions had never counted for much with anyone, really, had they?

A dart of pain just above her right eye announced the onset of a headache, and not to be outdone, every muscle in her shoulders and back began tightening. God, she felt so nervy. But maybe it was just pre-wedding jitters.

She heard a shriek of laughter and turned to see her mother, vibrant in a multi-coloured dress, regaling her friends with tales of how her Reiki instructor kept asking her out. Every so often, she glanced furtively at her husband, clearly hoping he was aware of her carefully contrived 'carefree' laughter. But Harold was busy admiring the numerous young women present, much to Meredith's outrage.

Isobel sighed. The green-eyed monster was alive and well and running rampant through her engagement party. Her gaze fell on Gemma, hovering at the edge of a small group, sipping a glass of champagne. Their eyes met and, for a second, they looked at each other grimly. Then the moment passed as, in perfect synchrony, they smiled.

But where was Dominic? She scanned the crowded room and finally located him, greeting some new arrivals and making sure they were mingling happily. Isobel smiled proudly. Not a single guest had arrived without him finding five minutes to spend with them. He was the perfect host, adept at making people feel at ease. And he was certainly the most attractive man there; most of the women in the room had been besotted with him at one time or another. So everyone was right, concluded Isobel. She was the lucky one.

She smoothed out an imaginary crease in her dress; a sensational slinky red designer number that Dominic had chosen. Strapless and practically backless, it fitted snugly over Isobel's newly streamlined curves. But although she weighed less than ever before, somehow the dress still felt tight.

Catching her eye, Dominic joined her and slipped an arm round her ever-shrinking waist. 'Doesn't she look stunning?' he demanded of the friends and family who were now swarming around them. 'I don't know why you girls go on about how hard it is to diet – just look how easily Isobel's managed it.'

Now he was positively glowing with pride over her weight loss and Isobel blushed. Everyone was staring at her, admiring her, appraising her, fussing over her figure. Before long, their voices merged into a meaningless, relentless babble.

Then, across the crowded room, Isobel glimpsed Byron. He was watching her with a sardonic smile, as though he knew exactly how she was feeling. She'd seen him earlier, engaged in a passionate debate with one of her father's friends. Byron was arguing against capital punishment. Fifteen minutes later, she had been intrigued to overhear him having an equally intense conversation with a fashion writer about that season's footwear trends. Half an hour after that, he'd been huddled in a corner with one of Dominic's cousins who happened to be a chess fanatic. Edging closer, Isobel had listened intrigued while Byron dissected the other man's strategies. Whatever the topic, Byron not only held his own but also spoke with conviction. It was an attractive quality.

Locating Dominic again, she watched her fiancé flirting with two exotic-looking girls he knew from way back. Isobel's stomach gave a sick little lurch as she saw him lean close to one of the girls and whisper something. She didn't mistrust him, she genuinely believed the kiss with Gemma had been a one-off, but even so she felt bitter.

Dominic had strayed.

Dominic had given in to temptation.

Dominic had enjoyed a moment's weakness. Why couldn't she?

Isobel drifted away from the circle of guests surrounding her and stood alone in the middle of the room. How strange; all these people were here for her, yet she felt distant. Detached. Now all the faces began blurring, as the voices had earlier. Only one remained clear. Byron's. His gaze was trained on her face like a searchlight. Isobel held his stare, held it properly for the first time, and as she did so, his smile faded. Slowly he approached her.

'Isobel,' he murmured huskily, 'you really do look out of this world.' His eyes caressed her.

She coloured and looked away.

Byron gave a throaty chuckle. 'And you're even cuter when you blush.'

Aware that Dominic was standing nearby talking to her father, Isobel gave Byron a reproving look. 'Stop it.'

'Why?'

'It's wrong,' she mumbled, wishing she could control the adrenaline skidding through her body.

He slipped his hand into hers, interlacing their fingers. 'Does it *feel* wrong?'

At his touch she smiled helplessly. 'No.'

He squeezed her hand, then sauntered away.

Isobel checked her watch. It was half-past eleven.

*

'Dominic.' Gemma touched his hand lightly and laughed when he almost jumped out of his skin. 'Hey, you, relax . . .' She lowered her voice teasingly. 'What did you think I was going to do?'

Dominic was relieved to see Isobel talking to Byron. 'Gems, hi. I've been worried sick about you!'

'Don't be. I'm happy for you and Isobel. I wanted you to know.'

Dominic was touched. 'That means a lot.'

'Yeah, well, you mean a lot – you and Isobel mean a lot to me, that is. Congratulations.' She kissed his cheek lightly then hurried off.

Dominic watched her walk away. Then he cursed himself. The touch of her lips on his cheek had reminded him yet again of what he mustn't want, what he couldn't want. Of what he wanted, still.

*

Gemma wandered around the party, feeling frail as a shadow as she drifted aimlessly from group to group. She shouldn't have come. Throughout the evening, she'd been alternating between guilt over sleeping with Dominic, and envy that he'd chosen Isobel, then back to shame over having betrayed her closest friend. Each time she saw Dominic, that sad little ache would begin inside her, spreading, intensifying and sharpening until she thought she would go insane. Every minute of every hour of every day Dominic was on her mind.

Lately she had cancelled more and more social arrangements, preferring to spend her evenings at home, curled up on the sofa, daydreaming about the two of them together, replaying his every look, his every word, his every touch that day at the gym. Sometimes Gemma could lose herself for hours in this fantasy.

Tonight that fantasy had splintered into tiny jagged shards. Like the slivers of glass with which Gemma sometimes cut herself. She closed her eyes, remembering the pain. Wonderful, magical pain, the only thing that could ever obliterate her hurt over Dominic. The cool kiss of the glass against her skin. The sweet sting of the glass as it worked its way *under* her skin.

Tonight she would go home, and she would make herself feel better. Suddenly Gemma giggled wildly. She was going to cut herself up – to stop herself being cut up over Dominic! Tonight, Gemma just wanted to curl up and die. Her eyes filled with tears.

*

Isobel had gone to the ladies' and removed her mobile from her tiny bag. Sure enough, there was another anonymous message:

Midnight. I can't wait.

She returned to the party and impatiently watched the hands on her watch creeping ever closer to the witching hour. Now, finally, it was ten to midnight. And still she had no clue as to who the messages were from. If it was Dominic, and he'd arranged some sort of surprise, he was doing a good job of acting normally. She was sure it wasn't him. So she shouldn't go.

But Isobel was gripped by an irresistible urge to make the rendezvous. Maintaining a glassy smile, she made her way slowly to the other side of the ballroom, heading for the door. And so, at precisely five minutes to midnight, one half of the perfect couple slipped unnoticed out of the party and through the flower-filled atrium. Ahead of her, through the hotel entrance, she watched the night sky turn a glaring white as sheet lightning sliced through it. Though it was still raining heavily, the air was sultry, crackling with electricity.

At the reception desk, Isobel asked for directions to room one hundred. The concierge smiled and led her back past the ballroom to an archway she hadn't noticed before. Isobel smiled her thanks, walked through it, and found herself in a long corridor. She followed it right to the end, where all that awaited her was a heavy black velvet curtain.

Somewhere behind her, a clock began chiming midnight.

Isobel hesitated, then peered behind the curtain and discovered a spiral staircase. The metal rungs echoed eerily under her high-heeled shoes as slowly she made her way up it.

At the top of the stairs she found herself in a dimly lit, narrow hallway, at the far end of which was a wooden door.

She slipped through it, shut it quietly behind her and turned to see a figure gazing out of the window. Her uninvited guest wore some kind of a flowing, deep blue cloak with a hood. Outside the sky was still seething and, as it lit up with another burst of lightning, Isobel glimpsed the person's reflection in the window-pane, the face a ghostly white.

Her brain reeled. What, in God's name, was Tempest St John doing *here*?

'The messages were from you?' Isobel queried nervously.

'Correct.' Slowly, the guru turned to face her; from inside the folds of her cape she produced an issue of *Primadonna* and flung it on the floor. It splayed open at the page containing Isobel's article. 'Not nice, Isobel.' She gestured at the magazine. 'Not nice at all.'

Isobel blinked. This was truly surreal. Finally she collected her wits enough to say quietly, 'I just reported what you told me.'

Tempest arched an eyebrow. 'You've twisted my remarks. You've changed my words. You've distorted my message.'

'Obviously I've paraphrased things.' Isobel glanced back at

the door, wondering how she could leave without causing further offence. 'That's journalism.'

'That's journalism, hmmm?' Tempest echoed, in a strange, lilting tone.

Outside, the sky shuddered as veins of blinding white lightning hurtled across it, followed swiftly by thunder. The lamp in the corner of the room flickered violently, then dimmed. Isobel jumped as, suddenly, the window gave a loud rattle. She glimpsed trees outside writhing under the weight of the storm, their leaves glowing faintly under the threads of lightning, their branches casting crooked shadows on the walls of the tiny room.

'You know what you did was wrong.' Tempest's voice was hushed. 'I gave up my time to help you. I answered all of your questions. And now you've written a piece making me out to be some kind of charlatan.' Her brilliant eyes blazed against her alabaster skin as she leaned closer, hissing, '*You've humiliated me.*'

'Er, don't you think you're overreacting? I wrote a factually accurate piece based on—'

'You've twisted my words and you know it!' Suddenly, inexplicably, Tempest's eyes softened and she smiled sadly, then reached out and gently touched Isobel's cheek, her fingers like ice. 'You foolish girl. Don't you know what you've done?'

Unnerved, Isobel shook her head.

'The law of karma states that whatever you give out, whatever you send out into the world you get back *threefold*. Isobel, do you understand?'

Now thoroughly disconcerted by Tempest's ramblings, Isobel edged towards the door. 'No, and I'm sorry, but I really don't feel this is an appropriate time to—'

'Oh, we're almost done.' Tempest's expression was strangely regretful. 'I have no desire to ruin your engagement party. And, besides,' again that odd smile, 'you're going to need all the luck you can get.'

Isobel tensed.

'Threefold,' repeated Tempest, violet eyes locked on Isobel's face. 'Watch yourself, Isobel. You've been lucky all your life. Now your luck's about to change. *And so are you . . .*'

Deciding she'd had enough of this ridiculous melodrama, Isobel rolled her eyes and turned towards the door. Obviously the woman was a raving eccentric. But in her haste she stumbled, bumping into the desk and knocking over the lamp. There was a resounding crash as it hit the floor. The bulb exploded with a bright blue flash, hurling the room into darkness.

And suddenly Tempest was beside her, whispering to her; whispering so quickly that at first the words were unintelligible, before they clicked into place in Isobel's mind.

'Good luck has been yours all these years; watch as joy now turns to tears. Where once fate to you was kind, from this day confusion you will find, with a change of heart, a change of mind, a change of heart a change of mind a change of heart a change of mind . . .'

Isobel staggered backwards and hit the wall, then groped frantically for the light switch and flicked it on with trembling fingers. Tempest had gone. Isobel frowned. She hadn't even heard the door opening. But, then, everything was confusing in the dark, wasn't it? Recalling the words of the whispered chant, she shivered.

She hurried out of the room and flew down the stairs on shaky legs, practically falling down the last few steps just as

Dominic appeared. 'There you are!' He slipped an arm round her waist and kissed her. 'I've been looking all over! *OK!* wants to take a few more photos. I'll tell them I've found you.' As Isobel prepared to tell him about her bizarre encounter with Tempest, he was leading her back into the ballroom, oblivious to her distress. Yet even as she was smiling at her friends and posing for photos, all Isobel could hear was Tempest's eerie whisper, her dark hints about Isobel's luck changing.

Fear wriggled along Isobel's spine.

It was rubbish, she reassured herself. Of course Tempest couldn't jinx her! She was just trying to freak Isobel out with her prophecies of doom, just trying to scare her by playing stupid mind games.

And it was working.

12

Sex, Lies,
and Libel Suits

Three weeks later.

Isobel peered warily through the leaves of the giant yucca plant. Good: no one had seen her. She'd just arrived at work – over an hour late. She surveyed the office and sighed with relief. Byron wasn't around. With any luck he was tied up in a meeting and would be none the wiser if she could just get to her desk without anyone noticing—

'*AAAGGHHH!*' She jumped as a hand grasped her shoulder.

'Isobel, what are you doing?' Byron had come up behind her and was regarding her suspiciously.

Isobel realised how peculiar she must look, with her arms wrapped around the yucca plant, her face buried in its lush greenery. 'Er, I was . . . talking to it.' She nodded earnestly. 'It's really important, Byron, to *communicate* with plants.' After all, they are living, breathing beings! So I was, well, just having a bit of a *chinwag* with this one.'

Now really warming to her subject, Isobel gave the plant an affectionate pat. 'He's called Christopher; I've named all the plants in the office, you see. Helps them feel more *important*. It says a lot about an office environment when the plants are happy and healthy and, you know, really feel like they're *part* of things and—'

'When you can tear yourself away from *Christopher*,' interrupted Byron crisply, 'perhaps you'd care to explain why you're over an hour late?'

'Late? I'm not late, oh, goodness me, no.' She tapped his hand playfully as though the mere idea was absurd. 'I've been here since eight thirty. You just didn't see me because I was so busy—'

'Chatting up a pot plant?' Byron's mouth twitched. 'You could at least come up with a more plausible excuse.' He looked at her sternly. 'Isobel, from now on you'll get here by nine like everyone else. Got that?' He stalked off.

Isobel hurried into her own office, just in time to answer the phone.

'Hello. Is—'

'Whatever you're doing this afternoon, cancel it,' barked Dominic.

'Why? What's wrong?'

'I just got a call from Jacqueline; she tried your work number but you weren't there. She's been burgled. Half of her wedding gowns have gone, including yours.'

Isobel groaned. 'You don't mean—'

'She'll have to start from scratch. I just hope to God she's got enough time.'

Isobel hesitated before saying carefully, 'Look, Dominic, it *was* a beautiful dress, but why don't I just wear something else? I'm sure we can find one that's al—'

'Don't be ridiculous!' Dominic tutted. 'The dress was perfect and you looked perfect in it. Jacqueline will just have to schedule a new round of fittings and you'll have to take time off work. Starting today. Look, let's meet for lunch before you see her.'

It was futile to argue so Isobel agreed and put the phone down.

A second later it rang again. 'Hello, Is—'

'My office. *Now*,' ordered Byron, and the line went dead.

Isobel wondered which cardinal sin she had committed since she had spoken to him a mere five minutes ago.

When she knocked tentatively Byron glanced up and beckoned her in. He was sitting behind his desk, staring at the last issue of *Primadonna*. Staring at her article.

She perched on the chair opposite and attempted a bright smile. 'Something wrong?'

'Oh, I think you could say that. Tempest St John is suing us.'

Her smile vanished. 'Because of my piece on her?'

'She's claiming defamation of character.' Watching the way she was now frantically gnawing at her fingernails, Byron decided to put Isobel out of her misery.

'I've spoken to our solicitors, and we shouldn't have too much to worry about. You were perfectly entitled to put a humorous spin on the piece. The real problem is with the bit about Tempest only caring about the money. But, hey, you only reported what she told you – just let me have the tape of the interview.' He rubbed his hands together with glee. 'We'll show her up for the liar she is! Runs off at the mouth like that and then tries to blame us? Defamation of character my *arse*!'

A violent wave of nausea hit Isobel. She shoved her chair

back and muttered something about not feeling well. In the sanctuary of her own office, she collapsed on to the sofa.

'Isobel?' Byron followed her through and sat down beside her. He laid a hand on her shoulder. 'What's the matter?'

Isobel didn't say anything. How could she tell Byron about the tape? He'd go ballistic.

'I can't help you if you won't talk to me.' Byron spoke more firmly. 'I mean it, I want to know. And I'm not going 'til you tell me.'

Isobel turned so that he couldn't see her face at all.

He sighed. 'Is this because of Tempest?'

She nodded.

'It's not your fault she doesn't like the article. If you're serious about journalism, you have to expect this sort of thing. Comes with the territory. You did a job and you did it well. You have nothing to feel bad about.'

Isobel knew she had to tell him, and better now than tomorrow, when the magazine's solicitor would want to hear the tape.

She forced herself to meet Byron's concerned gaze. 'It's the tape.' She managed to gulp before her throat constricted with fear.

'Don't tell me you've lost it?' Byron paled. '*Please*, tell me you haven't lost it?'

'No. I didn't lose it.' She shut her eyes tightly and blurted out quickly, 'I-didn't-lose-it-because-I-never-had-it-in-the-first-place.'

'Isobel, what the fuck are you talking about?'

She explained how she'd checked and double-checked the tape, how it had worked perfectly throughout the interview, how it had been blank afterwards. 'Byron, I know how it sounds, like I was just being my usual ditzy self, but I swear to you – that tape recorder was working. I don't know what happened. All I know is that for once it really wasn't my fault. You know how badly I wanted to do that interview. I would *never* have let you down, not in a million years.'

'I *knew* it! I knew I should have checked you could work the damn thing properly!'

'I did work it properly!' insisted Isobel.

'So, what are you saying – that Tempest put a spell on it?'

Isobel squirmed under his mocking gaze.

'So now it's your word against Tempest's. Do you have any idea how much this could cost us?' Byron groaned. 'Remember what happened with Tierney.'

Tierney Marshall was London's top Cool Hunter and wrote a regular column on trends for *Primadonna*. Right now she was enmeshed in legal proceedings, having brought a libel suit against a tabloid for alleging she was having an ongoing lesbian affair with a former friend and flatmate. The salacious story had almost wrecked her marriage to TV presenter Jake Sheridan. 'And the *Sunday Splash* can afford the best defence. We can't! All the jury will see is that we're a magazine and that Tempest is one individual taking on the media! This could *ruin* us!' Byron's voice was hoarse with despair.

He rubbed his eyes. 'Where's the tape now?'

'What?'

'I said, where's the tape?'

Isobel looked away, looked anywhere but at his face.

She heard him exhale slowly. 'Isobel, you've got three seconds to tell me where that tape is.'

'I threw it away. I didn't think I'd need it any more and I . . .'

Her voice trailed off as Byron turned a sickly shade of white. 'You did what?'

'I threw it away,' she whispered.

He hit the desk so violently that Isobel jumped. 'Are you congenitally *stupid*? Well? *Are* you?' His eyes conveyed a terrible mixture of disbelief and fury. 'I didn't think even *you* could be this careless! This *idiotic*! I should never have let you do that *fucking* interview in the first place.'

Isobel was trembling. 'But I told you what happened! The tape worked perfectly all through the interview but when I checked it later it—'

'For Christ's sake, Isobel!' His face radiated contempt. 'Do you expect me to sit here and listen while you come out with such blatant *crap*?' His lips curled with scorn and he pointed at the door. 'Go on, get the fuck out.'

'What?' Sheer disbelief made her smile. 'You don't mean—'

'Don't I?' snapped Byron. 'I said, get out! I don't want you here.'

Still Isobel didn't move, waiting for him to see reason. 'You can't—'

'Watch me.'

'But I'm—'

'A waste of space. I don't want you here!' Anger edged Byron towards spite. 'You've been a liability from day one. Now, because of you, we could lose everything. So yes, actually, I *do* mean it. ***GET THE FUCK OUT MY SIGHT!***'

Isobel stumbled out of the room. Back in her office she paused long enough to grab her coat then fled.

As she waited for the lift to arrive, she gazed at the bustling office. Lexie was typing so fast sparks were practically flying from the keyboard. Janine was putting the fear of God into a freelancer who had missed a crucial deadline. Adrian was trying to convince a model that fuchsia hair would suit her and look *divine* on January's cover. Julie was shoving plates full of organic chocolate in front of people and demanding to know which brand tasted best. Byron was on the phone. As Isobel stepped into the lift, no one noticed that she was leaving. Telling herself she didn't care, and knowing she cared desperately, Isobel hit the lift button and the door slid closed.

Glancing up just as she left, Byron told himself he was glad this had happened. He would be happier without Isobel around. He must have been insane to start caring about her. She'd suckered him in with those big green eyes and that cute smile, conned him into thinking she really did take journalism seriously. Now he knew differently. Just to get her by-line in the magazine, Isobel had now compromised the integrity and the existence of both *Primadonna* and everyone who worked on it.

Cursing, he began dialling another number. He had far more important things on his mind than Isobel. Like the small matter of trying to save this magazine and his career.

*

Outside in the street Isobel felt totally, utterly lost. Yet again she'd failed to prove herself. Oh, how everyone would laugh when they heard about this latest career crisis. It Girl? She was more like a *Twit* Girl.

As she watched her peers all around her, dressed in smart suits, talking earnestly into mobile phones while they hurried to and from appointments, Isobel felt a rush of envy. Career-wise, she'd achieved nothing. She was a failure. It was time to face reality; she could have all the ambition in the world, but what was the point, when it wasn't allied to ability?

She might as well go on the cruise with Dominic, and focus all her energies on being the perfect trophy wife. Isobel glanced at her watch. It was two hours before she had to meet her fiancé. Plenty of time to do some shopping, buy some new clothes for the holiday. But Isobel felt drained of energy. The mere idea of having to battle her way through busy shops and crowds of people was anathema to her. All she wanted to do was go home and crawl into bed. Her eyes were growing heavy at the idea. Even the thought of sitting with Dominic in a noisy restaurant seemed tiring. Suddenly she felt so totally, utterly exhausted that she could hardly be bothered to move. Perhaps it was simply an accumulation of stress that had built up over the past few months.

Isobel stifled a yawn. She'd just have to get through lunch and then she could go home and have a rest. Maybe if she could have a nice, long sleep she'd feel better about things.

A hundred years ought to do it.

13

Psychobabble

Isobel rested her head on the steering-wheel. The driver of the car beside hers shot her a sympathetic look. Ahead, the motorway was clogged with traffic as far as the eye could see, and in fifteen minutes, Isobel had to meet Gemma for lunch. Then she was due at the travel clinic to get her inoculations for the cruise. At this rate, she was never going to make it, and Dominic would be left waiting for her.

She punched his number into her mobile and turned down the radio. 'Dominic? Can you hear me? The traffic's terrible. Would you call the clinic and put our appointments back 'cause I'll never get there on time? Hello? Hello?' The phone cheerfully informed her that its battery was dead. Perplexed, she shook it a few times then threw it down on the passenger seat. She'd only charged it this morning. It should have been working perfectly.

But, then, why? Nothing else was. Ever since the engagement party, in fact, it had been one thing after another.

Isobel ticked off the events on her fingers. First, there had been the theft of the wedding dress and then her row with Byron, both of which had happened exactly three weeks after the party. She winced when she remembered how he'd thrown her out of the office. She'd been too terrified of his temper to return to work, which was absurd, given her financial involvement. But Isobel knew she was no match for Byron. And no doubt Lexie and the others knew about her incompetence by now. So Isobel was obeying Byron's order to stay away. Still, she jumped each time the phone rang, hoping he was going to to ask her back. But no one from work called. And with each day that passed, Isobel grew more despondent. She missed the routine of work. She missed the buzz of a busy office. She missed *Primadonna*.

Not working also meant she had more time to brood over Tempest's threats. Just thinking about the guru's hex gave her the creeps. Try though she might, it was impossible not to keep replaying that dire warning in her mind. Isobel supposed it was similar to voodoo – a self-fulfilling prophecy that worked purely because she believed it could.

Dominic wasn't helping. Although it was supposed to be bad luck for the groom to see the gown before the big day, he'd insisted on accompanying Isobel to Jacqueline's for the frenzied round of new fittings. 'I don't want to hear another word about all that superstition crap,' he'd informed Isobel angrily, when she'd begged him not to come. 'I am personally taking charge of this.'

As Isobel opened her mouth to protest he stopped her with a look. 'And I rather think you should be thanking me rather than arguing.'

'Thank you, sweetheart,' she had murmured meekly.

Isobel had never felt so isolated. There was no one she could confide in – who would take Tempest's outburst seriously? Even she knew she would do well to ignore it. Still, though, the guru's ominous warning continued to play on her mind.

Especially since a mere three days after Byron had thrown her out of his office, disaster had struck again.

'Darling, I'm afraid I have some terrible news.' Dominic had phoned Isobel from work, sounding choked up.

'Oh, God, what now?' She braced herself.

'It's my mother!'

Isobel had met Penelope Sakover-Forbes on several equally unpleasant occasions, and now her spirits lifted. 'Oh dear, has something . . . has something happened to her?' she asked hopefully.

'She's been *mugged*!' raged Dominic. 'In broad daylight! Two men attacked her in the street and took all her jewellery! I can hardly *believe* it!'

'Me neither,' muttered Isobel, impressed. God, the blokes must have been brave buggers to take on old Pen; she was built like a ruddy Sherman tank and could fell a grown man with one look from those malevolent grey orbs.

'Anyway, I said we'd go over there this evening, try to cheer her up,' announced Dominic.

Isobel opened her mouth and let out a silent scream. Penelope was going to milk this for all she was worth. 'Might have to give it a miss,' she said quickly. 'I have to have another dress fitting—'

'Even better. She can go with you! I know she'd enjoy it. And it'll take her mind off the trauma.'

Wondering how quickly she could commit ritual hari kiri with her Helena Rubinstein eyeliner, Isobel laid her head down and banged it gently against the table a few times.

Then, three weeks after the mugging, just when things seemed to be going smoothly, there had been the mix-up with the wedding date. The ceremony, reception and eleven-course dinner were to be held at an exquisite château in the South of France. Both sets of parents, plus Dominic, insisted it was the perfect choice; not only was it stunningly beautiful, it had a helipad – vital since several guests were flying in on the day itself. Everything was arranged and, though it wouldn't have been Isobel's first choice, she had to admit the place sounded charming.

Then came a frantic call from the owner's PA, informing them that another big wedding had been booked for the same date. Fellow society darling, Lucy Elliot, was also getting married that day. The families went to war and the papers reported gleefully on how each set of parents was battling to secure the venue for their daughter. By now Isobel was so stressed she would cheerfully have tied the knot in a telephone kiosk.

But when she dared to suggest settling for another venue, everyone was angry. Ultimately the Elliot family lost out, after Isobel's father did a secret deal with the owner.

Now, hurrying into the restaurant and searching for Gemma, Isobel realised that her only pleasure these days was to lose herself in one particular daydream in which she ran away to some unspecified location where everything fell beautifully, magically into place . . .

*

Tempest enjoyed the stir she caused as the lift doors opened and she breezed through the *Primadonna* offices. No one tried to stop her as she headed for Byron's room. They just stared. Her unruly mass of scarlet curls tumbled wildly around her face, which was pale but for bright red lipstick. Dressed entirely in black, Tempest looked like a woman who meant business.

She had to give Byron credit; the man hardly blinked as she

swanned into his office without knocking. He simply gestured to a seat, into which Tempest slid gracefully, flashing him her neon smile, then waiting a few seconds to achieve the full dramatic effect before finally announcing, 'You can relax. I've decided to drop the libel suit.'

*

As she listened to her friend chattering away, Isobel wondered what Gemma was on: she was manic, her face was flushed, her eyes too bright, her movements nervy. 'You feeling all right?' she enquired eventually.

'Absolutely!' Gemma beamed. Then she undid and retied her hair into a ponytail for the fifth time in an hour. She couldn't keep still. In the space of a few weeks she'd gone from depression to elation; it was unreal. Seeing Isobel's confusion at this change in her mood, she couldn't help laughing. 'Really, I'm fine. You?'

Isobel decided to broach what was worrying her. 'Actually, I wanted your advice.' Despite their problems, Gemma was still the only person she could talk to about this.

Now, having recounted her run-in with Tempest at the party, Isobel said sheepishly, 'I know how crazy this sounds, but you don't think she could have anything to do with all this bad luck I'm having, do you? God, I feel like an idiot for even suggesting it, but could she have put some sort of *jinx* on me?'

Gemma stared at her in amazement then shrieked with laughter.

'It isn't that funny.' Isobel folded her arms defensively.

'Sorry, it's just that Tempest would never do anything like that. She's one of the nicest people I've ever met.'

Isobel gaped. 'You *know* Tempest?'

Gemma nodded placidly. 'Met her a while back. I've been

taking some of her group meditation classes.' She paused. 'She's the therapist I've been seeing.'

Isobel clutched her friend's hand. 'Haven't you been listening to a word I've said? *The woman's a total headcase!*'

'You couldn't be more wrong. I'm telling you, Tempest is *magic!*'

'You're talking about the woman who's suing *Primadonna* and wrecking my career!'

Gemma looked contrite. 'I know, and I do feel bad over that. But she's helping me such a lot.'

So Tempest was the reason for Gemma's new improved mood. Isobel felt more uneasy than ever. 'How often do you see her?'

'Well, I've been having one session a week, but Tempest says we should make it two, 'cause now I'm like, you know, starting to deal with some seriously deep stuff.'

The idea of Tempest St John rummaging around in Gemma's delicate psyche made Isobel shudder. 'Not that I know anything about it, but don't you have to be careful with therapy? You can't let just anyone inside your head.'

'She's hardly "anyone",' protested Gemma.

While Gemma proceeded to reel off Tempest's qualifications, Isobel gulped down the rest of her wine. Something felt very wrong about all of this.

'What about the way she carried on at my engagement party? Turning up there uninvited, for one thing, then shrieking like a banshee? Hardly appropriate behaviour!'

'Actually, Tempest and I did discuss it.' Gemma looked thoughtful. 'I happen to know that she was very hurt, firstly, over the article, and secondly, because she wasn't invited to the party. She did go out of her way to help you, after all.'

'Yeah, well, you didn't see her. She was like a lunatic.'

'She was just expressing how she felt. You're always saying you wish you could be more assertive so you should admire Tempest for talking straight.'

Isobel fell silent. This was Tempest's logic, not Gemma's. Tempest had planted these thoughts in her friend's head, knowing that, inevitably, the two girls would discuss this topic. Tempest was clever. 'So, you reckon these sessions are really helping you, then?' she asked dubiously.

Gemma poured herself some more wine, and beamed. 'Absolutely! I don't know what I'd do without her.'

Observing her friend's glowing face, Isobel wondered. Sure, Gemma needed help, and perhaps as many as two sessions a week. But Isobel knew what an addictive personality her friend had. Could Gemma be getting hooked on Tempest, and whatever peculiar brand of help the guru was offering? 'What exactly do you and Tempest talk about?' she asked casually.

Gemma's expression was one of awe. 'Tempest *said* you'd be the first to ask me that.'

'She did?' Isobel knew she'd been outwitted again.

'Yeah, she warned me that it would probably be someone close to me who would try to deconstruct the process I'm going through.'

'Deconstruct?'

'Unravel. You see,' leaning forward, Gemma stared earnestly at her, 'when you go into therapy, it changes the dynamic you have with everyone else. The equilibrium is shifting. You're used to me being the weak one and, on some level, maybe it even suits you.'

'What?' Isobel was astonished. 'I've only ever wanted you to be happy.'

'On a *conscious* level, sure.' Gemma nodded sagely. 'But on an *unconscious* level, you like the *status quo*. We all do. And now I'm getting help, now that I'm *normalising*, you feel unsettled. And that, Isobel darling, is why you're asking all these questions about my therapy – you feel threatened. Tempest explained it all very clearly.'

'I bet she did.' Isobel watched her friend with an increasing sense of frustration. Talk about psychobabble. 'How long will you be in therapy for?'

Gemma shrugged. 'How long's a piece of string?'

'Oh, very helpful.'

'You're sceptical, just like Tempest said you would be,' Gemma marvelled. 'She's unbelievable!'

'Agreed,' murmured Isobel darkly. Tempest was one step ahead of her all the way. She'd just have to keep a close eye on Gemma and hope that, eventually, her friend would see sense.

'And, besides,' Gemma tapped her hand, 'if anyone's behaving strangely it's you. I mean, look at you, you're living in Cloud-cuckoo-land, thinking Tempest could put some sort of hex on you! How ridiculous is that?'

'But you have to admit that ever since the night of my party I've had nothing but bad luck.'

'Everyone has patches like that.'

'So you don't think that Tempest could jinx me?'

'No. I think you're looking for someone to blame your problems on.' Gemma glanced at Isobel's engagement ring. 'Are you . . . are you having doubts, Isobel?'

'Of course not. I love Dominic. I just want everything to be perfect, only it's all so stressful. Thank goodness we're going away on this cruise.'

'A few weeks ago you were dead against it,' Gemma reminded her sharply.

'Yeah, well, things change.' Isobel tried to pour more wine but the bottle was empty. While she tried to get the waiter's attention there was silence, both girls thinking about Dominic.

He was still on Gemma's mind but, with Tempest's help, she was accepting that he wasn't the answer to her problems. The guru had devised a plan to help Gemma get over him: now, whenever she felt herself weakening, whenever she knew she was close to contacting Dominic, Gemma simply called Tempest instead. And Tempest was showing her that she didn't need Dominic, or even Isobel, as much as she thought she did.

Isobel, meanwhile, kept telling herself – repeating it over and over like a mantra – that once she and her fiancé spent some quality time together on this cruise, she'd feel calmer. Better. Happier.

Isobel glanced at her watch and gasped. 'God, I'm going to be seriously late!' She summoned a waiter, paid the bill, kissed Gemma then sprinted out of the restaurant.

*

As Tempest dropped her bombshell, Byron assumed a look of mild interest. 'Forget the libel suit? Why would you do that?'

'You seem less than appreciative.'

'Just wondering what the catch is.' He lit a cigarette and his eyes glinted mischievously as Tempest coughed and waved away the smoke. 'I know there'll be one.'

'But a fair one. I'll withdraw the libel suit – if you print a full apology to me. And run another article, one that's favourable to me as a therapist.'

Byron tried to hide his relief. This was the best result he

could have hoped for. He'd write some glowing piece, thoroughly massage Tempest's ego, and she'd back down. Crisis over. 'You're right.' He held out his hand. 'That's perfectly fair.'

Tempest's cool fingers grasped his. 'Thought you'd agree.'

'Just let me know when it would be convenient for me to do another interview with you.'

Instantly her hand slid away from his. 'I don't think you understand.'

Byron frowned. 'I'm agreeing to what you want. And I'll be writing this article myself, so you won't have to worry about a thing.'

'But, you see, that's the problem.' She gave him a small, regretful smile. 'I want both the apology and the article to be by Isobel de RoseMont. After all, she did the damage. Now let her undo it.' Her eyes skimmed the faces watching them curiously through the glass walls. 'Where *is* Isobel?'

Byron was hardly about to admit that he'd banished her over the article, not least because Tempest was clearly determined to make this personal and embarrass Isobel as much as possible.

He sidestepped the question. 'Usually in cases like this the apology is on behalf of the publication as a whole. This is no longer simply between you and Isobel.'

'You're refusing to make her do it?' Tempest's tone suggested she hadn't been anticipating resistance.

'I will, of course, put the idea to her.' Byron remained amiable. 'We'll take it from there. I'll be in touch.'

'Make it soon, or I'll instruct my solicitors to go ahead with the libel suit,' she advised him brusquely. 'Only a fool would reject my offer. And you're no fool.' Ignoring the curious stares of the staff loitering outside the office, she left as swiftly as she'd arrived.

Byron considered his options. If nothing else, he had a good excuse now to phone Isobel, which he'd been wanting to do anyway. He was sure she'd apologise to Tempest, if it was the only way to rescue the magazine. Byron would apologise for losing his temper, persuade her to come back, then sweet-talk her into writing some glowing piece on the Gorgeous Guru.

Then they'd all be happy.

*

Isobel dashed into the clinic and found Dominic by the reception desk, chatting with a pretty nurse, who looked like she'd be only too happy to show him her bedside manner. When he saw Isobel he excused himself, took her arm and steered her into a waiting room. 'They'll be ready for us in a few minutes.' He frowned. 'Are you all right? You look a bit pale.'

'Just had a mad rush to get here.' Isobel wondered if now was a good moment to confide how despondent she was feeling. 'Actually, I'm not having such a good week. I miss work.'

'I know you do. But, Isobel,' smiling, he took her hand, gazing solemnly into her eyes, 'soon that might change. You might have something else to think about.'

A surge of adrenaline made her head spin. 'Really? Oh, my God, has someone said something about giving me a job?'

'No, nothing like that. I was just thinking we should start planning for the future.'

'The future?'

Seeing her puzzled expression Dominic laughed and kissed her. 'You're so cute! I'm referring to the patter of tiny feet.'

Isobel squealed with delight. 'You want to get a puppy? Oh, I'd *love* that.'

'That's not exactly what I meant.' Dominic smiled. 'What

I'm trying to say is that, well, you're almost thirty – surely the old biological clock's started ticking?'

'I think mine's on snooze mode, actually.' Isobel grimaced, then gasped as suddenly her heart fluttered violently. She tried to take a deep breath but a second later, another palpitation made her flush. 'I feel a bit light-headed . . .' she murmured, putting a hand to her forehead.

'You're probably just nervous about the injections.' Dominic looked at her in concern, then got up. 'I'll find a nurse.'

To her surprise, Isobel realised that, once she was alone, she felt better, her breathing relaxing somewhat. She wondered how serious Dominic was about having children. The thought caused another wave of dizziness.

Just then her fiancé returned, a nurse by his side.

'I'm fine, feeling much better,' Isobel said quickly.

'Sure? Tell you what, I'll have the jabs first, give you a chance to sit quietly.' Dominic gave her a quick kiss then followed the nurse across the hall.

Isobel grabbed a magazine and began to flick through it. Her stomach grumbled and she realised she'd hardly eaten any lunch. In fact, she had seldom felt hungry lately. Every time she sat down to eat, wedding nerves took over.

Ten minutes later Dominic reappeared, holding a wad of cotton wool to his arm. 'Your turn. I'll wait in here for you.'

Isobel walked hesitantly into the spacious cubicle and perched on a high-backed chair while the nurse prepared the injections. The lights were so bright and the room so *hot*. Suddenly her heartbeat skittered. 'Er, excuse me, could I have a glass of water, please?'

The nurse gave her a brisk smile. 'After the typhoid shot,

dear. Now, we'll give you the first injection, then you can go
and get a drink. Afterwards you'll need to come back for the
next one, okay?'

Isobel held out her arm and the woman swabbed it with
antiseptic. Isobel looked away as the needle pierced her skin. It
hurt. Glancing at her arm she blanched at the sight of the
needle burrowing into a slender blue vein.

'Feel sick!' she gasped, gesturing urgently at the nurse to
remove the syringe.

'Just a few more seconds now, dear . . . you're doing really
well . . .' The nurse didn't remove the needle, even when Isobel
began gagging and trying to clutch the nurse's arm to make her
stop. Just when she thought she couldn't bear it a moment
longer, the syringe slid out and the nurse slapped on a plaster.

'There. Not too bad, was it? Now, have that drink and sit
down outside for a bit,' she said kindly. 'Have a break before we
do the next one.'

Relieved that it was over, albeit temporarily, Isobel stood up
on shaky legs and headed out into the corridor. There was no
sign of Dominic so she went to the waiting room. But when
she sat down she was alarmed to find that she still felt dizzy.
And there was a horrible metallic taste in her throat. Her hand
flew to her mouth and she retched, looking round in panic for
someone to help her. But the room was empty, and though she
longed for some water, Isobel felt too weak to stand. She told
herself to keep calm and tried taking deep breaths. It was
probably just a reaction to the injection.

Closing her eyes, Isobel sat back and tried to focus on
something relaxing. But all she could see in her mind's eye
were tense, angry faces. Dominic pressuring her over the

wedding. Tempest cursing her. Byron screaming at her to get out of his office. Jon shouting at her down the phone from Brazil. Gemma kissing Dominic. Byron shouting. Dominic angry. Gemma kissing Dominic. Jon flirting. Dominic angry. Gemma crying. Byron furious. Dominic pressuring her. Tempest whispering. Gemma flirting with Dominic. Byron shouting. Tempest cursing her. Gemma sobbing. Jon shouting. Gemma kissing Dominic. Jon flirting. Tempest hexing her. Jon teasing. Gemma flirting. Dominic pressuring. Byron screaming. GemmasobbingTempestcursingherGemmaflirting withDominicTempestcursingherDominicflirtingwithGemma JonhatingDominichatingJonByronangryDominicpressuring ByronflirtingDominicscreamingJonflirtingGemmaangry ByronshoutingTempesthexingDominicyellingJonflirting TempestshoutingGemmacryingDominicangryByron screamingGemmasobbingDominicshoutingByronyellingJon flirtingTempestlaughingJonflirtingLexiemockingGemma sobbingTempestlaughingByronflirtingJonshoutingDominic pressuringByronscreamingGemmasobbingLexiemocking TempestlaughingDominicscreamingJonflirtingByronshouting GemmacryingDominickissingGemmaByron screaming—

Isobel clutched her temples. Her throat seemed to be closing up and again she retched. Blackness began seeping around the edge of her vision. Panicking, she staggered to her feet, desperate to find help. The floor lurched up to meet her. She cried out.

Dominic walked into the room just in time to see Isobel keel over and crack her head sharply against the corner of the table, blood trickling down her face as she lay motionless on the polished white floor.

Part Two

14

Sleeping
Cutie

Two weeks later

'They look like the three wise men gone wrong,' Dominic whispered to Isobel's parents as a trio of doctors filed into the consulting room. In a private ward on the other side of the sprawling hospital, Isobel continued to slumber peacefully, as she had for the past fortnight.

None of these three doctors inspired much confidence, decided Dominic. One was a young registrar from the hospital, another was a neurologist, and the third one was a specialist in sleep disorders. The registrar was the first to speak.

'Right, well, obviously you're anxious to know why Isobel is still unconscious,' he began. He didn't look a day over fourteen, wore a tie covered with polar bears, and judging by his perfect falsetto had himself sustained a nasty injury, in a delicate area. 'And the simple answer,' he continued, 'is that we don't know.' Seated beside him, the sleep disorder expert rolled his eyes, then assumed a complacent smile, as though he knew better. 'Right now,' the registar looked vaguely apologetic, 'Isobel is a medical mystery.'

Harold de RoseMont spoke first. *'What?'*

'As you know, we've run all the standard tests on your daughter. And several specialists have been called in,' the registrar glanced at the other two doctors, 'but they can't, er, agree on why she's still asleep.'

Dominic tried to control his rising panic. 'All right, then, why do you *think* she hasn't come round?'

The neurologist took over. He was a tall, lanky man with thinning hair and a nervous twitch whereby he would stare without blinking for several minutes, then blink three times in quick succession. Dominic was getting twitchy just watching. He tried to focus on what the man was actually saying.

'Well, personally I think that as a result of sustaining trauma to the head – when she hit it, in other words – Isobel has entered some kind of catatonic state, rendering her unresponsive to the normal stimuli. Such a state can also be the result of severe shock or stress.' He paused, staring into space, his eyes eerily still, while everyone fidgeted. Finally, after what seemed like an eternity, he blinked three times, and everyone relaxed. 'Had Isobel been particularly stressed prior to her accident?'

Flustered, Dominic, Meredith and Harold all turned to each other. Dominic coloured. Isobel *had* received a shock – the night she'd found him kissing Gemma. But that had been weeks ago; surely it couldn't have any bearing on what was happening now? And, besides, he could hardly mention it in front of her parents. Seeing that they were expecting him to answer the question, he shrugged. 'Sure, Isobel was a bit fraught, what with all the wedding preparations. But nothing out of the ordinary.' He crossed his fingers behind his back.

The neurologist nodded. 'It's also possible that the head

injury has left Isobel in a coma—' He jumped as Meredith screamed, then he continued quickly, 'The reason we've ruled this out is because the test results don't support this theory. None have indicated anything abnormal or worrying. But we're repeating some of them, just in case.'

'If she's in a coma, when will she wake up?' queried a subdued Harold.

'Impossible to say, I'm afraid.' He paused. 'There is another possible explanation . . .'

Right on cue the sleep specialist got up, took a sort of bow and began pacing. 'This is a most *fascinating* case!'

'Oh, we're *so* glad,' muttered Harold sarcastically.

'Yes, indeed, I am *convinced*' – the sleep specialist shot a withering look at the other two doctors – 'that Isobel has a condition called narcolepsy. People who suffer from this tend to fall into unusually deep sleeps and it's impossible to wake them.'

'But why on earth would Isobel suddenly develop something like that?' fretted Meredith. 'Is it because she hit her head?'

The specialist aimed another smug glance at his peers. '*They* will say no.' He puffed out his chest. 'But I have made it my life's work to study this condition. I know of a number of cases where a blow to the head seems to have triggered the problem. I'm also aware of a few, rare cases where the individual slips into a prolonged sleep, sometimes lasting for weeks.' He leaned forward again, clasping his hands together. 'Now, what I suggest is that we move Isobel to my clinic where I can make a full study of this intriguing case – it would make a *wonderful* topic for a research paper—'

'Forget it!' Meredith folded her arms. 'You're not dragging

my baby off to some kind of, oh, I don't know, dream factory, where you'll wire her up to monitors just so you can get a sodding article published!'

The specialist fixed her with a baleful stare, while the neurologist began blinking frantically.

'Let me make sure I'm understanding this properly.' Harold frowned. 'You're saying you can narrow the problem down to these three things, but you can't say which one it is, nor can you give us any idea as to when Isobel might wake up?'

'Er, actually there is a fourth possibility.' The registrar smiled nervously. 'Since so far we can't categorically say there's any *physical* reason for the prolonged sleep, the answer may lie in an emotional or psychological cause.'

'In English?' snapped Meredith.

'It's possible Isobel just doesn't want to wake up yet. Your daughter may simply have worn herself out.' He looked thoughtfully at Isobel's parents and fiancé. 'Sleep can be a form of escape.'

*

Dominic followed Isobel's parents into her room. Isobel lay on her back, chestnut hair spilling over the pillows. Her normally rosy face was now whiter than the bandage that covered the gash on her forehead and even her lips seemed a paler pink than usual. Dominic struggled to keep his composure. He wondered what his fiancée was dreaming about. She looked peaceful. *My very own Sleeping Beauty*, he thought. For this was what the media had christened her. The tabloids were in a frenzy. Isobel was a celebrity babe, she was young, she was beautiful, she was engaged to the most eligible bachelor in

Britain, and right now she was a medical mystery. It was a dream of a story.

Within hours of the accident, the papers had discovered which hospital Isobel had been rushed to, and a gaggle of reporters was now a regular fixture at the entrance, eagerly snatching shots of Isobel's friends and family as they left the grounds, shoulders slumped, faces despairing.

Now the registrar gestured to Dominic to leave the room with him. 'On an unconscious level, Isobel is still aware of everything going on around her so *talk* to her. Play music she likes. Read to her from her favourite books. Anything could stimulate a response. Ask her close friends to come in and chat to her. There's no way of knowing what, or who, could reach her.'

'What do I talk *about*?' Dominic felt foolish even asking.

But the doctor seemed to understand. 'Just talk about things you did before her accident. Films you saw together, parties you went to. Keep it light, keep it normal.' He smiled. 'Talk to your fiancée exactly as you would if she were awake.'

Dominic murmured his thanks and returned to Isobel's room. He glanced with concern at his future in-laws. 'Would you like to go and grab a coffee?' he offered. 'I'll stay here. I promise I won't leave her alone.'

Gratefully Isobel's parents nodded then kissed their daughter and left.

Dominic sank into the chair nearest the bed. He was riddled with guilt. He knew he hadn't caused Isobel's accident, knew that cheating on her hadn't made this happen. Christ, she didn't even know he'd slept with Gemma. Still . . . Isobel had been so anxious ever since the night she'd caught them kissing. The stress his betrayal had caused, combined with her frantic dieting, must have contributed to her accident. Must have worried her. Must have weakened her.

Again, he searched her face for a flicker of awareness, but there was nothing, only her eyelashes fluttering softly against high cheekbones which stood out like bruises against the snow-white skin.

'Isobel . . .' Dominic's voice cracked '. . . Isobel, I'm so sorry.' Silently he beseeched her to wake up and tell him that everything was going to be all right. But the only movement was the steady rise and fall of her chest. 'Isobel . . . won't you wake up . . . *please*?' He felt faintly absurd, pleading with her like this. 'Isobel, I swear if you'll just wake up, everything will be all right. I'll never let you be anything but happy – I'll do whatever it takes *if you'll just wake up*.' His voice trailed off. If she could hear him on some level, it wasn't evident from her face. And now Dominic was aware of an increasing sense of frustration. Why wasn't she responding to his voice?

And for one wild, weird moment, as he watched that tiny smile playing round her lips, he suspected she was *wilfully* disobeying him. Then he shook his head. Christ, he had to get a grip. This was just fatigue talking.

Making himself as comfortable as possible in the chair, Dominic closed his eyes, Isobel's pale face looming large in his mind. He stayed by her bedside for the rest of the night.

*

Week three
Gemma smiled her thanks to the nurse who showed her into Isobel's room. It was pleasant enough, with lemon yellow curtains and a matching carpet. Friends and relatives had sent

flowers constantly and the place resembled a florist's, vivid bursts of colour adorning every surface. She tried not to look at the transparent tube inserted into the back of Isobel's hand, providing her with liquids so that she didn't dehydrate.

Isobel lay perfectly still. She was frowning slightly. Gemma watched her intently. What was her friend thinking about, so far away, so lost in sleep? What was she feeling? What was she dreaming of? Her expression was definitely one of mild disapproval. Gemma shivered. Was it possible Isobel had guessed somehow about her little indiscretion with Dominic?

The weight of that shameful secret was crushing. It haunted Gemma. Ignoring the chair, she crouched down beside the bed, reaching tentatively for her friend's hand. Strange being here alone with Isobel like this. It felt like being in a confessional.

Maybe it was selfish, but Gemma was desperate to offload her guilt – not simply because she wanted Dominic for herself but because she was genuinely worried about Isobel, having watched her running herself ragged, changing her work routine, her opinions, even her shape, in a bid to become perfect wife material. 'Isobel, it's so awful seeing you like this. There's so much I want to tell you. I miss you . . .' How she yearned to confide in her friend. The confession was perched on the tip of her tongue and, as she gazed at Isobel's wan face, the shame of that illicit sex was overwhelming.

Gemma licked her lips, which were suddenly parched. 'Isobel, I need to tell you . . . need to tell you that I . . .' But the words wouldn't come, changing to, 'I'm scared . . . scared that when you wake up you'll carry on with Dominic even though I know you're not happy . . .'

But who was to say that Isobel *would* wake up?

Gemma's sense of loss was so acute it hurt. She sat on the floor and leaned weakly against the bed. 'Isobel, please wake up. The doctors say there's no reason why you shouldn't . . . I need you so much to wake up, Isobel. Can you hear me? If you can, show me!'

Not sure what she was expecting, Gemma held her breath and waited. Nothing. In the movies the patient always reacted some-how, but Isobel didn't move. Gemma sat beside the bed for another fifteen minutes, talking quietly to her friend. Then she gathered up her things. 'I'll be back soon, Isobel,' she whispered.

As she left, shoulders slumped under the weight of her lonely secret, she passed a nurse carrying a covered tray, a striking Oriental girl in her late twenties. She patted Gemma's shoulder, entered Isobel's room and swiftly closed the door.

*

Instantly her expression changed. She set down the tray briskly, and removed the cover to reveal a small camera. Then she positioned herself to one side of Isobel and began snapping away. 'Sorry about this, hon,' she murmured, 'but my editor's going to love me for ever!'

Lian knew she was one step ahead of her fellow hacks but, then – she chuckled – she always was. Her reputation as a top tabloid reporter – clinched by getting last year's scoop on Tierney Marshall's lesbian fling – was well deserved. Today was nothing that out of the ordinary. All it had taken was initiative; specifi-cally, getting hold of a nurse's outfit from a costume shop, then striding into the hospital looking as if she had every right and reason to be there. No one had given her a second glance. And these pictures were going to be something else.

Once she was sure she had enough material, Lian put the camera back on the tray, covered it carefully, and made her exit, pausing at the door. 'So long, Sleeping Beauty. See you on the front page.'

Isobel continued slumbering peacefully.

*

Outside it was dark, the moon a mere smudge of light. Gemma walked briskly across the deserted car park and was just unlocking her car when a hand grasped her arm. The scream died on her lips when she turned to find Dominic, his eyes bloodshot. 'She's not going to wake up, is she?' He was trembling. 'This is it.'

'You can't think like that.' Gemma took his hands and squeezed them hard. 'It's just over two weeks. We could turn up tomorrow and find Isobel sitting up in be—'

'But we won't, will we? I've lost her, I know I have – don't think I can bear it—'

To Gemma's alarm he turned away from her, shoulders hunched, and she realised he was crying. 'Dominic . . .' She hugged him tightly, closing her eyes as his arms slipped around her. For a few minutes they stood there, holding each other, both consumed with fear and disbelief at the events of the last few weeks.

Then Gemma stiffened. Dominic's arms had tightened around her, almost imperceptibly. She felt his lips brush her hair, then her forehead. '*No!*' She wrenched herself from his arms, and stumbled back. They looked at each other in confusion.

'I didn't mean – I wasn't – that wasn't—' stuttered Dominic. A shudder ran through him. 'Oh, God . . . Gems . . . I'm losing it . . .'

Now trembling herself from the effort of pushing him away, Gemma shook her head. 'Forget it. I'd better go.'

Wishing she could stay, and knowing she mustn't, she gave him a regretful smile, then got into her car and drove swiftly out of the car park. Dominic watched as the tail-lights faded. Then he walked back across the deserted car park towards the hospital.

15
Rude Awakening

Would Isobel want him here? Outside the hospital, Byron debated with himself. Only close friends and family were meant to visit, and he didn't qualify as either. Yet here he was because he couldn't stay away.

He walked into the reception area and shrugged off his coat. The air was hot and clammy, the thermostat turned up too high. Maybe the heat was making him yawn, but more likely it was lack of sleep; in the weeks since Isobel's accident, Byron had developed insomnia. Even when he did sleep, he just ended up dreaming about her.

Outside her room he hesitated again, images of the last time he had seen her flashing through his mind – terrible technicolour images of the way he'd thrown her out of the office, the harsh things he'd said, Isobel's stricken face as she'd fled. If she didn't come round . . . Byron hung his head. Regret was a constant companion, these days.

He opened the door and entered the room quickly, before he could change his mind. His face tightened at the sight of Isobel lying there, so still and pale. Something about the set of her features made her seem sad. Byron pulled the chair as close to the bed as he could, then sat down and looked at her.

What was going on in her mind, while she drifted in this seductive twilight of seemingly endless sleep?

'I don't know!' Speaking chattily, he reached out and smoothed a wisp of hair from her face. 'I let you out of my sight for five minutes and look at you!' His voice seemed to jar in the silent room. He waited, hoping to see a glimmer of something in her face. Still he saw only sadness. What would happen about the wedding? Perhaps Isobel would sleep right up to and through the big day? Byron had heard of people who had remained unconscious for long periods of time, for apparently no discernible reason, before suddenly awakening.

He glanced quizzically at the girl in the bed. Maybe Isobel just didn't *want* to wake up yet. Or perhaps he was just being stupid, believing what he wanted to believe because he couldn't cope with the idea of losing her.

A sour smile crossed his face. Lose her? She wasn't his to lose.

*

Week four

Heart pounding, Jon sprinted through the hospital. He'd just come straight from Heathrow, having jumped on the first flight back to Britain after getting a frantic call from Gemma. Isobel was in trouble.

Isobel needed him.

He couldn't get on a plane fast enough.

Just as he entered her room, a nurse approached him; the staff were being more vigilant since pictures of Isobel had been splashed all over a Sunday tabloid. 'Sir, excuse me, are you a relative?'

He stopped her with a look. 'I'm a family friend. Now get out.' The bemused nurse found the door being slammed in her face, as she was left wondering who this rugged, intense, rather good-looking bloke was. Still, she wasn't taking any chances. Picking up the phone, she dialled hospital Security.

Jon sat down on the bed and took Isobel's hand. He clasped it between his own, noting the icy coolness of her skin, the whiteness of her face. She looked like death warmed up.

He remembered the last time he'd seen her, at the office party – and the way he hadn't wanted to leave her, the strange inkling he'd had that something bad was heading her way. He leaned forward, and kissed her softly on the lips. 'My sleeping cutie . . . I'm here now, and everything's going to be all right. I know you can hear me, Isobel. And I'm not leaving until you wake up.' He clasped her hand tightly. 'So, you'd better get that gorgeous butt of yours out of this bed like *fast* – else you'll be stuck listening to me rambling on. I mean it. I don't care if I have to move into this sodding hospital and be here twenty-four seven – you **are** going to wake up!'

Willing her to wake up, he leaned forward and kissed her softly on the lips again.

Then the sound of a throat being cleared made him turn sharply. A haggard-looking Dominic was standing in the door-way. With an awkward smile, Jon got up and offered his hand.

Dominic ignored it. 'The nurse phoned Security. You're lucky it's me here and not them.' His eyes flickered disdainfully over Jon's faded jeans and black T-shirt, still crumpled from the plane journey. 'Thought you were out in the Amazon.' He wished Jon would get swallowed up by the rain forest and vanish for good. Anything rather than seeing him here, acting as though Isobel was still his.

'I was, but when I got back to Rio I heard about Isobel.'

'How?'

Jon noted that since entering the room, Isobel's fiancé hadn't even glanced in her direction.

'Well?' Dominic asked impatiently. 'Answer me! How did you hear?'

'*I* called him!' Gemma had arrived without either of the men noticing.

Jon knew that Dominic was feeling threatened. He wanted it to be *his* voice that triggered a response from Isobel. He was turning this into a fucking contest! He looked more closely at his adversary. Dominic was rather wild-eyed and his movements were unsteady, agitated. He looked as if he was losing his grip. Jon wasn't surprised; he'd always considered Dominic weak. And now, just when Isobel needed him most, he was cracking up.

He turned back to Isobel and studied her serene face. Suddenly, somehow, he knew that on some level she was all too aware of what was going on around her.

'You're not supposed to be here. It's relatives only.' Unable to bear the proprietory look Jon had just given Isobel, Dominic jabbed him on the shoulder.

Jon shook off his hand. 'Well, in that case, you'd better leave too.'

'Oh, I think you'll find that a fiancé qualifies as family.' Dominic picked up Jon's denim jacket. 'Yours, I believe? And don't worry, I'll make sure someone calls you if there's any news.'

Jon wanted to sling the jacket back on the chair and show Dominic he wasn't going anywhere. But this wasn't the time for a battle of wills and clash of egos. He had to do what was best for Isobel. Yelling wasn't. So he bit back a sharp retort and headed out into the corridor. Dominic followed him, determined to ensure he left.

'Security should never have let you in to begin with.' He glared.

'Your fiancé's lying there unconscious and all you care about is getting one over on me? God, Isobel really does need her head examining – for agreeing to marry *you*!'

'This isn't helping anyone.' Gemma had followed them outside in time to hear this last comment.

'You can talk!' Dominic rounded on her. 'It's your fault he's here!'

'Don't start on Gems, she was just being a good friend to Isobel, as always.' Jon put his arm protectively around Gemma. But as he said 'good friend' he saw a fast, furtive look flash between the other two. He looked suspiciously at them and wondered if something was going on here that shouldn't be.

A bit further along the corridor the lift doors slid open and Meredith de RoseMont appeared. Two morose hospital porters followed her, lugging a gigantic sound system and matching speakers.

'Hello, all! Dominic, be a darling and hold the door open.'

Curious, they followed her back into Isobel's room. Meredith opened her bag and produced a CD. 'One of Isobel's favourites.'

Bemused, they all watched as she slid it into the stereo and turned up the volume. 'This should get my baby up and about!' Her voice was tinged with desperation. Seconds later, everyone was covering their ears as Craig David came blasting out of the speakers. Everything in the room seemed to throb in time with the music.

'THERE YOU ARE, ISOBEL,' yelled Meredith, planting a kiss on her daughter's pale cheek. 'HEAR THAT, HONEYBUNCH? DOESN'T THAT MAKE YOU JUST WANT TO JUMP OUT OF THIS HORRIBLE HOSPITAL BED AND STRUT YOUR STUFF?'

Apparently not. Isobel remained motionless, while the music continued to blare out. Meredith's face fell, and Jon touched her hand. 'She's going to be all right,' he reassured her. 'Isobel will come through this. I know she will.'

'Not unless someone turns that God-awful racket off!' Harold de RoseMont strode into the room and lunged at the stereo. Glancing at Jon, his voice hardened. 'There really are too many people here.'

Byron chose that moment to come sauntering into the room.

Dominic looked daggers at the editor. 'This is too much. I am Isobel's fiancé, and I insist that everyone leaves!'

'I'll second that!' boomed Harold.

'*I* am her *mother*!' bristled Meredith. 'I am most certainly not leaving!'

'WOULD YOU ALL SHUT THE FUCK UP!'

For a split second, no one was sure who had spoken. Then Gemma gestured to the hospital bed. Now sitting up, Isobel was looking at them indignantly, her chestnut hair tumbling around her flushed face, her nightshirt slipping off one slender shoulder.

'That's better.' Her smile was sweet but her tone steely. 'Now, I think you should all leave. Anyone got a problem with that?'

16
Changes

A moment later everyone rushed forward in alarm, as Isobel blinked, put a hand to her head, then sank back against the pillows.

'My little angel! Thank heavens you're awake!' With a sob, Meredith flung her arms round her daughter. When Isobel pulled away, gasping for breath, Harold approached awkwardly, hovering for a few seconds before tentatively patting Isobel on the shoulder. Even now, Isobel noted sadly, he couldn't show her any affection.

Handsome face radiant with relief, Dominic made himself comfortable on the bed, still finding a moment to give Jon a smug look as he kissed Isobel's hand. Just then Byron reappeared with a nurse who instantly began ushering everyone from the room. 'I'm afraid you'll all have to leave.' Catching Dominic's gloating grin she added tartly, 'And I do mean all of you.'

Reluctantly, Isobel's friends and family edged out of the door.

The nurse took her pulse and checked her blood pressure. 'How are you feeling, young lady? Any dizziness?'

Isobel nodded. 'A bit. What happened to me?'

The nurse chuckled. 'You had a rather nasty bump on your head.' She glanced up as the registrar appeared, then left the room with a last kindly smile.

The doctor shone a pocket light into each of Isobel's eyes, then proceeded to examine her thoroughly. 'Do you remember how you got here?'

'I fainted, right? How long have I been in hospital? All night?'

'Five weeks.' He smiled at her shocked face.

'I slept that long? Why? What's wrong with me?'

'Nothing serious, though I'd like you to stay here for a few days so we can keep you under observation. We'll be running a few more tests just to be on the safe side. For now, try to rest, and be sure to let us know if you get any headaches or dizzy spells, okay?'

Isobel gestured at the IV tube inserted in her arm. 'Could we lose this?'

'Sure, I'll send someone in to remove it and bring you a light meal.' He patted her hand reassuringly. 'Your family and friends are outside, clamouring to see you. Feel up to some company?'

'Sure.'

Within seconds, Dominic and her parents were back in the room, crowding round the bed. 'God, I've been going out of my mind with worry!' exclaimed her fiancé.

Isobel's eyes bored into his like two emerald lasers. 'Have you?'

'Of course.' He waited for her to return his smile, but she simply continued staring at him.

The door opened and the others filed in one by one.

'Isobel!' Gemma hurried over to the bed. 'How are you feeling? Oh, you poor thing!'

But Isobel was looking past her to Jon, who was leaning nonchalantly against the door frame. She felt like a child on Christmas morning who, convinced her parents hadn't known what she most wanted, now opens her gifts and finds it there after all. Jon was here. He'd come back. For her. His presence seemed almost magical.

Abruptly, her elation subsided. Here she was, just waking up from a coma, and still all she cared about was that her ex was here.

Slowly, she smiled at him. 'Hi, stranger.'

'Hi yourself.' Jon ached to put his arms around her. Hold her tight. Never let her go. He wondered if Isobel could read his feelings in his face.

The door swung open and another nurse appeared. She beamed at Isobel. 'Well, you certainly gave everyone a shock! Now, let's get rid of this for you . . .' She fiddled with the IV tube, then ripped it off a tad sharply.

'*Careful!*' Isobel's usually sweet face twisted with temper, but a second later she was placid as usual, asking the nurse timidly, 'When can I go home?'

'Oh, in a day or two, I imagine.'

'You'll be coming home with me, babykins,' cooed Meredith. 'There's no way I'm letting you go back to that flat on your own. I'll be keeping an eagle eye on you from now on.'

'Actually,' Dominic cleared his throat, desperately trying to convince himself that Isobel hadn't just shared a long, lingering look with Jon, that he'd imagined it, 'I'm taking Isobel away for a few weeks. We've missed our cruise, but we can meet up with the others in the Bahamas. It's just what she needs – a change of scenery, rest, and sunshine. I'll take wonderful care of her. No need to worry.'

'She's not going anywhere,' thundered Harold, 'except to the Three Trees Hospital for a thorough round of tests.'

They began to bicker among themselves.

Jon decided Isobel's parents were incredibly selfish. And her fiancé was an emotional replica of her father. Oh, Dominic might seem to offer security, safety, and all the other things Isobel craved, but Jon wasn't fooled. Once they were married, Isobel's role would be that of a glorified geisha girl. She simply hadn't realised it yet.

Just then, Isobel smiled at him, and Jon felt the old spark reigniting. It was frustrating to feel the connection, to know they were more than friends, yet be barred from voicing these thoughts. Would she ever truly forgive him for leaving her all those years ago? Didn't he deserve a second chance?

He saw her watching her parents as they continued squabbling. Was he imagining it, or was there a certain glint in those gorgeous green eyes? A slight *edge* to her smile. A difference; subtle, slight, but there nonetheless?

'What on earth is going on in here?' The nurse had returned. 'I think that's enough excitement for one day. Now, if you all wouldn't mind?' She gestured to the door, her tone leaving no room for dissent. Even Harold looked sheepish as they all left the room. As the door closed, Isobel curled up under the sheets. Five minutes later she was sound asleep.

*

Jon shut the door to Isobel's room as quietly as possible. The others were three floors below in the hospital cafeteria, where

Dominic was busy reducing the catering manager to tears after finding a speck of soil in his salad. Harold and Meredith were exchanging evil looks. Gemma and Byron had tried to start a conversation that would involve the whole group, but had failed.

Unable to stand it any longer, Jon had slipped away. Now he gazed at Isobel lying in bed, her back to him. She must have been sleeping lightly, for suddenly she turned over and stretched. Her breasts pushed against the thin nightshirt as she yawned, then she sank back against the pillows, opened her eyes, and fixed him with a feline green gaze.

Jon sat down on the edge of the bed.

'Did you really come back from Brazil because of me?' Isobel asked softly.

'Yes.'

She waited for him to make the usual crack about liking to rescue damsels in distress, but he stayed silent.

'How long will you stay?'

Jon looked at her. 'Until I know you're okay.'

'But your assign—'

'You're more important.'

Isobel felt as though layers of hurt were suddenly melting away. That terrible, gut-wrenching sense of betrayal she'd been carrying around for three years was now dissolving. And in that second the world seemed to swing into sharper focus. She'd never got over Jon. She hadn't been asleep for five weeks, she'd been asleep for three years, ever since he'd left for Morocco. Isobel blanched. All this time, she'd been deceiving herself. Feeling tearful, she looked away, not wanting Jon to see. But, of course, he did.

His hand clasped hers and for a minute they just sat there. Jon felt torn. Was this the moment he'd been waiting for? Would Isobel now, finally, let him explain how intensely he regretted leaving her three years ago? He squeezed her tiny hand, feeling her skin warm against his, and then their fingers were interlocking. When Isobel finally looked up, Jon glimpsed the confusion in her eyes.

He let his hand slip from hers. Though there were things he longed to say, now was not the time. It would mean taking advantage of her vulnerability. And she was still engaged to someone else. No, he'd waited this long, he could wait a bit more.

'So how are you feeling?' he asked briskly.

'A bit strange, actually.' Isobel noted the change in his tone and frowned.

'What, you mean dizzy?'

'A bit.'

'Maybe I should get a doctor.' He started to get up.

'No, I'm fine, really.' The idea of Jon walking out of that door suddenly seemed unbearable. 'I just don't feel quite myself.'

'Well, you have had a shock to the system,' Jon reminded her gently. 'I'm going to get the nurse, just to be on the safe side.' He kissed her lightly on the forehead, and as his lips met her skin Isobel's eyes closed. She heard Jon leave. Now she couldn't stem the tears. It was the same old story: they took one step forward, then three back. Today they'd had a tiny window of opportunity, then he'd gone and slammed it shut. Why couldn't she just accept that she'd been right all along? He did love her, but he didn't love her enough.

At that moment, the door flew open to reveal her parents,

closely followed by a beaming Dominic. Quickly Isobel wiped away her tears.

'Great news! The doctor says you can come home the day after tomorrow!' Dominic kissed her firmly on the lips. 'Now, I've sorted out the hotel reservations. The Bahamas, here we come! We leave in a week. And don't worry about a thing. I've arranged for someone to do a little shopping and get everything you need.'

Meredith produced a pink silk robe from a vanity case and draped it over her daughter's shoulders. 'Before you go away, darling, you must find some time to spend at home with us. I want to make sure you're eating properly, for a start.'

'Oh, do stop *fussing*, Meredith!' Harold was exasperated. 'Isobel doesn't need to go putting all that puppy fat back on!'

'Isobel always looks beautiful,' said Dominic loyally.

As the three of them became embroiled in yet another heated argument, Isobel slid off the bed and slipped quietly out of the room.

*

'Ms de RoseMont?'

Half-way down the wide, bustling hospital corridor, Isobel heard a voice call her name. She turned and saw a doctor approaching her. In his early forties, he had thick, curly brown hair flecked with grey at the temples. His face was dominated by clear grey eyes and a wide, high-bridged nose. Underneath his white coat she glimpsed broad shoulders, plus blue jeans and a blue shirt, which was coming untucked.

'I'm Dr Paige, Carl Paige. No need to look so worried.' He placed a hand on her shoulder and steered her into an empty room.

'Is this to do with the test results?' asked Isobel anxiously, perching on the hospital bed.

'No, they're fine. But you had us all baffled for a while – there was no apparent physical reason for your prolonged sleep. So I thought we might have a chat. I'm a psychiatrist.' He paused, waiting for the inevitable horrified reaction.

Instead Isobel nodded placidly. 'Oh, fine. Only perhaps it's that lot in there you should be talking to.' She jerked her head in the direction of her room. 'I'm probably the sanest person in my family right now.'

'I see. And how are you feeling?'

'Good.' Isobel frowned. 'Well, perhaps I don't feel totally *me*.' Suddenly she lowered her voice teasingly, lay down and fluttered her lashes. 'Shouldn't I be lying down for this?'

Carl grinned. Then he became serious. 'Before your accident, were you under a lot of pressure?'

'I guess, what with the wedding and all.'

'You must be excited about getting married,' he probed.

'Sure. Who wouldn't be?' she said flatly.

He nodded. Her smile was forced. Her voice was dull. Something was definitely going on here.

'Well, Isobel, here's what I'd like to do. We're going to discharge you, but I want us to stay in touch. Maybe you could come back in a week or two for a proper chat, just to let me know how things are going. Would that be all right?'

'Is this, like, *therapy*?' she asked warily.

'Just aftercare. You had us all worried and I want to keep an eye on you.'

Isobel winked. 'Please do.' Then she blushed, wondering what was wrong with her. She'd flirted twice with him in the space of five minutes. It was totally out of character. But she did feel decidedly . . . *cheeky*.

To her relief, though, Carl threw back his head and laughed. He was probably used to women swooning in his presence, she concluded. Then she remembered something. 'My best friend's seeing a therapist. Tempest St John.'

He tensed. 'A friend? I mean, really a friend? It's not you?'

'As if!' She laughed scornfully. 'The woman's a raving psycho.'

'Yes, well, you might want to encourage your friend to seek help elsewhere,' Carl said.

'I've tried telling her that but she won't listen.' Her eyes narrowed. 'Hang on – I know why *I* don't rate Tempest, but what's your story?'

'Let's just say I take issue with some of her methods.'

'Meaning?'

'I probably shouldn't say any more,' he hedged.

She digested this, then frowned. 'But you *do* want me to start feeling better, right?'

'Obviously.'

'Well, then,' now Isobel was positively beaming, 'I *will* feel better *if* you'll just tell me a bit about Tempest. It'll stop me worrying about my friend, so I'll relax, feel better and then we'll both be happy.'

He relented. 'Let's just say that hypnosis is a valuable tool when used properly – and totally safe. Plenty of people have gone through operations under hypnosis without feeling any pain. But Tempest seems to use it with every client who comes to her. I think some of them become dependent on the treatment she's offering, and I would urge you to do everything possible to persuade your friend to stop seeing her.' He got up. 'There, I've said more than I should. Come on, let's go and tell your family to take it easy.'

Isobel wished he'd tell her more about Tempest, but she could see that the conversation was over. Sighing, she followed Carl back down the corridor and into her room where her family were still taking verbal swings at each other.

Isobel tutted and pushed her way past them until she was standing in the middle of the room.

'Right. I've decided what I want to do,' she said. There was silence as everyone looked at her. She noted that both her fiancé and her father were smiling complacently. 'I'm going back to work. And if you don't like it –' seeing the mutinous looks on her family's faces Isobel tilted her chin defiantly, and levelled her green gaze on them 'then *TOUGH*!'

17

Look Back
in Anger

'You're staying here!' Dominic snatched Isobel's bag out of her hand. 'You've only been out of hospital two weeks. You need to rest, not go shopping!' Hands firmly grasping her shoulders, he steered her away from the front door and back into the kitchen. 'Now, you sit down, and I'll make you a hot drink.'

'Dom, I really appreciate how you're looking after me, but honestly, I feel like I'm under house arrest!' protested Isobel. Ever since she'd been discharged, Dominic had acted more like a minder than a fiancé. He monitored her every move, analysed her every word, and would hardly let her out of his sight. Isobel was baffled by how obsessive his behaviour had become. The doctors had declared her fit and well and, more importantly, she felt fine.

Ignoring the chair he'd pulled out for her, she went back into the hall and put on her coat.

'My bag?' she asked him politely.

'You'll wear yourself out,' insisted Dominic.

'I need some fresh air, apart from anything else,' Isobel pointed out. 'Look, I know you're worried about me but, honestly, I'm fine. Now give me my bag – the sooner I leave the sooner I'll be back!'

'Except you won't, will you? Because you're seeing Jon this evening. I suppose you thought I'd forgotten?'

'Dominic, he flew back from Brazil to make sure I was all right, and I haven't seen him once since I came home from hospital.'

'Isobel, listen to me, I want you to stay here and take it easy today. You're not yourself at the moment. I don't care what the doctors say, I know you. You're all tense and tetchy—'

'Only because you're treating me like a child who can't make her own decisions!' Isobel decided this was getting ridiculous. She grabbed her bag from his hand. 'I'm going shopping. You're more than welcome to join me.' With that, she marched out of the front door, slamming it behind her.

Living with Dominic for the past fortnight had been a nightmare. Isobel felt like a lodger in her own home. He'd taken over completely. And if she'd tried to contradict him or regain any semblance of control over her own life, Dominic had flown into the most terrifying rages. On several occasions he'd reduced her to tears, at which point he'd instantly become contrite, apologised profusely, and sworn it would never happen again. It was becoming a pattern, and it frightened Isobel. Had Dominic always been this domineering? Surely she'd have noticed it before now? But then she'd never challenged him on anything before, so of course she'd never seen this side of his personality.

Now Isobel sighed. She'd finally woken up to the fact that her fiancé was a control freak.

And of course there was another reason why she was growing steadily more unhappy with Dominic: he wasn't Jon.

She'd tried hard to avoid reaching this conclusion. By the time she'd left the hospital, Isobel had almost convinced herself that the way she'd felt upon first seeing Jon again hadn't meant anything. She'd just been out of sorts, that was all.

But to be on the safe side, she'd agreed with Dominic's edict that she avoid her ex. Isobel had hoped that putting some distance between herself and Jon would give her a chance to regain perspective. Then this morning he'd called, asking to see her. Hearing his voice had made Isobel smile for the first time in two weeks.

Now she heard the front door slam again and turned to find Dominic hurrying after her. When they got to her car he automatically held out his hand for the keys.

Isobel smiled. 'Think I'll drive today, actually.' As he launched into his usual tirade about how she drove too slowly, she simply smiled sweetly and got into the car. Scowling, Dominic opened the door on the passenger side. Dreading yet another argument, Isobel switched on the radio and turned the volume up.

*

Three hours later
'Florence Nightingale on speed – that's you!' joked Isobel, as Dominic stopped in the middle of the crowded street to peer earnestly at her.

'You look tired,' he announced, 'and a bit peaky.' Placing a hand either side of her head, he turned her face this way and that. 'Yes, definitely a bit glazed around the eyes. Do you feel sleepy?'

'No, just bored with being asked how I am every five seconds,' retorted Isobel. 'What're you gonna do next – whip out a medical kit and stick a thermometer in my mouth?' She turned on her heel and walked down the street at an Olympic-style pace.

Catching her reflection in a shop window, Isobel stopped and stared: long beige skirt, classy but conventional. Soft, cream-coloured cashmere top, pretty but boring. Her hair had grown over the past few months and now hung to her shoulders but it was dead straight and dull. She groaned. 'I'm coming down with Blandular Fever!'

'I think I'll revamp my wardrobe,' Isobel told Dominic as he caught up with her, 'get some new clothes.' She beamed. 'Maybe have my hair done.'

She could see him tightening his jaw as he felt himself losing his hold over her. Instinctively, foolishly, he attempted to reestablish it.

'You're not cutting your hair again.' It was a statement, not a question.

Isobel grinned mischievously. 'Actually, I feel like having it all shaved off.'

Dominic's face went puce. 'I have no intention of walking down the aisle with a girl who has shorter hair than mine!' He waited for her to switch back into her usual placatory mode.

Instead, she made a face. 'And maybe I won't walk down the aisle with a man who tells me how to look.' With that, she turned on her heel and marched off down the street at a cracking pace.

Dominic stared after her, then sprinted off in hot pursuit. He caught her hand and turned her round to face him. 'Isobel, what the hell's got into you? We agreed you'd have long hair for the wedding photos.'

'Er, actually, *we* didn't agree,' she pointed out. '*You* decided, and *I* didn't argue.' Isobel could hear herself speaking but had no idea where the words were coming from, even as they tripped merrily off her tongue. 'Let's get something clear. Love me, love my hair!'

'Right. That does it,' decided Dominic. 'I'm calling the hospital. You need to be on something. Valium, maybe. You're hysterical.'

'No, I'm not.' Isobel shook her head vehemently. 'I'm *assertive*.' Tilting her chin in the air, she hurried off, ponytail swinging jauntily. Dominic's mouth fell open with shock. Squinting against the midday sunshine, he watched in bewilderment as his fiancé vanished into the crowds, turning briefly to send him a final, grave look over her shoulder.

*

Relieved that he hadn't followed her, Isobel checked her watch. She had three hours before she was due to meet Byron and discuss her role at work. Just enough time for what she had in mind. She turned down a side-street and walked until she reached a dark glass façade. It was the most exclusive hair salon in London. Isobel remembered the last time she'd walked nervously through these doors. She'd been so intimidated she'd not dared utter a word of criticism, almost suffering third-degree burns when the girl shampooing her hair had forgotten to add cold water. And as for the ridiculous haircut they'd landed her with!

But today was going to be different.

She pushed open the door and walked in with her head held high. Figures in pristine white gowns were seated in alcoves before mirrors, flicking through the latest magazines or eating from dainty little sushi boxes complete with gold-studded chopsticks, while an élite team of stylists quietly worked their magic. 'We don't just improve your Locks,' declared a sign on the far wall, 'we change your Looks. Your Luck. Your *Life*.'

An exceptionally pretty boy in his early twenties was lounging at the reception desk, busy polishing his cuticles. Isobel wondered how he could see what he was doing, since his bleached blond hair hung in hundreds of tiny plaits falling over his face to his shoulders. The tag on his white T-shirt revealed his name to be Rupert.

She cleared her throat and he glanced up with a look of acute boredom. 'Yes?'

Isobel smiled, but simply received an arctic stare. 'I'm afraid I don't have an appointment,' she began apologetically, 'but I was wondering if perhaps someone could squeeze me in.'

'*Squeeze?*' echoed Rupert, in disbelief. 'We don't *do* squeezing.' He blew on his nails, held them up to the light and admired them, then continued brusquely, 'Most of our normal clientele find it *does* help to make an appointment.' He did not deign to glance at her again before he began to file his nails with a vengeance.

Reeling from the disdain in his tone, Isobel headed for the doors. Then she stopped and turned back. She reached over, grabbed the nail-file and deftly snapped it in two. Rupert's eyes widened. Isobel smiled sweetly. 'Really, *Goldilocks*, is that any way to speak to a potential client? Now, my name's Isobel, and—'

'Isobel *what?*' he snapped, eyes flicking disdainfully over her again.

'De RoseMont.'

Disdain was replaced with a mixture of awe and terror. 'Isobel de RoseMont? *The* Isobel de RoseMont. You're marrying Dom—'

'There's a *clever* little bear!' Isobel couldn't help giggling. 'Perhaps you can squeeze me in after all?'

'Oh, Miss de RoseMont, please forgive *moi*!' He sprang out of his seat like a demented Zebedee and skidded round the desk to take her arm. 'Please, come this way and I'll find someone to attend to you *immediately*. May I get you something to drink? A bite to eat, perhaps? A manicure? Goodness, not that you need one – you have *divine* hands!' There was enough oil in his voice to rival a small Gulf state.

Byron and a few of the other journalists had adjourned to the pub up the street from the office for a long liquid lunch. Now he sat quietly, listening to them talking about the libel suit Tempest was still holding over their heads and the devastating effect it would have on them all. Guilt gnawed at him. Most of these writers had enjoyed prestigious positions on well-established magazines. He had lured them to *Primadonna*, enticing them with the promise of how exciting and satisfying it would be to build a publication from scratch. They'd believed him. They'd been wrong.

Sitting opposite, Lexie noted how subdued Byron was. The reassuring smile she sent him went unnoticed. Determined to get his attention, she began wriggling around on her chair, jiggling her breasts so frantically she feared her bra cups would catch fire from the friction. Still he didn't even glance her way.

Suddenly one of the men lounging at the bar gave a piercing wolf-whistle as the door opened and a girl sauntered in.

Byron did a double-take. Her black leather trousers were so tight they must have been poured on. His eyes lingered on the way they clung to her delightful *derrière*, outlining the pert rounded cheeks to perfection. Reluctantly, he hauled his eyes away to rest on the blood-red top clinging lovingly to her breasts, the plunging neckline drawing attention to the chunky silver cross that sparkled against her smooth skin. Sparkling green eyes met his, dazzling against a mass of coppery post-coital curls, tousled and sexy. Colouring, Byron tried to hide his reaction, but feared her mouth would prove his downfall, as he took in the bee-stung lips, plump, pouting, soft pink, and looking like they existed for the sole purpose of kissing and various other pleasures he now struggled not to think about.

Byron knew he was staring at Isobel, but he couldn't help it. And it wasn't just the clothes. It was something about the way she moved – the enticing sway of her hips as she walked, the sinuous movement as she slid on to a chair.

Seeing his response to her new look, Isobel gave him a wicked smile, and Byron sighed. Damn her! He couldn't get this girl out of his system. Even though Lexie, in a desperate attempt to hold his interest, was every night knocking herself out by staging her own sexual Olympics. But Byron knew he'd trade a thousand nights with Lexie for half an hour with Isobel.

'Thought I'd find you lot in here,' Isobel said. 'Don't look so surprised. I'm not about to sit back and watch *Primadonna* fold.'

'That's rich coming from *you*. You're the one who got us into this mess to start with by losing that sodding tape!' Lexie's dark eyes gleamed with malice. 'What a shame. Your one chance to make an impression.'

The other women tittered and exchanged catty smiles, while

several of the men smirked. Isobel shrugged. ' 'Cause of course, Lex, we all know how *you*'ve made your mark.' Her brilliant green gaze swept over the other girl, before lingering, deliberately, on Byron, then returning to Lexie. 'What's *your* work ethic? Give some head to get ahead?'

Gasps of amazement were followed by laughter and whispering. Lexie flushed crimson, visibly wilting, then turned to Byron in mute appeal. But his attention was riveted on Isobel, his mouth twitching as he fought the urge to laugh.

*

Seeing Lexie's mortified expression, Isobel felt a rush of shame. How could she have said something so insulting? Even if it was true. She opened her mouth to apologise, then shut it. Lexie had attacked her. Lexie had often been spiteful. Lexie had deserved this. And, as she glanced round at her colleagues, Isobel realised something else. They were looking at her differently; for once, she wasn't just some stupid rich girl with more money than brains. She sat up slightly straighter. She'd stood up for herself and it felt amazing.

Byron was looking wearily at both girls. 'I really think we have enough problems without the two of you having a verbal catfight. Right, lunch is over. You lot, back to work. No, not you, Isobel. You stay.'

The others stared curiously at them, then stood up and filed out of the pub, Lexie leading the way, her face pale.

Byron and Isobel looked at each other.

'So?' Isobel fidgeted. 'What are we going to do about Tempest? We can't let her take us to the cleaners. Listen to this . . .' She told Byron what had happened at the engagement party, describing how strangely Tempest had behaved.

'I must say, she does act bizarrely for a therapist. It sounds so weird,' said Byron.

'It was. And ever since that night I've had nothing but bad luck.'

'Isobel, I realise logical thinking is always a challenge for you, but if you try you'll find there are other explanations for what's been happening.'

'Like?'

'You're marrying a man with all the emotional depth of an ashtray, plus you've been putting the "die" in "diet". Look, I can see how Tempest has played on your fears, but that's all she's done. You're not hexed so stop worrying, all right?'

'I'll try.' But Isobel still couldn't shake the uneasy feeling that her accident had resulted from Tempest's jinx.

'Now, I have some news.' He relayed Tempest's demands for an apology. 'It's been several weeks since she came to see me, and I've just had an e-mail from her. If we don't agree to her terms, and soon, she'll proceed with the lawsuit. Anyway, now you're coming back and feeling better, I'm sure you won't mind writing a new piece on her and saying sorry.'

'You *are* joking?'

'No, of course I'm bloody well not!' snapped Byron. 'I don't mind telling you I was relieved when she offered this compromise. It's more than I ever dreamed of.'

'Well, it looks like we have a little problem then.' She leaned back and folded her arms. 'Because I'm not doing it.'

'Excuse me?'

His voice was so cold Isobel felt chilblains forming. But she stood her ground. 'You heard.'

*

For a few moments they stared at each other, Byron's rigid posture concealing his agitation. Impatience mounting, he waited for Isobel to back down, the way she always did. Normally he could intimidate her beautifully. Except now, it didn't appear to be working.

He sighed. 'Isobel, I don't think you *quite* understand—'

'Don't patronise me!' she cut him off furiously.

'*THEN STOP ACTING LIKE A FOOL!*' hollered Byron, not caring that the entire pub plus anyone within a ten-mile radius could hear him. 'We've got a chance to save this magazine – and we're going to take it! You ARE going to write that article and you ARE going to apologise and I don't give a *SHIT* how much you hate doing it!' He thumped the table. '*DO I MAKE MYSELF CLEAR?*'

'Finished screaming? Good.' She glared at him. 'Now, listen, because I don't intend to say this again. The days of you bullying me are **over**. Like it or not, I am associate editor of this magazine, not some little underling that you can just scream at whenever you feel like it.' Her voice hardened. 'I am not apologising to Tempest St John. I am not writing another word on Tempest St John. I don't give a flying fuck what Tempest St John wants or demands or expects. We're going to find another way of saving this magazine. So, Byron, why don't you stop bullying me and instead put your energy into helping me?'

Byron watched her in astonishment. She was so much *spikier* than usual. The old Isobel would have crumbled by now.

But it was okay. Scratch the surface and she'd be the same meek, malleable girl as before. Now he leaned forward so that she could see the resolve in his eyes. Byron was supremely confident. He'd triumphed over numerous adversaries far tougher than the girl sitting across from him.

'You're being absurd!' he said coldly. 'We're lucky Tempest is offering this compromise.'

'*Lucky?*' Isobel laughed in disbelief. 'The woman's certifiable! *You* might be prepared to sell out for the sake of a quiet life, but don't ask *me* to do the same! 'Cause, frankly, I'd rather lose the magazine and start over from scratch than promote Tempest to our readers!' As her gaze flickered over him, Byron found himself recoiling from the disappointment in those clear green eyes as Isobel added softly, 'It's a little thing called integrity, Byron. Funny. I thought you had some.'

Byron took a long, cool swallow of beer and gathered his thoughts. It was easy for her to talk about integrity, but what about all the journalists who would lose their jobs if *Primadonna* folded? Right now, integrity was a luxury they could not afford.

Still, he couldn't help admiring this new, gutsy Isobel. Now Byron remembered how he'd felt when he'd started out as a journalist, all fired up by idealism and a desire to change the world, to right the wrongs others didn't seem to care about. Somewhere along the way, he'd started worrying more about profit margins than ethics.

He raised his hands in a gesture of compliance. 'Fine. We'll try it your way.' Then, seeing her impish little smile, he glared. 'Don't push it.'

For a few minutes, they both sat lost in thought. Isobel was the first to speak. 'I think what we need to do is look more closely at Tempest's work as a therapist. Surely someone this weird can't be advising clients effectively? We should do a proper investigative piece, examine her methods, her background, the lot. I mean, how much do we really know about her? God, I shudder to think about the rubbish she's filling Gemma's head with! Maybe we should try and talk to some of her ex-clients.' Suddenly she remembered Carl Paige. 'And the psychologist at the hospital didn't rate Tempest too highly. There must be someone, somewhere who will speak to us.'

'Agreed.' Byron glanced at his watch. 'I have to get back to the office. Okay, I want you to start by contacting all the organisations to which Tempest belongs. Let's confirm that she really is affiliated to them. Meet me back at the office at eight. We'll go on the Net, see what we can come up with.'

'But what about the others? Don't you want them in on this?'

'They're all going to Pandora's birthday bash tonight. Looks like it's just us for the moment.'

'Fine.' Isobel waved goodbye and headed for the door. Byron's eyes were burning into her back so intensely she figured her clothes would develop scorch-marks.

'Isobel?'

She turned.

'If you ever . . . I mean if . . .' unusually, Byron found himself stuck for words. 'If you ever decide that Dominic isn't The One, then . . .' he met her eyes awkwardly '. . . let's just say I hope you'd let me know. I have a vested interest.'

Taken aback, she managed a subdued smile. 'See you later.'

*

Outside, Isobel walked slowly up the street. It was a bright winter's day, the sunlight glinting off shop windows. She felt unsettled. She was still attracted to Byron, and flattered that he

223

genuinely liked her. But whatever she felt for him, it couldn't compare with her feelings for Jon.

Where did that leave her and Dominic? Isobel couldn't believe how compliant she'd become over the two years they'd been together. She'd even agreed to be a passenger in her own car just because Dominic insisted she drove too slowly! Isobel made a face. How submissive could a girl get? But it was amazing what you could accept as normal if it happened gradually enough. When she'd first started seeing Dominic, she'd been feeling so lost. She'd loved the way he'd taken over and made all the decisions, from where they'd eat, to which film they'd see, to where they'd go on holiday. And she'd been so scared of losing him, of being alone, that she'd been desperate to please him.

Even the night they'd got engaged was an example of the way Dominic tried to control her, she realised now. Instead of giving her a bit of space to get over seeing him kissing Gemma, he'd backed her into a corner, insisting either she accepted his proposal or they were over. He'd never really acknowledged her hurt and anger over what had happened that night.

Suddenly Isobel stopped walking and gasped. 'Oh, my God. I'm marrying a man like my father. How have I let this happen?'

More to the point, what was she going to do about it?

18

Firsts

S illy to be nervous, decided Gemma, But it *was* her first
time. Still, Tempest had promised she'd enjoy it.

As if reading her mind, the guru gave her a reassuring smile,
slipped her hand into Gemma's then led her through the
spacious house towards the stairs. 'Relax. You're going to feel
wonderful afterwards. All the girls do. *Trust me.*'

On the second floor Tempest directed her to the end of the
hall and followed Gemma into a room, closing the door
behind them. The walls were pale peach, as was the carpet.
Aquamarine rugs were scattered around, the colour echoed in
the curtains that fluttered at the french windows. From somewhere music was playing; a soft silver melody full of harps and
whispered lyrics that Gemma couldn't decipher.

Against one wall was a huge four-poster bed. The soft silk
sheets in pretty pastel colours were pulled back invitingly, and
huge cushions, sky blue and lemon yellow, were arranged
neatly. A pale blue lacy canopy hung above the bed, and beside
it, on a tiny table, stood a little stone waterfall, the chiming of the
miniature waves blending perfectly with the music.

Gemma sighed with pleasure. 'What a beautiful room!'

'Knew you'd like it. I don't always use it but I wanted your first time to be special.'

'I'm a bit nervous,' admitted Gemma.

Tempest nodded. 'Understandable. Just think of this as an extension of the weekly meditation sessions you've been attending.'

'They've really helped.'

'And this will help even more.' Tempest smoothed Gemma's long hair back from her face. 'Your therapy's going well and I'm delighted with your progress. It isn't easy, looking inside oneself, remembering painful times. This session will help you cope with that. Help you see what's important. Help you feel good about yourself.'

Gemma nodded eagerly. The difference in how she had felt since meeting Tempest was amazing. That terrible dark void within her was finally starting to close. Occasionally she wondered how long the process would take, but whenever she asked, Tempest's responses were vague:

'It takes as long as it takes.'

'Everyone is different.'

'You've got years' worth of anger and hurt to work through.'

'Be patient.'

'*Trust me.*'

Over recent weeks Gemma had noticed that she was much better on some days than on others – the day after a session with Tempest, she'd feel fine – but as the time between appointments stretched on, panic welled up within her again. She'd reassured herself that this must be a normal part of the process – surely that was why Tempest had suggested these hypnosis sessions as well.

Now Tempest gave her another blinding smile. 'Make your-self at home and we'll begin.'

'Where do you want me?' Gemma glanced at the bed. 'Actually under the sheets or . . .'

'Just make yourself comfortable, most of my girls find lying on their backs works nicely.'

Gemma obliged.

'All right?' Tempest sat down on the foot of the bed and curled her legs beneath her. 'Let's do it . . .'

*

Jon paused outside Isobel's flat. He hadn't seen her since she'd left hospital, presumably because Dominic was being his usual possessive self. He had tried to put himself in the other man's shoes, but it was getting absurd. He'd flown back from Brazil to make sure Isobel was all right, and he wouldn't leave until he knew she was. Tonight would be the first time they'd been alone since he'd returned to London.

Now he rang the bell, and smiled as he heard hurried footsteps inside. Half a minute later Isobel flung open the door.

Jon's smile faltered. All she had on was a tiny pink silk robe that left little to the imagination. Her long, tanned legs were bare and her chestnut-brown hair fell in tight ringlets, tiny droplets of water shining like silver.

Isobel gave him a reproachful smile. 'I've hardly seen you.'

'You're pissed,' observed Jon, noting the way her words were slurred.

'Just a *tad*.' Isobel hiccuped, and ran up the stairs, beckoning to him to follow. 'I felt a bit tense earlier and a glass of wine seemed a good idea.'

Jon decided she must have drunk the whole bottle.

Suddenly her face lit up. 'This is *perrrfect* . . . you can give me a lift to *Primadonna*.' She rubbed her forehead. 'Can't drive like this.'

'You're going back to the office?' Jon tried to mask his disappointment. 'I thought we – Never mind. Why are you working tonight?'

'Got something big on,' came the cryptic response.

'How will you get home?'

'Oh, I'm sure Byron will be happy to take me.' Isobel led him into her bedroom. She stood before the walk-in wardrobe and stared intently at the contents. After a minute she pulled out an outfit and headed for the *en suite* bathroom. 'I'll just slip this on and then we can go, okay?' She frowned. 'I'm sorry to change our dinner plans. Tomorrow instead?'

'Fine.' Jon waited for her to change her mind – at least five times – over what to wear. To his surprise, she didn't. Another first, he noted.

'Don't know why I'm leaving the room to get changed.' Sending him a teasing glance she began shrugging off the robe. 'After all, it's nothing you haven't seen before.'

Jon stared, caught between anger at how she was teasing him, hope that she was still interested, and surprise at her behaviour. He waited for her to get serious, but she simply continued undressing. As the robe finally slipped to the floor, Jon looked away, his heart doing a fast, hard little tap-dance of anticipation. He stared resolutely in the other direction, battling the urge to turn round. Lust now had him in a vice-tight grip, like a pair of invisible, invincible hands trying to force his head round and make him look at Isobel.

228

'Such a gentleman.' Isobel hiccuped again.

'You certainly seem rather . . .' Jon paused '. . . *frisky*.'

Her laugh was low and lazy. 'Must be the effect you have on me.'

Lust won. Jon tilted his head a fraction of an inch, just in time to catch Isobel giving him a cheery smile before she sauntered unsteadily into the bathroom, wiggling her pert little bottom all the way.

He took a deep, shuddery breath and tried to calm his galloping pulse, then flopped on to the bed, hands behind his head, and gazed up at the ceiling. He liked being here, in Isobel's room – he felt more connected to her, somehow. Now he just had to figure out what the hell was wrong with her because something was. He'd glimpsed a slight difference back at the hospital, but had assumed it was just the after-effects of that crack to the head. But she was definitely acting strangely, and it wasn't just the alcohol. He really must keep an eye on her. Jon smiled. A close eye.

The bathroom door flew open and Isobel reappeared. Jon sat up slowly, staring. She wore a slip of a dress in some wine-red material; velvet, he thought. It skimmed her slender thighs while the bodice did up at the front with a series of delicate black laces that criss-crossed over her breasts. Looked like a tiny tug and those laces would fall open. Black knee-high leather boots completed the outfit.

'So, you like?'

'New?' Jon's voice was unsteady.

'Sure is.'

She began to walk towards him, pausing for a seductive little twirl. The skirt flared out around her, her body swaying slightly. Jon's eyes widened. Isobel looked dangerously close to performing the dance of the seven veils.

His heart started hammering frantically as she continued her slinky walk. Next moment she'd curled up on the floor beside him, resting her head on her arms and her arms on his legs.

'Jon.' Her voice held a pensive note. 'Do you ever remember . . . us?'

A stream of gorgeous, graphic images of the two of them together assailed him. 'Yes.'

Unable to resist, he reached down and began softly stroking her hair, his fingers trailing longingly through the silky dark skeins. Isobel gave a contented sigh, then started purring, a sexy, throaty little sound that made Jon close his eyes and reach for every last bit of will-power he possessed.

But his will was no match for his ex. Now Isobel had shifted position and was kneeling up, her brilliant green eyes locked on his face like some hypnotic spell, broken only by the occasional, languid flutter of those long black lashes.

Jon felt his own eyes growing heavy. He looked into hers and there was no mistaking the glitter of attraction there. Trembling, he pulled away.

Isobel's face flamed. 'What's wrong?'

'You! You're pissed! Not to mention being engaged to someone else! I don't want us to do anything you'll regret.'

She relaxed. 'Oh, I won't regret . . .' she kissed him softly on the lips '. . . a thing.' She kissed him again, lips and tongue enticing his. '*Promise.*'

'What about Dominic?' said Jon thickly, as her hand slid up his leg, fingers teasing the inside of his thigh.

Isobel didn't answer. Instead she ran a palm over his groin, her green eyes glittery again as they held his. Sliding her fingers between his she brought his hand down, pressing it against her thigh, smiling at his sharp intake of breath, then covering his hand with hers, easing it higher, still watching him with desire-darkened eyes.

Grasping every last scrap of resolve, Jon pushed her away, then jumped up.

Isobel fell back against the side of the bed.

Hurt, she turned away. 'Fine. You had your chance.'

He reached for her but now she was the one to shrug him off.

'Isobel, listen to me. I care about you too much to let something happen now, when you're all over the place and tomorrow you could decide it was a mistake. This isn't the right time.'

Still refusing to meet his eyes, Isobel shrugged.

'Sure. Whatever.' She grabbed her coat and started for the door. 'Shall we go?'

Without exchanging another word, they headed out to the car. The silence continued for the duration of the journey. Slumped in the passenger seat, Isobel brooded. Again he'd rejected her. Thinking about the way she'd come on to him just now, she cringed so violently that she almost dislocated a limb. Talk about making a fool of herself. But she'd wanted him so badly it had been impossible not to act on her feelings. It seemed that while she'd been in her prolonged sleep she'd lost all her inhibitions.

Fifteen minutes later they pulled up outside the magazine offices. Jon frowned. 'Why exactly are you coming back to work at this time of night?'

'I told you. Byron and I are working on something.'

'I'm happy to wait, then drive you home afterwards.' He was

starting to feel uneasy. Byron was an unknown quantity, and Isobel wasn't herself.

Half-way out of the car, Isobel turned. 'Don't worry.' She laughed, then gave him a look loaded with meaning. 'I can handle Byron.'

Jon mused that with Isobel in this mood, maybe Byron was the one he should be worried about. Because the sex kitten had grown claws.

*

Gemma was floating . . . her body suspended high in the night sky . . . a million stars shimmering around her . . . soft, milky white light streaming through her . . . the deep, dark night rippling over her . . . all her worries now fading . . . fading . . . spinning off into space . . .

The visualisation was working beautifully. Tempest's soft, clear voice was soothing her, lulling her into the sweetest sleep Gemma had ever known. Now her eyelids were so heavy . . . so very, very, *heavy* . . . her limbs too . . . her mind light and free to wander . . . drift . . . no need to even think . . . all she had to do was float . . . keep floating through the sea of stars . . . sea of silver stars . . . sea of silver . . . silver sea.

Tempest leaned over Gemma's slumbering body and checked for the signs that a deep state of trance had been achieved. They were all there: Gemma's eyelids were fluttering rapidly, she was breathing evenly, deeply, easily, and she wasn't responding to or disturbed by sounds from outside.

Perfect.

Tempest continued to speak softly, all the while watching Gemma's face. Oh, but she'd put a lot of work into this one and it would be worth it. The moment she'd met Gemma at the gym that day, Tempest had known who she was. She had recognised her face from the society pages of the *Tatler*. Over the years, Tempest had learned to be careful over whom she chose to work on and now she'd got it down to a fine art, could identify the right type of girl in the blink of an eye. They were all the same. Wealthy. Vulnerable. Bored. Gemma fitted the profile perfectly. Even so, Tempest had not rushed things. No, she'd taken her time, spent a few months on phase one of the plan. Now it was time to get things moving. She stared at the girl lying there before her, lost in trance.

Gemma, eyes shut tight.

Gemma, mind wide open.

Gemma, defences down.

Tempest smiled. Within the seemingly innocent, pretty trance imagery she had used were hidden commands; concealed instructions that – just by slightly altering her tone of voice – Tempest could emphasise and slot neatly into Gemma's unconscious.

'That's good, Gemma . . . and now you can really *let go* . . . and feel how wonderful it is to just *let yourself drift* . . . how relaxed you feel . . . Sometimes it's so good *just* to *drift away* . . . from the people and places that cause you pain . . . like Isobel and Dominic . . . and you know that seeing Dominic and Isobel together has hurt you . . . but now, lying here, you are starting to realise that you can feel so much better without these people, these negative influences in your life . . . and you feel much more relaxed without them . . . you can now just *drift away from them* . . . *drift away now* . . . and you know this is the right thing to do . . . to *distance yourself* from these negative, harmful influences . . . Take some time now, Gemma . . .

time to just think . . . drift . . . drifting and thinking . . . thinking and drifting . . . still feeling calm . . . still feeling safe . . . because, Gemma, you are safe . . . safely out of reach of those people who cause you pain . . . and so now you can just drift . . . just *leave them behind* . . . if *you want to* . . . and you feel so much better when you *do that* . . .'

Tempest paused, giving the words a chance to sink in. People were so impressionable, more than they themselves ever realised. When Gemma came out of trance, she wouldn't recall anything specific that Tempest had said. All she'd know was a vague feeling of detachment towards her friends and family, a feeling that Tempest would be sure to nurture. And once Gemma was isolated from the people she'd been close to, she would be far more amenable to Tempest's plans for her. Phase two had started. Her colleagues back in Australia were going to be delighted. Smiling again, Tempest continued to take Gemma deeper and deeper into trance. Not long to go now. Not long at all.

19

Foreplay

B yron knew that this was what he'd been waiting for. After months of wanting Isobel, of watching her, now he was alone with her in the silent, darkened *Primadonna* offices. She was sitting meekly beside him, staring at the glowing computer screen. This was the old Isobel; no sign now of the super-sexy girl who had sauntered into the pub earlier that day. No, right now her eyes were calm, her auburn curls tumbling around a serene face.

She'd slipped on a thick black chenille cardigan but Byron had glimpsed what was underneath. Get a load of that *dress*. The little red number was definitely out of character, and Byron's gaze lingered on the flimsy bodice, on the slim laces that criss-crossed prettily over her breasts. With each breath she took those laces seemed to give a bit.

He forced himself to look away. Must *focus* – they had work to do. And Isobel trusted him. She was gazing glumly at the screen, desperate to find something on Tempest. She was relying on him to help because *Primadonna* would fold if they didn't find a way through this predicament. Fast.

Now Byron took a deep breath and forced his mind to the

task at hand. This was not the time to be thinking about the girl beside him and what he'd like to be doing with her.

'Oh, this is hopeless!' wailed Isobel, oblivious to Byron's wistful scrutiny, 'Tempest's got enough letters after her name to start her own alphabet!'

'She's bound to have her own website.' Byron keyed in a new command. 'Don't suppose it'll tell us much but we may as well have a look . . .'

While they waited impatiently for the screen to change, Isobel busied herself printing out a load of material on therapists who had been struck off, on impulse widening the search to include countries other than Britain. It wasn't going to help them with Tempest, but she figured it would make good background reading when she returned home later that night. And maybe it would help take her mind off Jon, and the way he'd rejected her. Again.

'Look at this.' Byron beckoned to her. Tempest's PR machine was clearly an efficient one; the site was colourful. It included a striking photograph of the guru, whose violet eyes seemed to stare straight at them. Alongside the picture were testimonials from satisfied clients, as usual all of them women.

'Okay . . . let's try something else.' Byron's fingers flew over the keyboard. 'Let's enter the names of her more high-profile clients and see if anything interesting comes up.'

They spent the next hour calling up old newspaper stories.

'I don't get it.' Isobel frowned. 'She doesn't seem to have any *ex* clients.'

'Because they're all still seeing her,' Byron mused.

'Well, I guess therapy is an ongoing process?'

'Sure. But there comes a point when the client is much

stronger, and the therapist starts slowly to detach from them.' Byron frowned at the computer screen. 'According to this, some of these women have been seeing Tempest ever since she returned to the UK – six years ago! But why would they need to see her for so long? She's just a psychotherapist, not a psycho-analyst.'

Isobel slumped back in her seat. 'Something's wrong with this picture. If these women feel as great as they claim, why do they need to keep seeing Tempest? It doesn't make sense. Unless she's somehow making them dependent on her?'

Byron looked morose. 'The thing is, there probably *are* women who have stopped seeing Tempest and who weren't happy. We just can't find them. If they're not famous or they didn't lodge an official complaint, there's no way of tracking them down – short of advertising, and we can't do that without showing our hand. My gut feeling is there must be something on Tempest because she's so strange. But she's also clever. She's covered her tracks.'

Isobel bit her lip. 'So, what now?'

'Now I e-mail some contacts in Australia, see if they have anything on her. I've noticed that in all of her interviews she's quick to change the subject whenever her work there comes up.'

'She did that when I interviewed her too.'

'Maybe there's something that didn't filter through to the media in this country. It's a long shot, but it's all we have.'

'And if we don't find anything?' Isobel squirmed on her chair. 'We'll lose the case and *Primadonna* will fold. Oh, God, this can't be happening!'

'There is another option,' began Byron hesitantly. 'We could do what I originally suggested and apologise. Run some glowing piece on her. Then she'll drop the libel suit.'

Isobel bit her lip. 'I know maybe it looks like I'm being stubborn in not apologising. And I know I'm asking a lot of you, because if she takes us to court we may lose everything. But, Byron, I swear I didn't lie in that article! I would never do that! And if the only way we can keep this magazine going is to promote Tempest . . .' She shook her head. 'It just can't be right.'

'I understand how you feel. But we don't actually have any proof that she's up to no good yet.'

'The operative word being *yet*,' Isobel insisted. 'Look how she behaved at my engagement party. She turned up there uninvited, lured me to a meeting with her, then put a hex on me! That's a *horrible* thing to do to anyone. It's hardly normal behaviour for a therapist!'

Byron rubbed his eyes, his face betraying his fatigue. 'Agreed. And I hate the idea of apologising to her every bit as much as you do. But the bottom line is: I don't want this magazine to fold. And if we lose, we could end up having to pay her a fortune. Some libel cases have run into millions, Isobel. We must bear that in mind.'

'Sure. But we also owe our readers something.' Isobel smiled. 'I know we're a tongue-in-cheek read, but women still trust what we tell them. We can't let them believe Tempest is the Next Big Thing in mental health.'

'The legal fees could crush us,' said Byron quietly. He chose his words carefully. 'I'm loath to suggest this, but would you consider asking your family for help?'

'Not an option,' said Isobel firmly. She met his enquiring

look with a bitter smile. 'My father has made it painfully clear that he never expected me to succeed in the first place. There's no way he's going to bail me out.'

She recalled the strained telephone conversation she'd had with her father a few days ago. He'd spent most of it lecturing her on how stupid she'd been for investing in *Primadonna* to start with. And when Isobel had told him Tempest was bringing a libel case against them, Harold had been most unimpressed. He'd even accused Isobel of being an embarrassment to the family.

Now she sighed. 'My father won't help. And my mother's also being less than supportive.' She gave Byron a small, heart-melting smile. 'Guess I'm on my own with this one.'

'Not quite.' Instinctively, Byron put his arm round her shoulders and squeezed them gently in a gesture of support. To his delight, Isobel allowed her head to rest on his shoulder. Then she yawned.

'Tired?' He smiled fondly and lowered his head so that his lips just brushed her hair.

'A bit.' She yawned again. 'There really isn't anything we can do, is there?'

'Hey, we're not giving up, okay?' He smoothed back a stray ringlet from Isobel's face, his fingers lingering on her cheek. A tiny, tantalising touch. He knew he must remove his hand but he couldn't. He was physically unable to take it away.

'Isobel,' Byron could hear the anguish in his own voice, 'you're not going through with the wedding, are you? You're not really going to marry Dominic?'

Instantly she shrugged him off and sat up, her expression one of panic. '*Don't!*'

239

'Don't *what?*' demanded Byron, angry with himself for breaking the moment, and already missing the silken sheen of her skin against his fingers. 'Don't show any interest? Bit late to tell me that.'

'I don't want to talk about the wedding.' Her voice shook.

'You have to,' insisted Byron. 'We can't just pretend it isn't happening.'

'Can't we?' Isobel asked softly, green eyes imploring him.

Suddenly time, sound and movement seemed to freeze. They looked warily, hopefully at each other. One thought kept tripping through Isobel's mind: Jon might not want her, but Byron did.

Byron reached out and cupped her face in his hand, one thumb tracing the line of her cheek. Isobel's lips parted and softly she kissed his palm. An electric thread of lust wove its way through him.

Isobel began sucking the tips of his fingers, and her warm velvet mouth closed around them, her lips caressing his skin, until Byron was so hard for her it hurt. He slipped both arms around her waist, pulled her to him and kissed her lightly, not wanting to scare her away, yet not entirely trusting this new, flirty Isobel. But, of their own accord, his hands were wandering eagerly over her, luxuriating in the feel of her soft body against his. Then, abruptly, she was pushing him away, looking at him in horror and accusation, then jumping up and backing towards the door. 'I can't,' she whispered. She rubbed her eyes, trying to collect her fragmented thoughts.

'What's wrong?' Cautiously he started to close the gap between them.

'I don't know.' She shook her head and now he could see it

was the old Isobel again, all hint of mischief gone. 'I feel . . .
confused.'

'You're confused?' Byron's laugh was bitter. 'How the fuck
do you think *I* feel?'

He reached for her again and Isobel let him hold her for a few
heavenly seconds, before she pulled away. 'I'm sorry. I have to
go.' Then she bolted out of the door and down the hallway.

*

Isobel dashed into the lift. She was in love with Jon. She loved
Dominic. She liked Byron. She wanted Jon. She needed Dominic. She missed Jon. How could she have feelings for three
men at once? What did that make her?

'*Fickle!* It makes me *fickle*,' she lamented, collapsing against
the lift wall.

*

Back in the office Byron swore. Why the hell had she run
again? Uneasily, he recalled her lightning mood changes and
the bemused look on her face as she'd pulled away. Maybe he
really had taken advantage of her. Oh, but she'd been enjoying
it all right. And if she'd stayed, Byron was confident that he
could have fucked any lingering doubts clean out of her
system. Now he wouldn't see her until tomorrow, a lifetime
away. Well, he wasn't going to wait. He grabbed his jacket and
car keys.

Then he paused. What was wrong with him? This was mad,
chasing after Isobel like some lovestruck teenager – she'd jerked
on his heartstrings enough tonight. It was time to draw a line.
Then Byron smiled wryly. Who cared how ridiculous he looked
rushing after this girl? 'The man who has never made a fool of
himself in love will never be wise in love,' he murmured.

241

'Theodor Riek.' He snatched up his jacket and raced out of the door.

*

Jon watched in the rear-view mirror as Isobel hurtled out of the building. From her dishevelled hair and the way her cardigan was practically falling off, it didn't take a great leap of logic to work out what had been going on. Envy ripped through him. He'd waited for the better part of two hours, hoping she'd leave the building alone, because he hadn't wanted to leave things on a bad note.

Just then Isobel caught his eyes in the rear-view mirror. Her face registered surprise, then intense relief. A moment later she was rushing towards Jon's car, throwing open the door and falling into the seat before he could even speak. 'Just get me out of here,' she begged. 'Don't ask me anything – just take me home.'

Jon searched her face for a moment, then turned on the engine and went screeching away from the kerb.

*

Isobel closed her eyes tightly. She decided that if she couldn't see Jon, he couldn't see her, and although she knew this was irrational, she kept her eyes tightly shut for the entire journey as the car sped through darkened, rain-washed streets. It seemed like mere minutes before they were back at her flat. Slowly she opened her eyes without turning round, knowing Jon was watching her.

'I don't want to talk about it,' she announced, staring straight ahead.

Jon stayed silent.

'Nothing happened,' Isobel insisted.

242

He shrugged.

'It meant nothing.' Isobel turned and faced him.

Jon nodded.

'It isn't him I love,' she declared.

He smiled.

'Oh, why can't you just leave me be? *I told you I don't want to talk about it!*' She threw open the door, jumped out and stormed up the path.

Jon watched her go. Turning the key in the ignition, he sighed. It was almost time to return to Brazil. Isobel was obviously troubled. She didn't need him on the scene, confusing her even more.

He was so lost in thought that he didn't notice Byron's car entering Isobel's road from the opposite direction.

*

Byron slowed down to scan the house numbers for Isobel's. It was impossible to tell what she really wanted from him tonight. One thing he did know: she'd been up for it back at the office. He wasn't sure what had made her run, but he intended to find out.

He made out a house number, and realised that Isobel's flat must be right at the other end of the road. He decided to walk and pulled over. Maybe a bit of fresh air would calm him down, help him think more clearly. Except that thinking was the last thing he wanted to be doing tonight.

*

Inside the house Isobel was unbearably restless, pacing up and down, unable to keep still. It felt as though everyone in her life had turned traitor. She'd believed Jon still loved her, but he'd just rejected her, then fobbed her off with feeble excuses. She'd thought Byron actually cared about her, but maybe to him she'd just be one more office conquest. She'd thought Dominic wanted the best for her, but he was determined to control her. And always, in the background, lurked the gleeful figure of Tempest St John, determined to destroy *Primadonna*.

Turning on the radio, she flicked impatiently from station to station until she found something with a throbbing beat. She increased the volume then headed for the kitchen, opened a cupboard, and grabbed a pile of plates.

Isobel held the first one high above her head. 'THIS ONE'S FOR YOU, TEMPEST!' She hurled the plate to the floor, enjoying the sound as it shattered. 'AND FOR YOU, JON – CHEERS FOR BUGGERING OFF TO MOROCCO WITHOUT EVEN ASKING HOW I FELT!' Another plate smashed as, finally, years of pent-up anger and hurt found release.

*

Even as he was driving away, Jon couldn't shake the conviction that he could put things right with Isobel. No matter how strangely she was behaving, he decided to hang around and see her through the crisis with the magazine. And the wedding. Because until she walked up that aisle, they still had a fighting chance.

Was he just being a blind optimist? he wondered. If Isobel truly loved him why was she going through with the wedding? Jon's biggest fear was that Isobel cared more about actually getting married than about being with the right person. Him.

He braked, then reversed back down her road, telling himself he was just going to check on her, make sure she was all right. Deep down, though, Jon knew he was rationalising.

Because he wasn't going back just to make sure she was all right.

He was going back to finish what Isobel had started earlier that evening.

*

Isobel had destroyed every single plate, cup and glass in the flat. Now she sat in the hallway, head in her hands, her face scarlet, and her voice husky from all the screaming. She felt strangely exhilarated.

The doorbell rang.

Slowly, she raised her head, her breathing still ragged. Adrenaline throbbed through her veins, her pulse zigzagging crazily.

The doorbell rang again, this time more insistently. Isobel stood up and walked slowly down the hall. She knew it had to be either Jon or Byron. One of them was standing outside.

She took a deep breath, and opened the door.

20

One Night Stand

Within seconds of the door opening he'd pushed her back roughly until she was jammed up against the wall. Hands locked round her waist, he began to kiss her, giving her no chance to pull away. But she wasn't trying to. Instead she was pressing herself against him, her thigh trapped between his legs.

Glancing at her dress he smiled, before lowering his head and biting clean through the flimsy strands of lace, his lips brushing against her breastbone as the bodice of her dress fell away to reveal her breasts. He stroked them, and the rosy nipples hardened against his hand as he circled them with his thumbs before again lowering his head and sucking them, gently at first, then more insistently, teasing the deep pink buds with his tongue. Deftly he slid off her dress, then eased down her sheer black stockings, leaving her standing before him in nothing but a pair of skimpy black knickers.

He moved back, and let his gaze travel slowly, deliberately over her while she waited, trembling, face stained with colour, longing for his hands to make good on what his eyes were promising.

His stare came to rest on the wispy knickers. Lust tightened deliciously around her groin; she knew she couldn't wait another second. He knew it too. Suddenly he was ripping off her knickers and scooping her into his arms, carrying her over to the sofa where he pulled her on to his lap.

Her arms slipped round his neck, and she sighed. He stared into those clear green eyes, then at her full, moist lips, the coppery brown curls tumbling over her delicate, ivory shoulders.

Their eyes met again and seeing the slightly questioning look in hers, he began to kiss her, his hands playing over her curves, stroking the soft swell of her breasts, trailing lazily over her stomach, one hand moving lightly up and down her thighs, his hands never lingering long enough in one place but instead dancing over her skin, teasing her, testing her, rewarded by little gasps of pleasure, as he continued seeking out the most sensitive parts of her body, and, he smiled, there were so many . . .

She was exquisitely, unbelievably responsive to his touch. Fleetingly, he wondered if she was like this with Dominic too.

With feather-light fingers he caressed the fragile ridge of her spine; she shivered, pressing her breasts against his chest. He let his other hand slide down her back, over the sleek round of her buttocks. Now she was squirming with need, her thighs parting as his hand slipped between them and he began stroking her; then she was clasping his hand more urgently against her, showing him what she wanted, gasping when his fingers entered her, only to tease her by withdrawing again.

And all the while he was kissing her, his warm, knowing lips brushing her forehead, planting tiny kisses over her eyelashes, and enjoying the little sigh this evoked from her, smiling himself as he kissed her satin-smooth cheeks, trailing kisses around her jawline, before allowing his lips and tongue to trace the sweet contours of her mouth and, yet more soft, butterfly kisses along her neck, along the sensitive hollow of her throat, kisses fluttering over her slender collar bone, until she was dizzy with desire.

Then they were both tearing off his clothes, and he was pulling her on top of him again while she was raining kisses over his broad shoulders and muscular chest, covering his skin with her lips before pushing him down on his back. Raising his hips he entered her, caressing her breasts as, finding her pace, she began moving faster, her eyes closed, lips parted, head thrown back, long hair streaming over her shoulders, her face contorting with pleasure as she came.

He slid out, rolled her on to her back, his hips locking with hers, hearing her gasp as he entered her again. Then she was burying her fingers in his lush wavy hair and wrapping her legs around her hips, and he started thrusting harder, and faster, all the while kissing, licking and biting her, his tongue loitering over her fevered skin.

Her body was hot and slick under his; he began thrusting harder and she cried out, digging her nails into the backs of his arms as his hips plunged forward against her, his thrusts brutal, taking her closer and closer to the edge, until she was writhing in his arms and he was grabbing her hips and slamming even more deeply into her, her back arching as she moved with him until the world was shimmering, shattering around her, blood pounding through her veins and she was screaming with release, hearing herself crying and hating herself for it, knowing she'd never sounded this way with Dominic. A second later he collapsed against her, smoothing damp hair away from her face, kissing her neck and lips.

'Hey, it's okay . . .' Her eyes had filled with tears and Jon hugged her tightly. But something was wrong. Isobel was lying wrapped in his arms, so why did she suddenly feel more out of reach than ever?

She pushed him away, gathered up her clothes and dressed quickly. Jon did the same. Finally Isobel sat huddled at the other end of the sofa, not looking at him. She couldn't do this any more; she felt so much for him it frightened her. Dominic would soon be her past. Now she had to know once and for all: did Jon figure in her future?

She was shivering, and Jon reached for her, but Isobel shrugged him off. Finally, after a long silence, she said, 'I'm calling off the wedding.'

The words just seemed to hang there.

'Fine.' Jon's tone was matter-of-fact as he lounged comfortably at the other end of the sofa. 'So why not come back to Brazil with me? Nothing would make me happier.'

Funny how things changed, mused Isobel. A few months ago, such an offer would have been enough to cause a flutter of excitement. She would have taken it as proof that Jon still cared.

Now she saw it for exactly what it was: just a friendly invitation from a gorgeous ex who wouldn't quite let go and couldn't quite commit.

'Thanks, but I've got work to do here.' She lobbed the ball firmly back to his side of the court.

Jon nodded, realising she wanted him to define things. He

shifted position slightly, staring down at his battered old trainers. 'There was something I meant to tell you. It's, well, it's quite funny, actually. Remember the night you called me in Brazil, and told me you were getting engaged? Well, I tried to call you back. Your line was busy. I was going to ask you not to marry Dominic.'

Isobel beamed. All the years of missing him, of wanting him, of waiting and wondering, they were worth it.

But Jon hadn't finished. 'Yeah, I was going to – now don't laugh, okay? – I had this *mad* idea that we, you and I, should get married. I was all set to propose. I mean,' he chuckled awkwardly, 'how funny is that, right?'

'Hysterical,' said Isobel softly.

'Anyway, about five seconds later, I broke out in a nervous rash at the idea of it all,' continued Jon. 'You see, Isobel,' he took her hand and held it very very tightly, 'you've changed, but I haven't. I still don't want to get married. But that doesn't mean we can't be together.' He stroked her cheek. 'We *should* be together.'

She shook her head.

Abruptly he let go of her hand and stood up, pacing the room in frustration. 'You're being unreasonable. Look, I'm crazy about you. I don't need to go through some meaningless wedding ceremony to prove it. How I feel about you is a private thing. It isn't something I want to share with hundreds of people, most of whom don't mean a thing to either of us.' He rolled his eyes. 'And plenty of marriages end.'

'Yes, they do. But at least those couples entered into it with the right intentions and a belief they'd be different, that what they had was special enough to beat the statistics. Surely that must count for something?'

She took a deep breath, preparing to voice the secret fear that had always haunted her. 'Maybe you don't want to get married because I'm not The One. Maybe you'd feel differently about someone else. Perhaps you know, deep down, that you'd never honour those wedding vows with me. Face it, Jon, when have you ever stuck with anything for longer than five minutes?'

'That's a bit unfair.'

'*Is* it? God, you're like some knight in shining armour who comes charging into my life every time there's a crisis! You hang around just long enough to rescue me – then you pack up your shield and go racing off into the sunset, until the next time.' She laughed at the absurdity of it all. 'You know what? You're right. I *have* changed. I'm not some damsel in distress who constantly needs saving, not any more. Where does that leave you?'

'Precisely where I've always been: here for you. One hundred and fifty per cent. But not willing to spend the next twelve months planning some glitzy wedding that I know I'll hate.' He fixed her with one of his penetrating blue stares. 'Tell me something, Isobel, what's more important to you: getting married, or being with the right man?'

'Meaning?'

'It seems to me that all you really care about is having a wedding – isn't that why you agreed to marry Dominic?'

'No!' Isobel shook her head vehemently. 'Of course not! I loved him. I thought I was in love with him. I was kidding myself that I'd—' She broke off.

'Got over me?' suggested Jon wryly. 'But, Isobel, that's

exactly my point: don't let a marriage certificate come between us! Dominic will marry you in a second, but it won't make you happy.' His face darkened. 'If you really loved me, you'd want to be with me whether we got married or not.'

Isobel looked at him miserably. She'd spent her entire life not being acknowledged by her parents. If she and Jon didn't marry, if they just lived together, wasn't that also just another lack of acknowledgement? She wanted to be recognised as his wife. As the person he loved most in the whole world. When Jon travelled abroad on his assignments, she wouldn't always be going with him. When he was surrounded by stunning models, or alone in luxurious hotel bars, she wanted him to be wearing a wedding ring.

She looked at him. 'And if you really loved me, you'd understand how important getting married is to me.'

Jon looked bored. 'For God's sake, we're going round in circles! The bottom line is you shouldn't need marriage vows to know how committed I am.'

'Oh, *sure*,' said Isobel drily. 'I mean, it's not like you've ever bailed out on this relationship before.'

Jon looked away. For a few minutes he was transported back to the day he'd left for the assignment in Morocco. 'That was a long time ago,' he pointed out, 'and, believe me, there hasn't been a day since when I haven't regretted leaving you like that.'

She shrugged.

'Isobel, I was wrong. I know that now. I should have talked it through with you properly. Or even turned down the assignment. There would have been other jobs. But back then I didn't know that.'

'So why didn't you say any of this when you got back from Morocco?' challenged Isobel.

'You're kidding, right? From the second I returned, you gave me the cold shoulder. Christ, it was hard enough persuading you to be friends again, let alone anything more! I figured all I could do was try and be there for you as much as possible, and that in time, you'd, I don't know, *thaw*.' His smile was wistful. 'But you never did. And then you met Dominic.'

'You still didn't say anything,' she reminded him.

'You were happy with him,' said Jon simply. 'He could offer you the things I couldn't – then. Now I can.'

'Except marriage,' stated Isobel.

'Except marriage,' confirmed Jon.

They looked at each other with identical expressions, their faces a combination of frustration, hurt, and hope.

'I still don't see why you can't come back to Brazil with me.' Jon's lips formed a stubborn line. 'Come on, think about it. It would be fantastic. Then, when we get back here, we can see how it goes, take it one step at a time.' He paused. 'We could move in together.'

Isobel slumped back against the cushions. 'I want all or nothing. Either we go the whole way – by which I mean a wedding and a marriage and a real-life, grown-up relationship, with its ups and downs and problems and surprises – or we don't go anywhere at all. And certainly not to bloody *Brazil*!'

Jon scowled. Isobel was just like every woman he'd ever been involved with, interested only in frogmarching him up that aisle. And never mind that he was more loyal and more genuine than most of the men who said, 'I will.'

Well, they clearly weren't going to resolve this tonight. He pulled on his jacket. 'I'll call you tomorrow.'

'No.'

He frowned. 'What?'

She was blinking back tears. 'I'm moving on – either with or without you. If we're not going to be together, then we can't be friends. I can't handle it. I'm sorry.'

'You don't mean it. What is this? Some strategy you got from reading *The Rules* or something? You think if I can't see you at all I'll come to my senses and realise that I *do* want to get married?' He laughed scornfully. 'Thought you were beyond all that.'

Isobel stood up, walked past him, opened the front door and stood there. Finally Jon followed her. He paused, waiting for her to change her mind, to ask him to stay. And when she didn't he shook his head, his eyes bitter. 'No one will ever love you as much as I do.'

'Maybe. Maybe not. Guess that's a chance I'll have to take.'

He looked like he was about to say something else, then evidently changed his mind, shrugging helplessly before turning and hurrying down the drive. A moment later she heard a car spluttering to life somewhere in the distance. Then there was silence.

Isobel collapsed on to the sofa. She felt numb. But she had to pull herself together fast, because apart from anything else, she had a wedding to cancel. The thought of telling Dominic made her shudder. She could never tell him she'd slept with Jon; it would hurt him too much.

Suddenly guilt rose like bile in Isobel's throat. She legged it into the bathroom just in time to be violently sick. Twice. Then she staggered into bed, shivering uncontrollably.

Desperate to distract herself she reached into her bag and pulled out the sheaf of print-outs she'd got from the Internet earlier that evening. Halfheartedly, she flicked through them, knowing there wouldn't be anything helpful, but needing to focus on something. There were numerous stories about therapists who had been struck off. It made good reading, even if none of it related to Tempest. She glanced at one report for a second time. The therapist involved was nondescript-looking, with lank brown hair. Sighing, Isobel flicked through the others, yet her eyes kept returning to the picture of the bland brunette counsellor. Something about it bothered her. She read through the story again, but couldn't isolate the reason for her unease.

She held it up, and stared at it intently. Then she threw it on the bed. Two minutes later she grabbed it again, jumped up and rummaged frantically through her magazines for the issue of *Primadonna* with her profile of Tempest in. She knelt beside the bed, put the pictures side by side and leaned over them.

'*Oh. My. God.*' Her eyes widened. 'It is. It's *her.*'

The disgraced therapist was Tempest St John, *sans* violet contact lenses, flame-red hair, and dazzling smile.

At first Isobel was bewildered, then overjoyed. Now she could rescue Gemma from Tempest's clutches! A second later it hit her that she had a *scoop* – which, if handled properly, would save her magazine by forcing Tempest to drop the libel suit, *and* establish Isobel as a real journalist.

Instinctively she reached for the phone to share her news with Jon, the way she'd always shared everything with him, then stopped herself. The idea of never again being close to Jon . . . She couldn't take it in.

She forced her thoughts back to work. She couldn't call Byron either, not after what had happened at the office.

This time she really was on her own. The weekly *Primadonna* staff meeting was in two days. The perfect time to present her scoop and show her colleagues, once and for all, that she, Isobel, could cut it with the best of them.

Flopping down on the bed again, she curled up on top of the sheets. And whether it was the sheer relief of finding something on Tempest, or sadness over Jon, or a combination of the two, Isobel cried herself to sleep.

21

Hold the
Front Page

The atmosphere at the weekly *Primadonna* meeting was colder than a morgue. Tempers clashed as the team debated what to do about Tempest and her demands. Unable to look at each other, Byron and Isobel sat at opposite ends of the table, eyes meeting then richocheting away.

'The bottom line is this.' Byron pushed his unruly mane of sandy hair back from a face haggard with worry and lack of sleep. 'We can't cope with a libel suit. So, much as I loathe pandering to Tempest's every whim, we're going to have to apologise to her.' He paused. 'Specifically, Isobel is going to have to apologise, since that's what Tempest wants.'

A few others murmured agreement, and sent Isobel dirty looks. She met their gazes calmly, knowing they despised her for 'losing' the tape and placing them in this predicament.

Now she spoke slowly. 'There are two reasons why Byron is wrong. First, Tempest is at best a fake, and at worst dangerous. She plays with people's minds. We'd be betraying our readers' trust to promote Tempest and all her voodoo—'

'Oh, stop being so bloody melodramatic,' snapped Lexie. 'Just because you don't like the woman, that's no reason for this magazine to orchestrate a full-on vendetta against her. What, we're supposed to risk a libel suit because you're too stubborn to apologise?' She rolled her eyes.

Pandora was waving her hands for attention. 'I'm with Isobel on this one. Look, it's obvious that there's something wrong with Tempest – no normal person goes around placing curses on others! Isobel's right. It *is* dangerous to play with people's heads like that. If we apologise to Tempest, we're condoning her behaviour.'

'Yeah, but we've only got Isobel's word about what happened at her engagement party, haven't we?' said Lexie. 'No doubt Tempest would have a very different version of events.'

'Isobel's a member of our team, Tempest isn't,' pointed out Caroline, one of the other feature writers.

'We don't have any proof that Tempest is doing anything wrong,' Lexie insisted.

It was obvious the team were being swayed by Lexie. Isobel waited for them to quieten down again. 'I thought you'd react this way. And you'd be right to. If everything I said was unsubstantiated.'

She waited for the implication to sink in. Byron caught it first, his eyes narrowing. It didn't take long for the others to catch up.

'What are you saying?' Adrian set down his can of Pepsi. 'I mean, no one else seems to have any problems with Tempest. Christ, she's even got her own agony-aunt column.'

'All the more reason for us to reveal the truth,' Isobel pointed out.

Lexie sniggered. 'Hark at Little Miss Evangelist!'

Isobel opened the folder that lay on her lap, and handed out copies of the material she'd printed off the Internet two days ago. The first item was the picture of Tempest before she'd reinvented herself. Her colleagues stared at the photo of the bland brunette in silence. Next Isobel passed them copies of the news story, detailing how, nine years ago, while working as a therapist in Bristol, Tempest had been implicated in a client's death.

Isobel tapped her copy of the story. 'We all thought Tempest arrived in the UK for the first time six years ago. In fact, she worked here in the eighties as well, under the name Lili James. Anyway, there was a potential scandal over the way she handled one particular case. She was counselling a young woman, Amy, who was suffering from clinical depression. The girl turned up at Tempest's house, apparently in a terrible state, threatening to do something drastic. Instead of maybe arranging for her to be hospitalised or even alerting her family, Tempest just sent her home and told her to "work through" the crisis; she told her to meditate. That night, the girl swallowed enough sleeping pills to fill a pharmacy. She was found in her flat the next day by a friend. The parents wanted to bring a private prosecution against Lili but she disappeared. Went back to Australia and lay low, according to the newspaper accounts. Then, six years ago, she reappeared, as Tempest St John. No one realised that it was the same person.'

'You're winding us up!' Jess shook her head in amazement, staring at the pictures of Tempest from nine years previously. 'This is never her!'

Isobel passed around pictures of Tempest as she looked now, waiting while her colleagues compared them.

Watching Isobel, Byron was caught between confusion and pride. He didn't know what to conclude about their relationship, and kept remembering the way she'd looked at him in the office the other night.

Maybe it was good that they had this scoop to focus on; he could put all his energy into the story, and try not to think about Isobel. He glanced over at her again, as she described all that she'd found out about the Gorgeous Guru over the last two days.

Not for the first time, Byron marvelled at the change in her. Gone was the submissive, timid Isobel. Now her eyes were too bright, as if she was lit up from within, her cheeks rosy, her movements energetic as she paced before them, describing what she wanted to do with the next issue.

'Didn't know she had it in her,' muttered Adrian, one of the reporters, and Byron saw others nodding. No one had believed she could do it. Him included.

'This is what we'll do.' Isobel had been scribbling on some sheets of A4 paper, which she now held up. 'One possible headline will be: "Storm in a Teacup: Tempest St John exposed!"'

There was muted laughter, which quickly faded as she continued, 'Obviously we'll need as much background info on Tempest as possible, including more photos of how she used to look. We'll lead with the story of Amy Cooper, the client who committed suicide – we'll have to get a photo of the girl and someone should interview her parents. Profiles and pictures of Tempest's more famous clients would be good, plus some comments from other therapists.'

Lexie uncrossed her legs and leaned forward. 'About that background info on Tempest – we need the full story. And we really need to know what she got up to when she went back to Australia. What made her return here? Bet she's got a few skeletons in her closet out there too.'

Isobel nodded. 'Two people can fly out to Sydney and do a bit of digging.'

'Who?' persisted Lexie.

'Our two best journalists.' Isobel shuffled some papers. 'You and Byron.'

Byron raised an eyebrow in amusement. Isobel was practically pushing him into Lexie's arms! Presumably he was just a loose end that needed tying up. He looked at her. 'I won't be going anywhere, Isobel. And let me make one thing crystal clear: you may have found a good news story, but there's no way I'm letting you take charge of the entire issue. We can easily hire a good private investigator in Australia to get the dirt on Tempest. No need for anyone to leave this office.' He didn't notice Lexie's hurt expression.

Isobel met his eyes reluctantly. 'Fine.' She turned back to the others. 'Right, Lisa and Jeremy, you can go back through the archives and find out about various gurus and therapists over the last ten years. Put together something on that. Pandora, take over the info I have on other therapists who have been discredited. Steve, you can look into the legal situation regarding counselling in general. Let's put the situation with Tempest into a wider legal context.'

For a moment there was silence as suddenly it hit everyone that they had a seriously juicy story on their hands. For months now, the *Primadonna* team had struggled to make the magazine stand out against established rivals, watching while all the big celebs gave interviews to the better-known publications, such as *Totty*. Now they had a real news splash, and every person in that room was itching to do their bit.

Isobel grinned. 'Time to show *Totty* how it's done!' The team cheered.

*

Isobel gathered up her notes, and slipped away to her little glass-walled office, curled up on the sofa and rested her head on the window-sill. She couldn't stop thinking about Jon. Even while she had been busy at the staff meeting, her mind had lingered on her ex. Even though she knew she'd done the right thing, she was still full of regret for the way things had worked out. Not to mention queasy at the thought of calling off the wedding.

'Isobel.' Byron appeared and sat down, putting as much distance between them on the sofa as possible.

Isobel sighed. If he moved any further away he'd be on the floor.

'We need to revise the plans for the next issue. Obviously we'll need to enlarge the magazine. And I think we should spend more money on marketing – maybe even book some space on radio and TV to plug this edition. It'll cost a fortune but if this issue sells as well as it should, we'll be laughing.'

'Sounds great.' Isobel tried not to remember too vividly what they'd been doing the last time they were alone together. She darted a look at Byron, who was busy punching figures into a calculator, and wondered what he was really thinking.

He looked up, and caught her staring. There was a strained silence. Then he gestured at Isobel's notes. 'One thing I should mention, I won't officially give the go-ahead for this special issue until we've checked out the source of the story you got off the Internet. I want to know more about the journalist responsible. I'll check into that this evening and if it all pans out, tomorrow we'll get cracking for real.'

'What do you mean *if* it pans out?' asked Isobel anxiously. 'Why wouldn't it?'

'You can never tell with the Internet. Anyone can write anything. We need to be sure this isn't just someone with a grudge against Tempest before we spend tons on researching and advertising the next issue.' He glanced at his watch. 'Fuck, it's gone five already.'

'Shit.' Isobel jumped up and grabbed her coat and bag. She'd resolved to see Gemma tonight; her friend had been strangely distant over the last few weeks, never wanting to make arrangements. Isobel was worried about her.

'Right, well,' she smiled at Byron, 'guess I'll see you tomorrow.'

'Yeah.' He didn't glance up as she left.

*

Isobel arrived at Gemma's flat to find her leaving with a suitcase and a pile of paperbacks. They looked at each other, both feeling the weight of all that had passed between them.

Finally Isobel gestured at her friend's luggage. 'Going somewhere?'

'What's it to you?' Gemma's normally good-natured face was screwed up with resentment, and Isobel realised, with a shock, that she hardly knew the girl standing before her. Sure, Gemma had always been unpredictable, but you could still reach her. Now she was different, a strange, hard look in her eyes. She guessed Gemma was hurt because Isobel hadn't spent much time with her since being discharged from hospital. Isobel sighed. She'd done her best. Sometimes it seemed that however hard she tried, Gemma was always going to be upset or resentful over something. 'Where are you going?' asked Isobel again.

'To Tempest's country retreat.'

'A retreat?' echoed Isobel dully, her intuition shrieking.

'That's right.' Gemma brushed a fleck of cotton from her shoulder. 'I'm doing one of her intensive, week-long courses. They're only for clients who have attended her meditation classes for three months or longer. It's advanced material.'

Isobel was dismayed. An entire week locked away with Tempest and her nutty disciples and Gemma would lose whatever semblance of common sense she had left. Suddenly she felt scared for her friend. 'Er, Gems, do you really think this is a good idea?'

'Why wouldn't it be?'

'Look, I know you believe this woman is helping you but, please believe me, she isn't. She's not who you think she is.' Isobel longed to reveal what she knew about Tempest, but knew she couldn't until they ran the story. 'You only *think* you're feeling better! All that's happening is that you're replacing the drugs and drink with Tempest. *You're getting hooked on her.* Please, listen to me. Please, stay here and let me help you.'

'You don't know what you're talking about. Why are you always slagging Tempest off? Okay, so she didn't like your precious article – get over it!'

'But she's—'

'A brilliant therapist! Listen up, Isobel. You're the one who's been saying, for years, that I needed help. Well, now I've found it. And, frankly, I'm fed up to the back teeth with your constant criticisms.'

'I'm just trying to help.'

'Well, don't!'

Gemma felt so negative towards her. She wasn't sure why. 'Gems?' Tentatively, Isobel held out a hand. 'Can't we just sit down and talk? Can't you just delay going to this retreat? Please, stay and talk to me.' She willed the other girl to take her hand.

And, for a moment, Gemma seemed to waver, her face softening. Then her gaze slid past Isobel, who turned to find Tempest standing behind her, smiling serenely.

Isobel was aware of anger coursing wildly through her, just like the night when she'd destroyed all the crockery. But this was different. Because this rage was sure and specific and centred on one person.

'Everything all right?' Tempest turned to Gemma.

'Everything's fine.' Without even realising it, Isobel clenched her fists. 'This is a private conversation.'

The guru's smile didn't falter. 'Sure. If that's what Gemma wants.'

Both Isobel and Tempest looked at Gemma.

'You seem stressed.' Tempest looked anxiously at her client. 'Has Isobel been upsetting you? You remember we've talked about this—'

'Oh, you *have*, have you?' Isobel rounded on her furiously. 'Had fun poisoning my best friend's mind, have you?'

Tempest shot Gemma an I-told-you-so look, and moved towards her.

'*I'm not finished!*' yelled Isobel. And at that moment something inside her snapped. As Tempest moved to stand between the two girls, Isobel lost control and pushed her out of the way. Tempest stumbled but managed to stay upright.

'Isobel!' Gemma gave her a furious look.

'You can't go with her to this retreat,' Isobel insisted.

'Interesting,' murmured Tempest, 'the way you try and control Gemma.'

'*What?* Talk about the pot calling the kettle black!' Isobel scowled at the guru, alarmed at how she managed to twist everything. 'Gemma, please, she's not what you think—'

Gemma tutted, picked up her suitcase, and followed Tempest out to her car. All Isobel could do was watch helplessly as her best friend got in and sped off into the distance, securely in the clutches of Tempest St John.

Isobel walked slowly back to her own car and collapsed in the seat. With a demented little laugh, she mused that life had gone haywire. She was about to cancel the society wedding of the decade, she'd come *this* close to committing GBH on Tempest, and now her closest friend believed she was some kind of lunatic. After twenty-eight years of repressing her temper, it was now unleashed and on the rampage!

But it was all Tempest's fault, wasn't it? Tempest had spooked her so much, that's why Isobel had hit her head and fallen asleep in the first place – up until then she'd been a normal, rational woman who would never have dreamed of raising her hand to anyone. Sure, she might have been a doormat, but at least her life had made some kind of sense.

Isobel decided the safest place for her was at home in bed. Alone.

*

Gemma got out of Tempest's car and stretched her limbs, which were aching after the three-and-a-half-hour journey. Then she stood very still and gazed at her surroundings, allowing the cool, clear country air to flood her lungs. Eyes widening appreciatively, she gazed into the horizon, where the moon was a shimmering white disc floating amid waves of crimson and turquoise.

The retreat turned out to be a huge, sprawling house, reminding Gemma of a girls' boarding-school. The evening sun threw amber and red rays on to the sandy-coloured walls and pristine white window-frames. All around them lay lush green fields, the nearest village a good mile away.

'It's stunning.' Gemma followed Tempest across the car park to the back of the house where, tucked away in a corner, a tiny flight of stone steps led to a large reception area with a cobbled floor. A few women of about Gemma's age were chatting away while checking notices of upcoming lectures and classes. Seeing the newcomer they all smiled cheerfully.

'Tomorrow I'll give you a guided tour,' Tempest collected Gemma's room key and beckoned for her to follow, 'but for now I'll let you get unpacked. You'll be wanting to meet your room-mate. She's been here before and she's a lovely girl, great fun. She'll show you the ropes.'

And, indeed, Gemma took to Fran the moment they met.

'This your first time here at the retreat?' The other girl hurried to help Gemma with her bags.

'Yeah, I'm really looking forward to it.' Gemma surveyed the room with delight. The twin beds were covered with flower-patterned linen, and lots of plump white cushions. A stunning arrangement of hot-pink orchids filled a slender glass vase on the table.

Gemma went over to the french windows at the other end of the room, pushed aside the lacy white curtain and stared out across a beautiful green garden that stretched into the distance. Just metres from the room was a narrow, winding river and beyond that a waterfall, which glowed softly under the rays of the moon. From the rooms on either side of theirs, Gemma caught laughter, could hear radios playing and laughter rippling. Already her tension was dissipating.

Fran joined her at the window. 'There are get-to-know-you drinks at seven, then dinner. Afterwards there's a pool party, and tomorrow the classes and lectures begin.' She handed Gemma a clear plastic pouch filled with information sheets and a bright yellow timetable.

Gemma was amazed by the range of activities she'd been put down for – everything from t'ai chi to table tennis, not to mention three private and five group sessions with Tempest, plus countless talks and seminars. 'I'll hardly have a minute to myself!'

'This is a week you won't forget in a hurry.' Fran smiled warmly. 'Trust me.'

*

'*Go away!*' Jolted awake by the phone, Isobel sat up in bed and groaned as she caught sight of the time. It was six fifteen in the morning. She'd slept restlessly, plagued by nightmares about Gemma and Tempest. Now, cursing, she snatched up the phone.

'About time,' snapped Byron. 'We need you here ASAP.'

'Now? Why?'

'I've been here half the night checking your story on Tempest. Seems we have a slight problem.'

Isobel sat bolt upright in bed. 'What problem?'

'I spoke to the journalist who filed the story and he's put me in touch with a man called Darrell Sanders.'

'Who is?' Isobel was growing more uneasy by the moment.

'Darrell Sanders is a founder member of an organisation called Cult Scan.' Bryon paused. 'Seems there's more to Tempest St John than we thought.'

22

Mind
Games

Darrell Sanders was one of those people who instantly inspired confidence. Behind a pair of shiny round glasses, his grey eyes were shrewd, and his voice was assured. Owing to the time difference, it was evening in Australia, but he'd agreed to a video-conference link-up. Now he listened carefully as Byron outlined the story *Primadonna* was preparing to run on Tempest. Foot tapping impatiently, Isobel interrupted every two minutes, anxious about Gemma's involvement with the guru. Finally, when they both fell silent, Darrell leaned forward, took off his glasses and stared into space. When he spoke, Isobel's skin prickled.

'Understand this, Tempest St John is more than just a therapist. She has a cult following in the literal sense of the word – she is part of a cult.'

Byron flashed him a sceptical look. 'So why is this the first we're hearing of it?'

'Because she's never been publicly aligned with it in the UK. The Tempest you know, that is. Out here we know her under another name and, believe me, she's one of the group's most active members. As you know, she worked in Britain in the eighties, which makes her the perfect choice to spread the word there. No one suspects a thing.' His smile was faintly exasperated. 'You guys have such a simplistic idea of how cults present themselves – bet you still think they all run around banging tambourines, wearing inane smiles and wearing flowing orange robes.'

Byron and Isobel exchanged sheepish looks.

Darrell nodded wryly. 'We've been monitoring these groups for years. In the run-up to the new millennium, we saw a real proliferation, and they're becoming far more sophisticated in how they scout for and recruit new members.' He leaned forward, his expression earnest. 'Look, think of Tempest as the reconnaissance. Slowly, surely, she's creating a base for the British chapter. Her colleagues are doing the same in the States.' His face darkened. 'As for this "retreat" your friend has gone to, well, it's just a watered-down version of the commune they have out here.'

'Oh, *fabulous*! This gets better by the minute!' Isobel looked at him accusingly. 'If you know all this, why aren't you doing anything to stop it?'

To his credit, Darrell didn't react defensively. 'There's nothing *to* stop right now. Remember, this cult doesn't exist officially in Britain. Tempest runs a legitimate practice as a therapist. If her clients elect to attend this retreat, hey, that's their business. She doesn't pressure them, she doesn't demand they cut ties with friends and family – or, at least, not openly. There's no coercion. No one's deprived of food, water, sleep or contact with the outside world. And Tempest's transition from therapist to guru to charismatic leader is happening so gradually that no one's even questioning it.'

'I'd still like to know why you haven't alerted the British media.' Byron's tone conveyed disapproval. 'That would seem a logical step. It's an incredible story – someone would have run with it.'

'We did consider it. But we were scared of tipping off Tempest and her associates. That happened before, in the States a while back, and it resulted in her doing one of her vanishing acts. We lost track of her for almost three years. At least now we can keep tabs on her. The only reason I'm talking to you is because one of our own informants has let us know she's close to securing the funding she needs to start things moving over there.'

'My God, I just don't believe I'm hearing this.' Agitated, Isobel began to pace the room. 'My best mate thinks she's at a sodding health farm, while it's actually more like WACO, THE SEQUEL!' She yelped. 'Next you'll be telling us they're into suicide pacts and think that if they all kill each other they can get on board a giant UFO which is currently orbiting the earth and sending them messages hidden in *EastEnders*.' Her green eyes widened in horror. 'They don't believe that, do they?'

Stifling a chuckle, Byron turned back to the screen. 'What *do* the cult members actually believe in? And what name do they go by?'

'They go by several, which makes tracking them harder,' explained Darrell. 'In Australia, they're known as "The Sisterhood", while in America, they've been nicknamed "Babes", because most of the members are young women. As for what they believe in, well . . .' He paused, frowning. 'Basically, they take recruits through ten "levels". And of course, each level involves a deeper commitment to the cult.'

'So what will they be telling Gemma?' persisted Isobel. 'How do they dupe so many women into joining? It's mad!'

'Well, for starters, remember this group preys on people who are unhappy or dissatisfied with their lives. They tell potential recruits that all their problems can be overcome by achieving Peace Of Mind; one of their catch-phrases, if you like.'

'And how exactly are they supposed to do that?' Isobel was intrigued.

'Through heightened self-awareness—'

'Which is where Tempest's counselling comes in, I suppose?' cut in Byron, with a wry look at the other two.

'Precisely.' Darrell nodded. 'Level One involves getting the women to attend group meditation sessions. Level Two is then all about intensive hypnotherapy; Tempest uses this to plant suggestions in the women's minds about their no longer needing their friends and family. Before long, they'll feel no one really understands them.' He shrugged. 'From here, it's very easy to take them to Level Three—'

'The retreat where Gemma is now!' Isobel thumped the table.

Darrell looked grim. 'Yes, and Level Three is a crucial one. It involves replacing Gemma's normal support system – you guys – with other cult members. Tempest will use the term "sister-hood" a lot, creating almost a pseudo-feminism. She'll have planted "stooges"; long-term cult members posing as clients. They'll get close to Gemma and the other genuine clients; they'll befriend them, learn more about them, and feed this information back to Tempest. She'll then use it in the indivi-dual group sessions she has with each client. Soon Gemma will feel almost as if Tempest can read her thoughts. Pretty powerful stuff. And there will be tons of "lovebombing", whereby Gemma will be showered with affection by the stooges. In addition, I would expect her to be taking part in lots of team-building exercises. Tempest will want to bind them together, turn them into a family—'

'Aaagh!' Isobel let out a piercing shriek. 'What is this woman? A female Charles Manson?'

'Er, no,' said Darrell drily. 'To the best of our knowledge, she doesn't qualify as a mass murderer. Anyway, as I was saying, your friend will also be enticed into donating a whacking great sum of money. At each successive level, she'll be required to give up something – starting with certain foods. The cult leaders will make out they're helping the women to eat healthily. Since most women diet at one point or another, this is a non-threatening place for the cult to start exerting an influence. Of course, they don't really care about the food – it's just a way of getting the women used to listening to them, and changing their lifestyles. It builds compliance. And this will start at the retreat. Further down the line, the leaders will persuade the women to reject all sorts of material possessions. Then their jobs. Eventually, the women will have renounced the outside world without fully realising it. The only place left for them is the cult.'

His face darkened. 'And of course, the cult leaders will have their own ways for the women to bring in lots of money.' Seeing their sceptical expressions, he sighed. 'I know. It all sounds melodramatic. But remember, this all happens very gradually. It's insidious. You wouldn't believe some of the things I've seen women do for this group. *I* can hardly believe it.'

Isobel was bewildered. 'But it's all so . . . so . . .'

'So slick?' Darrell smiled bitterly. 'Yes, it is. *She* is. Tempest St John is trouble. Your friend has no idea what she's getting herself into.'

'Right. That does it.' Isobel got up and began pulling on her coat. 'We've got to go and get Gems out of this *nuthouse!*' She headed for the door, where she stopped to fix Byron with an imperious stare. 'Well? What are you waiting for?'

'Isobel, chill. It's only seven in the morning. We can't just go charging off into the country and kidnap Gemma! First we need more information from Darrell. Then we have to brief the rest of the team, get them working on this new story. It's massive, surely you see that? *Then* we'll go and get Gemma.' Seeing the mutinous light in her eyes, he spoke sternly. 'Isobel, I'm still editor-in-chief. And this is how it's going to be.'

*

It took almost two hours to brief the *Primadonna* team. Isobel saw that Byron had been right to insist they waited, since the ramifications of this new information were enormous. Their story had now taken off in an unexpected direction.

Byron relayed to everyone what Darrell had said. 'It seems that, to a certain extent, our original story would have been doing Tempest an injustice. It's true that in the eighties one of her patients *did* commit suicide – but Tempest did nothing wrong. The girl was seriously disturbed, and Tempest knew that. She was trying to arrange for her to see a specialist, a psychiatrist, because she knew she couldn't help. Then the girl went and topped herself. Well, of course the family went mad and blamed Tempest. According to Darrell, she was devastated. At that point, she was a bona fide counsellor, and had no connection to this cult. She'd worked incredibly hard to qualify as a therapist and she took her work seriously. When the client died things began to go horribly wrong. She chucked in her practice here and went back to Australia.'

Byron shrugged.

'Exactly what happened when she got back there, I guess we'll never know. Presumably she was vulnerable and the cult got its claws into her. Apparently they offered her some sort of volunteer work as a therapist, told her she'd be helping young runaways or something. They helped her regain her confidence – Darrell says she was terrified of treating anyone because of what had happened here. Anyway, by the time she knew what the group was really about, she'd been thoroughly brainwashed. She changed her name to Tempest, and has been with them ever since.'

The team had listened, their faces grave. And while Isobel had been stunned at this new information, in her mind it still didn't excuse what Tempest was doing now.

'But isn't it weird,' Lexie was intrigued by the story, 'that a therapist of all people should get sucked into a cult? Surely she should have sussed their tricks. I mean, I can understand if she'd been some idiot, but . . .'

Byron nodded. 'That's what I thought. But Darrell says this is where most of us fail to understand how cults work. We all assume we'd be intelligent enough to see through them. Because of that, we're confident enough to enter into a discussion with them in the first place. Once you do that, they're half-way to recruiting you. And, if what he says is true, cult members are often of *above* average intelligence, that's why these groups' sophisticated ideology appeals: recruits have enquiring minds and these groups *seem* to offer rational answers.' He smiled at the expressions on his colleagues' faces. 'Talking to Darrell was an eye-opener, let me tell you. We're just scratching the tip of the iceberg. These groups are clever. And,' his smile widened, 'this is one shit-hot story!'

As the others began smiling too he continued, 'Darrell has given me a name and number for another ex-patient of Tempest. This girl, Claire, was on a working holiday in Australia seven years ago when she came into contact with Tempest. Darrell's calling her right now and he thinks she'll agree to talk to us.'

He glanced down at a page full of scribbled numbers. 'We're increasing our print-run for next week's issue because of this exclusive on Tempest. It'll cost, but I think we should do it. I've also had to retain an advertising agency to organise radio and TV coverage. Again, we can't really afford it, but it should pay off.' He grinned. '*Primadonna*'s first exclusive!'

Later, as Isobel and Byron headed out of the building, their thoughts were still on Gemma. Byron jangled his car keys. 'I'm parked right across the street. Come on, I'll drive.'

'Gemma will be all right, won't she?' fretted Isobel. 'She won't get sucked into this cult?'

'No. We'll get to her in time,' Byron reassured her, but she wondered if he truly believed it.

*

Lexie clamped her hand over the phone and looked daggers at her colleagues before yelling, 'For fuck's sake, will you lot keep it down? I'm trying to get the dirt on Tempest and all I can hear is you guys.' As a hush fell over the room, she uncovered the mouthpiece again, her voice now syrup-sweet, 'Claire, *so* sorry about that. You were saying?'

Not for the first time, Lexie thanked God she knew short-hand. At first Claire had been reluctant to open up. Her involvement with Tempest almost seven years ago still caused her embarrassment, and she resented anyone raking up bitter memories after so much time had elapsed.

Even Lexie's hard little heart had softened. But there was a juicy story here, and she was going to get it. So for the next hour she was sympathetic. Supportive. Shocked in all the right places. And gradually, bit by bit, it came out.

Lexie felt a glorious surge of adrenaline. She chewed viciously on her pen whenever Claire paused or strayed from the essential thread of the story. The story of how Tempest had befriended a young backpacker who was in Sydney for a few weeks, and had then tried to suck her into a cult. Gently but firmly, Lexie extracted quotes bursting with emotion, colourful soundbites that were going to make this story leap off the page. Soon she was writing so frantically her wrist hurt.

Satisfied at last, Lexie thanked Claire profusely, then jumped up, clutching her pad to her chest. She could hardly wait to start typing, but first she wanted to check the angle of the story with Byron. Half-way to his office, though, her steps slowed, as Lexie remembered he wasn't there. No, he was too busy running round with Isobel.

Now the hurt she'd felt at the staff meeting, temporarily numbed by the thrill of chasing a scoop, hit Lexie with full force. Sitting down before her computer and sipping a luke-warm mug of coffee she gazed thoughtfully at the blank screen. It was always going to be like this: her watching Byron watching Isobel. Lexie forced her mind back to the job at hand, and began to type. Before long, she was lost in the story. The story every hack would kill to get hold of.

*

Almost four hours later, Byron's car screeched to a halt in the driveway of the retreat, sending gravel flying. For a minute Isobel and he just sat there in silence, staring at the enormous house and the beautiful grounds.

'Impressive.' Byron rolled down the window, and inhaled the sweet country air.

Isobel reached for the car door. 'If I'm not out in an hour, come and get me.'

'Not so fast.' He yanked the door shut again. 'I don't like you going in there alone.'

'Hey, relax.' She grinned. 'What's Tempest going to do? Turn me into a frog?'

Byron laughed, but then turned serious. 'Listen, you *mustn't* let on to Tempest that we know about her involvement with the cult. Feelings are going to run high once you get in there, but promise me you won't let it slip, however much she riles you?'

Isobel nodded. 'I don't intend to stay long. I just want to see Gemma.' With that she jumped out of the car.

Small, unobtrusive signs indicated the way to the main reception area. Inside, Isobel paused to take in her surroundings. The lobby consisted of a polished wooden reception desk, behind which were seventy cubby-holes, bursting with letters, timetables and information for each guest. On the opposite wall hung a huge picture of Tempest, wild red curls framing her face, violet eyes gleaming.

Surreptitiously, Isobel gave it the finger.

'Can I help you?' chirruped the girl behind the desk.

'I'm here to see Gemma Cartwright.'

Although the girl's smile didn't waver, her eyes grew a tad more watchful. 'I see. You're a guest here, then?'

'No, actually.' Isobel smiled pleasantly. 'Which room is she in?'

'I'm sorry, I'll need to take your details before I can disturb Ms Cartwright.' Still smiling, the girl produced a card and pen. 'Name?'

'Look, it's taken me half a day to get here. I don't have time to—'

'It's all right. I'll take care of this.' Tempest had appeared. 'Isobel, if you'd like to come with me?'

Silently Isobel followed her through the reception area. The ground floor comprised three long corridors that formed a triangle. In the centre there was a dance studio, consulting rooms, and a larger room where various beauty treatments were taking place, women reclining on chairs and wearing white towelling robes.

Tempest turned off down a side corridor and showed Isobel into a pretty room with pale green walls, and a table set with what looked like tea for two.

Though her host gestured to a chair, Isobel remained standing. 'I'd like to see Gemma.'

'Why the hurry? Wouldn't you like something to drink?' Tempest picked up a cup.

'I'd rather see my friend.'

Tempest put down the cup. 'Goodness, so bolshie. What's the problem, Isobel?'

'You're a fake, and we both know it.' The words left

Isobel's lips before she could stop them. Inwardly she cursed herself.

'Ah, but do we?' Tempest made herself comfortable on the sofa, and indicated that Isobel should join her. 'You're so sure I have nothing to offer as a therapist. Why not let me prove you wrong? Only fair to give me a chance. Only fair to find the truth. Isn't that what quality journalism is all about, hmmm?'

And, though Isobel failed to realise, Tempest's smile contained a trace of anxiety. For suddenly, inexplicably, she found she actually cared about being accused like this. Whatever mistakes she'd made over the years, whatever compromises she'd made in the name of a greater cause, nothing altered the fact that she was good at what she did. Tempest prided herself on her insight into the women she treated. And Isobel de RoseMont was no different from the rest. Easy to read? The girl might as well be transparent.

Isobel perched on the edge of a chair. 'What do you mean, give you a chance?' *A chance to do what?* she added silently. Darrell's words kept running through her mind. *She's slick.*

'Well, you're so sure that I don't know what I'm doing so let's put it to the test. Then maybe you'll drop this absurd witch-hunt. Come on, let me prove you wrong. Right here. Right now.'

'How?'

'Oh, that's easy.' Tempest chuckled. 'By telling you about yourself, telling you the things you thought no one else could possibly know.'

Isobel glanced at the door, which was ajar. She should leave; she hadn't come here to become a player in one of Tempest's seductive little mind games. Yet the temptation to stay was intense. The desire to have someone strip away the layers and

. . . And what, precisely? What was it she wanted from this woman?

Peace of mind, that's what. Isobel couldn't shake the idea that only Tempest could reverse her bad luck, and remove the hex. Tempest had triggered all the chaos and changes in her life so maybe talking to her was okay. And, after all, she reasoned, it was only human nature to want to hear about oneself, wasn't it?

Tempest observed Isobel's face and body both relaxing ever so slightly. The girl was close. The girl was tempted. The girl was hers.

'How about it, Isobel?' Tempest suggested softly. 'What's the worst that can happen? After all, they're only words . . . Isobel de RoseMont . . . Let's see now, reluctant It Girl. Daddy's girl. Stuck-up little rich girl. A girl who's never had to work for anything in her life, never had to prove herself.' Her eyes narrowed. 'Oh, but you'd like to. For isn't that what secretly scares you? On those nights when you lie there wrapped in your cool silk sheets, in that chi-chi little flat of yours, staring out at the sky. Yes, you lie there and you wonder. Wonder where you'd be, wonder what you'd be, without that grand old family name and all the doors your family's cash kicks open for you . . . Wonder what you'd be without all that money. Wonder if you would, in fact, be anything much at all . . .'

Gradually, Tempest's voice was getting lower, softer, wheedling its way into Isobel's mind.

'Yes, I'll tell you what frightens you. It's knowing, deep down, that you'll never go it alone. Never turn your back on that name and that wealth. Never know what you could have been, left to your own devices. Oh, you whinge on about how tough it is being rich and famous and privileged, but deep down you wouldn't have it any other way. Take away the expensive clothes and exquisite manners and what's left underneath, hmmm? Nothing. What would happen if, tomorrow, you lost all that surface polish and those material comforts? I'll tell you what would happen. You'd fold' – Tempest clicked her fingers sharply – 'like *that*!' She nodded thoughtfully. 'Yes, what terrifies Isobel de RoseMont is knowing that she isn't a real person, she's a *stereotype*!'

Isobel sat rigidly, her face white. Tempest's voice rose in triumph. 'And isn't that what really *gets* you about Dominic wanting Gemma? Though you'll never admit it, you know why he was drawn to both of you. It's because you're the same! Pretty rich girls with more money than character. No wonder he's confused. No one's ever taken you very seriously, have they, Isobel? And you know what? Deep down, way deep down where it counts, *you don't blame them!*'

Isobel felt as if someone had plunged a sliver of ice straight into her heart, then started twisting it. She attempted a nonchalant shrug. 'It's hardly my fault that I was born into a wealthy family. And, for your information, I've had to work' – her voice broke – 'had to work twice as hard as anyone else to prove I'm none of the things you're suggesting.'

'Have you?' challenged Tempest, her violet gaze never leaving Isobel's face. 'I bet Daddy found you every job you've ever had. And then there's *Primadonna*.' She laughed in delight at the name.

'*Primadonna* must be very important to you. How you must have hated me for threatening to bring that libel suit and ruin everything. Poor Isobel.'

Seeing that hatred glinting in Isobel's eyes, Tempest smiled. 'Still can't do it, can you? Not surprising. As I said, stuck-up little rich girls usually are low on character.'

Isobel frowned. 'Can't do what?'

'Still can't admit you were wrong.'

'About what?'

'The article you did on me. Come on, Isobel, you twisted my words and you know it!'

Isobel saw herself interviewing Tempest: the guru had been nothing but friendly and helpful. Then she saw herself sitting in her car afterwards, the rain lashing the windows, the heater on full blast, the interview tape blank. She recalled scribbling frantically, certain she was recording Tempest's remarks accurately. Had she unwittingly tweaked the guru's comments?

Now unsure, Isobel looked searchingly at Tempest. Her gut feeling was that the guru had switched the tapes. Had she decided Isobel was an easy target, and decided to fleece *Primadonna* for as much money as possible? Or maybe it was the opposite. Maybe she'd been worried that Isobel had seen through her, and wanted to keep the tape in case she'd given something away that Isobel might later pick up on when she listened to the interview.

Isobel tensed. Could her intuition be wrong? Had she herself simply screwed up by pressing the wrong button on the tape recorder? Perhaps her memory was not as good as she thought and she'd put an unfair spin on the guru's comments. Her face turned red with shame.

Or was Tempest now manipulating her? Confused, Isobel rubbed her eyes. Even though she'd not taken to Tempest at the initial interview, she'd tried to be scrupulously fair in her reporting. Now she glanced up to catch a tiny, amused smile on the other woman's face. Isobel stared. Tempest was just playing mind games. That's what was going on here. This was her way of getting Isobel to doubt herself. Before she knew it she'd be doubting everyone and everything else too, and Tempest would have a hold on her. In that moment Isobel could see precisely how this woman enticed people like Gemma to trust her.

'Nice try.' Isobel smiled. 'You almost had me believing you. Now I wonder: can you turn that relentless perception on yourself? Let's take a closer look at Tempest St John. And let's start with you admitting that no reputable therapist would behave the way you did at my engagement party. I suppose you thought it was funny, putting that hex on me? It's all just one big game to you, isn't it? You wanted to freak me out and never mind the effect it had on me or who got hurt in the process!'

To Isobel's surprise, Tempest burst out laughing. 'Oh, *please*, spare me the righteous indignation! My so-called hex was the best thing that ever happened to you. I've been hearing all about it from Gemma. Come on, Isobel, it's just us here. Let's talk straight. You and I have our little tiff, next thing you know you have your accident, and suddenly Isobel de RoseMont is standing up for herself like never before! My "jinx" gave you an excuse to do all the things you really *wanted* to do. *That crack on the head was a wake-up call* – even if it did send you to sleep for a while first!'

Isobel frowned. *All the things you really wanted to do.*

Oh, God, it was true, wasn't it? She'd had gorgeous, riotous sex with Jon. She'd asserted herself at work. She'd even slammed the phone down on her father. She had finally found her temper. Isobel blinked. Tempest, damn her, was right. The hex had liberated her.

Then Isobel shook her head. 'But you couldn't have known your little stunt would have positive effects. You were just playing with my mind – because that's what you do. Well, you know something? All I really care about is Gemma, and I want her to come home with me.'

Tempest nodded. She looked tired suddenly. 'Sure. I'll take you to her room myself. Gemma is free to leave at any time she chooses. Unlike you, I don't try to pressure her into things. You'll probably find she's quite happy to stay here.'

'Only because you've been filling her head with crap about her not needing her friends and family any more.' Isobel headed for the door. 'I want to see Gemma. Now.'

*

Gemma's wonderful new relaxed mood evaporated the second she opened her bedroom door and found Isobel standing there.

'Mind if I come in?' Without waiting for a response, Isobel marched past her friend and into the room. She wasted no time in explaining why she was there. Listening, Gemma decided Isobel had well and truly flipped her lid. Fancy following her all the way down here just because she didn't like Tempest!

'Give me one solid reason why I should even consider leaving,' Gemma said.

Isobel recalled her promise to Byron not to reveal what they knew about Tempest and the cult.

'Won't you just take it on trust?'

'No, I won't.'

Catch-22. Isobel searched for some inner flicker of intuition to guide her. Maybe telling Gemma the truth about Tempest's plans would persuade her friend to leave. More likely, though, she'd just run straight to Tempest, which would ruin everything. Isobel felt sick at the choice she was being forced to make. She was going to have to keep quiet and leave Gemma here for Tempest to toy with her mind even more.

But this was about more than helping Gemma, wasn't it? Isobel had to keep the secret about Tempest: she owed it to the team at *Primadonna*, all now working round the clock to put this story together. She owed the women who read their magazine. And she owed it to those Tempest would, in the future, try to lure into her cult.

'Gems, please,' she tried one last time, knowing it was futile, 'I have *good* reasons for asking you to come with me. You mustn't stay here. You think it's doing you good but, trust me, it's not. I just can't tell you the full story, not right now. Please, just believe me. Please, just come home with me.'

But Gemma was shaking her head incredulously. 'You're jealous. You can't bear me having something you're not part of. Well, I've got news for you – I'm not interested!' With that she ushered Isobel out of the room and slammed the door in her face.

Isobel stood in the silent corridor, trying to ignore the curious stare of a maid piling bed-linen outside a nearby room. She half expected to turn round and find a gloating guru waiting, but Tempest was nowhere to be seen. In fact, the place seemed deserted. Slowly, she made her way back down the corridor, past the treatment room and the dance studio, where a notice announced that a primal screaming class was now in progress. She shuddered at the piercing shrieks of ten adult women who were holding their heads, skipping round the room and wailing.

No one glanced her way as she wandered back through the lobby and out into the car park, where she paused. Everywhere she looked girls were chattering happily, some collecting bikes and tennis rackets, others comparing timetables. Hard to believe that beneath this wholesome façade women were being seduced into parting with their money, their sanity, their friends and families. And, for a split second, taking in the animated, carefree faces, Isobel wondered if maybe she and the others had got it all horribly wrong.

But then she pictured Gemma, and knew they weren't wrong at all.

She opened the car door and saw that Byron was ready to start firing questions. She gazed at him, dejected, and he kept quiet. As the car moved down the long drive, she said quietly, 'We're running the story. It's the only thing we can do now.'

23

Primadonna

'Ladies and gentlemen,' Byron's eyes lit up with pride as he looked at his team, 'I give you *Primadonna*!' From behind his back he produced their bumper edition, amid cheers and whistles from the staff. Isobel felt a quiet sense of satisfaction as she glanced at all the happy faces. The magazine looked fabulous.

Deciding to break with tradition, they'd opted for a jet-black cover, against which Tempest's photograph stood out dramatically, her flaming red hair curling wildly, lush lips curved in a triumphant smile. Her face was angled slightly downwards, so she was gazing up through lowered lashes, brilliant violet eyes gleaming.

Lauren, their picture editor, had spent hours scouring the archives for the perfect photograph, and everyone had agreed that this was definitely it. The magazine's name was emblazoned in silver, as was the shout-line running beneath the picture: 'FAKING IT'. The effect was simple, striking and sexy.

'We've doubled our print-run.' Byron was gazing dreamily at the magazine. 'This time next week five hundred thousand copies of *Primadonna* will hit the stands. If anyone wants one, there are loads in the storeroom. Just help yourselves.' There was a moment's hesitation and then, like a pack of excited children, the team giggled and went flying down the corridor, each returning with a copy of their own.

In her office Isobel flicked through the smooth pages. God, it looked good. The story had come together perfectly. They'd profiled all the main players: Tempest; the patient who had died; Claire, the backpacker; other major leaders of the cult. Lexie and Byron had done most of the writing, but they'd assigned Isobel the section dealing with Tempest's former career in Britain, and she was thrilled to see her byline. They'd also added a separate section 'Gurus Are Us', profiling various other charismatic leaders from the UK and around the world.

And if the photographs were superb, well, that wasn't surprising; to Isobel's surprise, Jon had offered his services. Not that she'd seen him, thank goodness. For the last week he'd been busy shadowing Tempest, snapping picture after picture, as well as getting plenty of her Harley Street office and her home. He'd also gone to the retreat and taken pictures there with a zoom lens.

Now there were only two days before this issue of the magazine went on sale. Isobel was incredibly excited. The radio and television space had been booked, and Byron had primed several tabloid reporters, who would pick up on the story the moment *Primadonna* hit the shelves. Operation Storm, as it was now known, was well and truly under way.

Isobel was so absorbed in the magazine that she jumped at a loud rapping on her door. Dominic was peering through the glass. Her stomach lurched. She'd been psyching herself up all day to call him.

Now, as he strode in and leaned forward to kiss her, Isobel steeled herself. 'Dominic, we need to talk, but not here.'

'I agree. I've hardly seen you lately. I'm going to cook for us tonight.'

'You really don't need to—'

'No arguments!' he declared.

'But, Dom—'

'Isobel.' He looked at her reproachfully. 'I've already gone out specially and bought all your favourite things. I know you've had a stressful few weeks at work but, darling, surely you won't disappoint me?'

Isobel felt her resolve weakening. She could hardly break off their engagement here. Better to wait until tonight, then tell him in the privacy of his own home. 'Dinner would be lovely,' she said quietly.

'Great. What time do you finish?' He flicked his wrist, admiring his new Rolex. 'It's almost five. I'll wait for you and we can go home together.'

Isobel heard the eagerness in his voice, and looked at him. For a few moments, they stared steadily at each other. She saw that he knew all was not well but that he didn't want to address it. He'd rather pretend everything was fine.

'No, it's fine,' she said. 'I'll meet you at your place. Around eight.'

'Can't wait.' He went to kiss her on the lips. Instinctively Isobel moved and he ended up kissing her cheek.

*

'Where *is* it?' Fran flew round the room like a whirling dervish, slamming drawers and emptying bags, while Gemma watched.

'What are you looking for?' she enquired. Her new room-mate usually seemed so serene.

Fran flopped down on her bed, sighed and punched a cushion. 'My cheque-book. I owe Tempest.'

'Oh?' Gemma frowned. 'Didn't you pay the fees before you got here? I thought we had to.'

'Oh, sure, of course.' The other girl gazed round the room then pounced on an old denim bag she'd stuffed into the wardrobe. 'Got it!' She sat down again, scribbled then ripped out a cheque. Seeing that Gemma was confused, she smiled patiently. 'It's a little pressie for Tempest. She likes to reserve a few places here for women who can't otherwise afford it, so those of us who can give a bit extra. It's sort of a tradition.'

'Oh, I had no idea.' Flustered, Gemma glanced round for her own bag.

'Of course you didn't. That's why they put you with me, so I could show you the ropes.'

'Er, how much? I mean, what would you suggest?'

Grinning, Fran held up her own cheque. Gemma barely contained her shock. She'd never spent that much money in one go in her life. Then she scolded herself. It wasn't as if she didn't have the funds. And, besides, what else did she need it for? Quickly she wrote out a cheque for the same amount. 'Thanks for telling me,' she smiled gratefully. 'God, I would have been *mortified* if no one had mentioned it and I'd been the only one not to give anything.'

'Don't worry, someone would have said something.' Fran held out her hand. 'Here, give me yours. I'm going to see Tempest so I'll take them both with me, save you the trip. You've got a group-therapy session in five minutes, right?'

'Cheers. I owe you one.'

Fran waved as she shut the door quietly behind her. As she walked down the corridor, her fingers were busy ripping her own cheque into bits. Tempest was right. Gemma was going to be a very welcome addition to their group.

24

Saving
Face

T he only parking space Isobel could find was at the end of
Dominic's road. As she walked slowly up the street, the
Wedding March kept sounding in her head. Apt, since it was
time to face the music. Time to look her unsuspecting fiancé in
the eye and tell him there would be no marriage.

It had to be the coldest night for ages. Isobel was glad she'd
worn her new cashmere scarf. Peering up at the sky, she made a
bet with herself that there would be snow before the week was
out.

The trees lining the street were all bare, their branches
reaching down at jagged angles, like fingers pointing at her
in accusation. Isobel was dreading breaking the news to Dominic. She kept picturing herself alone at home later, curled up
on her bed, having cancelled the wedding. Kept picturing
herself alone. If she couldn't be with Jon . . . Well, the thought
of being with anyone else was unbearable.

She jumped as a car alarm suddenly sounded, the siren
echoing in the deserted street. Glancing at the houses she
was passing, Isobel glimpsed figures moving in rooms, saw
televisions flickering, heard doors slamming. Right now, she'd

cheerfully swap places with any one of these people, tucked away in their homes, presumably settled and happy and secure in their relationships.

She turned in through Dominic's gate, and almost lost her nerve but forced herself to keep moving. Before she could press the bell, the door flew open and a beaming Dominic ushered her inside and helped her remove her coat and scarf. 'Your timing is perfect.' He wrapped her in a tight hug. 'Dinner will be ready in about ten minutes. That okay?'

Isobel extricated herself from his embrace. Better do it quickly. She had to be cruel to be kind. 'Dominic, we have to talk.'

'Sure.' Seemingly oblivious to the tension in her voice, Dominic skipped back into the kitchen, leaned over the cooker and peered earnestly into a saucepan. 'Think the soup needs a *dash* more cayenne . . .' Sprinkling pepper into it he closed his eyes and sighed. 'Perfect!'

'Dominic,' Isobel's face was resolute, 'I need to tell you something.'

'Let me guess. It's another diet, right? You've become a vegan. Oh, but not tonight, darling?' Frowning, he inspected the spice rack. 'Hmmmm . . . think the fish needs a little something . . . maybe a *pinch* of turmeric . . .'

Struggling to keep calm, Isobel took his hand. 'Can we sit down? Now?' He allowed her to lead him to the table, where she pulled out two chairs and placed them close together.

'Dominic,' she began, 'I don't really know how to say this. There's, well, there's no nice way to do this.' She took a deep breath and looked him straight in the eye. 'Here goes. I can't marry you.'

To her astonishment, Dominic grinned. 'Okay.'

'Excuse me?'

He smiled. 'Really, it's okay, I've been expecting this.'

'You have?'

'Absolutely. Pre-wedding nerves. I knew we'd never make it
to the church without you having some sort of panic attack or
last-minute crisis.' He smiled lovingly. '*Bless.*'

'No, you don't und—'

'Isobel, darling, I understand perfectly. And it's only natural.
It's going to be the biggest day of our lives.' He gave her an
indulgent smile. 'I don't blame you for feeling jittery. For
having some tiny niggling doubts even. It'll pass.' He sprang
up. 'Must check on the dessert – I made your favourite, crème
brûlée! Now, I'm just going to drip some spun sugar over the
top and—'

'Dominic, please, stop playing *Ready Steady Cook* and *listen* to
me.'

'Sweetheart, r-e-l-a-x . . .' He kissed her cheek tenderly. 'I
promise, your nerves will pass and you'll be itching to walk
down that aisle next month. Now, can I get you a drink?'

Bemused, Isobel watched as her fiancé poured them both a
glass of white wine. Good Lord, he was even singing softly to
himself, his mood not in the least dented by what she'd been
trying to say.

But why was she surprised? After all, wasn't this the ultimate
proof of how badly suited they were? For here they were,
actually in the process of breaking up – but only one of them
realised it. Here she was cancelling their wedding, and Dominic was totally misreading her. It was as if the emotional connection between them had short-circuited.

She watched as he brought the wine to the table, pausing only to beam at her again, before proceeding to bustle around checking on the dinner, spooning sauce over the fish, stirring the soup, whistling cheerfully to himself all the while.

Isobel began to cry. She was sitting in her fiancé's kitchen, while he prepared a fabulous meal yet didn't notice that the woman he supposedly loved had tears streaming down her face.

It was surreal. One day, she was sure she'd look back on this and see the funny side. But right now, it hurt. Isobel had never felt so alone. How could Dominic profess to love her yet be so oblivious? Sure, he had his back to her, but couldn't he *feel* her distress?

She willed him to turn round. But Dominic continued to scurry around the kitchen, fetching fruit juice from the fridge and pouring it carefully into a jug. Silently, she beseeched him to pick up on her mood. But he was now consulting one of his many cookery books, running his finger down the page, apparently checking that he'd done everything correctly.

Jon would have turned round. Jon could finish her sentences for her. Jon often knew how she was feeling before Isobel even realised herself.

'Dominic.' Isobel stood up. 'You don't understand. I'm not having last-minute nerves.' Her voice shook. 'Dominic, look at me. *I'm crying.*'

Finally he turned, and instantly his face softened. 'Oh, you're so cute when you're upset! Your cheeks get all pink!' He kissed her again. 'I knew you'd get over-emotional once the big day drew near.' He went to the oven and took out a tray with two massive sea bass, their glazed, pale eyes seeming to stare at Isobel with reproach. 'Now, I've made two rather exquisite sauces,' Dominic announced proudly. 'One with lemon grass and one with—'

'OH MY GOD! WILL YOU SHUT UP ABOUT THE SODDING FOOD AND FOR ONCE JUST *HEAR* WHAT I'M SAYING?' Isobel clutched her temples. 'I DON'T WANT TO MARRY YOU! THERE ISN'T GOING TO BE A WEDDING!'

He stared at her, his face strangely devoid of expression. Then Isobel noticed that he was gripping the tray of fish so tightly that his fingers were white. A nerve twitched under his left eye, as Dominic gazed down at the sea bass like they were suddenly going to start speaking and explain to him what was happening here.

'Dominic.' She took the gloves and eased the tray from his grasp, then set it down on the worktop. 'Let's go and sit down.' She led him back to the table. 'I'm so sorry, I know this is a terrible thing to do, so close to the wedding, but I can't go through with it.'

'But I don't understand. We're engaged. You said yes.'

'I shouldn't have. It was a mistake.' Isobel guessed that Dominic was in shock: his brown eyes were staring blankly into hers. 'Dominic, it would be wrong for us to get married. We wouldn't be happy together.'

'We have seven hundred guests coming. Vlad, the Nearly Naked Chef, is doing the catering. He's organising an eleven-course meal. The staff at the château are expecting us. The honeymoon is booked. Jacqueline has knocked herself out trying to get your dress ready. Our families are ecstatic. *OK!* and *Hello!* are both sending photographers. What on earth do you mean, there's not going to be a wedding?' He seemed genuinely puzzled. 'Is this some sort of joke?'

Isobel reached for her glass of wine. God knows, she needed it. But Dominic's hand shot out, his fingers closing around her wrist, jerking her hand away from the glass. 'You're serious?'

She nodded. 'I'm sorry. More than sorry.'

'But why? Why now? I don't get it. Has something happened?' His eyes searched hers frantically for some clue. 'There must be a *reason*.'

'I know this is hard to understand but . . . I genuinely thought I could go through with it, or I would never have said yes in the first place. But I've realised we're not right for each other.'

He let go of her hand and sat back. 'So that's it? You've simply decided we're "not right". Just like that?' His mouth tightened with barely controlled anger. 'I see. And when did this revelation hit you?'

'What?' Isobel wriggled nervously on her chair.

'I said, when did this life-changing revelation hit you?'

'Well, there wasn't one precise moment. It's been a gradual thing.'

'But when *precisely* did you decide to call off our wedding?' pushed Dominic. 'How did it happen? What, you just woke up this morning and decided, "Oops! Can't marry Dominic! We're wrong"? You were happy enough with me for the last two years. What's changed?'

'I don't . . . I can't . . . I don't know.' How could she explain to Dominic what she barely understood herself? 'Maybe *I've* changed.'

'You haven't been yourself lately, that's for sure. Ever since the accident, in fact. That's probably why you're being so ridiculous now.'

Vintage Dominic, realised Isobel. Putting her down the moment he didn't like what she was saying. 'I don't think I'm being ridiculous.'

'Don't you?' His face was flushed. 'That crack to the head's knocked all the common sense out of you. Why can't you accept that you're not thinking straight right now, that this has nothing to do with the wedding?'

Isobel decided she'd better sit on her hands or she might throttle him. 'Dominic, pleeeeease – try and actually *hear* what I'm saying. *I can't marry you.* Simple as that. It's nothing to do with my accident. It has to do with *Us.*'

'But you can't do this,' insisted Dominic, his mouth quivering like a petulant child. 'Everything's in place – the church, the flowers, the guests, the paparazzi. You don't have the right to do this. You *have* to be there – you can't back out, not now! You don't have the right to just cancel everything!'

'I don't?' Isobel was horrified. 'Do you realise what you're saying? Surely I have *every* right to choose who I do or don't marry.'

Dominic's eyes narrowed. 'And who *do* you want to marry, Isobel? If I'm not The One, who is?'

His perceptiveness caught her off guard. Instantly, Isobel looked away, but realised he'd caught the tell-tale blush. 'So that's it,' he murmured. 'I should have known. This has nothing to do with a gradual realisation as you so charmingly put it. This is about Jon. Ever since he turned up at that hospital, you've been all starry-eyed.' He began pacing up and down. 'I see how it went. You knew he'd never commit so you figured you might as well make do with me. But then you had your accident and, suddenly, Jon is terrified he might lose you for good – as were we all.'

He stopped pacing, and looked at her as though she'd just stabbed him through the heart. 'All this time, all those assurances you gave me that you were over him, it was all just *bullshit*. Tell me something, Isobel, did you ever love me, or was I always just a stop-gap until Jon grew up enough to handle a proper relationship?'

'It isn't like that,' insisted Isobel. But she knew her voice lacked conviction. For wasn't Dominic right? Had it not been for her accident, would she ever have woken up to the fact that she was still in love with her ex? Or would she have spent the rest of her life in denial?

'Save your pathetic excuses and flimsy apologies! It's all very simple.' Dominic's lips curled with scorn. 'You're dumping me for your ex. You *bitch*.'

Isobel flinched at the venom in his voice.

A buzzer screeched. Dominic gestured at the cooker. 'It's the timer. Dinner's ready.'

In the silence of the house the timer seemed excruciatingly loud.

'How do I switch it off?' Isobel waited for Dominic to answer but now he was just staring at her, his face ashen.

'Do you know how this is going to look, cancelling the wedding four weeks before the big day?' Dominic winced at the idea of the embarrassment, the gossip, the sheer and utter humiliation of being jilted. 'Have you any idea what this is going to *do* to me?'

'I'm sor—'

'You can't. You can't do this to me!' Suddenly he was beside her, clasping her hands. 'You can't put me through this. I'll look like a fool. Everyone will know I've been jilted for Jon. I'll never live it down.' He seemed to shrink before her eyes.

'I know it will be horrible for both of us, but there's nothing I can do. I'm so, so sorry. And I know it doesn't help to say this but, Dominic, I swear I *did* love you. I never meant to hurt you. I genuinely thought I was doing the right thing by agreeing to get married.' Now she too was close to tears. 'I'd give anything to turn back the clock, to avoid hurting you like this. Anything.'

But he didn't seem to hear her. Head bowed, palms clasped together as though in prayer, he sat down at the table. 'Okay. I think I've found a way to get through this.' He took a deep breath. 'We have to go through with the wedding. Give everyone the day they've been waiting for. Allow me to retain a modicum of dignity. Then, after a few weeks, we quietly have the marriage annulled, citing irreconcilable differences, and go our separate ways.'

'I can't—'

'*You owe me!* I never asked for this to happen and I sure as hell don't deserve it. I've never been anything but honest with you, while *you*, you've done nothing but use me!'

Then his voice softened. 'And you know the worst bit? That even after all this, if you wanted, I'd stay with you. Even knowing I'd be second best. I'd do that, if that's what it took to keep you.' His tone changed, becoming more conciliatory. 'Isobel, think about it. We can't simply cancel a wedding this big at the eleventh hour. Apart from anything else, the cost to your parents would be astronomical. And to be honest,' his voice faltered, 'I don't think I could cope with the shame when, five minutes after you cancel the wedding, you're seen running round with Jon. I can't handle it.'

'You want me to go through with the ceremony, recite those vows, when it wouldn't be for real?'

'Isobel, *think* about it. If we go through with the wedding, no one has to be embarrassed. And once the actual day is over, we won't be in the public eye so much any more. But you cancel it now and the media will never leave us alone.' He shuddered. 'I can see it now, all the things they'll write about us. All our secrets will come out. Everything. We can kiss goodbye to privacy. I'm telling you, you cancel this wedding now, and I don't think I could take it.'

'I'm sorry, I can't—'

'*Please*, Isobel, you have to do this for me.' He gazed at her beseechingly. 'I never asked for any of this to happen. All I wanted was to marry you and make you happy. It's bad enough that you're dumping me for someone else. Please don't publicly humiliate me as well.'

Isobel realised she couldn't refuse him. What he was suggesting made her feel sick but, as he said, didn't she owe him? After all, he was the innocent party. It wasn't his fault she was still hung up on her ex. She'd agreed to marry him and, by God, she was going to have to go through with it.

'Okay, I'll do it.'

'Thank you.' Dominic closed his eyes with relief. 'And we can't tell anyone. I mean it, not a soul. One careless word, and that's it.'

She nodded numbly, feeling like the old, submissive Isobel, giving in to someone else's demands out of guilt. She allowed herself a bitter smile. Might as well enjoy the wedding. It would probably turn out to be the only one she ever had.

How distorted her life had become. The man she loved refused to walk up the aisle and say the vows. And the man she didn't love cared more about the wedding day than about her. Everything Jon had said about a wedding being the least important thing was true. He was right. Here was the proof.

Right now, though, all she wanted was to get away from Dominic. She glanced at him; he still looked shell-shocked. 'I have to go.'

'All right. I'll speak to you soon. We'll have to act as if nothing's wrong for the next month. When others are around, I mean.'

'Sure.' She headed out into the hall. Dominic made no attempt to follow her. As she opened the front door, Isobel heard him scraping the dinner into the bin, chucking the cutlery into the sink, closing the oven door. She felt desperately sorry for him – and also for herself.

It was so ironic. The whole world was waiting with bated breath for their wedding day, believing them to be the golden couple. In reality, it would have been better if they'd never met and never got involved. Because she and Dominic were more than just wrong for each other.

They were bad luck.

25

Scoop!

The next day Isobel woke up and instantly wished she hadn't. Seeing the winter sunlight streaming through the windows, she made a face. Pity she couldn't pick weather to match her mood: all dingy grey skies and torrential rain. Isobel knew she should be feeling great; tomorrow *Primadonna* hit the stands. But instead she was consumed with nerves over the impending sham of a wedding. Yawning, she dragged herself out of bed and into her pretty pale green *en suite* bathroom.

She flicked on the radio, not sure why she was bothering since every song just reminded her of Jon, and every lyric seemed to contain some hidden meaning just for her. Isobel showered and dressed in a total daze. Outside it was a chilly but brisk February. Pulling on her fake-fur coat, she meandered towards the tube station, her thoughts drifting as she saw herself in a few years' time, when she would no doubt still be broken-hearted over Jon.

Yes, decided Isobel morosely, there she'd be, wandering down perhaps this very street, when her eyes would meet those of a gorgeous man walking towards her. They would

309

both slow, stop, and greet each other awkwardly, for it would be Jon. Then he would introduce her to the girl whose hand he was holding. His wife. Isobel would, however, hold her head high and treat the couple to a nonchalant smile before sauntering off.

Now she grimaced. In reality she'd be far more likely to slip over and go sliding down the street on her bum, leaving Jon and his no doubt terribly elegant wife laughing their heads off about what a narrow escape he'd had, and how relieved he was not to be with his klutzy, scatty ex-girlfriend.

She turned a corner, and got ready to shove her way through the crowd thronging around the subway entrance. At the steps, she paused to give some change to the row of homeless men lying against the railings. As she stood up again, she spotted the magazine stand: the latest edition of *Totty* had arrived. Unable to resist, she wandered over to take a quick peep at *Primadonna*'s biggest rival.

'What the—' She blanched, mouth falling open in shock as she lurched forwards, grabbed a copy of *Totty* and stared at it in horror. Life had one sick sense of humour.

'Oy, luv, you buyin'?' The vendor glared.

'Excuse me? Oh, right . . . here you are.'

Her buckling legs just managed to propel Isobel to the side of the road, where she collapsed against a building, staring grimly at the magazine. There on the cover was a picture of Tempest and alongside it, in big red letters, the caption 'Storm in a Teacup: Tempest St John Exposed!'

Her caption.

Frantically she flicked through the glossy pages, face darkening as she skim-read the text. Not that she really needed to – for

Isobel knew the story inside out. The *Primadonna* team had written most of it. She groaned, the magazine slipping from her hand. It was all there, all the information they'd been gathering and piecing together.

Totty had scooped them.

Oblivious to the stares of those around her, Isobel hurtled back towards the tube station, knocking people aside in her haste, swinging her bag like a lasso as she pushed her way through the crowds of commuters. She was going to find out who had stolen the story. Now she shook her fist at this as yet faceless foe. The old, meek Isobel might have taken this lying down but the new, improved-formula Isobel de RoseMont – *she was going to find the culprit and wring their fucking neck*.

*

Gemma was bored. Tempest had left early that morning to run some sort of workshop, leaving her alone in the enormous house. After the paradise of the retreat, her return to London had been a shock to Gemma's system. She wasn't coping too well. Exactly how poorly she was coping had been brought home to her earlier that week, when she'd headed out for the day, planning to spend some time in Harvey Nicks, her spiritual home.

Except she'd never made it there. The train had been so crammed that Gemma couldn't bear it: all those bodies pushing, shoving and pressing against her, and the clammy heat that made it impossible to breathe. Her heartbeat had quickened painfully, and her throat clogged with panic. With a muffled cry, she'd hopped off just before the train doors snapped shut.

Finding herself alone on the grimy platform, Gemma had walked slowly to the edge and stared down at the glinting metal track. She experienced a sudden, scary, seductive little urge to just hurl herself forward and put an end to the constant panic, the endless sadness.

But she hadn't. Instead she'd gone running to the one person, the only person, whom she trusted. Tempest had gone through some relaxation exercises with her, then done a bit of hypnosis, after which Gemma had felt much better. And when Tempest had suggested she stay with her for a while, Gemma's relief had been so acute she'd sobbed.

Now she wandered into the beautiful guest bedroom she'd been using, and sat down on the bed. Trouble was, as time went by she seemed to need more and more help from Tempest. Two sessions a week had become four yet somehow that still didn't seem to be doing the trick. The guru kept insisting that Gemma was doing brilliantly, that she was really making progress, so why, Gemma wondered, didn't she feel any better?

She scolded herself for being disloyal. Hadn't Tempest been right about so many things? She'd shown Gemma how bad Isobel and Dominic were for her, and Gemma would always be eternally grateful for that. She sighed. The bottom line was: she still felt lousy.

But there was one thing to look forward to. Tempest was so impressed with Gemma's progress at the retreat that she'd offered her the chance to go to Australia and take part in an intensive two-month self-awareness course run by her colleagues there. Gemma couldn't wait.

She switched on the television and changed channels a few times, looking for a movie. Suddenly she glimpsed a familiar face. Smiling in surprise, she turned up the volume, leaned forward and listened intently. It was one of the morning chat shows and they were showing a clip of Tempest at one of her workshops. A news reporter was talking about the guru.

Then the chat-show host began recapping for new viewers and, as it became painfully clear what was happening, Gemma sat very still, eyes locked on the television screen.

*

All activity at *Primadonna* had come to a standstill. Copies of *Totty* were strewn around the office and one had been turned into a dart board, which was proving rather popular. Computers stood silent while journalists clustered in small groups, lamenting their lost work and condemning their rival publication. In his office, Byron was sprawled at his desk, reading *Totty* and cursing so violently that the air around him was practically turning blue.

A few people looked up as the lift doors opened and Isobel appeared. Ignoring their sympathetic stares and subdued greetings, she marched across the room, flung Byron's door open, then let it slam shut behind her. 'Well? What the fuck happened?' She threw her copy of *Totty* on his desk. 'Who the hell gave them our story?'

'I don't know, but when I find them, they're going to wish I hadn't.' Byron scowled.

'Why would anyone here do it?' Impatiently she shrugged off her coat and threw it carelessly on to the chair. 'It doesn't make sense. Everyone here was so involved with this issue, *why* would someone stab us in the back like this?'

'For money.' Byron waited until she'd sat down, then continued quietly, 'I've seen this before. Journalism is a cut-throat business. Shit happens. Everyone here knew *Totty* would pay mega-well for this scoop. It could have been anyone.'

His mouth twitched at the way Isobel stood there, hands jammed on her hips, green eyes blazing, her cheeks two rosy little patches of rage, as she declared, 'I WANT TO KNOW WHICH DOUBLE-CROSSING *GIT* STOLE OUR STORY! THEN I WANT TO BOIL THEM ALIVE IN A VAT OF HOT MARMA-LADE!' She growled and clenched her fists. 'Ooh, just let me get my hands on them . . .'

Comparing this murderous rage with how timid Isobel used to be, Byron's eyes creased with mirth. Isobel shot him a reproachful look. Suddenly she frowned. 'Hang on, where's Lexie?' Jumping up, she opened the door and stuck her head out. 'Hey, you lot, anyone seen Lex?'

No one had.

She sat down again. 'I'm assuming you've called Lexie to tell her what's happened? Or maybe you didn't need to call her. Maybe she was already at your place this morning?'

'What do *you* care?' demanded Byron furiously.

'I *do* care if because of your on-off-on-again relationship Lexie got pissed off and stole our story!'

'Oh, so suddenly this is all my fault?' Impatiently, Byron pushed his mane of sandy hair back from his face. 'I really don't like what you're suggesting, Isobel. I can assure you I'm every bit as upset as you are over this.'

But she wasn't listening. Something was clicking into place in her mind, as she remembered what Gemma had told her, ages ago, about Byron's bedroom, about all the magazine covers on the walls. About the covers of *Totty*. Byron had worked there for five years. Byron had dreamed of editing it. Perhaps his loyalties were still with his old magazine.

'Maybe Lexie had nothing to do with this. Maybe it was *you*.'

Isobel gulped. 'Byron? What happened? Did you get cold feet, decide to bail out? Did you do some deal with *Totty* as insurance in case things didn't work out here?' Thoughts spinning wildly, Isobel stared at him in horror. It all made perfect sense. Everyone knew that his career meant the world to Byron. He'd risked everything to join *Primadonna*. But was he ruthless enough to sacrifice them all just to get back in with *Totty*? It didn't make sense, given how much he'd invested financially in *Primadonna*.

But surely, if she was wrong, he'd be angry at being accused like this? 'Well?' She looked at him suspiciously. 'Aren't you even going to try to deny it?'

Hurt flickered in his eyes. 'I shouldn't have to.'

But she was staring at him as if he'd just shot Bambi. And suddenly Isobel realised how greatly she valued Byron as a friend, how devastated she'd be if he'd betrayed them all. '*Was* it you? Did *you* sell us out to *Totty*?'

'No, he didn't.'

Lexie was dressed in a black coat, her glossy dark hair scraped back untidily from a face uncharacteristically devoid of cosmetics. She closed the door and took a deep breath. 'I know Byron didn't do it because . . .' she looked Isobel straight in the eye '. . . because it was me. I did it. I sold your story.' She reached into her pocket and produced a slim white envelope. 'My letter of resignation. I'll go and clear my desk.' She turned back to the door.

'Why?' Isobel had to ask.

Lexie stood still, then slowly turned round. 'You really want to know? Because I didn't see myself having much of a future here. I slogged my guts out at *Totty*, working sixteen-hour days, weekends, holidays, the lot, and I was really getting somewhere. But when Byron asked me to follow him here, I didn't think twice.' She looked at him. 'You asked me to come and support you on this new project, and I did. I thought that at least you'd understand how much I was giving up to do that! My God,' she shook her head in apparent wonder at her own flawed choices, 'leaving a leading women's magazine for an unknown? It was an insane move to make! But I figured it was better to be a big fish in a small pond, that we'd build the magazine into something special, that I'd have a shot at making editor one day, the one thing I really wanted.'

She swung round to face Isobel. 'Then, out of the blue, you decide it's time to play at being a career girl. You even tried to take over the celebrity column – my project. You see, Isobel,' her dark eyes glinted with resentment, 'we don't all have enough money to buy ourselves magazines and make ourselves associate editors. Some of us work for years to achieve what you got with a click of your fingers. So, if you really want to know, the idea of working for you made me *sick*!'

Isobel looked at her ruefully. 'And you made my life miserable here from day one. Did it ever occur to you that maybe my life isn't as picture perfect as you so glibly assumed? That maybe I've missed having the chance to prove myself – that maybe I would have loved the chance to fail or succeed on my own merit?' She leaned forward and gripped the back of her chair. 'You're just like everyone else, so busy being jealous of me that you didn't give a shit how unhappy I was actually feeling. We could have worked *together* – there's plenty of room for us both. Don't suppose that idea ever occurred to you?'

'It did, actually.' Lexie smiled slightly. 'And, believe it or not, there were times when I felt bad about how I treated you.'

'So why didn't you stop?'

'Because,' Lexie glanced quickly at Byron before looking away again, 'because I'm in love with a man who spends his whole time watching you. So you see it's been a bit hard to like you, what with one thing and another.'

Byron felt a hot, fast rush of shame as he observed Lexie's wan face. He did care about her. As a friend. A friend whom, he blushed, he'd used to make Isobel jealous. He'd behaved like a bastard. Who could really blame Lexie for being so furious? No one had ever stopped, for a single moment, to consider her feelings in any of this.

'But why sell the story to *Totty*?' Byron asked quietly, knowing Isobel was wondering the same thing. 'I mean, why not just leave? Why betray us like this?'

Lexie shrugged. 'There's no one reason. It was just that when Isobel revealed the info she'd found on Tempest at the staff meeting something inside me snapped. I think it was when she suggested you and I go to Australia to dig up the background dirt on Tempest. You were so quick to dismiss the idea. It was obvious you couldn't bear the thought. Suddenly I realised that if I stayed here, it would always be like this – me watching you watching Isobel. I wanted out.' Her cheeks reddened. 'And I guess I . . . wanted to hurt you. I thought *Totty* would give me my old job back if I proved I was still loyal to them. I knew it was wrong, but that didn't stop me.' Her smile was wry. 'For what it's worth, I'm not proud of myself.'

'And have they offered you your job back?' queried Byron.

'No. Guess they figured if you couldn't trust me they probably couldn't either.'

'How did you actually get the material to give them?' persisted Byron.

Lexie blushed again. 'I went into your office and took the file with the final proofs in it, just before they went off to the printers.'

Byron's eyes were suddenly very still. 'You mean the red folder? On my desk?'

'Yeah, I'd been watching you, I knew you'd put everything in it.' Lexie gave a nervy little laugh. 'I felt so bad I just grabbed it, jumped in the car and drove over to *Totty*. Anyway, I was there for all of five minutes, just long enough to hand the file over. I didn't want to hang around to see their faces when they saw all the work. They'll probably get in touch at some point today.'

'Oh, I doubt that.' Byron grinned. 'Because you see, Lexie, you didn't give them anything.'

'But she just said—' Isobel threw up her hands in confusion. 'What d'you mean?'

'I moved the final proofs. I put them in my case before I left that night, took them home to give them one last read through. I wanted to make triple-sure everything was word-perfect.'

'So . . .' Lexie had paled '. . . what was in the red folder?'

Byron grinned. 'Next week's horoscopes.'

'But if Lexie didn't give them the story, who did? *Someone* did.' Isobel groaned. 'We're back to square one – it could have been anyone!'

Lexie picked up her bag. 'Anyway, I'm glad I had the chance to tell you. Better go get my things.'

Byron and Isobel glanced at each other. He raised an eyebrow, Isobel thought for a moment, before shrugging and smiling.

'Lexie,' Byron got up and stopped her opening the door, 'look, you didn't actually give them the story. There's no reason for you to leave. Stay.' As her eyes cut to Isobel he added quickly, 'We both want you to.'

'But I *meant* to give them the story!' Lexie's eyes shone with tears. 'I really thought it was in that file! I appreciate your offer but to be honest, I think I could do with a fresh start.' She glanced swiftly at Byron again, and Isobel understood: it was too painful for Lexie to be around him day in, day out. In silence, she and Byron watched as Lexie quietly slid her letter of resignation on to the desk and then, with a small smile, left his office for the last time.

'Much as I hate to admit it, she's probably doing the right thing,' Byron said briskly. 'And she'll find something else, as long as it never gets out that she tried to sell our story to a rival. We'll have to make sure no one ever knows.'

'I can't believe I'm saying this but,' remarked Isobel wryly, 'it's a shame she won't stay. Anyway, what are we doing to do? *Primadonna* hits the stands tomorrow! God, we're going to look like total morons – it's got "exclusive" all over the front page. We'll just be running the same story as *Totty*. Who's going to buy us now?'

'And we increased the print-run.' Byron covered his face with his hands. 'I'd better get on the phone to the ad agency and see if they can rework the ads, at least change the wording. This is all going to cost.'

'Can't we just cancel this week's issue?'

'No. We may possibly benefit from the "halo effect". If

people are intrigued by what *Totty* are saying about Tempest, they might want to read more about it, and buy us.'

'We'll have to make sure next week's issue is something really special,' suggested Isobel.

'Next week?' Byron looked at her. 'There is no "next" issue of *Primadonna*.'

'What are you talking about? Why not?'

'Because we have no money left.' Byron looked bitter. 'Two days ago I attended an emergency board meeting; I didn't tell anyone because I didn't want to worry any of you. The bank wanted to pull out, since we're still running at a loss. Anyway, I explained to them that we were about to scoop all our rivals with the story on Tempest; I managed to persuade them that this issue would be a turning point. But now we're actually going to lose money on it. We used up too much, what with the increased print-run, the extra pages, not to mention all the media space I booked, and the ad-agency fees. It seemed like a necessary gamble at the time. It didn't work. So now, the bank are pulling out. There's no money left.'

'I still don't understand. What do you mean "no money"?' Isobel was looking at him blankly.

'It's not that hard. Look, we started off with a certain amount of money, and now it's all gone.'

'But *where* has it gone?' Green eyes narrowed, Isobel gazed expectantly round the room as though waiting for little wads of notes to suddenly come limbo dancing out from their respective hiding places.

'Dear God, give me strength.' Placing his hands together in supplication, Byron directed a beseeching gaze heavenwards.

Maybe if he used really simple language . . .

'Isobel, There Is No Money Left.' He spoke slowly and loudly. 'And One Reason Why There Is No Money Left Is Because You Spent It All.'

'Really?' She looked utterly mystified. 'What did I spend it on?'

'What didn't you spend it on?' Byron stared at her in exasperation. 'For months I've been pleading with you to cut back on your so-called "necessities", but would you listen? No, you had to have your precious car park! And those *stupid* voice-activated computers! Oh,' Byron's voice was pure acid, 'and let's not forget your "corporate bonding" sessions at the most expensive blinking health farm in Europe.' He continued wearily, 'Then there's your state-of-the-art flotation tank – which, by the way, is leaking and has short-circuited every light on the floor below. As for your expense account . . .' He winced, remembering exactly how much money Isobel had frittered away.

'But . . . but . . .' Isobel was having trouble getting her head round the idea that their funds had run dry. 'There must be *something* left.'

'We have just enough to pay this month's salaries and the electricity bill. After that, we've had it.'

'Oh, but couldn't we just make the next issue a teeny-weeny tiny one? Then it would cost less.' Isobel smiled hopefully.

'No.' He spoke through teeth clenched so tightly they were probably welding together permanently. 'We cannot make it a smaller issue. We don't have enough money. That is what I have been trying to tell you. We do not have money to do anything. We have no money, period. None. Zilch. Zero. Nada. *No money*.'

He watched while Isobel digested this information. First she stared earnestly into space, then she frowned as though deeply puzzled, before finally assuming a look of mild irritation. And Byron could have sworn the phrase *does not compute* flashed briefly in her eyes as she turned to him again.

'How about if we make it a black and white issue? Tierney swears monochrome is the Next Big Thing. That would cut costs, right?'

'We can't produce *any* type of magazine. Not even one page.'

'Couldn't we borrow some money?'

'I can't borrow any more money, that's for sure.' Byron got up from behind his desk and began to prowl as restlessly as a caged tiger. Isobel noticed that even his golden mane of hair seemed wilder than normal. He stood still suddenly, eyes bleak. 'I don't know what to say. Looks like . . .' his voice caught '. . . looks like this is it.'

Gutted, they stared at each other. Isobel gulped. So, when push came to shove, it all came down to cash. Or lack of it. What a joke. Her entire life she'd had too much of it, been stereotyped because of it, and now the one time she needed it she was broke!

'How are we going to tell the others?' she wailed. 'All the work everyone's put in and now they're all out of jobs. Oh, God!'

Byron reached out to touch her – then his hand dropped to his side. 'Isobel, I know this feels like the end of the world, but it isn't. We did our best – and that's all anyone can ever do. We're not the first magazine to fold, and I promise we won't be the last. Don't take it too hard.'

She nodded, not trusting herself to speak. She could just

imagine how people would greet the news of her failure. Well, it was only what everyone had expected, so they wouldn't be disappointed.

'Hey, there'll be other chances.' Byron couldn't bear her dejected expression. 'Let's just get through one thing at a time, okay? Right now, we need to organise an emergency meeting to explain the situation to the team. I want to schedule it for tomorrow afternoon.'

But Isobel was no longer listening. Her face had turned a ghastly shade of white. 'Gemma,' she whispered. 'Oh, my God . . .'

Understanding instantly, Byron got up and grabbed their coats. 'Come on. I'll drive.'

They fled from the office. Isobel felt dread unfold inside her. Gemma was unbalanced anyway: how would she cope with discovering that Tempest was a total, utter fake?

26

Suicide Blonde

'This place is *huge* – you'd need distress flares in case you starved while looking for the kitchen!' Byron jumped out of the car and stared at Tempest's house.

After trying Gemma's mobile once more, Isobel joined him and together they gazed at the guru's home. Huge and white, it was set back from the road by a winding gravel driveway. It loomed against the dull grey sky, chimneys rising like turrets.

'What if Gemma isn't here?' Isobel asked fearfully, as they dashed up the drive, the gravel crunching under their feet.

'Well, we've tried everywhere else,' Byron shouted back, the bitter winter wind dragging his words away.

At the top of the path Isobel struggled to unlatch a black wrought-iron gate. She was so nervous her fingers were all over the place and Byron pushed her aside. He had it open in seconds. Then they were racing towards the ornate front door, shouting for Gemma and ringing the bell. Byron attacked one of the front windows with his fist. 'Gemma? *GEMMA?* If you're in there, just let us know you're okay. *GEMMA?*' Still there was no response.

Isobel's face brightened. 'Listen – hear that? There's a radio or TV on somewhere inside. She's here!'

'Not necessarily.' Byron didn't want to get her hopes up. 'Maybe Tempest left it on by mistake.'

Just then, they heard the squealing of tyres and a car door slamming. A few minutes later Tempest was flying up the path towards them, her face like thunder, a voluminous blue dress billowing around her, her Titian hair in disarray.

'Well, well . . .' drawled Byron, folding his arms and leaning against one of the ornate white pillars that adorned the front of the house. 'If it isn't the Galloping Guru . . .'

As Tempest came hurtling towards them, they caught the sound of screeching brakes, out in the street, and more doors slamming, and a little knot of journalists appeared, brandishing cameras as they gave chase. Byron and Isobel watched as, reaching the little wrought-iron gate, Tempest gave up fiddling with it, simply leaping straight over instead. Isobel blinked. This was getting surreal.

'OUT OF MY WAY,' screamed the shaman, face contorted with panic. Producing an impressive cluster of keys she fumbled with the lock. Please, God, prayed Isobel silently, let Gemma be here. The door finally opened and Tempest tried to bar them from entering. 'Bugger off!'

'Not bloody likely!' Byron wedged one large foot in the door, and Isobel pushed her way into the house.

'Gemma? GEMMA?' She turned to Tempest. 'Where is she? Tell me where Gemma is, or we'll let that little lynch mob in.'

Tempest glanced at Byron, who smiled grimly and opened the door a fraction just as the journalists reached the wrought-iron gate. 'Last I saw of her she was upstairs,' snapped Tempest, then shot through a door at the end of the circular hallway and disappeared.

Isobel tore up the stairs on legs so heavy it felt like they were dragging dumb-bells. It was as though she'd been sucked into the archetypal nightmare: she needed to hurry but her body was resisting, every muscle, joint and limb conspiring to trip her up and slow her down. And all the while, this terrible feeling of foreboding. Isobel had experienced whispers of intuition in the past, but never anything like this: the icy certainty that Gemma was in danger.

When she reached the second floor, she found herself at the end of a long landing, with several corridors leading off it. Isobel looked around in confusion. 'Gemma?'

She began to throw open doors, but all she found behind each one were large, white, high-ceilinged rooms, scattered with large, pastel-coloured cushions.

Before long Isobel was ready to scream with frustration; each time she thought she'd looked everywhere she came across yet another door, or another narrow little corridor winding its way to yet more rooms. 'This isn't a house – it's a maze!'

Byron, meanwhile, had disappeared up another flight of stairs. Now she heard him calling her name. Isobel ran upstairs and practically fell into the room where he was waiting for her. The bed was strewn with Gemma's clothes, and make-up littered a vanity table in the corner. An overflowing ashtray lay on the bed.

'She's obviously been here,' Byron sighed heavily, 'but it doesn't appear as if she's still in the house.' Seeing Isobel's look of despair he touched her shoulder lightly. 'Listen, chances are she heard the news about Tempest and has just gone back to her flat. Bet she arrived there minutes after we left the place.

You'll get home and find half a dozen messages from her.' But his cheerful tone sounded forced.

While Byron tried Gemma's home and mobile numbers again, Isobel sank wearily on to the bed. There was no point in trying to explain how she felt right now, Byron would just accuse her of being a typical neurotic female.

Byron clicked his phone shut. 'No answer. Let's head back to her fl—' He broke off abruptly. He was staring at the window-sill. Isobel followed his gaze. There, propped against the pane, was a ragged piece of paper, folded in half, the sunlight filtering through the window behind it and making it glow a gentle golden. Covering the room in two big strides, Byron snatched it up, glanced inside then handed it straight to Isobel. 'It's for you.'

*

It was crucial, Dominic decided, to act like everything was fine. After all, there was no way he could know what was in the latest issue of *Totty*, was there? So there was no need to appear anxious, or buy the magazine, since it certainly wasn't something he would normally read. And if anyone saw him doing so, it might trigger suspicion.

For the entire morning, Dominic carried on at the gym as though nothing was wrong. Then, at lunchtime, while having a drink with some colleagues, he spied his chance. A copy of *Totty* was tucked into one of the girls' bags.

'Theresa, mind if I have a quick flick through?' Dominic smiled sheepishly. 'It's the main rival to Isobel's mag. I should take a look, see why she's always banging on about it.'

'Sure.'

'Cheers.' Dominic looked casually through it, then stopped

at the section on Tempest. He allowed himself one carefully timed loud gasp.

'What's wrong?' James, one of the trainers, looked at him quizzically.

Dominic assumed an expression of outrage, and flung down the magazine. 'They've nicked Isobel's story!' Whipping out his mobile, he cursed a few times for good measure as he punched in his fiancée's office number. He was relieved to get her voice-mail.

'Isobel, darling, it's me.' He was acutely aware that the others were watching him. 'I've just seen *Totty*. What on earth happened? You must be devastated. Anyway, I'm worried about you. Call me as soon as you get this message.'

He cast a final, anxious look at his phone, as if praying Isobel would ring back that second, then picked up the magazine and pretended to read the story, shaking his head in disgust, as his colleagues peered over his shoulder. He tried not to think too hard about how Isobel must be feeling right now. What he'd done was wrong, and Dominic knew it.

And the truth was, he regretted it. But after Isobel had left his house the night she'd broken things off, Dominic had lost control. He'd never felt the need to hurt anyone like this before.

That night, in the kitchen, Isobel had no idea how close he'd come to losing control, to smacking her round the face, which is what he'd felt like doing once he'd realised she was dumping him because of Jon. For the first time, he'd understood why crimes of passion had once been a special category. He felt like killing her.

Instead, he'd decided to get even.

It wasn't hard. People at *Primadonna* were used to seeing him waiting in Isobel's office, so it had been the work of minutes to get into her computer and find the lead story for the forth-coming issue. Passing it to *Totty* had given Dominic a few minutes of satisfaction; a sense of righting a wrong, of regaining an element of control.

That feeling hadn't lasted. The following day, he'd despised himself for what he'd done. More, for what he'd become. But by then, it was too late. *Totty* had the story. The damage had been done.

*

Isobel struggled to make sense of Gemma's note. The writing was strange, the letters spindly, the spacing between the words uneven, sentences meandering across the page with no order or logic.

'Isobel?' Byron had remained silent but now curiosity got the better of him. 'What does it say?'

She handed the note to him and he scanned it swiftly, trying to piece together the disjointed sentences. He glanced at Isobel. Her delicate brows were knitted together in a slight frown. Byron turned back to the note. It was impossible to tell from Gemma's tortured ramblings exactly what was going on in her head. But one thing was crystal clear. Learning the truth about Tempest had sent her over the edge.

'I *knew* Tempest was going to damage her! We have to find her!' Isobel burst out.

'Let's try her flat one more time,' Byron suggested.

'No, she won't have gone back there.' Isobel tapped the bit of paper thoughtfully. 'See this bit where she talks about finding somewhere quiet, away from everyone and everything? That wouldn't be her flat because she knows it's the first place we'd look.'

Byron opened his mouth to voice his fears, then thought better of it. But Isobel caught the fear which darted into his eyes for a split second. 'What? Byron, what is it? Tell me!'

He said nothing, his eyes returning to the note.

'Byron, you're scaring me . . .' Isobel's voice trailed off as she, too, looked at the note again. 'Oh no, you don't seriously think . . .' She shook her head vehemently. 'It couldn't be . . . I mean it's – it's not a *suicide* note.'

'I don't know,' Byron said uneasily. 'If you look at her words one way then I agree, it's just a note asking for some space. But if you look at them another way – see this bit here about her going somewhere peaceful, finding somewhere with no pain or people, this part about her not wanting to actually *feel* anything any more . . .'

'Oh, my God, what do we do? Call the police? What do we do?' Now half crazed with panic, Isobel clutched the note, staring wildly at it as though if she looked for long enough, the words would rearrange themselves to reveal Gemma's whereabouts. 'What do we *do*? We have to do something!'

Byron had no patience with female histrionics. 'Isobel – stop being such a total *girl*. Calm down, and let's think clearly. We're going to make some calls. You're going to contact Gemma's parents and any friends you think she might turn to in a crisis. I'm going to put in a call to an old mate of mine who's with the Yard, see if he can suggest anything. Then we're going to look for her.'

They spent the next fifteen minutes on the phone, then hurried outside to Byron's car. As they were turning out of the street Isobel gasped. 'The note! Give me the note!' She snatched it from Byron's hand and stared intently at one line. 'I think I know where she is. She talks about going somewhere "beyond" all this upset, somewhere where she can get a "different perspective".' She grabbed his arm, and the car swerved sharply. 'There's one place that fits. Her parents have this flat in town. It's a penthouse with the most incredible view right across London. When we were kids, Gems always used to go there when she was upset over something. She used to say she could look out of the window and put her problems in perspective! That's what she means! That's where she is!'

*

They weren't going to give up. In her study, Tempest listened to the journalists outside the house, calling her name and thumping on the door. She could hear their mobile phones ringing as news desks and editors across the country ordered their hacks not to show their faces again without this story.

She glanced over at a small wooden cupboard behind the door. Deep down, she'd always known this day would come. And knowing, Tempest had made her plans. She had set up several bank accounts in different names, and acquired two passports and driving licences, also in different names. It was so much easier than most people realised.

Opening a drawer, Tempest smiled.

Now for the fun part.

*

Isobel and Byron ignored the concierge as he tried to detain them at the entrance. When the man became more forceful, Byron put him in a headlock. 'Go for the lifts, quick!' he ordered Isobel, and, though rather concerned as the concierge's face turned an unhealthy shade of red, she did as she was told. She was soon joined by Byron, who had left the concierge spluttering with anger and lack of oxygen.

In silence, they counted the seconds until the lift reached the penthouse. The door was ajar. Byron and Isobel glanced at each other then burst into the hall, automatically going in opposite directions to find Gemma.

'Oh, thank *God*!' Isobel laughed with relief. Her best friend was curled up on the window-seat, smiling serenely, her hair glinting in the evening sunlight, her slender frame wrapped in a bulky jumper.

'Gems, we've been frantic!' Isobel gave her a hug. But Gemma didn't reciprocate, and when Isobel pulled away, it was to find her friend still smiling impassively.

'She's okay,' Isobel called out to Byron. 'Crisis over.'

'I don't think so.' Byron tore into the room. He held up an empty pill bottle. 'I found this in the bathroom with half a glass of water. She's overdosed.'

*

Tempest reached into a large make-up bag, which contained numerous packets of brand new contact lenses. She slid out the violet ones she was wearing, and replaced them with a blue pair, blinking a few times until they felt comfortable. Then she stared at herself in the mirror. Quite a difference already.

Now for her hair. Quickly she secured her lush red waves into a neat bun at the nape of her neck, then back to the cupboard, this time pulling out a sleek grey mannequin's head, on which was arranged a wig, an ice-cool blonde bob. Synthetic, yes. Sexy, all the same.

She tipped her head forward, and pulled it on, then arranged the fringe so that it fell prettily over her forehead, a few strands framing her now sapphire-blue eyes. Strutting over to the mirror again, she whistled appreciatively. 'Hello *baby* . . .' Now for her clothes. She swapped the blue dress for a pair of jeans and a red T-shirt, her shoes for a pair of trendy trainers. Now it was time to make her move. Everything she needed was in a suitcase behind the study door, prepared a long time ago, for a day like this. She'd already spoken to her partners back in Australia, and they were expecting her. She'd be able to lose herself back home in no time. But first, Tempest grinned, she was going to enjoy a nice long holiday, somewhere hot. Maybe visit her friends in the States.

So, while the journalists clustered at the front of the house, Tempest slipped quietly out the back. Running alongside the enormous garden was a secluded narrow path that widened into an alley and led into the next street.

At the alley's mouth, Tempest looked back at the house. The hacks' voices floated towards her, their mobiles trilling faintly.

'Goodbye, Tempest St John.' She chuckled, her Australian accent already more pronounced. 'G'day, Melody Mitchell.'

*

'We're going to have to get her to hospital, and there's no time to wait for an ambulance.' Byron carried Gemma out of the room and into the lift, with Isobel behind him.

As they reached the lobby and stepped out of the lift, the concierge began to hurl abuse at Byron, who ignored him as usual. Isobel struggled to get Gemma through the revolving glass doors.

'Isobel, listen carefully, because this is important. I want you to sit in the back with Gemma and make sure she stays awake. Whatever happens, don't let her fall asleep.'

It was a journey Isobel knew she'd never forget. Gemma's eyelashes were fluttering, her face was deathly pale, and her breathing was strained. Isobel slipped an arm round her friend, and smoothed the matted blonde hair off her face. 'Hang on, Gems, we're almost there . . . Oh, please, hang on.'

Byron was driving like a madman, tearing round corners, barely stopping for lights.

'Byron, slow down! If you crash it won't help Gemma!' gasped Isobel as they narrowly avoided colliding with another car.

Eventually they screeched into a hospital car park. Byron did not bother to switch off the engine before he hauled Gemma out and carried her into the overly bright, hot A & E unit. Within minutes she was being lifted on to a trolley, and then all Isobel could do was watch helplessly as her friend vanished amid a flurry of white coats and shouted commands.

She and Byron perched in the waiting area on cold, shiny red plastic seats. 'Seems like only five minutes since we were here to see you,' noted Byron, recalling how frantic with worry he'd been.

'Don't remind me.' Isobel was biting her fingernails. 'Gems will be okay, won't she? I mean, we did get here in time?'

'I hope so. But this wasn't a case of crying wolf – Gemma really was trying to kill herself.'

'When I get my hands on Tempest . . .' Isobel made a strangling motion with her hands.

'I know how you feel, but it isn't really her fault.'

'Isn't it?' Isobel bristled. 'Messing around with people's heads? All she cares about is collecting souls for her flaming cult.'

Byron nodded thoughtfully. 'I reckon there are probably lots of people in Gemma's situation. They need help and think they're in safe hands because someone has a few letters after their name. Practically anyone can set themselves up as a counsellor.'

'Are you thinking what I'm thinking?' Too edgy to sit still, Isobel began pacing. 'This would make a *brilliant* campaign for *Primadonna*! I know *Totty* has done the sensationalist aspects with the Tempest exposé, but we could do it properly. We could lobby for tighter checks on therapists and organisations that claim to monitor them! And we can make sure that what happened to Gemma doesn't happen to anyone else.'

Byron smiled pensively. 'If only we still had a magazine.' He got up. 'Look, you stay here and wait for news of Gemma. I must go back to the office and organise tomorrow's emergency meeting. We have to let everyone know what's happening. It's not fair to keep them in the dark. But you've got enough to cope with right now. You don't have to come to the meeting. I'll handle it.'

Isobel looked at him. She knew Byron wanted to spare her the shame of facing her colleagues and admitting she'd failed. 'Byron, I appreciate the offer, but I intend to be there. Just do me a favour and make the meeting as late in the day as possible. Then I can come here to see Gemma in the morning.'

'Sure.' He seemed about to add something, then obviously changed his mind. Isobel watched as he walked out of the hospital, hands in his pockets, head bowed. Suddenly it occurred to her that the magazine's failure was worse for Byron than for her. After all, he had a reputation to maintain. He was the one who had created *Primadonna* and placed his career on the line. It would be hard on his pride to have to work for someone else after being the boss.

But she was too worried about Gemma to think about *Primadonna* for long. The girl on reception was singularly unhelpful, telling her with an officious smile, 'Sorry. Only relatives are allowed to be given inf—'

'I'm her sister,' fibbed Isobel.

The girl's face turned sceptical. 'Really? You didn't mention that when she was admitted.'

'I sincerely hope you're not calling me a liar,' Isobel smiled sweetly.

'No, of course not.' The girl picked up a phone and gestured to her to take a seat again.

Ten minutes later an exhausted-looking doctor materialised.

'You're here for Gemma Cartwright?' he asked.

'Yes – is she going to be all right?'

'She'll pull through. We'll keep her in until tomorrow.'

Isobel relaxed slightly. 'Can I see her?'

'In a bit. Right now she's being evaluated and we're arranging for her to see a clinical psychologist.' He looked at Isobel gravely. 'She's lucky you found her when you did.'

*

Twenty minutes later Isobel was peering into a small room, which was in darkness but for a tiny nightlight in the corner. Gemma lay in the bed, her face turned towards the window. Even from that angle, Isobel could see the sadness etched into her friend's features. 'Only me,' she whispered. 'Are you up to some company?'

Gemma nodded.

'How are you feeling?' Isobel sat down carefully on the end of the bed.

'Terrible. I had my stomach pumped.' She put a hand on her abdomen.

Isobel felt an overwhelming sorrow. Gemma was young, and intelligent – she should have everything in the world to look forward to. 'Oh, Gems, this is horrible. Why did you do it?' She winced at the reproach in her own voice. 'Please, just tell me why you . . . how this . . . how things got so bad that you *did* this to yourself?'

Gemma was silent for a long time. Then she said, 'It's hard to explain. Everything just seemed to be collapsing in on me. Nothing was . . . *solid*. I trusted you, only you ended up going out with Dominic. I trusted Tempest, but she turned out to be the biggest sham of all. I started panicking. And it kept on getting worse. You can't imagine how it felt, how bad it was. In the end, I just wanted it to stop, and I didn't care *what* made it stop, as long as something did. I just wanted not to feel that way.'

Isobel was stuck for words. She couldn't relate to what her friend was saying. Sure, she'd gone through a bad patch recently, but that was nothing compared with what Gemma had been experiencing. Gemma, she knew now, had been lost for a long time. But no one had noticed. 'Gems, I won't say I know how you're feeling, 'cause I don't. But that doesn't change the fact that I'm here for you. Always.'

'Doesn't matter now.' Gemma attempted a faint smile, then looked down at her hands, summoning up the strength to tell Isobel the truth about having slept with Dominic. She hadn't been able to bring herself to put it in the letter. But now she was being given a second chance to do the right thing and confess. 'Isobel, there's something I—'

A knock on the door made them both glance up. A moment later Carl Paige was entering the room quietly. 'And how are you feeling, young lady?' He looked intently at Gemma, then sent Isobel a swift smile.

'Better than when I first got here,' responded Gemma drily before her face crumpled. 'And terrified of feeling that bad again.'

'Which is where I come in.' Carl eased his muscular frame into the nearest chair. 'I'm going to suggest we set up some counselling sessions. And I promise you'll feel better soon.'

She shrugged. 'That's what Tempest said.'

'Yes, well, I won't guarantee instant miracles. You're suffering from clinical depression, and it's certainly not going to vanish overnight. But we can start by undoing some of the damage Ms St John has done. You *will* feel better, but it'll take time. I'd like to help you, though. What do you say?'

'I guess.'

'Good girl.'

Gemma tried to smile back. But she could see Isobel watching her with such concern. It would be selfish to tell Isobel the truth about her fiancé; they were getting married in less than a month. And she obviously wasn't meant to tell her, because each time she tried, something happened to stop her.

Beneath the sweltering hospital sheets, Gemma shivered.

She was going to have to live with her guilty secret for a very long time.

*

The television flickering in the corner of her bedroom was the only source of light. Not that Isobel was actually watching it.

No, she was gazing out of the window at the night sky, a huge black canopy dotted with stars. Then she became aware that a news bulletin had started, and looked back at the television screen.

'A mystery deepens tonight after Tempest St John, celebrity guru and shrink to the stars, has vanished – apparently into thin air! The thirty-seven-year-old therapist had been hiding out following relevations in *Totty* magazine concerning her link to an Australian-based cult. She is believed to have slipped out of the back door of her house even as journalists camped on her doorstep. Ms St John is thought to be abroad. For a full report, join us tomorrow night at ten.'

Isobel switched off the television, and flopped on to her bed, staring into the darkness. Gemma was lying in hospital with a damaged psyche while Tempest had swanned off to God knows where using God knows what name, free to play her headgames with yet more unsuspecting women. It was hard to stomach.

She lay awake until the early hours, eyes finally drifting shut as a pale, cool dawn seeped into the room, the exact same shade of purple as Tempest St John's eyes.

27

Money,
Money, Money

'Serves her right, swanning in here and acting like Lady Muck.' Pandora leaned over the row of shiny white washbasins and peered lovingly at herself in the mirror as she applied lipstick. 'Thinking she could run a magazine when she's never even worked on one! Christ, no wonder they've called an emergency meeting. We're going under. It's obvious.'

Beside her, Jess nodded gloomily. 'Yeah, well, it's all right for Isobel, she's marrying money. What does *she* care? Wish I'd never heard of poxy *Primadonna*. Should have stayed in my old job. Last time I ever listen to Byron Harrington about anything.'

'Yeah, you and the rest of the world.' Satisfied that her lips were now the perfect shade of blood red, Pandora unscrewed her mascara. 'He's so *over*. I mean, think about it, what's he going to do? Go crawling back to *Totty*? No, he's finished.'

Watching as her colleague's eyelashes grew steadily spikier with each painstaking application, Jess recalled how enthusiastic Byron had been at the start of the venture. 'Shame, though. He's a good journalist.'

'And a typical bloke – thinks with his dick. Isobel had him

wrapped round her little finger. If he'd been on top of things she'd never have been able to lose all this money.' Pandora's raucous laugh echoed around the room. 'He was too busy trying to get on top of *her*!'

They sauntered out of the cloakroom, still tittering, and the door slammed shut behind them.

In a tiny cubicle at the end of the cloakroom, Isobel smothered sobs of hurt by clamping a hand tightly over her mouth. The insults, coupled with her current emotional exhaustion, had been too much for her. She'd spent most of the morning at the hospital with Gemma, rushing home only to change outfits and psych herself up for this emergency meeting.

Her mobile and answerphone were, once again, clogged with messages, this time from Dominic and Jon, both of whom knew about *Primadonna*'s imminent demise. She was avoiding them both. Talking to Jon wasn't an option. She'd made her decision and she was going to stick to it. Talking to Dominic just reminded her that the wedding was drawing closer. If she hadn't given him her word that she'd go through with it, Isobel would have called the whole thing off by now.

And today was proving even tougher than she'd expected. The moment she'd arrived at the offices, Isobel had felt her colleagues' hostility and had scuttled into the cloakroom, intending to hide out there until the meeting started. Now she felt sick with nerves at the prospect of facing everyone, seeing her own inadequacy and failure mirrored in their accusing eyes. She'd let everyone down and she was right back where she'd started. No one respected her. No one wanted her here. Her life lay in shreds around her. Her best friend was suffering from clinical depression, and her marriage was going to be a sham. Meanwhile, her father was puffed up with delight at having predicted Isobel's failure from the outset. Oh, yes, Isobel reflected bitterly, the family grapevine was sizzling with gossip about how, yet again, she'd screwed up.

Isobel felt like running away. She did some mental calculations, and worked out that she had just enough left in her personal bank account to buy a plane ticket. And Go Somewhere. Anywhere.

She left the cubicle and went over to a washbasin, trying to cheer herself up by imagining all the beautiful places she could go to for a month or even more. She wouldn't tell anyone except Gemma. Then she gave a hollow laugh. Who would notice that she'd gone? She checked herself in the mirror. Sadness and defeat loomed in her big green eyes for all the world to see.

Suddenly Isobel's expression changed. No, she *wasn't* quite back where she'd started six months ago – because that was the old Isobel, the Isobel who had allowed herself to be dominated by Daddy and bullied by her boyfriend. And, yes, that Isobel probably would have run away. 'But now I'm different!' she insisted to her reflection. The girl in the mirror flashed her a defiant look. Okay, so this magazine had failed. But it wasn't entirely her fault. She couldn't be blamed for someone having sold her story to *Totty*. And, sure, Isobel shrugged, she had frittered away an awful lot of money, but she'd learn from it and wouldn't make that mistake again.

Run away? Now the girl in the glass gave a mocking smile. Like fuck she would! What, and give Pandora and Jess the satisfaction of calling her a coward as well as a fool? No, she was going to walk into that meeting with her head held high.

And later, when she was home, alone, she would cry if she needed to. Then and only then.

She opened her bag, and pulled out her little cosmetics case. Then, just as Pandora had done a few minutes before, she carefully applied her war-paint.

*

'Your presence here really isn't necessary,' snapped Dominic as Jon eased his lanky frame into the last available seat in the crowded conference room. 'After all, your photos don't even appear in *Primadonna*.'

Jon made himself comfortable then gave Dominic an amiable smile. 'First, several of my pictures have been in this magazine. Second, even if they hadn't, I'd be here to show my support to Isobel on what is indisputably a difficult day for her. Third, I don't like you at the best of times and I'm certainly not in the mood for your snide remarks today. Now, I suggest you shut your trap before I take great pleasure in shutting it for you.'

By the end of this pleasantly delivered put-down, Dominic was practically spitting venom. Jon turned his back on him and surveyed the room, wondering where Isobel was. He'd debated long and hard about being here today. She probably wouldn't want to see him, but he couldn't bear not to show her some support. Old habits were hard to break.

The conference room was packed. The long table had gone, replaced by rows of chairs. Even though the meeting was due to start in less than five minutes, people were still filtering in and searching for vacant seats.

Jon wondered how many people in the room knew why the meeting had been called. He suspected that the majority

344

realised the magazine was in crisis, but expected Byron and Isobel to salvage things. Everyone was talking in hushed voices, and malicious gossip was rife.

For the umpteenth time, Jon checked his watch. Then, just as the little hand flicked on to three, silence stole through the room. He saw Isobel appear, and heads snapped round to stare as she walked in.

*

Isobel willed herself to keep moving when she longed to scarper. All these people, judging her. She could feel their eyes sliding over her face and body. What was she? The star attraction in some freak show?

Just then, a giggle escaped from somewhere near the back. Isobel's steps faltered, her cheeks stinging with embarrassment. Her eyelashes trembled with tears.

To her right, she registered Jon and Dominic sitting stiffly beside each other. She wished neither had shown up. Then she was standing beside Byron. Her glance took in the piles of *Primadonna*s, stacked on shelves around the room. It seemed impossible that all their hard work, their optimism, should come to this.

Byron glanced at her, then turned back to his audience. His voice was heavy with disappointment. 'I think you all know that, owing to recent events, this magazine is in dire straits. Basically,' he took a deep breath, 'we're broke. We've tried to secure additional funding, but haven't succeeded. I'm sure I don't need to tell any of you how competitive a market this is, or how many publications fold within the first year. So—'

A loud buzz on the intercom interrupted him. At the back

Tierney Marshall jumped up and hurried out into the reception area. A few minutes later she returned, clutching a slim white envelope. 'It was a courier. This is for you, Isobel.'

Perplexed, Isobel ripped it open. She did a double-take. In her hand was a letter from a prominent solicitor, attached to a cheque for an obscene amount of money. Someone wanted to save *Primadonna*.

'I don't understand . . .' She held out the cheque in trembling fingers. The people sitting in the front rows craned their necks to read it, and others rushed forward to see what the fuss was about. Soon everyone was talking at once, voices raised in excitement and confusion.

'But *who*?' Isobel looked at the cheque again. 'I don't get it. Come on – someone here must know who this is from.'

But no one knew anything. Isobel continued to stare in sheer disbelief at the cheque. Things like this simply didn't happen in real life.

'I *have* to know who did this,' she declared, scanning the room for a flicker of embarrassment or pride. 'I can hardly accept this amount of money without knowing who it's from.'

'Why not?' Pandora challenged. 'Whoever it is obviously has it to spare.' She giggled. 'And when you find out his name, give me his number!' A few of the other women laughed.

Isobel frowned. 'Whether he – or *she* – has the money to spare is hardly the point. This goes way beyond generous. This is a small fortune.'

'Look, whoever it is clearly wants to help.' Jon was still lounging comfortably beside a tense Dominic. 'They've gone to a lot of trouble to do this and they obviously prefer to remain anonymous. Why don't you use the money to save the magazine? Eventually, when you find out who sent the cheque, you can repay them.'

This made perfect sense and she knew it. Now Isobel looked at him suspiciously: was Jon her mystery benefactor? He was certainly wealthy enough. And coming to her rescue was his forte. But this wasn't his style; he was far more direct. Besides, Jon's blue eyes met hers openly. No secrets there.

Her gaze switched to Byron, now chatting with Jess. He gave Isobel a wry smile then resumed his conversation. Isobel felt sure that he, too, would have been more direct if he'd wanted to bail her out. Anyway, he'd stated categorically that he'd have loved to help, if only he had the money. Isobel shook her head. It wasn't him.

Unless . . . She frowned. Unless all Byron's remarks had been deliberate! A double-bluff to conceal today's generosity. It was possible. And yet Byron, like Jon, had looked her straight in the eye.

'Someone here must know *something*! Tell me!' Isobel begged, but only blank faces confronted her. Isobel's eyes lingered on Tierney Marshall, sitting cross-legged on a chair, twisting a lock of silky blonde hair round her index finger and watching Isobel with a sympathetic smile. The Cool Hunter was one of the magazine's most loyal writers and always had been. This was just the sort of sweet, generous thing she would do. But Tierney needed every penny she had in case she lost her libel suit against the *Sunday Splash*. And, besides, her clear blue eyes were as puzzled as everyone else's.

'Okay.' Isobel threw up her hands in resignation. 'I give up.

347

Come on, let's get on with organising copy for the next issue –
now it looks like there'll be one.'

*

'Can I bum a cigarette?' Byron grinned at Jon.

'Sure.'

For a few moments they stood in companionable silence.
Then Byron asked cautiously, 'So, are you planning to go to
Isobel's wedding?' Seeing the other man's face darken, he
grimaced. 'If it's any consolation, I can't stand Dominic either.'

Jon shrugged, not revealing that Isobel had told him she was
going to cancel the wedding. 'As long as she's happy.'

'She should be, with that cheque. Guess she must have a
fairy godmother.'

'Guess she must.'

Something in Jon's voice made Byron look at him more
carefully. 'It's you, isn't it, Jon? The money's from you.'

Jon simply looked at him.

'Hey, it's cool, I won't say anything. And I appreciate why
you want to keep it quiet.' Byron's smile turned sheepish.
'You're not the only one with feelings for Isobel.'

'I'd noticed,' responded Jon drily.

'Yeah, well, only wish I'd been able to help her out. Why
aren't you telling her? Oh,' he answered his own question,
'guess you don't want her feeling beholden to you.'

'Something like that.' Stubbing out his cigarette, Jon remembered Isobel insisting that she didn't want him playing knight
in shining armour to her damsel in distress any more. 'Look,
mate, cheers. I appreciate you keeping it quiet.'

'No worries.'

*

348

They were so involved in their conversation that neither Jon
nor Byron noticed Dominic hovering nearby. Hearing this
latest revelation about the money, Dominic could also hear
something else. And it was a truly magical sound – opportunity
knocking.

He smiled to himself. If Jon was stupid enough to keep quiet
about his generosity, more fool him.

And lucky, *lucky* Dominic.

*

Isobel was still lost in thought when Dominic's insistent
rapping on the door startled her.

'Hi,' she said, without much enthusiasm.

'How's Gemma?' He sat down beside her.

'She's pretty down.' Her mind's eye was filled with her
friend's wan face. She changed the subject, and gestured at
the cheque. 'I'm in shock.'

'Understandable.'

'I'd so love to know who I should be thanking. It doesn't feel
right . . .' Her voice trailed off.

'You're really upset about all this, aren't you?'

'I know it seems silly but, yes, I am. I can't bear not knowing
who's rescued us.'

Dominic fell silent for a few moments, then asked quietly,
'And you really, really want to know who it is?' A tiny, modest
smile appeared on his face. 'Okay . . . Well, then, actually
you're looking at him.'

Her eyes widened. 'You? I don't understand.' The world must
be going haywire.

*Look at her – she's overwhelmed! This has got to be my best move
yet . . .* Dominic congratulated himself. 'I know how much the

magazine means to you. And when we were together, I wasn't always as supportive as I should have been. So, this is my way of making it up to you, and saying thank you for agreeing to go through with the wedding. I know it's asking a lot.'

She felt choked up. 'You didn't have to do this. I never expected . . . You're so kind.' Isobel smiled as Dominic leaned forward and hugged her. God, this man should be wearing a halo! She'd broken up with him four weeks before their wedding, as good as admitted she was still in love with her ex, yet he could still do something like this for her. For a split second Isobel wondered if she'd done the right thing in finishing with him. Jon was never going to commit. Dominic was the one who really loved her, who looked out for her.

'I don't know what to say.' She smiled at him again, and when he met her eyes, she didn't look away or resist when Dominic kissed her softly on the lips. It was so familiar. So easy.

Then she pulled away, confused.

'I know I'm not Jon,' he spoke hesitantly, 'but, Isobel, he can't love you more than I do. I've only ever wanted you to be happy. And, if you give me a second chance, I'll prove it.' He laughed. 'Look, here's an idea. After the wedding, we could still go on the honeymoon. No pressure, no strings. Just see how it goes. It's all booked. I'll get a separate room and you don't have to see me for the whole four weeks, if you don't want to. It's just an idea.'

'Maybe.' Isobel had to admit that, right now, it sounded tempting.

He looked at her solemnly. 'Isobel, will you do me one favour? Don't tell anyone the cheque is from me, okay? I think it might just reinforce the idea of you being bailed out by your rich soon-to-be-husband. And it would be, well, rather *embar-rassing* for me. Can we keep it just between the two of us?'

'Sure.' Isobel was surprised by this unexpected modest streak. But he was right, if the *Primadonna* team knew Dominic had rescued them, she'd never hear the end of it. 'I'm glad things are better between us,' she said suddenly.

He kissed her hand. 'Me too.'

*

Jon had been observing them through the office's glass wall and raised an eyebrow. So Isobel wasn't calling things off, after all. All she cared about was getting married – and if he wouldn't do it, she'd settle for Dominic. Jon was surprised. Obviously he didn't know her as well as he'd thought.

That realisation hurt almost as much as losing her.

28
My
Way

On the morning of the wedding Dominic awakes early. For a moment he just lies there, noting the unfamiliar surroundings, wondering where he is. Then he remembers. He's in one of the numerous luxurious bedrooms at the château. Somewhere, not too far away, is Isobel.

He thinks back to the previous night. That was some stag party. He'd been sorely tempted to enjoy himself with one of those strippers. But even though he had known today's ceremony would be a charade, Dominic had refrained from indulging himself, somewhat to the surprise of his best man. Now he congratulates himself on his restraint. He is hoping that there's still a chance that today, when Isobel makes those vows, she will be making them for real. Ever since the emergency meeting at *Primadonna*, her attitude towards him has been warmer. They've been getting on so much better. Almost . . . now Dominic smiles wistfully . . . like when they first met. And as far as he can ascertain, Jon is no longer in the picture. Though Dominic doesn't know the details, he senses that Isobel and her ex have finally come to a parting of the ways. So now, despite everything Isobel said at his house the night she called things off, Dominic is hopeful.

Tonight maybe Isobel will be in the marital bed, his wedding ring glinting on her hand as her slender fingers work their magic. Tonight, muses Dominic, might be the first time he fucks her as a husband. And, he lets optimism run riot, if so, then tonight he's going to get that blushing new bride doing things she's never done for anyone else, things he never quite dared suggest when they were going out. Because now they will be married. Now she will be his.

Perhaps.

Stretching lazily, Dominic watches the sunlight skitter through the room. Somewhere outside in the château grounds the pensive wail of a peacock fills the air, a plaintive, high-pitched cry. It seems to reach some unbearably tender, vulnerable place in him, and his smile falters.

Shaking the sensation off along with the bedsheets, he jumps up, strides over to the window, and gazes out over lush green vineyards that roll into the distance as far as the eye can see. An azure sky greets him, not a cloud in sight. It is a dream of a day.

Still, though, he cannot stop his thoughts wandering back over the last few months. He is bemused by the degree of ruthlessness he's shown in making this wedding happen. He's used Gemma, deceived Isobel, and undermined all the hard work she's put into her magazine. He's stooped so low he's practically hit the floor. And he isn't proud of his behaviour. But it's the only way Dominic knows. As a child he'd often felt giddy from watching his father run rings round his mother. And he'd vowed not to repeat the pattern. Yet here he is, doing just that. He's slipped into it without even realising. It it such a terrible thing? he wonders. After all, his parents are still together, unlike those of most of his friends.

A jolt of savage panic assails him. Is it possible that he could have behaved more honourably, and still have ended up marrying Isobel? For real?

No matter. Regret is a wasted emotion – it's not as if he can change things. The important thing is to focus on getting through today.

*

In an equally luxurious room three floors up, Isobel too is gazing out of a window, her eyes resting on the same glistening green fields and baby-blue sky as Dominic's. Like him, she, too, is lost in thought, wondering whether she has been right to let things get this far.

She checks her watch. Many of her friends and relatives have stayed overnight in the bustling yet picturesque town a few miles away. All those people, so *excited* about today, so *thrilled* for her. All those people with no idea what is really going on beneath the surface glitter of her life.

Isobel still cannot get over the way Dominic has rescued *Primadonna*. His generosity and his understanding of what the magazine means to her make her wonder if she's got it all wrong. After all, she was mistaken over Jon – she had been sure he was The One. Her intuition is not infallible.

Despite everything, she still cares about Dominic. It's hard to erase two years. So now, like countless women before her, Isobel asks herself: I am not in love with him, but I love him. Is that enough? He truly loves me – is that enough for both of us?

But Isobel knows the answer. Nothing and no one else will ever make her happy. Only Jon.

*

'My little chemical friend . . .' murmurs Gemma, gazing at the tiny blue pill in her hand. Three of these each day keep away the heavy black chains of depression. Just.

The first lot of medication they'd put her on had been a disaster; she had felt constantly sick, and couldn't sleep. After five days, she was a wreck. Then Carl Paige changed the prescription, and now she is happier. And, of course, the therapy is helping. How can it not? Carl is *wonderful*. At times, Gemma even wonders if all the trauma has been worth it for, after all, hasn't it brought them together? She'd tentatively voiced this thought to Isobel, but her friend had reacted with horror, accusing Gemma of getting addicted to Carl. Gemma laughs at the mere idea. How absurd.

She sits on her bed. She is worried, cannot shake the feeling that in marrying Dominic Isobel will be making the biggest mistake of her life. Gemma is not privy to the fact that today's ceremony will probably be a sham. And so she frets, sure that Dominic will cheat on Isobel again. But not with Gemma.

*

Byron loathes travelling by Eurostar. He can't help feeling nervy at the thought of being under all that water. He tells himself it's just like being in any train in any tunnel. But he still hates it. At least this way he'll be on time for the wedding. Not that he's especially keen to watch Isobel shackling herself to Dominic. But if that's what makes her happy . . .

He's certain that Isobel still wants Jon, and equally sure that

Isobel will never want *him*. Byron shrugs, sits back, and closes his eyes. It's a funny thing; he's always been unlucky in love.

*

Isobel and Gemma are enjoying a walk in the beautiful grounds, both smiling as the breeze plays with their hair, while the early-morning sunshine warms their faces. They stroll slowly past the château and into the gardens, drinking in the vibrant flowers and intense green of the grass. They walk in silence, enjoying just being together.

Isobel slips her arm through Gemma's. It is a casual, spontaneous gesture. And there is something so natural, so trusting about it, that now Gemma feels something – some emotion she cannot name – welling up inside her.

'I slept with Dominic,' she says suddenly.

'What?' Isobel pales. They stop walking. They separate, their arms falling to their sides.

'I slept with Dominic,' repeats Gemma quietly. 'Before you got engaged. Before the night you found us kissing. It happened at the gym. I've been wanting to tell you—'

'You sure picked a hell of a time!' Emotions spinning crazily, Isobel suddenly feels unbearably cold. Then she glances at Gemma's anguished face and knows what keeping this secret has been doing to her friend. 'Is that why you . . .?'

'Tried to top myself?' Gemma nods. 'It was part of it. I'd become so obsessed with Dominic, I couldn't think straight. I'd even started convincing myself that you'd taken him away from me, that I had a right to try and get him back. I've hated myself ever since we . . . ever since he and I . . .'

Isobel's mind flashes back to the night Dominic proposed, the night she found him kissing Gemma. Now she feels light-headed with anger, as she realises just how thoroughly he has deceived her, how he looked her straight in the eye and promised he didn't want Gemma. Her face burns. The *lies* he's told.

Then Isobel flushes again, this time with shame. After all, she too has been unfaithful, she too has slept with someone else. Is she any better than Dominic? Yes, because as soon as she'd indulged in that extra-curricular sex, she'd cancelled the wedding. Tried to, anyway. And, God knows, she never would have slept with Dominic after being with Jon.

Oh, but *Dominic* . . . He'd acted as though *she* was paranoid for not trusting him! He'd fucked with her mind and, Isobel winces, he'd continued sleeping with her even after being with her best friend. He'd screwed her every which way.

'I know it doesn't help to say it but I'm so sorry—'

'Forget it,' says Isobel briskly, 'I know you weren't yourself. And I know you've wanted to tell me.'

'What are you going to do?'

Isobel turns to her. 'How many hours until I have to be at the chapel?'

'Oh, you've got bags of time.'

'You remember the town we passed through on the way here?'

'Sure.'

'They had all the usual shops, right?'

Gemma is now totally confused. 'I think so.'

'Good. Now look, I want you to tell everyone I'm in my room and don't want to be disturbed, okay? I'm going to enjoy some retail therapy.' Seeing how puzzled Gemma is, Isobel smiles. 'You'll see.'

*

Dominic watches yet more guests arriving as he chats with Toby, his best man. A field with a large red H set into the middle adjoins the château's gardens; three helicopters and a private jet are circling, queuing in the sky until receiving clearance to land.

Meanwhile, those guests who have stayed overnight in the house are now climbing into quaint little horse-drawn carriages waiting to take them to the chapel.

'Got the ring?' Dominic turns anxiously to Toby for the umpteenth time.

'Will you relax?' Toby pats him heartily on the back. 'Come on, I think it's time we made a move. Isobel will be down any second now and we can't have you seeing the bride before the ceremony. Bad luck and all that.'

Dominic manages a sickly smile.

He knows that if Isobel had even an inkling of the lies he has told, the things he's done, then today would not be happening. She would never have agreed to go through with this and help him save face.

Because, oh, the things he's done.

He's fucked her best friend.

He's stolen her story.

He's lied about the cheque.

And Isobel has no idea.

Now Dominic realises that even if by some miracle she agrees to stay with him after today, he will be languishing in a little mental prison cell, his secrets holding him as securely as bars, separating him from the woman he has married.

He's just like Tempest St John. *A total fake.*

*

Seven hundred guests squeeze into the ornate chapel, exclaiming in delight at the beautiful blue and amber stained-glass windows. Tiny candles are dotted throughout, and flowers trail prettily around each pew, and over the door.

In the front row, Meredith de RoseMont sits quietly, listening as Penelope Sakover-Forbes delivers her own glowing sermon on Dominic, the world's greatest son and, if his mother is to be believed, a man eligible for sainthood. 'He's so *staunch*,' booms Penelope. 'Not many people have Dom's loyalty. His compassion. His strength.'

'Handsome bugger too, if I say so myself,' chortles Sebastian Sakover-Forbes, preening.

'Yes, well, he's jolly lucky to be marrying my Isobel!' Meredith is astonished to hear herself declare. Then she falls silent again, unsure what has prompted her little outburst, and hoping her daughter's marriage will prove happier than her own.

*

Gemma smoothes out a crease in her dress, enjoying the way the soft cerise silk ripples over her skin. She imagines Carl's response to the way she looks today. Would he like her dress? Having appraised all the men present, Gemma knows her therapist is more attractive than any of them. Even Dominic is nothing special by comparison. She wonders why she ever thought he was.

*

Sitting there at the back of the chapel, Jon is surprised to find himself caught up in the atmosphere. He normally boycotts weddings. But now, looking around, he notes the emotions flitting across all the faces; excitement, pride, envy, hope. He imagines Isobel walking down the aisle, imagines her making the vows. He wants to be the man standing beside her. For the first time, it hits him that maybe the ceremony is about more than just convention. Maybe he's been wrong all this time.

Jon knows that, for Isobel, the vows she makes today will be binding. He forces himself to sit still, though what he really wants to do is get up, run out, and stop her from marrying Dominic. But he won't. He wants to see if she'll actually go through with it. If she does, then she must truly love Dominic.

*

'I fail to see the joke.' Harold de RoseMont's fingers close around his daughter's arm as they stand at the entrance to the chapel. 'But whatever it is, it's gone far enough. Now go back and get changed.'

'It's not a joke.'

Sheer shock at being disobeyed silences Harold. But not for long. 'If you think I'm walking down that aisle with you looking like that, you're wrong.'

'Then don't,' says Isobel softly.

'I SAID, GO AND GET CHANGED!' her father bellows.

'No. This is my day. We'll do things my way.'

Deadlock.

'You know something,' Isobel regards her father steadily, 'you're my father, and I'm sure that on some level, I love you. But I don't like you very much, and you don't like me. That's the truth of it. So if you choose not to accompany me down the aisle, that's all right.' She gives him a sad smile. 'In my whole life, you've never supported me once on anything – *why start now?*'

She turns on her heel and walks alone through the chapel doors.

29

Nice Day for
a White Wedding

The first notes of the Wedding March rang out; instantly there was a stirring and rustling as every guest turned towards the doors, eager for their first glimpse of Isobel. The photographers from *OK!*, *Hello!* and *Primadonna* stood ready to capture the images that would enthrall and delight women across the country. Dominic held his breath. Meredith dabbed at tear-logged eyes. Gemma smiled with glee, for now she knew what was about to happen. Byron shifted impatiently in his seat, wishing he was the one marrying Isobel.

Then Isobel appeared. And seven hundred guests gasped.

There was a stunned silence, then murmuring, which grew louder, then frantic clicking, the cameras going crazy as, chin tilted proudly, Isobel walked down the aisle, wearing a wedding gown that looked as if it belonged on a catwalk.

Dominic's eyes bulged.

Instead of the traditional long white dress that had been specially made for her, Isobel was clad in a parody of a wedding gown. The only thing he recognised from the numerous fittings he'd attended was the veil. His eyes were practically out on stalks as he took in Isobel's bare shoulders, the only item adorning her top half being a white bustier decorated with tiny, candy-pink kisses. It was cut low, Isobel's cleavage to the fore. Horrified, he lowered his gaze then wished he hadn't: her midriff was showing and – Dominic shuddered – she'd had her bellybutton pierced! Through his fingers, which were clamped over his eyes, Dominic could see the bottom half of the 'dress': long, sheer, with a slit up one side to her waist. Tied snugly around one tanned, firm thigh was a blue silk garter.

By the time Isobel reached him, his face and neck were a mottled red, his mouth opening and closing like a bewildered goldfish. 'You – you—' he spluttered, raising a tremulous hand and pointing to where Isobel's auburn mane had shimmered over her shoulders. Now it was all gone, and in its place was a short, sharp, geometrical cut; a sleek, shiny, dark cap of hair tapering into Isobel's long, creamy neck, and enhancing her enormous emerald eyes.

Isobel stopped beside him, waited a beat, then turned and faced him for the first time since entering the chapel. She said nothing. She didn't need to. Because the look she gave him said it all. And in that precise moment, catching that cool, green, measuring stare, Dominic realised something.

She knew.

Somehow, she knew about the lies he'd told, the way he'd manipulated her. She'd found something out. Whether it concerned Gemma or the money for her magazine, he couldn't be sure. But she knew something.

And rather than simply cancelling the wedding at the last minute, she'd decided to teach him a lesson. She had re-invented herself in line with all the things he loathed. She was visible, beautiful, proof that he could lie, cheat, manipulate and still – if he chose – deceive everyone here and marry her, but that even if he did, Isobel would be one elegant step ahead of him, all the way.

As they stood there, watching each other silently, Dominic realised something else: that Isobel was silently throwing down the gauntlet. After all, apart from his mother only he had seen the original wedding dress? No one else was aware that she was deviating so dramatically from their plans.

As far as all their friends and family were concerned, Isobel had simply chosen a quirky wedding gown and decided to have a radical haircut. They might not approve, they might be surprised, but they couldn't know what her choices represented.

The priest cleared his throat. As Isobel watched him, Dominic realised more fully what she was doing: she was letting him decide if they were to go through with this sham of a ceremony. Now Dominic felt his throat catch with tears – Isobel was trusting him to have enough integrity *not* to go through with the wedding.

He blinked. Everything in his line of vision seemed to sway. He had to decide. He could continue with what they knew to be a charade. No one would know anything was wrong until a few weeks later, when the couple would announce their separation. Or, he felt sweat break out on his forehead, he could do the honourable thing and stop it now. He was aware of a grudging admiration for the woman standing silently beside him. He thought he'd been so clever in manipulating her, yet she had beaten him at his own game.

Suddenly it struck Dominic that this was the first time he'd ever felt respect for Isobel. Oh, he'd loved her, and wanted her, but he'd never respected her as he did now. The irony was like a physical blow. In that minute, Dominic wanted Isobel more than ever, even as he knew it could never be.

*

Standing there quietly beside him, Isobel knew that Dominic understood what she was doing. That one, initial look which passed between them had told her that. Now she took a deep breath. This was one hell of a gamble. If Dominic really didn't have a shred of decency, he might call her bluff and go on with the ceremony. And she hated the idea of saying those vows when she didn't mean them, hated the idea of being married to this man even if it only lasted for a day.

Again the priest cleared his throat, beaming at the couple standing before him. 'Perhaps we might beg—'

'No.' Dominic spoke firmly. 'No. We can't.' He looked at Isobel with tears in his eyes, before raising her hand to his lips and kissing it gently. Then he said, very loudly so that everyone present would hear, 'There isn't going to be a wedding. Because I don't deserve this woman. I never have.'

And as seven hundred guests watched in total confusion, the groom turned and walked out of the church, leaving the bride smiling sadly. A minute later, a car started up outside and, still in shock, everyone just sat there in total silence.

Then, as if by some invisible signal, all hell broke loose.

The first person to move was Penelope Sakover-Forbes who bounced out of her seat and thundered towards Isobel with the light of battle gleaming in her eyes. 'Isobel, you foolish girl!' she screeched hysterically. 'I want to know what you've done to upset my son like this.'

'Penelope,' Isobel smiled politely, 'might I make a suggestion?'

The older woman nodded and Isobel's smile widened. '*Shut up.*'

Friends and family accosted Isobel from all sides, some of them practically clinging on to her veil as she tried to make her way from the chapel. At the door she paused. 'Perhaps someone might like this?' She threw her bouquet high in the air, and watched as it landed in Gemma's hands. Then Isobel bolted into the chapel grounds, laughing with relief.

'*Love* the dress,' drawled an amused voice and Isobel stared at Jon, who was lounging against the limo that would have whisked the happy couple off on honeymoon.

'Thought you'd gone back to Brazil!'

Jon walked over and slid his arms round her waist. 'What, and miss this? No way.' He sighed. 'Isobel, I'm a stubborn git. I loathe admitting when I'm wrong. But I *was* wrong.'

'About what?'

'Getting married.' He smiled sheepishly. 'I don't know, it was weird. Sitting there in the chapel, watching you walk down the aisle, suddenly I understood a bit more. It's not just about convention. It's about making a statement. Isobel, will you marry me?'

She burst out laughing.

'Not exactly the response I was hoping for,' said Jon, with a grin.

'It's just that when I was in the chapel, I realised *I* was wrong. I don't need a ceremony to prove that we're committed to each other – it's just words. You were right, it's not the wedding that matters, it's being with the right person. I don't want to get

367

married. I just want you.' Now she was laughing and crying at once.

Just then the chapel doors flew open and a crowd of people spilled out, then stopped short at the sight of the bride in another man's arms. But Isobel was past caring, clinging on to Jon as everyone swarmed around them. Amid the chaos, a tap on her shoulder made her turn to find the priest. 'Do you suppose the groom might be returning?' he ventured, giving Isobel and Jon a dubious look. 'Only I have an exorcism in thirty-five minutes?'

Isobel shook her head. 'No. He won't be coming back.'

'Come on,' Jon tugged at her hand, 'let me take you away from all this!'

Isobel hesitated. 'Can you wait two weeks?'

'Why?'

'For our honeymoon, Dominic and I were going to Hawaii, and I have the tickets! God knows I could do with a break.' She lowered her voice. 'I thought I'd take Gemma. She's been through such a lot.'

'Okay, but only if I can fly out and join you both there for the second week,' insisted Jon. 'We've spent enough time apart. Besides, you always get into so much trouble when I'm not around to look after you!'

'True.' Isobel glimpsed Gemma in the crowd and grabbed her hand. 'Fancy a holiday?'

Linking arms, the two girls headed for the limo driver, who was watching events with fascination. Isobel smiled at him. 'We'd like to go back to the château, then on to the airport.'

And before the shell-shocked onlookers could say a word, Gemma and Isobel were getting into the car.

'See you in a week.' Jon leaned through the window and gave Isobel a long, lingering kiss.

Then he frowned. 'Hang on, you never answered my question and I was serious – will you marry me?'

Isobel winked. *'I'll have to sleep on it . . .'*

Epilogue

'This is *heaven* . . .' Yawning, Isobel settled back on her sun-lounger.

'No arguments here!' agreed Gemma, sipping a cold drink and trying to decide if she had sufficient energy for another dip in the hotel's Olympic-size outdoor pool.

Hawaii had proved even more stunning than they'd imagined, and even one week away had done wonders. For one thing, they both looked better than they had in a long time. Isobel's skin was now softest, smoothest cinnamon, against which her green eyes seemed aquamarine.

Gemma also looked good, her dark-blonde hair now streaked with gold. Much to her alarm, the sunshine had brought her out in freckles, though everyone assured her they looked adorable.

Now she beamed. 'It's wonderful here.'

Isobel sighed. 'Paradise.'

Most importantly, they were getting on brilliantly, though there had been some tricky moments. Conversations about Dominic. Times when one or both girls had cried. The occasional recrimination. But there was also plenty of laughter, and any damage the friendship had sustained was healing nicely.

To her delight, Isobel had even found time to do some writing. She had faxed two articles back to *Primadonna*. One was a light-hearted travel piece about Hawaii. The other was a spiky piece about the down-side of being born into a wealthy family. Entitled *A Rich Bitch Writes*, it dealt candidly with Isobel's experiences at work and how people had judged her without knowing her. The day after she'd faxed it, Pandora had e-mailed her at the hotel, saying how much she loved it, and admitting that it had made her feel ashamed of her behaviour towards her.

Now Isobel got up, shielding her eyes from the midday sun as she squinted in the direction of the bar. 'I'm going to get a drink. Want one?'

'No, I'm fine,' Gemma mumbled, half asleep.

Wincing as the concrete burned her bare feet, Isobel hopped over to the bar, stumbling headlong into a tanned blonde woman wearing the obligatory designer shades and a bright red sarong.

'Sorry!' Swiftly Isobel put a hand out to steady her fellow sun-worshipper.

The blonde grinned, gesturing to indicate it was no problem. The bartender handed her a receipt. 'Just sign there, please.'

Isobel smiled as the woman made space for her at the bar. She glanced at the woman's sprawling signature. *Melody Mitchell*. Pretty name. Isobel glanced again at the blonde as she headed towards the pool. Something about her was vaguely familiar, but she couldn't put her finger on it. Shrugging, Isobel began placing her own order, deciding on a triple scoop of organic chocolate-chip ice-cream, heaped with hot butterscotch sauce, whipped cream, and sprinkled with nuts.

*

Gemma sat up and began to apply more sun lotion. She admired her bronzed limbs. In one week they'd return to London, and she'd be resuming her therapy sessions with Carl Paige. Would he notice her tan? While away, Gemma had thought about him a lot. Picturing him had helped her, for she'd had a few difficult days. Once, when the tablets hadn't woven their usual chemical spell around her brain, she'd taken one more than she was supposed to. She'd carried on doing that for the rest of the holiday. But maybe now that she and Carl would be seeing each other again, she could cut back on the pills. Maybe all she needed was him.

Gemma began rubbing lotion over her slender thighs. She wondered if Carl was married.

*

'Isn't that . . .' Sitting up, Isobel shielded her eyes. 'Isn't that . . . It's Jon! But he's not supposed to be here until tomorrow!'

'He was obviously missing you too much.' Gemma also sat up.

Beaming, Isobel jumped to her feet and ran to greet him. He laughed and dropped his bags. 'Thought I'd surprise you.' He kissed her, then looked at his watch. 'Right. You have exactly two hours.'

'Er, until what?' Isobel looked at him warily.

'Until we tie the knot!' He grinned as his girlfriend gasped.

'I don't understand! What are you talking about?'

'I know you said you'd changed your mind and having a wedding didn't mean anything to you any more, so I've arranged a ceremony with a difference. And it's starting in two hours.'

'What? Where, you lunatic?'

'Right here, by the pool. I've organised a civil ceremony. We get to write our own vows – I've already done mine. I've spent all week on the phone to the hotel. They're going to provide food, drinks, music, and they've arranged for an authentic hula dance to celebrate!'

Isobel threw her arms around him. Then she gasped. 'What will I wear?'

'Come on, we'll go and find something.' Gemma grabbed her hand. Jon laughed as the two friends went dashing into the hotel, squealing with excitement.

Sensing that he was being watched, he glanced round. Over by the other side of the pool, an attractive blonde was staring at him. Jon was sure he'd seen her somewhere before.

Something was tugging at his memory. He tried to place her, but couldn't. Shrugging, he gave up. It wasn't important.

Melody Mitchell, aka Tempest St John, continued watching Jon intently for a moment. Then she chuckled to herself, before gathering up her suntan oil, towel, and a pair of pretty pink Jimmy Choos, and sauntering away towards the beach.